The Secrets of Hawthorne House

Donald Firesmith

Awards for The Secrets of Hawthorne House

2020 TopShelf Magazine Book Awards – 1st Place Winner in three Categories (Fiction/Paranormal, Young Adult/Fantasy, and Young Adult/Paranormal) and Finalist in two Categories (Fiction/Supernatural and Young Adult / Coming of Age)

2020 International Book Awards – Winner in the Fiction: Fantasy Category

2020 Author Shout Reader Ready Awards – Top Pick

Winter 2020 Pinnacle Book Achievement Award – Best Books in the young adult fantasy category

2019 Readers' Favorite – Silver medal in the urban paranormal category

American Book Fest 2020 Best Book Award – Finalist in Fantasy

Independent Author Network 2020 Book of the Year – Finalist in the Paranormal/Supernatural Category

ReadFREE.ly's Top 50 Indie Books of 2019 – Third place

2020 Purple Dragonfly Book Award – Honorable Mention in the Science Fiction / Fantasy Category

PRD Book Cover of the Month – July 2019

Praise for The Secrets of Hawthorne House

"The complexity and depth of *The Secrets of Hawthorne House*, as well as its incorporation of magical elements with realistic struggles and confrontations, create a captivating story that is hard to put down, original, and satisfyingly unique. Its lessons about different cultures and backgrounds, the process of grief and recovery, and the acceptance of ideas and realities a bit different from the norm... creates a powerful interplay of mystery, intrigue, and healing that will keep all ages thoroughly engrossed." – *Midwest Book Review*, D. Donovan, Senior Reviewer,

"As an adult, I found *The Secrets of Hawthorne House* truly enjoyable even though it's for teen readers. A commendable work from Donald Firesmith, and I look forward to the sequel." – *Readers' Favorite*

"The author's prose is lucid and descriptive... A satisfying tale that aptly balances teen drama with a bit of magic." – *Kirkus Reviews*

"A fun, exciting mystery for younger teens." – *The Wishing Shelf Book Awards*

"There is a lovely lyrical quality to Firesmith's prose, the authorial voice is strong, and the author has a penchant for rich description." – *BookLife Prize Critic's Report*

"*The Secrets of Hawthorn House* was wildly entertaining. It's the story of kindness, friendship, and starting over, all wrapped up in two mischievous teenage boys. I can't wait to read the next book." – *Sherry's Book Confessions*

"I enjoyed reading *The Secrets of Hawthorne House*… I was drawn in from the beginning… There is humor, sorrow, adventure, mystery, love and realistic, relatable characters in this book. It's a middle school YA read, but I think just about anyone would enjoy reading it!" – *United Indie Book Blog*

"I loved it! I'm definitely looking forward to reading the next in the series!" – author *J. Aislynn d'Merricksson*

"*The Secrets of Hawthorne House* was a great book, and I'd recommend it to fans of mysteries, YA readers, and people who enjoy stories with paranormal elements… Definitely check it out!" – author *Jasmine Bryner*

"I love the story and the characters… This is a great, clean and entertaining story for middle grade and young adult kids who like mystery, treasure hunts, and magic. It is nicely done by Donald Firesmith. I would keep my eyes out for the next book in this series." – author *Anna del C. Dye*

"Hawthorne House is an easy read and a page-turner. Enjoy and keep an eye out for the sequels." – author *Kelly Zimmer*

"I totally enjoyed the book and recommend it. The author did an excellent job." – author *Thomas Trimble*

"I really enjoyed this tale… This magical narrative so reminded me of the books I enjoyed speeding through in Junior High and High School. Adventure. Druids. Supernatural spells. Secrets buried in the house. Witches. Goddesses. Even a rich history of the family going back thousands of years. And as a coming of age tale, I love the idea Matt and his friend Gerallt have the ability to cast spells on bullies and get them into all sorts of trouble. I think this is perfect fun for a 15 or 16-year-old, and I highly recommend it to young readers." – author *Gary Seigel*

"A well-written children's tale with likeable characters and detailed descriptions. It's definitely worth reading!" – author *Billy Burgess, Ramblings of a Coffee Addicted Writer*

The Secrets of Hawthorne House

Copyright © 2019 by Donald G. Firesmith

All rights reserved.

All rights reserved. No part of this publication may be reproduced, distributed, or transmitted in any form or by any means, including photocopying, recording, or other electronic or mechanical methods, without the prior written permission of the publisher, except in the case of brief quotations embodied in critical reviews and certain other noncommercial uses permitted by copyright law.

This book is a work of fiction. Any similarities to real people, living or dead, is purely coincidental. All characters and events in this work are figments of the author's imagination.

You may purchase autographed books by contacting the author via:

Magical Wand Press
20 Bradford Avenue
Pittsburgh, PA 15205

http://donaldfiresmith.com

This book is typeset in Times New Roman.

Cover design by Rudy Parfaite www.rudyparfaite.com

Interior design by Donald G. Firesmith

Edited by Donna Kelley and with the editing applications, Autocrit® and Grammarly®

Table of Contents

Chapter 1: First Day of School	1
Chapter 2: The House Next Door	28
Chapter 3: Gerallt Moves In	45
Chapter 4: Rescuing Gareth	58
Chapter 5: Best Friends	68
Chapter 6: Herbology and Magic	83
Chapter 7: Trick or Treat	91
Chapter 8: Inside Hawthorne House	107
Chapter 9: Colin's Revenge	123
Chapter 10: The Principal's Office	135
Chapter 11: Grounded	146
Chapter 12: What to Do?	155
Chapter 13: Matt's Marvelous Plan	170
Chapter 14: An Unexpected Anthem	178
Chapter 15: Freedom	189
Chapter 16: Modron and Miracles	206
Chapter 17: Gerallt's Revenge	219
Chapter 18: Spending the Night	234
Chapter 19: Tina and the Tree Branch	246
Chapter 20: The Inadvertent Investiture	256
Chapter 21: Laid Off	268

Chapter 22: Moving In	278
Chapter 23: The Stolen Amulet	293
Chapter 24: The Secret Search	315
Chapter 25: Searching for Treasure	336
Chapter 26: The Hidden Tunnel	353
Chapter 27: Unexpected Announcements	377
Epilog	393
Thank You	394
Map	395
The Characters	396
Druidic Spells (Prayers to Modron)	401
Maine Accents and Idioms	406
Family Trees	409
Acknowledgments	411
Dedication	412
About the Author	413
Cataloging in Print (CIP) Data	414

Chapter 1
First Day of School

It was that magical moment when the warmth of day grudgingly gives way to the chill of night. Matt knew it was nearly dinnertime. He imagined his mother standing at their back door, wondering whether to call him in for supper or to let him enjoy a few more minutes of freedom.

He watched the setting sun balance briefly on the western horizon, transforming the restless surface of the sea into a bed of liquid gold. The waves rolled and crashed with the sound of distant thunder as they rushed up the beach before retreating into the sea. Searching for their dinner, sandpipers raced in and out with the waves, constantly keeping their tiny feet mere inches from the frigid water. Overhead, ghostly gulls floated motionless in the gathering gloom, crying mournfully as if lamenting all the sailors lost at sea.

Twilight fell swiftly, and the early evening breeze blew colder as the land cooled and the forest darkened. Matt stood up and brushed the sand from the seat of his cut-offs. He breathed deeply and smelled the surf's salty spray mixed with the decay of kelp and small, dead creatures washed up on the shore. He started slowly up the sand dunes toward the hill where his home lay nestled in a grove of wind-sculpted evergreens.

In a matter of moments, twilight became evening and then night. Although Matt had walked the well-

Chapter 1 – First Day of School

worn path for as long as he could remember, it somehow seemed unnaturally dark and long. The low trees were twisted into forms so strange and fantastic that even the strong winds blowing steadily in from the sea could not have shaped them. He heard his mother calling his name, calling him in from the darkness to the cozy and well-lit rooms of their small sea cottage. She called again, but her voice was garbled. Each time she called, the wind grabbed her words and dragged them away into the black shadows beneath the twisted trees.

Matt tried to run, but the sharp edges of the sawgrass sliced the skin of his bare legs, and thick brambles blocked his path. He tried to push past them, but they tripped him, winding tightly around his legs. He heard his mother's scream, a single, long piercing cry of pain and fear. Then, nothing but the sound of the wind blowing, the trees creaking, and the waves thundering upon the rocky shore...

"Matt!" his twin sister Tina shouted through his bedroom door, waking him from his recurring nightmare. "I called you at least 10 minutes ago. Get up! The school bus will be here in 20 minutes, and I'm going to be on it, even if you're still in bed. And don't expect Dad to drive you; he's already left for work. You miss the bus, and you're walking."

"Alright, Tina, I'm up," Matt muttered as he tugged at the sweat-drenched sheets and blanket that were tightly wrapped around him like some wrinkled snake. It took him a moment to remember where he was.

Then the terrible meaning of the nightmare came crashing over him. He remembered the town drunk who had lost control of his beat-up pickup. How he'd struck his mother as she was picking the wildflowers that grew along the side of the narrow coastal highway. He remembered the endless hours and days in her dreary hospital room, taking turns reading aloud his mother's favorite book in a vain hope that she would hear and wake from her coma. And then the rest blew over him like a wild winter storm, one from which he could neither run nor hide. The dreadful day the doctors declared her brain dead. How his father, Tina, and he had cried as they said goodbye to her before the doctor turned off her ventilator. She had simply stopped breathing.

The days that followed were a blur. There was the terrible funeral followed by a reception with friend after friend and neighbor after neighbor saying a hundred variations of "I'm so sorry." Not knowing what to say, Matt merely nodded as tears silently ran down his cheeks. Finally, he remembered their sudden, unexpected, and unwanted trip to Hawthorne, Indiana, where his father had lived as a child. Some twenty-five miles northwest of Fort Wayne, it was about as far from the ocean as his father could have possibly moved them.

Matt sat up and shook his head, trying to toss off the terrible memories. Quickly combing his hands through his straight blond hair, he put on his glasses and dressed in the blue jeans and flannel shirt that he had selected the night before.

Stopping in the bathroom on his way down to breakfast, he glanced in the mirror and briefly considered his reflection. What he saw was a fifteen-

Chapter 1 – First Day of School

year-old boy of average height and build whose gray-green eyes stared back at him through small oval glasses. While his sister, Tina, was pretty and looked like a younger version of their mother, Matt resembled their father whom Matt felt was neither handsome nor unattractive, merely average.

As usual, Tina had already finished eating. Her single, small strawberry yogurt container sat empty on the counter as she brushed her straight black hair into a long ponytail.

"Is that all you're having?" Matt asked, although he already knew her answer. He couldn't help noticing that the high cheekbones she had inherited from their mother seemed to grow more pronounced each week. Tina had been slender before their mother's death and had been slowly losing weight ever since. Matt was beginning to worry and wondered whether their father had noticed.

"I like yogurt," she replied. "Besides, not everybody eats a mountain of Frosted Flakes to tide them over 'til lunchtime." She took a compact from her purse and quickly checked her spotless face for non-existent pimples. Satisfied, she smiled. "Can you believe it, Matt? It seems like we've been waiting forever for this day, and it's finally here. High school! Football games, school dances, and parties."

It's the first day at a new school in a new town, Matt thought, *and she acts like it's still summer, and she's just going down to the boardwalk to meet friends. How can she wall off her memories and act like everything is normal?*

Then Matt remembered what had happened several nights earlier. He had gotten up to use the bathroom and had heard the soft sound of crying coming from Tina's room. If he had seen light shining under her door, he might have gone in. As it was, Matt returned to his bedroom and his own dark memories. At breakfast the next morning, her blue eyes had been red and puffy. She might be better than he was at hiding her feelings, but the loss of their mother ate at her, just as it did at him.

Matt wolfed down his cereal and grabbed his backpack. He joined Tina at the curb just as an old yellow school bus turned the corner and passed the dilapidated Victorian mansion next door. The bus stopped in front of them, and Matt followed Tina up the steps.

"Fantastic," he muttered to himself as he looked down the aisle of the nearly-packed bus. Tina paused at the free seat next to an older boy wearing a letterman jacket. He smiled up at her and quickly moved his books so that she could sit down next to him. They were happily flirting before Matt even managed to walk past. That only left three "free" seats. The first was next to a huge hulk of a boy, who sat sprawled across both seats. He looked up at Matt with a bored stare. It reminded Matt of a lion that had recently feasted and was lazily deciding whether a passing antelope was worth leaving the comfortable shade of its acacia tree. Lion boy turned to look back out the bus window and made no move to slide over. Farther back, an older girl looked right through him as if he didn't exist, although she quickly laid her

Chapter 1 – First Day of School

schoolbag on the empty seat next to her. That left one last free seat near the back of the bus, next to the biggest, homeliest girl Matt had ever seen.

Smiling somewhat hopefully and self-consciously through crooked teeth, the girl looked up at Matt. "You're new here," she observed.

"Yes," Matt replied, uncomfortably aware that she extended several inches onto the empty seat. Feeling somewhat embarrassed, he sat down next to her. He would have to ride the rest of the way to school with only half his bottom on the hard, worn-out bus seat.

"I'm Sarah Duffy," she said.

"Matt. Matt Mitchel."

"So, have you seen Old Lady Hawthorne yet?"

"Who?"

"Old Lady Hawthorne. She lives in the old mansion next to your house."

"No. Why?"

"No one's seen her in ages. Not since she murdered her husband."

"What?"

"She murdered her husband and the woman who lived in your house."

"What? You're kidding, right? Wouldn't she be in jail, or something?"

"They never found the bodies. Most people think she dumped them into Quarry Lake, but I think she probably buried them in her basement."

"Wait. I get it. Feed the new kid in town a story about the house next door, and see if he falls for it."

"No, really. It's true. You can ask anyone."

Matt gave Sarah a skeptical look. "Right..." He turned away and silently studied the other students on the bus.

After a short drive, and picking up a final student, the bus pulled up in front of the school. Matt ended up as one of the last ones off the bus. Half of his rear had gone to sleep and tingled painfully as he limped down the bus steps to begin his first day at Hawthorne High.

The high school was huge compared to the middle school that Matt had attended back in Port Orford, Oregon. The cold Indiana winters had worn the edges off the gray sandstone blocks that trimmed the two-story red-brick building. The tall, columned archway over its front doors was cracked and missing small shards of stone.

After attending a welcoming assembly for ninth-graders in the school's huge auditorium, Matt headed to the office where an overly-friendly guidance counselor gave him his class schedule and locker assignment. After searching several long and crowded hallways and asking a couple of very busy teachers, he finally found his locker and stashed his coat.

The first period's warning bell rang as Matt shut his locker door. He reached into his pocket and pulled out his padlock. The key should have been in the lock's keyhole. It wasn't. Thinking the key had fallen out, he reached into his pocket, but the key wasn't there. He tried his other pocket, but it was also empty. Starting to panic, he thought back. The last time he remembered seeing the key, it had been lying on his desk next to the

Chapter 1 – First Day of School

padlock. In his rush to dress and get downstairs for breakfast, he must have overlooked it.

With no time to consider what to do, he carefully lined up the padlock's rounded shackle with the hole and hoped that no one would notice that it wasn't really locked.

Then Matt was off, searching through the rapidly-emptying hallways for his freshman American history classroom. After a few false turns, he found it just as the final bell rang.

There were only three empty desks left in the room. Grabbing an empty chair next to a window, Matt picked up the history textbook that had been lying on the desk and quickly flipped through its pages. It was thicker than his books back in middle school, and the print was smaller. Clearly, classes were going to be harder now that he was in high school.

Matt opened his backpack and removed the file folder of printer paper that his father had given him the night before. He made a mental note to remind his father that he really needed notebooks rather than some office supplies his father had brought home from work.

To prepare for class, he took out a sheet of paper and placed it on his small, graffiti-covered desktop. Halfway through writing "American History" and the date at the top, the tip of his pencil suddenly jerked sideways, tearing right through the paper. Angrily lifting it, Matt saw the name "Clayton Cartwright" crudely carved into the surface of the desk. Wondering why anyone would be so stupid as to ruin his own desk, Matt crumpled the torn paper, took out a new sheet, and began searching for a smooth place to write when the teacher rose and introduced himself.

"Good morning class. My name is Marcus Thompson, and I will be teaching American History this year." Tall, with the build of a basketball player, the teacher was in his early twenties. He looked as though he should still be sitting in a college classroom rather than standing in front of a class of his own. He picked up a piece of paper from his desk and continued, "Raise your hand and call out 'here' when I read your name."

Matt looked around his new classroom as the other students responded one by one when they heard their names. It was strange to not recognize a single face. They all stared back at Matt when Mr. Thompson spoke his name. *I guess they think it's weird having a stranger in their room, too*, Matt thought to himself.

He wasn't really paying much attention to the steady recitation of names until the teacher said the name "Clayton Cartwright," and a deep voice answered "Here."

Matt turned around, and there at the desk immediately behind the empty chair next to him, he saw the same big and muscular boy who had taken up two seats on the bus. It suddenly dawned on Matt why the desk directly in front of Clayton had been empty when he entered the room. Apparently, everyone else had known better than to sit in front of Clayton. The carving on Matt's desk made it utterly obvious that this wasn't Clayton's first year at Hawthorne High. In fact, given his size and the fact that he needed a shave, Matt guessed that Clayton had been held back more than

Chapter 1 – First Day of School

once. While a couple of students passed out the books, Matt idly wondered how old Clayton would be by the time he eventually graduated.

Once the roll call was complete, Mr. Thompson walked around to the front of his desk. Leaning back against it, he swept his eyes over his students and began. "In this class, we will be studying American history. Now many of you probably expect to be spending the year memorizing names of presidents and dates of wars, things that happened long before you were born and have nothing to do with you. I wouldn't be surprised if some of you are expecting history to be boring, irrelevant, and something you just have to tolerate because the State of Indiana requires it for graduation. Well, that is not an unreasonable expectation." He paused, glancing briefly around the room to gauge his students' reactions. Several students stared back with a mixture of surprise and confusion, having never heard a teacher say anything negative about his own class.

Mr. Thompson continued. "It is true that I will be teaching you the *who*, *what*, *when*, and *where* of important historical events. But in this class, we are also going to dig a little deeper. I intend to teach you the *why* of historical events. Why did these events occur, and why should we care that they did? Why is America the way it is today? Without understanding the past, it's very difficult to understand the present and almost impossible to predict the future."

"Because I just moved to Hawthorne, and we're all new to Hawthorne High, I thought it might be interesting to spend one class looking at the local history of our town before we take on the history of our entire country. So with that in mind, I met last week with some members of the Hawthorne Historical Society. I spent several hours at the public library going through back issues of the town newspaper. Of course, I also spent quite a bit of time googling Hawthorne on my computer. In other words, I did a little historical research, and what I discovered is quite interesting."

Mr. Thompson looked around the class. "How many of you know why the town is called Hawthorne?"

No one raised his hand.

"No one? Okay, how about this? You all know the Hawthorne House, our town's infamous haunted house. Can anyone tell me why it was built?"

Matt's ears picked up when he realized that the teacher was talking about the old mansion next door to his house.

One student tentatively raised his hand.

Mr. Thompson glanced at his roster of students. "Yes, Mr. Harper. Do you know why it was built?"

"Er... So someone named Hawthorne could live there?"

Several students snickered and one muttered, "Great guess, Captain Obvious" under his breath.

"Well, that's true as far as it goes, but there's more to the story. We come now to perhaps the most interesting question. Does anyone care to guess why it looks abandoned when one might expect that someone would have fixed it up and turned it into a fancy bed

Chapter 1 – First Day of School

and breakfast?" He paused, looking once more around the room. "Anyone?"

"Well, here is what a little historical research revealed. The town of Hawthorne was founded in 1826 by a man named Ezekiel Hawthorne when he opened a general store for local farmers. As the area's largest landowner, Ezekiel was also the wealthiest man in the county. He was not known for being a modest man, so he named the small village that grew around the store after himself." Mr. Thompson smiled and said, "So now we have the answer to our first question. Ezekiel Hawthorne, the man who founded it back in the 1820s, named our town after himself." Mr. Thompson walked to the blackboard and wrote, *Ezekiel Hawthorne named our town after himself.*

"Ezekiel Hawthorne built a large home for his family here in town, but it was not the Hawthorne House we have today. A book I borrowed from the Hawthorne Historical Society had an old picture of the two-story wooden house that stood on the same site where the Victorian brownstone mansion now stands. When Ezekiel Hawthorne died, his eldest son, Harold, inherited everything. Known as an ambitious man, he worked very hard to increase his family's fortune. I found some old land titles and deeds that show that Harold Hawthorne soon owned most of the town including two saloons, a hotel, stable, and several other businesses. During the Civil War, the growing town of Hawthorne supplied men, wheat, and corn to the Union Army. But in those days, the town was not yet connected to any of the Midwest's railroads. To sell their crops, the local farmers had to haul them using nothing but horse-drawn wagons that weren't much faster than a slow walk. It would have taken farmers nine long hard days to make it down to Indianapolis or twelve days to reach Chicago, where they might be able to sell their produce for a higher price than they could locally. That is why Harold Hawthorne invested most of his family's fortune founding the Northern Indiana Railroad Company. And it was a good investment. Within a couple of years, his railway lines connected Hawthorne to Indianapolis, Chicago, Detroit, and Cleveland."

While Mr. Thompson paused to take a sip of water from the bottle on his desk, Matt tried to imagine what it was like to make such a long trip without a car or even modern roads. What did the farmers do for food and drink? Did they just pull off the side of the road at night and sleep under the wagon? What did they do if it rained?

Mr. Thompson looked briefly at his notes and continued. "Upon Harold's death, his eldest son, Henry Hubertus Hawthorne, inherited the family fortune and businesses. Henry Hawthorne was a proud man who felt that he had outgrown the town his family had built. He left Hawthorne and moved to Chicago, where he became a member of that city's elite."

"Now, here's another question for you. If the Hawthorne family left Hawthorne for Chicago, then who built the Hawthorne House mansion? The answer involves a chance meeting that ended in an unlikely marriage. You see in 1910, Henry was on a hunting and fishing trip along the coast of Maine. There, in the small fishing village of Deer Isle, he met Rhiannon

Chapter 1 – First Day of School

Llewellyn who by all accounts was a very charming young woman. Henry extended his stay, and one month later, the two were secretly married against the wishes of her parents. Apparently, they did not trust the stranger who wanted to take their daughter far away where they might never see her again. And Henry did indeed take his new bride back to Chicago, and there is no record that the two ever returned to Deer Isle or that she ever saw her parents again.

"But in Chicago, things did not go as Henry planned. Despite living in what must have seemed unimaginable luxury to Rhiannon, entries in Henry's journals clearly show he was worried that his wife was falling into a deep melancholy. First, she was never accepted by the members of Chicago's *nouveau riche*. Their marriage was quite scandalous, partially because their engagement was appallingly short according to the customs of the time. More shockingly, she was from a poor family from a tiny village in Maine that no one had ever heard of. Rhiannon also found Chicago to be far too crowded, noisy, and full of strangers. She longed to live in a small town that was more like the village where she grew up.

"Henry must have truly loved his wife because he gave up Chicago and all the business opportunities it offered. One year after their son Morgan was born, the couple returned here to Hawthorne, which had barely a fifth as many people a hundred years ago as it does today. No longer satisfied with his old family house, Henry had it torn down in 1912 and had the Hawthorne House built in its place. According to the Hawthorne News Gazette, he spent what the townspeople felt was an outrageous amount of money building his new mansion. According to a website I found on famous mansions of the Midwest, Henry had the brownstone brought all the way from Wisconsin, the Art Nouveau stained-glass windows from Tiffany's in New York, and the paintings and furniture from France. Six years later, Henry and Rhiannon's daughter Vivianne was born in their new mansion on Hawthorne street. And thus, we now have the answer to another of our questions. In 1912, Henry Hawthorne built Hawthorne House for his wife Rhiannon because she wanted to live and raise her children in a small town like Hawthorne instead of a big city like Chicago." Mr. Thompson turned and wrote the words *Henry Hawthorne built Hawthorne House in 1912* on the blackboard.

"And now for our final question. Why has Hawthorne House been allowed to fall into such a state of disrepair that many now think of it as Hawthorne's haunted house? This question is harder to answer than the others because the facts only provide circumstantial evidence. According to the newspaper articles and legal documents I found, the downfall of Hawthorne House began in 1937 when Henry and Rhiannon were killed in an automobile accident. Their 26-year-old son, Morgan, inherited the house, but he didn't want to live in a place that constantly reminded him of his parents. He gave the house to his 19-year-old sister, Vivianne, and moved to his mother's ancestral home on Deer Isle, Maine. Unlike her brother, Vivianne Hawthorne chose to stay in Hawthorne and eventually married a man named John Carter in October of 1941.

Chapter 1 – First Day of School

Two months later, the Japanese attacked Pearl Harbor, the United States entered World War Two, and John Carter was drafted. When the war ended in 1945, John Carter returned home, and nothing out of the ordinary happened until two years later when John Carter and a young woman named Mary Collins mysteriously disappeared. According to newspaper articles of the time, Ms. Collins lived next door to the Hawthorne House and was Vivianne's closest friend. Shortly after their disappearance, Vivianne Hawthorne filed for divorce, claiming she had discovered her husband was having an affair with Mary Collins, and that they ran off together when she confronted her husband. The divorce was granted, and Vivianne Carter once again became Vivianne Hawthorne. And today, she still lives alone in Hawthorne House, a recluse who no one sees except for the man who delivers her groceries."

Mr. Thompson paused to let the class consider what he had told them. "So where does that leave us? We know that in a relatively short time, Vivianne Hawthorne lost her parents, her brother moved back to Maine, and her new husband was drafted and away for four years. To top it all off, he had an affair and left her for her best friend. In other words, Vivianne Hawthorne had been abandoned by everyone she had ever cared for. Alone inside her home, why should she care how her yard and the outside of her house looks to others?"

Mr. Thompson ended his lecture and remained silent for a minute, while his students considered for the first time what it might be like to be "Old Lady Hawthorne," the 'witch' of Hawthorne House. Matt did not have to wonder what it was like to lose someone you really loved. He already knew.

"And that, class, is an example of historical research. It deals with all five Ws: not just with the questions of *who*, *what*, *when*, and *where*. It also seeks to answer the question *why*. Why an event happened and why it's important." Mr. Thompson walked back to the chalkboard and wrote those five words.

"Now it's your turn to write about a historical event. Take out a piece of paper and spend the rest of the period writing a paragraph about a past event that was important to you. The event can be anything. It can be something good like the birth of a brother or sister, the move to a new house, one of your parents getting a new job, or a special family vacation. It can even be something bad like an accident, injury, illness, or even the death of a pet. Just remember the five Ws and write *what* the event was, *when* and *where* it happened, *who* it involved, and *why* it mattered. That way, you can begin to get a feel for what history is all about before we start with American history tomorrow." He looked up at the wall clock and continued, "You have 15 minutes 'til the bell rings. Hand your papers in on your way out." With that, the teacher turned back to the classroom and began erasing the chalkboard.

Matt had stopped listening when Mr. Thompson said the word "death." *What am I supposed to write?* Matt wondered. *That Mom went out to pick flowers and never came back? That I spent an eternity at the local hospital waiting for her to wake up, and she never did? Maybe I should write about how Dad changed when he realized that she was gone forever*

Chapter 1 – First Day of School

and knew he would never see the ocean again without thinking of her. Or how he'd fled to Hawthorne, taking Tina and me back to this little town where he grew up.

Matt couldn't stop his awful thoughts from rushing through his mind. *No more beaches and climbing on the rocks. No more sand dunes. No more forests and hills. No more long walks alone along the cliffs. No mother!*

What did I do last summer? Last summer, I watched my Mom die, and now I feel like I died, too. But unlike her, I'm still breathing, and there's no ventilator to turn off.

Matt felt a big finger poke him in the shoulder, dragging him back to the present and the blank sheet of paper on the desk in front of him. "Hey, new kid, what's wrong with you?" Clayton's low voice whispered from behind him. "Are you having some kind of fit or something?"

Matt saw the teardrops splattered on the paper and realized he had been silently crying. Clayton must have seen his shoulders shaking. Matt angrily turned around and hissed, "Mind your own business!"

Clayton fell silent for a second, surprised that anyone would dare speak to him like that. But then he noticed the tears rolling down Matt's cheeks. "What's the matter?" Clayton whispered back, "Is the little crybaby going to throw a temper tantrum just because he's got to write an itty-bitty paragraph?"

All the pent-up emotions of the last few weeks welled up and washed over Matt. "I told you to mind your own damn business!" he shouted, jumping from

The Secrets of Hawthorne House

his seat and turning to stand with his hands balled into fists, glaring down at Clayton.

"That will be quite enough, Mr. Mitchell!" Mr. Thompson commanded as he walked swiftly over to stand between Matt and Clayton. "We do not allow that kind of language here. You can discuss losing your temper and your inappropriate choice of words with Principal Tanner." He wrote a brief note, handed it to Matt, and walked back to his desk.

Matt could feel everyone's eyes watching him as he shoved his history textbook, pencil, and paper into his backpack. He wondered how many heard Clayton whisper, "I'll deal with you later" as he turned and stalked out the door. *Damn*, Matt thought, *this is just great! My first day, and I'm sent to the principal.*

Matt trudged to the school office, nervously asked to see the principal, and was told to take a seat. After waiting for what seemed like forever, the bell marking the end of the first period rang, and the principal's door was still closed. A few minutes later, the bell rang again, marking the beginning of the second period. Ten minutes later, Mr. Tanner finally walked in, opened the door, and motioned Matt into his office.

"So, what brings you to me on your first day of school?"

Matt silently handed him his teacher's note.

"Losing your temper and cursing in class. I assume that Mr. Thompson has informed you that such behavior will not be tolerated here at Hawthorne High."

Matt nodded sheepishly.

Chapter 1 – First Day of School

"Do you want to tell me what happened?"

Matt thought it over for a second. One day in, and he was already getting a reputation as a crybaby who couldn't control his temper. The last thing he needed was to get a reputation as a snitch too.

"No, sir. It was something personal. It won't happen again."

"See that it doesn't, Mr. Mitchell. As this is your first day and first offense, I will let you off this time with just a warning. However, one more outburst or incident of cursing, and you will have an in-school suspension, and I will have a talk with your parents. Are we clear on this?"

"Yes, Sir," Matt muttered, hoping that Clayton would forget his threat and let Matt keep his promise to the principal about no more problems.

"Okay, Mr. Mitchell," the principal replied, looking up at the clock on the wall. "You can go. Stop by the front desk, and Mrs. Fletcher will give you a hall pass for your teacher, explaining why you're late." Matt picked up the note and left to wander the empty hallways in search of his Algebra I classroom.

When Matt finally found his class, only a few empty desks remained. He looked around the room but didn't see Clayton, who must have had a different class that period. Matt handed the principal's note to his Intro to Algebra teacher and took an empty seat, trying hard to ignore several students from his American history class who were staring at him. He opened his book and did his best to fade into the woodwork for the rest of the period.

Third-period biology went significantly better. For the first time, Matt shared a class with Tina, who liked all things science, almost as much as he did. "Hey, Sis," he said, as he took a seat next to her.

"Hi, Matt. How's your morning been?"

"It sucked. How was yours?"

"What? Your first day in high school isn't even half over. How could it suck?"

"I'll tell you later."

"Okay..." Tina said, giving him a skeptical look.

By the end of the period, Matt was pretty sure biology was going to be his favorite class, although he wasn't looking forward to dissecting a frog. The only animals he wanted to cut were the ones that were cooked and ready to eat.

After class, Matt decided to drop off his morning books in his locker on his way to the cafeteria. But as he approached, he noticed that his locker door was slightly ajar. Rushing up, he yanked open the door to discover that his new coat was gone. Matt's trick of lining up the shackle of the padlock with the hole hadn't fooled at least one young thief. Matt slammed his locker door in frustration, but it clanged back open. Adding insult to injury, the thief who had stolen his jacket had also locked his padlock to his locker so that the door couldn't shut. Afraid the same thing that happened to his coat would also happen to his books, Matt left them in his backpack, closed his locker door as far as it would go, and stormed off to lunch.

By the time Matt finally arrived at the cafeteria, it was crowded with scores of students talking and

Chapter 1 – First Day of School

eating. The lunch line was long, and by the time he got to where they were serving the food, the pizza and tacos were gone. Matt was forced to settle for a piece of overcooked meatloaf that looked as if it had been left over from the previous school year. One of the cooks added some cold, crusty mashed potatoes topped with gravy with the consistency of pudding. Matt picked up a couple of cartons of milk, paid for his lunch, and carried his tray into the cafeteria to look for a place to sit.

Matt scanned the room for Tina, hoping to tell her about his run-in with Clayton and being sent to the principal's office. The cafeteria was almost twice the size of the one at their middle school back in Oregon, so it took a while for him to spot her. He finally found Tina near the back of the cafeteria, sitting quietly at one end of a table filled with girls who were all talking with each other. Some of the girls were giggling as they watched the boys at the next table when they thought the boys weren't looking.

Matt shook his head with a mixture of frustration and concern. Tina was smart, maybe even smarter than he was, although he'd never admit it to her. She excelled in math, taking Algebra II while Matt took Algebra I. He also knew that both of them would ace biology. Looking at the giggling girls sitting at her table, he couldn't help hoping she'd find some friends who viewed school as more than just a place to meet boys.

Matt turned and eventually found a seat at the end of a table next to a bunch of older students. The meatloaf had dried out and tasted as bad as it looked.

Somehow that seemed appropriate, given how his day was going. Matt was washing his third bite down with his milk when he heard a familiar voice coming from the end of the next table. He looked up from his tray to see Clayton Cartwright, sitting with his broad back to him and talking to two other boys. He recognized one of the two from his algebra class. The pointy-nosed, little ferret-faced freshman was Dylan Jones.

"Colin, did you get a look at the fat pig sitting at the table behind you?" Clayton asked the tall blond boy with a cruel face who sat opposite him. "She should hide her face in a bag if she's going to come in here where people are trying to eat."

Matt looked over and noticed it was Sarah, the girl he'd sat beside on the bus ride to school. Although she tried not to show it by looking down at her lunch, it was clear from the pained expression on her face that she'd overheard Clayton's cruel remark. Matt felt a twinge of guilt remembering how he'd been embarrassed sitting next to her. Okay, so she could lose a few pounds and get braces, but no one deserved to be treated like that.

Clayton's friend, Colin, glanced over his shoulder at Sarah and then turned back to continue eating. "Sooey, pig, pig, pig!" he called between mouthfuls.

Dylan laughed and said, "Oink, oink."

A few seconds later, Matt and Clayton both noticed a short, skinny boy wearing glasses who was walking towards them carrying his tray of dirty dishes.

Chapter 1 – First Day of School

"Nerd alert," Clayton said to Colin, who had his back to the boy. "Nerd approaching, arriving in three, two, one."

The countdown reached zero just as the small boy passed Colin, who suddenly stretched out his foot. The boy tripped, his tray of dirty dishes and leftovers flying from his hands in a low arc straight at Matt. Time seemed to slow as Matt began to push himself back, but Matt wasn't nearly fast enough. The boy's tray crashed into Matt's, sending the remainder of both lunches cascading into his lap. When Matt stood up, he was wearing blobs of mashed potatoes while streams of milk and gravy ran down his pants and onto the floor. In disbelief, Matt looked up to see all three of the bullies laughing at him.

"Good one, Colin! Killed two birds with one foot!" the little toady Dylan crowed, grinning like he'd cracked the funniest joke of all time.

"Hey, it's the crybaby from first period I told you about," Clayton taunted. "Did you enjoy your little talk with the principal?"

Matt was fuming and about to yell something nasty about Clayton's IQ equaling his age when he saw the cafeteria monitor quickly walking his way. Leaving the trays where they were, Matt abruptly turned and stormed out of the cafeteria, trying hard to ignore the snickers and stares of the students around him.

On reaching the hallway, Matt ran to the nearest bathroom, hoping that no one in the hall would notice he was wearing what was left of his lunch. Once there, he looked around for a paper towel dispenser, but the school had hot-air hand dryers instead. With no other choice, Matt went into a stall, wadded up some toilet paper, and used it to wipe the food off his pants. Although he'd successfully removed most of the mashed potatoes, the toilet paper disintegrated when he tried to scrub off the gravy stains, leaving his pants covered in dozens of white flecks of wet paper. By the time he'd wiped them off with his hands and stood for what seemed like forever under the hot air dryer, Matt was left with a damp food stain on the front of his pants and painful calf muscles from standing on tiptoes so that the hot air from the dryer could reach his crotch.

The rest of Matt's day wasn't much better. He got lost twice trying to find his afternoon classes and was late both times. Colin, Clayton, and Dylan were in several of his other classes and made a point of loudly commenting on his stained pants as he entered each class.

Eventually, Matt's first day at Hawthorne High was over. His mood was as dark as the storm clouds rolling in overhead when he walked out the school's front doors. The wind was rising and the temperature dropping as Matt searched for his bus and any sign of Colin and his minions among the crowd of students that had gathered there. His only decent luck during the entire catastrophic day was being able to quickly find his bus, sit down near the driver, and have the seats around him taken by the time Clayton finally sauntered up the steps. The bully was unable to do more than make a rude remark as he passed. Matt couldn't wait to get home.

Chapter 1 – First Day of School

"What happened to your coat?" Tina asked, as the twins exited the bus in front of their house. "And what did you do to your pants? You look like a slob."

"I forgot it at school," Matt lied, hoping that his coat would turn up later in the school lost and found.

Standing on their front porch while Tina unlocked the door, Matt glanced past her at the dilapidated Victorian mansion next door. Wet and shivering, he felt like he had about as much of a chance of fitting in at school as the Hawthorne House had of fitting into their neighborhood with its neat rows of cookie-cutter houses.

Over dinner, Matt told his father and sister about his horrible day. But he didn't mention his missing coat. Although he and Tina weren't supposed to know, Matt had overheard their father discussing the family's finances with Uncle James. Their mother's massive medical bills, the outrageous cost of her funeral, and their move to Hawthorne had wiped out all of his mother's meager life insurance and much of the family's savings. Without the income from their mother's pottery shop, the family was barely making ends meet. There was no money for a new coat unless absolutely necessary.

After Matt had finished, Tina gave her brother a concerned look. "When we were in biology class, and you said your morning sucked, I thought you were probably overreacting. I was wrong. Your day really did suck."

Exhausted from a stressful day at work, their father was considerably less sympathetic. "Now, Matt, you can't let your first day get you down. From what I've been told, Hawthorne High is an excellent school that'll do a great job of preparing you for college if you just apply yourself. Besides, every school has bullies. You'll just have to stand up to them or learn to stay out of their way.

"Matt, the best thing to do is to make some new friends," Tina added, trying to act as if she were several years older than him instead of the actual seven minutes that separated their births. "Find your own group and try to fit in."

Easier said than done, Matt thought. Matt's father had never been as sympathetic as his mother, and the conversation just made him miss her more.

Matt left the dinner table early, went up to his bedroom, closed the door, and turned on his computer. He selected a playlist to fit his dark mood, and *The Sea Cries Salty Tears* by the indie rock band Death Watch began to play. *"Your hand grows cold, and they close your eyes. The ocean moans, and the sea bird cries."* Listening to the lyrics, Matt decided that he hated Indiana and Hawthorne High School. And he hated Clayton Cartwright most of all.

Chapter 2
The House Next Door

The rest of the week wasn't quite as bad as Matt had feared. His coat turned up three days later in the lost and found, dirty but otherwise unharmed. Because Colin, Clayton, and Dylan had a large group of students they regularly picked on, Matt could often safely hide among the rest of the students. He also met a few students who were okay, although none of them seemed to have much in common with him other than a general dislike for the school and Colin's gang.

The one possible exception was Paul Stephens, a student in Matt's English class. Like Matt, Paul had lost his mother to a car accident, although it had happened eight years earlier when Paul was only in the second grade. With no mother and a father who drowned the pain of his wife's death in an endless river of beer, Paul had grown up to become a loner. Giving up on fitting in, he instead turned his interests to the occult. Although Matt didn't share Paul's obsession with vampires, ghosts, and other demons of the night, he could understand Paul's fascination with death.

"Is it true?" Paul asked, when Matt mentioned that his house was on Hawthorne Drive.

Matt nodded.

"Whoa! You seen the old witch yet?"

"You mean the old woman who lives in the Hawthorne House? No, not yet."

"Of course, that's who I mean," Paul replied as though it were obvious. He glanced around to see if any teachers were near enough to overhear, then leaned forward and whispered, "Old Lady Hawthorne. She's an actual, honest-to-God witch."

"Come on, Paul. This isn't one of your graphic novels, and Halloween's not 'til the end of next month. Besides, my American history teacher told us about the Hawthornes and Hawthorne House on the first day of school. She's only an old woman who has had shitty luck. She's probably just hiding from everyone because she doesn't trust people after her parents died and both her brother and her husband left her."

"I'm not kidding, Matt. I don't care what your teacher said, 'cause everyone 'round here knows the real story. Fifty years ago, Old Lady Hawthorne found out her husband was having an affair with her best friend, the neighbor lady next-door. Old Lady Hawthorne was so pissed off, she poisoned him. Then she cut out his heart, cooked it up in a stew, and invited her former friend over for dinner. After her rival had eaten a piece of her husband's heart, Old Lady Hawthorne put a curse on her." Paul leaned even closer and continued. "She cast a spell that turned the woman into a dog. Sometimes people still see the phantom hound late at night, prowling around the graveyard looking for what's left of her lost lover."

"You've been watching too many horror movies," Matt said, shaking his head in disbelief. "There's no such thing as witches. Besides, if she'd really done

Chapter 2 – The House Next Door

what you said, she'd still be in jail for murder instead of living next door to me."

"Next door?" Paul asked, sounding really impressed. "Wicked! You actually live right next to the Hawthorne House? That means you live in the exact same house where her husband's mistress lived! They say Old Lady Hawthorne still holds a grudge against anyone who lives in that house. No one has ever stayed there for more than a few months before being forced to leave for one reason or another. You'll be gone before Christmas."

Matt didn't buy a word of it. He wasn't naïve enough to still believe in witches, spells, and spectral dogs haunting graveyards at midnight. Still, there was no denying that there was something strange about the old Victorian mansion next door.

Later, when the school bus dropped the twins off in front of their home, Matt couldn't help walking over to the Hawthorne House's front gate and taking a good long look. At three and a half stories, the dilapidated old Victorian towered over the other houses in the neighborhood. Unlike the one and two-story wooden homes around it, the Hawthorne House was fashioned from large blocks of brownstone, making it appear more like a castle than a mere mansion.

The house's most distinctive features were its three towers. The single circular window in the strangely-shaped roof of the square central tower gazed like a cycloptic eye over the neighborhood. On the left corner of the house stood an octagonal tower, while a round tower stood on the right. Both were topped with conical black slate roofs that looked remarkably like giant witches' hats.

Although mostly hidden behind the corner towers, Matt could see the very tops of a pair of massive red-brick chimneys that ran up the center of both sides of the house. An ornamental iron grill stood atop the slate roof while ornate wrought-iron lightning rods topped the twin corner towers. Fancy gingerbread trim lined the slate roof of the ground floor's wrap-around porch. The final distinguishing feature of the house was the stained and cut-glass panels along the top of each window, above and on either side of the front door, and forming the ornate center windows of the second and third floors.

In its prime, the Hawthorne House must have been truly magnificent. Now, the only evidence that the Hawthorne House had not been abandoned years ago were the thin streams of smoke rising from the row of narrow black chimney pots of the chimney facing Matt's home. Most of the paint on its porch and window frames had long since peeled off, and parts of its gingerbread trim hung loosely while several pieces were completely missing. The stained-glass panels were covered with so much grime that it was hard to tell their original colors. Finally, the yard looked like it hadn't been maintained since the house was built. An army of weeds had long ago conquered the flower beds, and in places, the grass would require a scythe instead of a lawnmower.

Now that he thought about it, Matt realized that he'd never actually seen the old woman who supposedly lived there. He'd never seen a car parked in

Chapter 2 – The House Next Door

its driveway or on the street in front of the house. The only signs of the recluse were the occasional smoke from the chimneys, what appeared to be flickering candlelight coming through some of the windows in the evenings, and the man who delivered bags of groceries every Saturday.

As the days passed, Matt became more and more curious about the old house. He asked Tina, but she'd only heard the same stories he'd heard from Paul. One night over dinner, Matt decided to ask his father about the house and its mysterious occupant. "Dad, was the house next door like it is now when you were growing up?"

Sam Mitchell finished chewing and swallowing his roasted broccoli before saying, "Pretty much. It's looked more-or-less abandoned for as long as I can remember. Why'd you ask?"

"Just curious, I guess. My American History teacher said the old woman who lives there is probably a recluse because she's lost her parents in a car wreck, her brother left town, and her husband ran away with her best friend. But the kids at school say she's a witch who murdered her husband."

"That's what I heard, too," Tina added. "Kathy Perkins from Spanish class swears one of her brother's friends saw Old Lady Hawthorne flying on a broom over the lake a few years ago.

"Now, kids, don't tell me you still believe in witches," Sam said, as he looked incredulously at the twins.

"No, of course not," Matt replied somewhat indignantly. "But you got to admit the house is creepy, and just because she isn't a witch doesn't mean she didn't kill her husband."

"Now, you can stop right there," Sam said with more than a little annoyance. "She was never charged with any crime, and you should assume people are innocent until proven guilty. I want the two of you to promise me you'll mind your own business and not spread cruel rumors about our next-door neighbor. If she wants to be left alone, then we need to leave her in peace."

Matt didn't know it, but he was going to meet Old Lady Hawthorne very soon. The reason was money; he didn't have any. He and Tina hadn't been getting their weekly allowances in the three months since their mother died.

One evening as Matt was finishing loading the dinner dishes into the dishwasher, Matt asked, "So Dad, how's work going?"

Sam looked up from his laptop and the computer books covering the kitchen table. "Okay, I guess. I'm a little rusty, and I'm not up to speed yet on some of the newer technologies, but I'm getting there."

"I don't suppose there's any chance you've been given a raise yet?"

Sam shook his head. "Matt, I've only been working there a couple of months. People don't usu-

Chapter 2 – The House Next Door

ally get raises until they've been working for at least a full year. What's this about?"

"Well, it's been some time since you've been able to give Tina and me allowances. When do you think we might start getting them again? I can't buy any new CDs or video games, and I'm getting really bored with my old ones."

"Matt, do you have any idea how incredibly expensive your mom's medical and funeral bills were? By the time they were paid, we barely had enough money left over to make it here and cover the first month's rent and the deposit on the house."

"I know, Dad. I overheard you talking to Uncle James about it. I just hoped that maybe things weren't quite as bad as they sounded."

"I wish they weren't, but without the money from your mom's pottery, we're basically living month to month. We just can't afford any unnecessary expenses right now, and I'm afraid that includes allowances. I'll have to get a raise first, and I'm not sure how I'm going to do that until I get a lot better at writing and debugging software. Creating real code is a lot harder than teaching intro to programming back at Port Orford High, and I'm competing against co-workers practically half my age who are twice as fast as I am."

"That's okay, Dad. I understand. But I've got to get some money somehow. I'll go crazy if I don't get some new CDs and video games."

"Well, son, how about getting yourself a job?"

"But, Dad, no one's going to hire me. I'm only fifteen, and you have to be at least sixteen to work at a fast-food restaurant or grocery store. Besides, between my homework on weeknights and not being old enough to drive, who's going to give me a job?"

"Matt, I'm sorry, but you're just making excuses. Tina has started babysitting, and you can mow lawns like I did when I was your age. You could help people with house and yard work. Maybe you can find something here in the neighborhood, and you can always ride your bike to jobs."

"But..."

"I know! Tomorrow's Saturday, and you can begin by going next door. Introduce yourself to Mrs. Hawthorne, and offer to help her with her yard. Given the nasty things that kids have been saying about her, I bet she'd appreciate some help."

Matt gave his father a dubious look.

"Just think about it, okay? If you want the money badly enough, you'll find a way to make it happen. In the meantime, do what I do and listen to music on YouTube. It's free, and you can find just about everything."

"Okay, Dad. I'll think about it." Matt finished loading the dishwasher and went upstairs. He grudgingly started on his homework, but not before spending half an hour exploring YouTube's massive repository of music and discovering several new groups.

The next morning after breakfast, Matt put on some old work clothes and walked next door to the

Chapter 2 – The House Next Door

Hawthorne House. Although he was curious to finally see what his next-door neighbor looked like, he also had to admit to himself that the house got creepier the closer he got to it. The weather-worn gate creaked loudly as he opened it, and a few enormous spiders wove webs in the weeds and dead rosebushes behind the fence. Several of the ornate spindles under the wrap-around porch railing were either missing or hanging loosely at an angle. Climbing up the front steps, he carefully stepped over a broken board and walked up to the front door.

Matt looked for a button to ring the doorbell but couldn't find one. There was only a large ornate doorknocker in the shape of a laughing gargoyle on the old oak door. He lifted it and let it fall. The resulting thud was much louder than Matt expected, but nothing happened. He let the knocker fall again.

After a few seconds, he heard footsteps and saw a shadow through one of the two narrow stained-glass windows that bordered each side of the door. An old woman's wavering voice demanded, "Who's there?"

"Excuse me, Mrs. Hawthorne," Matt said, addressing the shadow through the glass. "My name is Matt Mitchell, and I live next door. I was wondering if you might have any jobs I could do for you. I could cut your lawn or work on your flower beds."

"Just a second, young man," the shadow behind the glass said, speaking with an accent Matt didn't recognize. Then he heard the clicks of four separate locks and the scraping sound of a deadbolt sliding back. The big oak door slowly creaked open a few inches before being stopped by a thick safety chain.

With the curtains closed, the room behind her was as dark as a long-abandoned crypt, but the cool air from inside smelled of lavender and candles.

An old woman peered out at him from behind the chain that hung between the door and its frame. Her snow-white hair and pale complexion from decades hidden from the sun stood in stark contrast to the old-fashioned black dress that covered everything but her head and hands. Emerald eyes gazed out from skin that was heavily wrinkled with age and loneliness.

"Let me take a look at you, young man," she said, gazing intently at him over her half-moon reading glasses. "Are you sure that you'ah not just heah tah play some sick joke on a helpless old woman? Did Colin O'Connell or Clayton Cartwright put you up tah this? Why are you really heah?" She glared over his shoulder for any sign of someone hiding behind the trunks of the old oak trees lining Hawthorne Drive.

"No one has put me up to anything, Mrs. Hawthorne, except maybe my father," Matt replied, trying not to flinch under the powerful gaze of her deep-set eyes. He was definitely insulted at her suggestion that he would be swayed by the likes of bullies who delighted in making him miserable. "I'm Matt Mitchell, and I live next door. I really need to make some money, and my father suggested I might be able to earn some by helping you with your yard."

"We'll see," Mrs. Hawthorne said skeptically, apparently satisfied for now that Matt was alone. "I'll tell you what. You work on my dooah yahd for an hour, and if you work hahd and do a good job, you're hired." The old woman spoke with a strange accent

Chapter 2 – The House Next Door

that stretched out some words and softened the letter 'R' to the point where it occasionally vanished. "If not, then you can just go back and tell your friends you've seen and talked with the infamous Old Lady Hawthorne, the murderer of wayward husbands and caster of wicked spells." With that, she chuckled and shut the door in Matt's face.

"Well, I'll be," Matt muttered to himself, wondering what to do next as he listened to her relock each lock and slide the deadbolt back into place. And what did she mean by *dooah yahd*? Did she mean her front yard? He almost decided to go somewhere else, but then it dawned on him that this might just be her weird way of testing him. In the end, her remark about him being a member of Colin O'Connell's gang decided the issue. He'd rather pass her test than live down to her poor expectations of him.

Since she hadn't offered him the use of her lawnmower (if she even had one), he went back home, gassed up his father's lawnmower, and started cutting the grass in her front yard. It definitely wasn't easy work. The yard was so overgrown that every few feet, Matt had to push down on the handle to lift its front end to keep the blades from stalling. Later, he returned home to get his father's rake and lawn bags for the mowed grass.

Before long, sweat was dripping onto his glasses and into his eyes. *This is ridiculous*, Matt thought. *At this rate, I'll never get done.* But then he remembered how she'd asked him if he was one of Colin's minions. That only made him even more determined not to quit. Thirsty, Matt was about to head back home for a drink when he heard Mrs. Hawthorne call.

"Boy, come over heah," she said, her head framed behind the partially open door.

Wiping the sweat off his forehead with his shirtsleeve, Matt walked up onto the porch. "Yes, Mrs. Hawthorne?"

"I've been watchin' you, young man," she said, handing him a drink under the door's security chain. It was a tall, thin glass of homemade lemonade, cool and refreshing with just the right mix of fresh-squeezed lemons, sugar, and just a hint of honey. "It seems that I owe you an apology," she continued after he handed back the empty glass. "Apparently, you really ah interested in earnin' some spendin' money. You can work six hours each Saturday, and I'll pay you five dollars an hour, plus an extra dollar foah each hour that you work as hahd as you have so far this mornin'. Deal?" She extended a thin age-spotted hand through the narrow opening.

"Deal!" Matt answered, shaking her hand. The old woman's grip, though bony, was surprisingly firm.

"Well, you can start weedin' the flowerbeds when you finish mowin' the dooah yahd, and I'll pay you when you'ah done for the day." With that, she calmly closed the door, and Matt could once again hear the turning of locks and the sliding of the deadbolt.

During the remainder of the morning, Matt mowed the front lawn, raked until his arms ached, and dragged what seemed like an endless succession of overflowing lawn bags out to the road for the garbage

Chapter 2 – The House Next Door

men to pick up. Matt was starving by the time Tina called him home for lunch.

"Well, I see you've followed my advice," Sam said, smiling approvingly as he watched his son wolf down a second sandwich. "I looked over a couple of times this morning, and it looks like you've been doing a great job so far. So, how much are you making?"

"She's paying me five dollars an hour plus an extra dollar an hour as long as I keep working as hard as I have today," Matt replied between mouthfuls. "And she's letting me work six hours each weekend. At this rate, I'll have enough to buy one of the video games I've been wanting by the time I'm finished this afternoon."

"So, Matt, what's Old Lady Hawthorne like?" Tina asked.

"I don't know," Matt answered, stopping to think. "Old, I guess... old and strange."

"Strange? How so?" she asked.

"Well, she's kind of paranoid. She must have half a dozen locks on the door, and she only opens her door a couple inches to talk to me. And she stands right behind the opening like she's trying to keep me from seeing inside."

"Sounds to me more like she was afraid of you," Matt's father countered. "An old lady living alone can't be too cautious around strangers."

"Maybe," Matt replied. "Then, there's also her funny accent.

"Her accent?" Tina asked, more curious about that than the multiple locks on their neighbor's door. "What's she sound like?"

"The most obvious thing is she usually doesn't pronounce the letter *r* on the ends of words. She'll say things like *fathah* instead of *father* and *youah* instead of *your*. And she doesn't pronounce the *g* on words that end with *ing*. She'll say stuff like *workin'* instead of *working*."

"You know," Sam said, "there are lots of people who don't say the g's on the ends of words."

"Yeah, Dad. I know," Matt said. "But it's really obvious when she does it. And that's not all. She stretches out some of her vowels, so they sound like they're two syllables long." Matt paused to think of a good example. "For instance, she'll say *doo-ah* instead of *door*, *fo-ah* instead of *for*, and *he-ah* instead of *here*. I've never heard anyone do that before."

"Strange," Tina observed.

"And that's not the strangest thing. She calls her yard a door *yahd*."

"That is weird," Tina said. "Me, neither."

"I'm not sure," Sam said, "not having ever spoken to the lady myself, but it sounds to me like she could be from someplace in New England. Maybe Maine. Regardless, remember it's not polite to call someone's accent funny. After all, from her point of view, you might be the one with the funny accent."

"Okay, Dad," Matt said. "I did hear in school that her mother was from Maine, but she was born right here in Hawthorne, right next door in fact. But if she

Chapter 2 – The House Next Door

grew up here, then why does she have a different accent?"

"Well, you got me there, Matt," Sam said. "Once you get to know her better, why don't you ask her? I bet she'd appreciate someone showing a little interest in her after all these years living alone. Old folks usually like talking about their experiences when they were young. Just remember to be polite about it, and who knows what you might hear."

Ten minutes later, Matt was back at the Hawthorne House mowing the backyard. There was far too much for him to do to get bored, and the rest of the afternoon passed surprisingly fast. A small ornately-carved table holding a glass and a cut-crystal pitcher of fresh lemonade had appeared on the porch, and Matt felt amazingly refreshed and invigorated after each time he paused to drink. Although he never saw Mrs. Hawthorne step outside of the house, the jug was always full and inviting.

Matt was amazed at his progress. He completed the mowing and started on the front flowerbeds. He cut and pulled weeds until he had several more lawn bags standing out by the road. Although the yard still needed a lot of work before it would look as good as those of the other houses on the block, it no longer looked like it belonged on the set of a horror movie.

Overall, Matt was pleased with himself, even if his hands and arms ached from all the work he'd done. When his six hours for the day were over, he stepped up on the porch, but before he could lift the doorknocker, the front door creaked opened a few inches to reveal Mrs. Hawthorne's smiling face behind the security chain.

"I must admit that I'm impressed, young man, and that is not somethin' that happens very often when you're as old as I am," she said, glancing over his shoulders to her newly transformed front yard. "Next Saturday, I shall tell you which of the plants tah dig up and how tah trim the ones that are worth keepin'. If you continue workin' like this, then we may yet complete the flowerbeds before the first frost." With this, she held out three crisp ten-dollar bills and the additional six one-dollar bills she'd promised for his continued hard work.

"Thank you, Mrs. Hawthorne," Matt said, taking the money and stuffing it into a pocket of his dirty jeans. "I'm glad I could prove to you I'm not one of Colin O'Connell's gang."

"And thank you, Mr. Mitchell, for the good, honest work you did. And for lettin' me prove tah you that I'm not the wicked old witch they say I am," she said, with an odd little smile before she once more closed, locked, and bolted her front door.

The next morning, Matt awoke with sore arms and back, but also with a sense of pride in the obvious difference he'd made in his neighbor's yard. As he lay in bed enjoying his feeling of accomplishment, two things dawned on him. He hadn't fallen asleep missing his mother, and his reoccurring nightmare hadn't terrorized his sleep.

And so it continued each Saturday in September. Matt weeded and replanted the flowerbeds, trimmed

Chapter 2 – The House Next Door

dead branches from the trees, and scraped and repainted the picket fence in front of the old Hawthorne House. He even replaced the broken board on the front steps and fixed a couple of window shutters that needed new screws. Each Saturday morning, Mrs. Hawthorne gave him new chores, and rain or shine, he worked his six hours. Each Saturday afternoon, Matt returned home, exhausted but thirty-six dollars richer. But not once did she fully open her front door or invite him in.

Chapter 3
Gerallt Moves In

The first Saturday in October, the air was crisp and full of yellow leaves and acorns falling from the old oaks that lined Hawthorne Drive. The previous week, some men had repaired the gingerbread trim and broken spindles on the Hawthorne House's wraparound porch so Matt could paint them. He had spent the morning and half of the afternoon sanding and scraping off old paint when he heard the familiar clicking and creaking of Mrs. Hawthorne unlocking and unbolting her front door. Putting down his paint scraper and removing the dust mask his father made him wear because of the lead in old paint, he turned to find her in her usual place behind the security chain of the partially-opened door.

"Can I do something for you, Mrs. Hawthorne?" Matt asked, quickly brushing paint dust and chips from his hands and shirtsleeves.

"Ayuh, Matt," she replied from within the darkness of her foyer. "Somethin's come up, and I was wonderin' if I could talk you intah workin' a few extra hours today."

"Sure, Mrs. Hawthorne," Matt answered, thinking about the new sound system for his room that he'd finally be able to buy. "I could probably work an extra two or three hours. I might even be able to work a few hours tomorrow if you need me to. I'll have to ask my dad first."

Chapter 3 – Gerallt Moves In

"Just today, if you don't mind," Mrs. Hawthorne answered, absentmindedly running a hand through her long white hair. Then she looked back at Matt. "Tomorrow I'll be right out straight. My niece and her three children will be arrivin' from Maine. In fact, they will be movin' in tah stay with me, and I'd really like tah have this old house lookin' its finest for them. It would be wonderful if you could finish paintin' the veranda today."

Matt looked up and down the length of the large front porch before nodding. "Sure thing, Mrs. Hawthorne. It may take a while, but I should be able to get at least the first coat of paint on before dark."

"Well, do what you can, dear. I have so much work tah do myself, gettin' their rooms ready and such." With that, she quickly closed and relocked the door, leaving Matt to wonder about Mrs. Hawthorne's niece and especially her three children. Over the next hour, he finished scraping off the old paint, swept up the paint chips, and started applying the first coat of paint to the porch. He was still working when Tina called him in for supper.

"We're going to have some new neighbors," Matt announced as he joined his father and sister at the dinner table. "Pass the spaghetti, please."

"New neighbors?" Tina asked, handing Matt the pasta and sauce. "Who?"

"Mrs. Hawthorne's niece and her three children are flying in tomorrow from somewhere in Maine," Matt replied, dishing up a huge plate of spaghetti. "They're moving in, and that's why I worked until dinner. She wants me to return once I'm done eating to finish painting the porch so the house will look nice for them."

"I thought you worked late today," Sam said. "It's amazing how good the place is beginning to look."

"Thanks, Dad. It's been a huge amount of work, but it feels great to look over there and be able to say I've done it all by myself. I've even noticed that my arms are stronger, and I don't get tired as fast as I used to."

"Yes, Matt," Sam said, "You can be proud of yourself. I'm glad you stuck with it."

"And I'll have earned enough for my new sound system by the time I'm done tonight," Matt remarked between mouthfuls.

"Has she let you inside the house yet?" Tina asked.

"No. She never even opens the door more than a few inches and stands in the opening, so I can't see past her. And she still locks and bolts the door as soon as she closes it. Kind of weird, like she is hiding something."

"Sounds more like she's just scared," Tina suggested.

"Possibly," Sam said. "Still, an old woman living alone has the right to protect herself. Besides, she's bound to pick up some unusual habits after being by herself for so many years."

After dinner, Matt returned to his painting. The sun had set, and it was getting dark and cold by the time he finished the last of the gingerbread trim. He cleaned the brushes, put away the remainder of the paint, and knocked on the front door. It was a while

Chapter 3 – Gerallt Moves In

before Mrs. Hawthorne opened it, paid him, and bid him goodnight. Exhausted, Matt fairly collapsed when he returned home, but the fifty-four dollars in his pocket made it all worthwhile.

The next day, Matt found lots of reasons to spend time in his front yard or ride his bike up and down the street. He was curious to see Mrs. Hawthorne's niece and especially to learn more about her three children. But the morning and afternoon passed without a taxi from the airport or the arrival of a moving truck. As far as he could tell, it was just another peaceful Sunday on Hawthorne Drive. The old house next door was as quiet as a graveyard.

Eventually, bedtime came, and Matt fell asleep long before the grandfather clock in the library of the Hawthorne House struck midnight. Had he been awake and looking up at the narrow Gothic windows of the third floor of the mansion's round tower, he might have seen a strange green light flash four times from behind the thick lace curtains. Later, he might also have noticed the dim glow of candlelight in the newly occupied bedrooms.

Monday morning dawned, and Matt and Tina were out early in front of their house waiting for the school bus. Before long, the newly-stained oak door of the Hawthorne House silently swung open, and three children dressed all in somber black strode solemnly down the front walk toward the bus stop.

Tina gave Matt a questioning look, but he merely shrugged his shoulders. Though Vivianne Hawthorne typically wore an old-fashioned black dress, neither of the Mitchell twins expected that her grandniece and nephews would follow suit.

First in line was a tall, slender girl, a couple of years older than Matt and Tina. Matt thought she was very pretty in a sad sort of way. She had dark green eyes and straight black hair that nearly hung down to her waist. She was quite pale as though she had rarely spent time in the sun. Next in line was a boy about Matt's height and age with the same green eyes and raven hair as his sister. Unlike her, his hands were rough, and his broad shoulders lent him the look of someone who had spent the entire summer working outdoors. The youngest was a small, shy boy who also shared the green eyes and black hair of his siblings. Dressed just like his brother, he could have been an identical twin if he were only three or four years older.

"Good mornin' tah you," the girl said, as she slowly appraised the Mitchell twins. "You must be Matt and Tina Mitchell. Ahnt Vivianne has told us about you. My name is Gwyneth Hawthorne, and these are my brothahs, Gerallt and Gareth," she said, gesturing to her brothers. Like the older Mrs. Hawthorne, she spoke with the unusual accent, only stronger than that of her great-aunt.

Gerallt, the older boy, nodded hello, while Gareth merely stared nervously at Matt and Tina from behind his big sister.

Chapter 3 – Gerallt Moves In

"Hi," Tina said, staring at their somber, almost sinister, black clothing. Gwyneth wore a simple, long-sleeved Victorian dress and black leather shoes with narrow toes, short square heels, and big brass buckles. The boys were also dressed entirely in black from their shirts to their sturdy leather shoes. The three looked like they could have stepped out of a Gothic novel or a hundred-year-old painting. Their clothes were plain and appeared homemade with black wooden buttons instead of zippers. Their simple black shoes had likewise never seen the inside of a shoe store.

Gwyneth and her two brothers reminded Matt of the Amish people who he sometimes saw driving into town in black, horse-drawn carriages. He was about to ask them if they were Amish but decided that they might think he was being rude. "I didn't see you arrive yesterday. I was kind of wondering if you'd made it and would actually be here this morning."

"Ayuh," Gwyneth replied, pausing as if carefully considering what to say next. "It was quite late when we arrived last night. Perhaps you were sleepin'."

Noting that there wasn't a car parked in front of Hawthorne House, Matt continued, "So did you take a taxi all the way from the Fort Wayne Airport? That must have been expensive."

"What was your flight like?" Tina added. "When we came here from Oregon a couple of months ago, we had to drive the whole way, stuffed into a big U-Haul truck and pulling our car behind us. I wish we could have flown, too."

The two younger Hawthorne children glanced nervously up at Gwyneth before she replied. "Our trip was nothin' unusual, although we have nevah traveled so fah in the past."

"So what grade are you in?" Tina asked, changing the subject when it was clear that they weren't going to divulge anything more about their trip.

"I'm a junior," Gwyneth answered. "Ahnt Vivianne tells me Matt is the same age as Gerallt. Gareth is twelve and will be attending the middle school."

Matt was going to ask more questions, but the school bus rounded the corner and pulled up in front of the children. The Hawthornes ended up sitting separately in the remaining free seats, preventing any further discussion.

Upon arriving, the two oldest Hawthorne children went into the school office to register while Gareth walked next door to the middle school. Unable to ask any more questions, Matt and Tina went to their lockers and first-period classes. Midway through American History, Mr. Thompson was describing the causes of the Revolutionary War when the door opened. Gerallt entered, walked up to the teacher, and handed him the note he'd been given at the school office.

"Class," Mr. Thompson said, after quickly reading it, "we have a new student. This is Gerallt Hawthorne, who has just transferred here from Deer Isle, Maine. I'm sure that you will all give him a big Hawthorne High welcome. You may take a seat now, Gerallt."

Chapter 3 – Gerallt Moves In

Spotting Matt as the only familiar face in the room, Gerallt walked over and sat at the empty desk next to him. It also happened to be the chair directly in front of Clayton Cartwright.

Waiting for the teacher to face the chalkboard and turn his back to the class, Clayton leaned forward, stretched out his arm, and poked a sausage-sized finger into Gerallt's back. "Hey, new kid," Clayton whispered. "Where'd you get the Halloween costume? What're you supposed to be, some kind of Goth druggie?"

Gerallt ignored Clayton. Matt glanced sideways, the memory of his own initial run-in with Clayton still fresh in his mind from the first day of school.

"What's the matter with you?" Clayton continued, leaning forward to poke Gerallt again. "I'm talking to you. You deaf? Or stoned!"

Gerallt glanced over his shoulder, gave Clayton a look of utter contempt, and then turned back to read what the teacher was writing on the chalkboard.

"Oh, I get it," Clayton whispered, giving Gerallt a third poke in the back. "You're one of these Amish kids who don't believe in fighting. Believe in turning the other cheek, do you? Or maybe you're just a coward." He gave Gerallt a shove to the back of the head. "Just wait 'til after school, Bible boy, and I'll give you a little something on each cheek."

This time it was Gerallt who made sure the teacher was still busy at the blackboard with his back to the class. Then he turned and whispered in the same unusual accent as his sister, "My great ahnt warned me about you, Clayton Cartwright. It will take more than the likes of you tah frighten me. And I promise you this. Poke me one moah time in the back, and you won't be poking anyone foah a very long time." Then Gerallt turned his back on Clayton, swiftly slipped his fingertips between the wooden buttons of his shirt and began to whisper something too softly for Matt to hear.

"Is that so, Bible boy?" Clayton replied angrily, just loud enough for the teacher to hear. Mr. Thompson turned around just in time to see Clayton lean his considerable weight forward to poke Gerallt once more in the back.

Clayton's finger had barely touched Gerallt's back when there was a loud crack as the front legs of Clayton's chair snapped. Suspended motionless for an instant, his entire body pivoted forward on the chair's remaining legs, and his nose smashed into the back of Gerallt's chair with a sickening, yet strangely satisfying, crunch. Next, his outstretched index finger, driven by the whole weight of his body and desk, hit the floor with such force that the resulting snap was heard clearly by everyone in the room. This was followed instantly by the crash of Clayton's desktop, body, and books onto the floor followed by an unexpectedly high-pitched scream of pain. After a second of shocked silence, the class erupted as everybody started talking and yelling at once.

Mr. Thompson ran over to Clayton, who lay sprawled and whimpering on the floor. Blood was gushing from his nose while his right index finger was bent backward at a bizarre angle. "Class, I want you

Chapter 3 – Gerallt Moves In

all to remain in your seats while I escort Mr. Cartwright to the nurse's office," he said, helping Clayton to his feet. "You may continue reading and working on your next assignment." Then he turned and helped the dazed Clayton stagger out the door, leaving a trail of blood drops every few inches along the floor.

Everyone seemed to be talking at once except for Gerallt, who calmly scooted his chair back to where it had been before being pushed forward by the force of Clayton's face.

"Wow, did you see that?" one girl asked. "Clayton's finger was pointing straight up."

"Did you hear what the new kid said?" Paul Stephens asked, leaning over to Matt, who was silently staring at Gerallt. "He told Clayton to stop poking him or else he wouldn't be poking anybody. And the next thing you know, the big idiot pokes him and crash! Clayton sure won't be poking anyone now. That was fricking awesome!"

"Lucky, you mean." Matt corrected Paul, before turning to Gerallt. "Man, you got to be careful talking to Clayton like that. What would you have done after school if he'd shown up with his buddies Colin and Dylan?"

"Well, luckily for them, Colin and Dylan won't have tah find out," Gerallt answered. Then with a satisfied smile, he opened his textbook and calmly began to read the assignment that the teacher had written on the board.

The Secrets of Hawthorne House

Later, Mr. Thompson returned with the janitor, who mopped up the blood from the floor. Once the class had settled down, Mr. Thompson told them that Clayton had been taken away in an ambulance, suffering from a broken nose and broken finger. He also left the school with a severely damaged reputation. The rest of the day was filled with far more rumors than schoolwork. By lunchtime, the story was that the new boy had beaten Clayton up, given him a concussion and broken his arm. Gerallt had become a hero to half of the school.

Between being seen getting on the bus in front of the old Hawthorne House and having Hawthorne as his last name, it didn't take long for the students to put two and two together. The news spread swiftly, and Gerallt's hero status melted faster than frost on a sunny morning. Now, the rumor was that Gerallt had taken out a magic wand, levitated Clayton to the ceiling, and then dropped him so that he broke both arms falling onto the floor. By the time school was over, most of the students looked on Gerallt with more fear than admiration.

Everyone stopped, stared, and got out of his way when Gerallt walked by. Everyone, that is, except Matt.

"So, Gerallt," Matt said, sitting next to his new neighbor for the bus ride home. "That was quite a first day at school. I thought my first day was rough. I was sent to the principal's office for losing it with Clayton in history class, and then in the cafeteria, Colin O'Connell tripped some kid so that I ended up wearing my lunch. But you definitely have me beat."

Chapter 3 – Gerallt Moves In

"Ayuh," Gerallt muttered, shaking his head nervously. "Now, I've gone and stepped in it. My mothah and great ahnt are goin' tah skin me alive when I get home."

"But why?" Matt asked, wondering what reason they could have for being upset with Gerallt. "You didn't do anything wrong. It was Clayton who started everything by picking on you. And he only has himself to blame for falling on his fat face and finger. If he hadn't been leaning his chair so far forward and putting all his weight on its front legs, they wouldn't have broken. Regardless of what they say about your family, it's not like you cast some spell to break his chair."

"Uh... ayuh." Gerallt paused before responding to Matt's question. "It is our way. We ah taught that it is wrong tah mix with outsidahs, and when we must go among them, it is ah custom tah be quiet and not draw attention tah ourselves. It is a bad thing tah bring unnecessary trouble on oneself, one's family, and one's people. Besides, there ah already too many stories about us Hawthornes without me addin' anothah one."

The bus pulled up in front of their houses, and the Mitchell and Hawthorne children got off. Matt was going to invite Gerallt over, but before he could speak, Gwyneth turned to her brother. "Well, Gerallt, can you guess what I heard today? It seems that durin' his very first class, a Hawthorne got intah a fight with one of the school bullies and sent him tah the hospital. Just wait until Ahnt Vivianne hears about this. And you know how upset Mothah's been since the accident. You'll be lucky if she doesn't confine you tah yoah room for the rest of the year."

"Gerallt didn't do anything," Matt interrupted as Gwyneth paused for breath. "I was sitting right next to him and saw the whole thing. Clayton did it to himself and got what he deserved for picking on Gerallt."

"Did he, now?" Gwyneth asked skeptically, looking over at Matt with a mixture of caution and surprise. "Still, Gerallt knows bettah than tah call attention tah himself and our family name. It's good that he's found someone tah stick up for him, but that doesn't really change what has happened. A boy was injured, and a Hawthorne was involved." She turned back to Gerallt and Gareth. "Come along, boys. Mothah is waitin' for us, and Gerallt has some explainin' tah do." The three Hawthorne children silently filed through the gate, up the front walk, and into the Hawthorne House.

"So what really happened?" Tina asked Matt once the others had left.

Matt told his sister the entire story and retold it to his father over dinner. All in all, it had been a most interesting day, and Matt decided that he liked not being the newest kid anymore. He admired how Gerallt had stood up to Clayton without losing his temper and especially without getting into trouble. Matt also liked the fact that Clayton wouldn't be bothering anyone for the next few weeks while his nose and finger healed. Although they'd just met and he hardly knew anything about him, Matt decided that he liked Gerallt Hawthorne.

Chapter 4
Rescuing Gareth

The next morning, Matt rushed through breakfast and went out early to wait for Gerallt at the bus stop. Curious about how Gerallt's mother and great-aunt had taken the news regarding Clayton, Matt was more than willing to put in a few good words if Gerallt thought it might help. The more Matt thought about yesterday's events, the more he admired Gerallt's self-confidence in spite of Clayton's taunting and Gerallt's refusal to let the rampant rumors of witchcraft get to him.

The minutes passed slowly while Matt waited for the school bus. Tina joined him by the curb, and Matt was beginning to think that the Hawthorne kids were not going to come out in time. It wasn't until he heard the bus in the distance that the front door to the Hawthorne House opened and the three Hawthorne children silently filed out.

"Morning," Matt said, as Gwyneth, Gerallt, and Gareth walked up to the now waiting bus. "Gerallt, how did it go with your mom and great-aunt? Did you really get in trouble?"

Wearing a somewhat embarrassed expression, Gerallt solemnly nodded his head but said nothing as he turned and followed his sister and little brother onto the bus. Matt climbed the steps, hoping to sit next to him and find out what had happened.

However, the bus was crowded, and Gerallt ended up sitting several seats away.

Upon arriving at school, Matt and Gerallt went to their lockers to drop off their coats and afternoon books. It seemed as though everyone in the hallways stopped and stared at Gerallt. They whispered behind his back, and a few of them even made a point of walking out of their way to avoid getting too close to him as he and Matt headed to their first-period class.

As the boys entered, the history classroom suddenly grew silent as all eyes turned on Gerallt. Even the teacher seemed somewhat at a loss as to how to react. Matt glanced around the room, noticing that all signs of yesterday's accident had been removed. Clayton's broken school desk had been replaced with a new one, and the entire floor had been mopped.

"Okay, everyone, let's all take our seats," Mr. Thompson said, even though it was still several minutes before the first bell would ring. "Take out your books and open them to where we stopped yesterday."

Gerallt and Matt sat down and opened their books as Mr. Thompson began speaking about drafting of the United States Constitution. The first time the teacher had his back to the class, Matt leaned over to Gerallt and whispered, "Well, how'd it go at home?"

Gerallt looked over and put his index finger to his lips, signaling Matt to be quiet.

Matt was silent for a while, before leaning over again and whispering, "Do you want me to talk to your mom and great-aunt for you?"

Chapter 4 – Rescuing Gareth

Gerallt glanced over at the teacher, who was still busily writing on the blackboard. "I appreciate what you're tryin' tah do," he whispered back to Matt, "but it won't help." He paused to look around the room. Several of the students were eying them suspiciously. "I'll talk tah you later, but not durin' class. I have tah be on my best behavior. If I get in a gaum, Mothah's sure tah ground me 'til Yuletide."

"In a gaum?"

"In trouble." Gerallt turned away and refused to even look at Matt for the rest of the class.

Matt was curious about why Gerallt said Yuletide instead of Christmas but decided it must just be another aspect of the culture in which Gerallt was raised. Mr. Thompson finished and turned around to face the class, forcing Matt to stop asking questions.

The rest of the morning went much the same. Matt tried a couple of times to talk to Gerallt between classes, but he remained silent and merely shook his head. Gerallt seemed to be doing everything in his power to keep a low profile, but it didn't seem to help. Everywhere they went, the other students stopped and either turned to stare at him or turned their backs as if hoping he would disappear.

When the lunch bell finally rang, Matt went to his locker to drop off his morning books. He picked up the lunch bag he'd been bringing ever since that first day of school when he'd ended up wearing meatloaf, potatoes, and gravy. By the time he got back to the cafeteria, Gwyneth had already found Gerallt, and the two of them were sitting all by themselves at a table in a corner of the room. Matt was about to join them, but the stern glance Gwyneth gave him made it very clear that she didn't want them to be disturbed. Matt sighed and headed outside with his lunch bag.

Hawthorne High School and Hawthorne Middle School were built next to each other, with the high school football fields and the middle school playgrounds lying between them. During good weather, some of the high school students would eat their lunches on the football bleachers so that they could avoid the crowded cafeteria. Matt found that it was also an excellent way to avoid Colin, Clayton, and Dylan, who usually ate hot lunches and were too lazy to walk outside with their trays. Sometimes, Matt liked to gaze over at the middle school children playing outside and remember the fun he'd had playing touch football after school the year before his mother had died.

It was a crisp fall day, and the sun was shining brightly as Matt climbed up on the bleachers. He took a seat with his back to the breeze and unwrapped his tuna fish sandwich. Because he was wondering how to get Gerallt to open up and answer a few questions, several minutes passed before Matt noticed the unmistakable sounds of seagulls coming from overhead. It was the cry of his favorite birds, driven down from Lake Michigan by an advancing autumn storm. He smiled, remembering all the times he had lain with his back on the dunes, listening to the surf thundering on the sand and watching the gulls floating motionlessly, suspended like kites in the wind.

However, the plaintive calls of the seagulls were interrupted by the cruel sounds of teasing coming

Chapter 4 – Rescuing Gareth

from the nearby middle school playground. Matt looked over the low chain-link fence separating the schools and saw four boys standing in front of a smaller boy wearing nothing but black. He heard the name "Hawthorne" and realized they were picking on Gareth.

Ordinarily, Matt avoided confrontation whenever possible, but remembering how Gerallt had stood up to Clayton Cartwright, he wasn't about to let a bunch of middle-school bullies-in-training pick on Gareth. He had jumped down from the bleachers, climbed over the fence, and marched toward the group. Scavengers that they were, several seagulls swooped down to bicker noisily over what remained of Matt's forgotten sandwich.

"What's the matter, witch boy?" the biggest boy asked, pushing Gareth in the chest. "Where's your broom? We want to see you fly." The other boys started chanting, "Fly! Fly! Fly!"

Matt jogged over, placing himself between Gareth and the other kids. "Back off!"

The young bullies stepped back in surprise at being confronted by an angry high-school student who had rushed to Gareth's defense.

"Who are you?" the biggest boy demanded, still feeling powerful with his three buddies backing him.

"I'm someone who's fed up with bullies ganging up on people," Matt countered, putting his fists on his hips.

"We're not bullies," the boy retorted indignantly. "Besides he's a Hawthorne," the boy continued as though that were the only explanation required. "We just wanted to see the little witch do some magic."

"Aren't you kids too old to believe in witches?" Matt asked, shaking his head in disbelief. "If you want to see magic, go watch a magician on TV. There're no such things as real magic or witches."

"But we heard how his brother hexed some kid and put him in the hospital," the boy argued.

Matt was about to say he'd been there when he heard the sound of someone climbing the fence behind him. He turned around to see Colin O'Connell and Dylan Jones strutting up.

"What's the matter, new kid?" Colin taunted, looking amused at the younger boys standing around Matt. "Decided high school's too tough, huh? So, who are your little friends? Can we play too?"

"He's no friend of ours!" the leader of the middle school kids said indignantly. "We were just asking the new Hawthorne kid here to show us some magic when *he* comes over and starts butting in," the boy continued, pointing his finger at Matt.

"Is that so," Colin sneered. "Sticking up for a Hawthorne? That's not very smart in this town, especially after yesterday. Seems to me like someone needs to teach you how to mind your own business. Seems like maybe that someone should be me." He stepped forward, stopping with his nose a few inches from Matt's face. "Why don't you little kids go somewhere else for your magic lesson while I give the new kid here a lesson of my own," Colin continued, never looking away from Matt's eyes.

Chapter 4 – Rescuing Gareth

"I don't think so," Gerallt's voice said from the far side of the fence. He quickly climbed over and jogged up to stand shoulder to shoulder with Matt. "No one is givin' anyone lessons in anythin' unless perhaps you wish me tah give you a lesson in courtesy."

Colin was momentarily stunned, and Dylan actually seemed a little afraid as he looked into Gerallt's resolute face. "You were lucky yesterday, Hawthorne," Colin said. "Clayton would have pulverized you if he hadn't been such a klutz and fallen off his chair. You want to teach me something? Then go right ahead. I'm not afraid of you or any Hawthorne!"

Gerallt gazed steadily back into Colin's eyes. "Well, you should be." Gerallt paused, glancing up at the top of Colin's head. "What's that on yoah hair?" he asked, with the hint of a smile.

"I'm not falling for that old trick," Colin answered, raising his fists in case Gerallt was planning to sucker-punch him if he were to feel the top of his head for some imaginary bug.

"Really?" Gerallt asked, carefully taking a step backward while raising his right hand to his shirt. "I'm sure I see somethin'." Gerallt slipped his fingers between the buttons and began muttering something barely audible.

"What's that, witch boy?" Colin demanded, glancing down from Gerallt's face to his hand. "Got yourself a cross and think praying's going to protect you? Or am I supposed to believe you're casting some kind of spell? Well, neither is going to save you now."

Colin drew back his right fist and was about to step up to Gerallt when a large wet blob fell from the sky to splat loudly on top of his head. The bully gingerly reached his hand to his hair. When he brought it back down, it was dripping with white and green bird poop. Colin looked up to see several seagulls hovering like avenging angels in the autumn breeze. Dylan, who had not yet looked up, started to laugh at Colin just as another gull unleashed its smelly payload over Dylan's head and shoulders. Soon, other seagulls began to dive-bomb the middle school bullies, who ran screaming for the distant doors. More gulls dove on Colin and Dylan who cursed and sprinted for the fence and the safety of their own school building. None of them made it inside without several more hits by the squadron of angry seagulls.

Gerallt started to chuckle, followed by Gareth. The Hawthorne boys looked over at Matt, who was initially too surprised to say anything.

"What the heck just happened?" Matt asked, stunned by the bizarre behavior of the birds.

"I guess it's like the bumpah stickah," Gerallt answered, looking innocently from Matt to Gareth and then back again. "You know ... Shit happens."

Matt couldn't help himself. Despite his shocked surprise at the improbable bird bombardment that blasted the bullies while leaving the Hawthorne brothers and him untouched, Matt started chuckling. Soon, the three boys were all laughing so hard that they could hardly stand.

Chapter 4 – Rescuing Gareth

Just then, the bells rang, signaling the end of both the middle school recess and the high school lunch period. Gareth thanked Matt and Gerallt and headed back inside, while the older boys climbed back over the fence toward the high school.

"Matt, I want tah thank you foah helpin' Gareth," Gerallt said, briefly resting his hand on Matt's shoulder. "I really appreciate it. Once I saw Colin and Dylan stickin' their dirty noses in, I was afraid things would get serious befoah I could reach you."

"You're welcome," Matt said. "And thanks for backing me up when you did. I thought for sure Colin was going to beat me up." The two walked on for several moments in silence. "Gerallt, what just happened? Clayton getting hurt I can chalk up to klutziness and luck. But I have no idea what just happened with those birds."

Gerallt continued walking for a few seconds before replying, "Hard tellin'. Maybe I'm just very lucky. And then again, maybe the seagulls just had tah go." He stopped to look into Matt's eyes as if wondering whether he would buy the explanation.

"Maybe," Matt replied skeptically as they turned and continued back across the football fields, "but it sure was one heck of a coincidence." He paused for a second before continuing. "So, what are you doing after school?"

"Just my homework," Gerallt replied.

"Do you want to come over to my house?" Matt asked. "I can show you some of my stuff, and we can play video games. That is if you're not grounded."

"Mothah got ugly on me, but Ahnt Vivianne told her about catchin' Colin and his gang paintin' 'wicked witch' on the sidewalk in front of the house."

"What? Ugly on you?"

"You know. Mad. Angry. Anyway, I was able tah convince them that Clayton was merely bein' gommy and did it tah himself. Mothah only sent me tah my room without dinner, so I got off easy. Anyway, I'll ask her once I finish my homework. Who knows? Ahnt Vivianne likes you, so maybe Mothah will let me come, especially if I don't stay too long."

The second bell rang as they entered the building, making them both tardy for their next class. Neither of them seemed to mind.

Chapter 5
Best Friends

As soon as he got home, Matt rushed inside and dove into his homework and afternoon chores, finishing them in record time so that he could get his room ready for Gerallt's arrival. He tossed the blankets back over his bed, threw his dirty clothes into the laundry hamper, and shoved everything else into his closet or under the bed. He had just laid out a pair of his favorite remote-control cars when the doorbell rang. Dropping everything, Matt raced down the stairs and was halfway to the door when Tina beat him to it.

"Oh. Hello, Gerallt," she said in surprise, as she opened the door and stepped aside so that Gerallt could come in.

"Hi, Gerallt!" Matt said, running up to stand in front of his sister. "Come on in."

"Hello, Tina. Hi, Matt," Gerallt said somewhat awkwardly, looking around the entryway with open curiosity. "Thanks for invitin' me ovah."

"Who's that?" Matt's father called from his recliner in the family room, where he sat watching the news on the family's big screen TV.

"It's Gerallt from next door," Matt said, as he led Gerallt into the room. Sam muted the sound and stood up to greet their guest. "Gerallt, this is my father. Dad, this is Gerallt Hawthorne," Matt said, introducing his friend, who stared in amazement at the screen as if he'd never seen a TV before. "I've got my homework and afternoon chores done. Gerallt and I are heading up to my room for a while, okay?"

"Hello, Gerallt," Sam said. He reached out to shake Gerallt's hand, but the boy's eyes were still fixed on the face of the silent set. Sam Mitchell dropped his hand. "So you like it, Gerallt? My wife bought it for us a few months ago with the proceeds from her last pottery exhibition."

"Definitely, Mr. Mitchell," Gerallt said, finally turning his eyes back to Matt's father. "I didn't know televisions could be so big. But then, I've nevah actually seen one up close befoah," he added a bit sheepishly.

"Oh, really?" Matt's father said, somewhat at a loss for words.

"Come on, Gerallt! Let's go," Matt interrupted, dragging Gerallt out of the room.

Gerallt followed Matt upstairs to his bedroom. Once there, Gerallt stood transfixed in the open doorway. "Savage!" Gerallt exclaimed, staring enviously at Matt's TV, video game system, CD player, and three-year-old desktop computer. "Is this all youahs?"

Matt nodded, surprised at his friend's unexpected question.

"I nevah dreamed you had so many gadgets. What's this?" Gerallt asked, pointing to the game system and its two controllers.

"That's my game system," Matt said proudly. "I got it last Christmas. What system do you have?"

Chapter 5 – Best Friends

"Uh ... I don't have any of them," Gerallt replied, somewhat uncomfortably. "My family doesn't believe in such things, and we've nevah had electricity."

"What?! You mean you've never watched TV or played video games before? I was wondering about that when I didn't see any lights on at your house, but I thought it was just your great-aunt being eccentric. You really didn't have electricity back at your home in Maine? Jeez, what do you do for fun?"

"Well, we read lots of books," Gerallt replied, defensively. "Gwyneth, Gareth, and I play cahds and board games. We used tah play family games like charades. We all play the piano, and my Ahnt Vivianne has a wind-up gramophone and a huge collection of 78's." He paused as a wistful, homesick look came over his face. "Back home in Maine, I'd spend a lot of time outside when the weather was good. I'd go hikin' up in the hills and walk alone along the cliffs above the sea. And in the evenings, I used tah..." He hesitated briefly. "Well, anyway, there's lots of stuff you can do that don't need electricity."

"I suppose... But what did you do for light after the sun goes down?"

"We have oil lamps, and Mothah used tah make these really wonderful candles."

"Wait. What the heck did you do with your food? How'd you keep it cold without a refrigerator?

"Well, we had our root cellah for the vegetables and the food Mothah canned. Every day when Fathah got back tah port, he'd bring home a few of the fish he'd caught so Mothah could cook them for suppah. Occasionally, we bartered fish for meat, and she'd always cook it before it went bad. We had a neighbor who gave us fresh milk in exchange for fish. I guess we nevah needed one."

Midnight, the Mitchell family's cat, marched majestically into the room. Ordinarily quite cautious around strangers, she walked right up to Gerallt and began lazily winding herself around his ankles.

"That's strange," Matt observed. "Midnight usually hides whenever anyone comes over and only comes out after the person is gone."

"Maybe she smells our cats, Nightshade and Belladonna," Gerallt said, sitting down on the floor so that he could get a better look at Matt's cat. Midnight looked up into Gerallt's eyes and gave a welcoming meow, before she rolled over on her back and stretched, silently demanding that he rub her belly. Gerallt obliged and meowed right back at Midnight before making a purring sound that matched Midnight's contented purr. Then, he looked back up at the Game Cube. "How about showin' me how tah play one of youah games?"

"Is that allowed? I mean, given how your family feels about electricity, wouldn't your mom get upset if she found out?"

"Ayuh, she would. She'd get ugly on me for sure."

"So?"

"So we don't tell her. I'm tired of always being told what I can't do. It's just a game."

Chapter 5 – Best Friends

"Okay, Gerallt. Here's your controller," Matt said. He spent the next hour teaching Gerallt how to use a game controller while playing Super Smash Brothers Melee.

"Ahnt Vivianne told us that you just moved tah Hawthorne too. So where did you live befoah movin' heah?"

"I grew up just outside of Port Orford," Matt replied, carefully keeping his eyes on Donkey Kong as he controlled his character's movements. "It's a little fishing town on the southern Oregon coast. We had a little cottage at the foot of a hill overlooking the ocean. I used to spend a lot of my free time walking on the beaches or hiking up into the Coast Range. It was wonderful, especially in the fall after the tourists had gone home. I could hike for hours and never see a single soul. Just me and the seagulls."

"I know what you mean," Gerallt said, hoping that Matt's mention of the gulls wouldn't turn the conversation back to the mysterious bird attack on the school fields. "We didn't live in town eithah. And I know what you mean about it being bettah once the summah tourists leave and things aren't so crowded. We lived out in the willie wacks, and our nearest neighbahs in The Colony were a quartah mile away. We could be ourselves and do whatevah we wanted." Gerallt paused briefly before changing the conversation. "So, why'd you move tah Indiana?"

"My mom...," Matt started to answer. His fingers, which had been flying over the buttons on the game controller, froze along with his video game character on the TV screen.

"Oh, I'm sorry," Gerallt said, noticing the look on Matt's face. "I just assumed she was away from the house, grocery shoppin' or somethin'. Are your parents divorced?"

"No," Matt answered, forcing himself back from his painful memories. "Mom was one of the town's local artists and had a small pottery shop where she'd sell her work to the tourists. She'd pick up seashells on the beach and gather leaves from interesting looking plants. Before she fired her pieces, she'd press them into the wet clay so they'd leave an impression." Matt sighed. "Anyway, last summer she was walking along the coast road, picking plants for her pottery when the town drunk ran into her with his pickup. She was in a coma for several weeks before the doctors told us she was brain-dead and would never recover. The next day, Dad let them take her off the ventilator, and she just stopped breathing."

"*Magna Dea*! What ah pissah!" Gerallt exclaimed.

"Dad says I'm a lot like her," Matt said, somewhat surprised by Gerallt's weird curse. "I guess because we both liked to spend our free time walking along the beach or up in the hills. Anyway, she was beautiful, slender, and nearly as tall as Dad. She was also one-quarter Native American, with long straight black hair. And she always seemed to have potter's clay under her fingernails."

"She sounds nice. But you still haven't told me why you moved tah Indiana."

"Once Mom died, Dad got really depressed." Matt could feel the sorrow welling up inside him like the

Chapter 5 – Best Friends

rising of the tide. "He said that everything kept reminding him of her: our house, the coast, the sea. He couldn't see anything without thinking about her. Pretty soon, Dad couldn't stand it anymore. One day, I think he just sort of snapped and told us he'd taken a job here where he grew up. A couple of weeks later, he sold our cottage, and we left. I think Dad wanted to move us as far away from the ocean as he could.

"How about you?" Matt asked, diverting their discussion from his own painful memories. "Why didn't your dad come with you? Are your parents divorced?"

"No," Gerallt said heavily. "Fathah was the captain of a small fishin' trawlah. He was killed last summah in a freak accident. Somethin' happened with the engine. The boat caught fiah, and the fuel tank exploded. He was burned over 90 percent of his body and died before the Coast Guard could reach him and his crew." Gerallt looked over at Matt, who stared back at him in shock. "Anyway, Mothah sort of shut down and stopped carin' about anythin'. Gwyneth and I tried to take ovah, but there was only so much we could do without the fresh fish and income from Fathah's fishin' boat. When Ahnt Vivianne heard how bad things had become, she talked Mothah intah movin' us heah tah live with her."

"Wow. We do have a lot in common."

"Matt and Gerallt," Tina called from downstairs, interrupting their conversation. "Dinner's ready in ten minutes! Come on down. And Matt, it's your turn to set the table. Hurry up, or else Dad and I will eat it all."

"What time is it?" Gerallt asked in alarm, looking around the room for a clock.

"About a quarter to six or so," Matt said, as he switched off the game. "What's wrong?"

"Whew," Gerallt said with relief as they headed downstairs. "I'm supposed tah be back home by six. I lost track of the time and was afraid I was goin' tah be late. Mothah wanted me back in time for suppah, and I'll bet she's got tons of questions. We'ah hardly ever allowed tah go to other people's houses. Thank the Goddess, Ahnt Vivianne put in a good word for you."

"Why don't you phone home and see if you can stay for dinner?" Matt suggested, surprised to hear Gerallt say "Goddess" instead of "God."

Curious, Matt almost asked Gerallt what he meant but decided not to risk getting into a religious discussion with his friend. Because Matt's mother had been into Native American religions and new age spirituality, she had taught him to respect other people's beliefs and never say anything negative about them. Matt's father had also warned him to avoid discussions about religion. As an atheist, his father believed religious discussions were a waste of time, mainly because most people would never change nor even question their beliefs.

"We're having tacos," Matt continued. "Tina always makes more than we can eat, so I'm sure we'll have plenty."

"That sounds great," Gerallt said. "But we don't have telephones. I'll have tah go home and ask in

Chapter 5 – Best Friends

person, but that's actually good. Mothah's more likely tah say 'ayuh' if I ask her in person."

Gerallt walked back home while Matt set the table, adding an extra place setting just in case. Matt had just finished when the doorbell rang. He ran over and opened the door to see Gerallt standing on the porch. He had a big smile on his face and was carrying a large clay jug and wicker picnic basket.

"What's that?" Matt asked, as he led Gerallt into the brightly lit dining room.

"Mothah and Ahnt Vivianne wanted tah thank you for havin' me ovah for dinner," Gerallt said, placing the jug on the table and handing the basket to Tina. "My ahnt sent ovah some of her homemade hot spiced apple cidah, and Mothah sent one of the pumpkin pies she just baked. Be careful, they're both really hot, and the pie needs tah cool befoah we can eat it."

They sat down at the table, and Matt's father passed Gerallt a ceramic baking dish full of taco shells partially filled with steaming spiced ground beef. This was followed by bowls of chopped lettuce, diced tomatoes, grated Mexican cheese, and picante salsa. Meanwhile, Matt and Tina were helping themselves to the refried beans and chips. After putting the ingredients on his plate, Gerallt waited and watched curiously as the Mitchells made their tacos before carefully copying what they did. He looked skeptically at the refried beans and chips but put some on his plate to be polite.

"This is wicked good," Gerallt said, as soon as he had taken his first bite of taco. "You have tah tell me what spices you use; I've nevah tasted anything like them befoah. I'm sure Mothah and Ahnt Vivianne would love tah know what they are."

"You mean the taco seasonings?" Tina asked, somewhat surprised by the question. "It's mostly chili powder, I guess. Maybe some dried onion. I'm not sure, but the ingredients should be listed on the package. Do you mean you've never had tacos before? I thought everyone ate Mexican food. What do you usually eat?"

"Now, Tina," Sam said. "Not everyone eats the same thing, especially foreign foods."

"But, Dad," Tina said, "We're not talking about anything exotic here. This is just basic Mexican food. They even serve tacos at school every now and then."

"That's okay, Tina," Gerallt said. "I'm not offended. I guess they haven't had tacos in the cafeteria since I arrived. Anyway, I guess we ate traditional New England meals at home. We always used tah have fresh fish every day befoah Fathah died."

"Gerallt's dad was a captain of a fishing boat," Matt explained. "He died in a boating accident."

"I'm sorry to hear that," Sam said.

"Anyway," Gerallt said, not wanting to talk about his father, "we had a large chicken coop, so we'd have lots of fresh eggs and maybe a chicken once every month or so. Mothah would always bake different kinds of bread every day or two. We also had a good-sized garden, so we always had potatoes, corn, string beans, squash, and pumpkins and berries for pies.

Chapter 5 – Best Friends

And, of course, each fall, we'd have apples and pears from our trees for cidah, tarts, and pies."

"That sounds wonderful," Sam said. "It's cool that you grew most of your own food. Reminds me of when we used to stay with my grandmother when I was little. She had a huge garden and grew all sorts of stuff. She'd always be canning something or other. I remember that she had this amazing pantry full of mason jars filled with nearly every fruit and vegetable you could think of." He paused, sipping some steaming spiced apple cider from his mug.

"Wow!" Sam continued, taking a deep breath of the fragrant steam that curled out of his cup like fog from a winter pond. "This is definitely the best cider I've ever had. It smells heavenly and tastes just like McIntosh apples..." He paused to stare in surprise at the sparkling golden liquid in his glass. "Strange, I've never been able to tell what type of apple was used before. Is that a McIntosh apple tree in her backyard?"

"Yes, sir," Gerallt said.

"I taste cinnamon," Sam said, "but your great-aunt is also using some spices I've never tasted before. Whatever it is, I like it. You are going to have to thank her for me. Now I understand what Matt means when he talks about how good her lemonade is." Everyone smiled as the exotic spices in the cider filled their stomachs and hearts with the warm feeling of home and happiness.

"If you like home cookin' from yoah own garden, then you'd feel right at home eatin' with us," Gerallt said, as he helped himself to more tacos and beans. "We also had a big pantry of food that my mothah canned, and we brought it all with us when we came. In fact, in the spring we're plannin' tah put a large garden out back so we can have fresh vegetables and herbs. Matt, it's goin' tah be a honkin' big job, and I'm sure Ahnt Vivianne will want you tah help us."

"That would be great for you," Sam observed, "learning how to put in a proper garden. I always liked going out with my grandma and gathering food for dinner. We'd pick the vegetables, snap the green beans, shell the peas, and shuck the corn. There's nothing quite like fresh corn on the cob straight from your own garden! Store-bought vegetables just can't compare with homegrown."

"So why didn't we ever have a garden?" Tina asked, somewhat surprised by her father's reaction to Gerallt's description of his family's garden and the foods they grew. Other than the occasional meal out, for as long as she could remember, they'd always eaten food that they had bought from the grocery store.

"I don't know," Sam said. "Your great-grandmother lived in the Willamette River valley where there's a lot more sunshine than on the coast where we lived. You need plenty of direct sunlight if you want a good garden, and we had quite a few cloudy days on the coast." He paused and then admitted somewhat sheepishly, "That and a large garden's a lot of work. I guess your mom and I just found it was easier to buy everything at the store. Looking back on it now, though, I think that was a mistake."

"Gerallt, please pass the tacos," Tina said.

Chapter 5 – Best Friends

Glancing at the slightly uneven stitches on Gerallt's shirt sleeve, Sam suddenly realized that it had been sewn by hand. "Gerallt, did your mother make your shirt?"

"Yes, Mr. Mitchell. She makes all our clothes."

"Well, then, she's quite a seamstress. They're very nicely made. She must be very talented and self-reliant."

"She is," Gerallt said. "I think she can do almost anythin' if she sets her mind tah it. She makes almost everything we need. And anythin' that she couldn't make, she could usually barter foah. Back in Maine, she used tah have her own candle and scent shop for the summah flatlandahs. She'd make all kinds of scented candles, soaps, lotions, and packets of herbs. She used tah' do all sorts of stuff."

"So why did she stop?" Tina asked.

"She hasn't felt like doin' much of anything since Fathah died," Gerallt answered sadly. "I thought maybe she would get bettah once we moved in with Ahnt Vivianne. The two of them could talk and do things togethah, but it hasn't really helped. So now, she mostly just sits by herself in her room and stares out the windows."

"I'm sorry to hear that," Sam said, feeling somewhat uncomfortable hearing such private information about Gerallt's mother. "I know exactly how devastating it is to lose a spouse. I couldn't do anything for the first month or so after my wife died. I think I'd still be sitting in a dark room if I hadn't gotten a new job and moved back here to start over again."

After dinner, they cleared the table and sat back down to sample the pumpkin pie Gerallt's mother had made. Like the apple cider, it tasted both familiar and somewhat exotic, as if it contained unfamiliar herbs and spices.

By the time they finished their meal, Gerallt said it was getting late and that his mother wanted him home so he could get plenty of sleep before school the next morning. But he promised to come again, as often as Matt could have him over and his mother would let him come.

After cleaning up from dinner and watching an hour of TV with his father and sister, Matt went happily off to bed. It had been a wonderful day. He had saved Gareth from the middle school bullies, and somehow Gerallt had saved him from Colin and Dylan with the unexpected help of a flock of seagulls. Gerallt had even been able to come over to hang out and have dinner. Lying in bed, he stroked Midnight who purred contentedly, especially when he scratched her under her chin. Mostly, though, he wondered what it would be like to live without his electronic games and TV. He also wondered how seagulls from the Great Lakes had managed to get lost and show up at school just in time to relieve themselves all over Colin, Dylan, and the middle school bullies, while totally avoiding Gareth, Gerallt, and himself. Matt drifted off to sleep, thinking that this day had been about as perfect as it could possibly be.

Chapter 5 – Best Friends

In his own bed at Hawthorne House, Gerallt was feeling the same as he fell asleep.

Chapter 6
Herbology and Magic

From then on, Gerallt came over two or three times a week. Although they still occasionally played video games, usually they would go for long walks around the neighborhood, or stay in and listen to Matt's CD collection when it was raining or too cold outside. They talked for hours about how much they missed the parents they'd lost, how much they missed living on the coast, how much they disliked Colin, Clayton, and Dylan, and how much they felt like they didn't really belong at Hawthorne High School. Matt was surprised to learn that Gerallt, Gareth, and Gwyneth had always been home-schooled in Maine. He was curious about what that had been like, but Gerallt was always vague about just what it was that they studied.

By October, Matt and Gerallt were inseparable. They sat next to each other on the school bus and at lunch. They did their homework together and played video games at Matt's house. And every Saturday, they worked together at the Hawthorne House.

Once the boys finished working on the yard, Gerallt's mother had them clean and repair the windows of the Hawthorne's small greenhouse. The following Saturday, Matt arrived to find dozens of small pots holding herbs that needed to be transplanted into larger pots. Each little pot was carefully labeled with the name of the plant, which Matt read as he and Gerallt moved the plants and

Chapter 6 – Herbology and Magic

added potting soil to their roomier pots. Many of the herbs were familiar spices such as parsley, sage, rosemary, thyme, and oregano.

However, quite a few of the plants had strange names that Matt had never heard of. The boys transplanted belladonna and foxglove with their purple bell-shaped flowers, mandrake with its thick multi-limbed roots, wormwood with its tiny yellow flowers and parsley-shaped leaves, and even wolfsbane with its bright blue blossoms and large leaves.

"Is your mother worried that werewolves will come trick-or-treating on Halloween?" Matt jokingly asked as the pair transplanted the wolfsbane.

"Of course not," Gerallt replied indignantly. "Mothah was the best herbalist back on Deeah Isle. She knows all of the uses of every plant in this greenhouse, and she knows the uses of lots of plants that are too big tah fit in heah. Some of these herbs have natural medicinal properties, and she uses them tah make poultices and potions. For example, a very dilute infusion of wolfsbane is useful for fevahs, colds, croup, and asthma."

"Wow! I thought it was only useful to protect you from werewolves."

"Seeing as werewolves aren't real, I guess wolfsbane wouldn't be very useful if that was all it was good foah," Gerallt said with a smirk. "She makes all manner of concoctions, decoctions, tinctures, and infusions from some of these plants. She also uses some in her soaps tah help cure various skin conditions, and she adds others just because they make the soap smell good. She would hang some of the ones with a strong smell up tah dry so that she could use them tah make potpourris and incense. Everyone in the colony used tah come tah the house foah the stuff she made. She even sold some tah flatlanders during the summah tourist season."

Gerallt's mother had taught her children herbology while home-schooling them, and Gerallt was happy to share what he'd learned. By the end of the day, Matt was sure he'd learned far more than he'd learn all semester in his freshman biology class.

Once the boys had finished with the repotting, Gerallt was rewarded by finally being allowed to spend the night at Matt's house. During dinner, Matt introduced Gerallt to the joys of pepperoni pizza with extra cheese.

Afterward, the two friends went upstairs to Matt's bedroom where they watched one of the many Halloween-themed movies being shown in the weeks before the holiday. Actually more of a comedy than a horror movie, it involved a teenage boy and girl coping with a trio of bumbling witches who returned from the dead to steal the souls of the local children. Matt thought that it was pretty funny, but Gerallt often snickered at inappropriate moments and then got offended when the witches talked about being hungry and wanting to cook one of the children.

"Matt, how can you think that's funny?" Gerallt asked when his friend laughed during a particularly silly scene. "That's just sick, and besides, witches aren't anythin' like that."

Chapter 6 – Herbology and Magic

"Come on, Gerallt. It's only a movie; it's all make-believe. And anyway, it's not like witches are real."

"No, Matt, you're wrong; witches ah real," Gerallt said indignantly, as if Matt had said something personally offensive. "And the movie's lies about eatin' children ah just the kind of propaganda that used to get people burned at the stake."

"What are you talking about?" Matt asked, surprised at the unexpected vehemence of his friend's reaction.

Suddenly remembering where he was, Gerallt looked over at his friend with a mixture of embarrassment and fear on his face. "Nothin'," he answered nervously, quickly turning back to face the TV. "Let's just watch somethin' else."

"Not so fast," Matt said, unwilling to let it drop. "You don't really believe in witches, do you? It's all just superstitious nonsense."

Gerallt turned and looked closely at Matt. "If I tell you somethin', do you promise not tah laugh?"

"Sure," Matt replied hesitantly.

"I mean it, Matt. You have tah swear you'll nevah tell anyone what I'm about tah say," Gerallt said, with a look that showed he was dead serious. "And you especially can't tell anyone from my family."

"Sure," Matt answered, unclear where the conversation was going or why Gerallt was suddenly so serious.

"Okay. Then ayuh, Matt, I do believe in witches. And I don't mean the Wiccans with their modern pagan superstitions like the ones who'd shop at my mothah's little candle store back on Deah Isle. I mean the hidden truth behind it all: the worship of the Great Goddess. It's an ancient religion and way of life that's just as good as any othah."

"Wow!" Matt said, not sure how to respond.

"Think of it this way. Foah hundreds and hundreds of years, the people you call witches were discriminated against, persecuted, and killed for theah beliefs. Why else do you think Ahnt Vivianne would live like a recluse?"

"You don't mean she really believes she's a witch?"

"Ayuh, Matt, that's exactly what I mean. But it is moah than that. It's not just something she believes. She knows she's a witch." Gerallt paused and looked deeply into his friend's eyes as if deciding how much he could really trust him. "In fact, Matt, all of us Hawthornes ah."

"Are what? Witches?" Matt was stunned. He had gradually grown to accept the Hawthorne's eccentricities but had assumed that it was merely a cultural thing. To Matt, it had seemed like how his mother, a member of the Coos Indian tribe, had been raised to believe that spirits inhabited the trees and hills of her ancestral lands along the southern Oregon coast.

"But, you don't mean that you actually believe in magic spells, curses, and riding on broomsticks, do you? I mean, how can anyone still believe that stuff after everything we've learned and accomplished with science and engineering? Except for things like a

Chapter 6 – Herbology and Magic

magician's illusion and sleight of hand, there's no such thing as magic."

Although Matt's mother had weakly held some Native American and New Age beliefs, his father was a no-nonsense secular humanist. Allowed the freedom to choose, Matt and Tina eventually decided to follow their father. He'd taught them to place their trust in science, technology, and humanity's ability and responsibility to fix humanity's problems rather than relying on faith that some deity would solve them for us. Thus, for Matt's father, the supernatural was for the superstitious and gullible, and a religion was merely a myth that hadn't yet died out. But living as atheists in a mostly Christian culture, Matt had also learned to be tolerant of other people's beliefs, which he knew from experience were rarely open to argument or change.

"Ayuh, Matt, I do," Gerallt said. "It's what I believe and who I am."

"Still, even if your family worships some goddess, it doesn't mean that magic's real," Matt said, not ready to concede any more. "If it were true, it would violate all sorts of physical laws. If it were real, surely someone would have proved it a long time ago, and we'd be studying it in school. I think you'd need to give me some serious proof before I could believe that spells actually work and that you can really fly around on broomsticks. You wouldn't care to show me something truly supernatural, would you?"

"Then what about Clayton's chair?"

"What, you're trying to say you made that happen? You're just trying to take credit for something that was an accident. Clayton's big, and he was putting all his weight on the front two legs of his chair when they broke. It was probably old and ready to break when he leaned on it. You could have just gotten lucky that it broke when it did."

"And the seagulls?"

"Well, I have to admit that was really weird. Still, birds do poop on people, and it could have been just another lucky coincidence. How about proving you can do magic by doing a spell right now?"

"I can't," Gerallt replied, shaking his head.

"I thought so." Matt grinned in triumph.

"It's not that I'm not able tah. It's that I'm not allowed tah, not in front of an outsidah. Mothah would skin me alive. In fact, she'd probably ground me forever if she knew that I'd even been talkin' tah you about it. After hundreds of years of being hunted and burned at the stake, we've learned tah keep tah ourselves and avoid doing anything that would arouse suspicion. That's why what I did with Clayton's chair and the seagulls was so stupid. I lost my tempah and could have ruined everythin' for all of us."

Gerallt paused for a second and shook his head at the magnitude of what he'd risked. "Besides, I can't do anything you would call magic now even if I dared; I can't without something that's at home in my room."

"Okay, Gerallt, have it your own way," Matt said, giving up the argument and turning off the TV. "We don't have to watch the movie, and it's getting late

Chapter 6 – Herbology and Magic

anyway. Let's go to sleep, and you can show me some real magic when and if you finally decide to."

"Okay," Gerallt said, unrolling his sleeping bag on the floor.

Once they were ready and Matt reached over to turn out the light, Gerallt looked at his friend and said, "I'm sorry Matt. Someday, I hope I can."

Chapter 7
Trick or Treat

By the final week of October, the tall oaks lining Hawthorne Drive had reached the peak of their colors, and the first yellow leaves slowly tumbled down to lie on lawns and sidewalks. All along Hawthorne Drive, the modest one- and two-story houses had been turned into happy Halloween haunts. Throughout the neighborhood, bright orange lights framed windows and doors, and small fluttering ghosts hung from the branches of many of the smaller trees in peoples' yards. Black plastic spiders sat on the cottony cobwebs that shrouded every bush, while jolly Jack-O-Lanterns stood silent guard at every porch. Front yards had become graveyards, and the occasional inept witch hung where she'd crashed headlong into a tree or the side of a house.

Yet the morning of Halloween had arrived with no change to Hawthorne House, making it appear decidedly underdressed with no sign of Halloween decorations.

"So Gerallt, doesn't your family celebrate Halloween?" Matt asked, as the Hawthorne children joined him and Tina at the bus stop. "You haven't put up any decorations, and I haven't heard you mention it all month."

"Of course we observe Halloween, only we call it Samhain," Gerallt said, exchanging wary glances with his sister. Unlike Wiccans, who pronounce the

Chapter 7 – Trick or Treat

holiday as *Sow-in*, Gerallt pronounced the Gaelic word meaning the end of summer as *Sahm-wan*. "It's just that for us, the holiday doesn't start until dusk and we always wait until then tah decorate."

"Tonight is very special tah us," Gwyneth added solemnly.

"It's our new year," Gerallt continued. "We have a feast tah welcome the spirits of those who will be born in the comin' year and tah celebrate the lives of those who have passed in the previous year. Tonight, we'll celebrate the life of our fathah and welcome his spirit when he visits us from the Spirit World..."

Before Matt could decide how to respond to Gerallt's unexpected expectation that his father's ghost was going to visit him, Gareth said, "Samhain 's my favorite holiday. I love trick-or-treatin' and all the candy. Can I go with you and Gerallt tonight? Please? I promise not tah be a bothah or anythin'. Please, Matt?"

"Okay, Gareth," Matt said, his mind still spinning with what his friend had said. "So, Gerallt, what are you going to go as this year?"

"Thank you, Matt!" Gareth said, thrilled at the thought of joining the two older boys on their rounds through the neighborhood. "Gerallt and I will be wearin' wizard cloaks and hats. How about you?"

"I'm going as a vampire. I have a cool red and black cape and fake fangs from last year, and Dad bought me a vampire makeup kit with fake blood."

"What about you, Gwyneth?" Tina asked. "One of my friends is having a big party, and she said each of us could bring a friend. You want to go with me while the boys are out trick-or-treating?"

"Thank you, Tina," Gwyneth answered. "It is very kind of you tah invite me, but I really must help Mothah with the decoratin', hand out the treats, and help prepare for our Samhain celebration. Hopefully next time."

Just then, the school bus turned the corner, pulled up before them, and ended their conversation, once more leaving Matt with more questions than answers. The day passed quickly with class parties and endless discussions of costumes and the best routes for collecting the most candy. Then, it was back into the buses for the trip home, a quick dinner, and getting dressed for trick-or-treating.

The sun had just set as Matt, now transformed into a young vampire, walked out his front door to join Gerallt and Gareth for their planned evening of house-to-house candy extortion. Rising in the east like a pale pumpkin in the sky, a full moon peeked out from behind wispy translucent clouds. The temperature was dropping rapidly, and Matt drew his cheap black and scarlet cape around him with a flourish before striding out into the gathering darkness.

A thin mist was rising from the dew-drenched grass, forming a low layer of fog that darkened the shadows beneath the row of oaks lining Hawthorne Drive. Matt looked next door at the old Victorian mansion and was amazed by its transformation. Each tall window of the Hawthorne House framed a single colorful candle, burning with flickering flames of yellow, orange, or red. A few candles even burned

Chapter 7 – Trick or Treat

with the same sickly shade of green that illuminated the bottom of the twin streams of smoke rising from the mansion's massive stone chimneys. The green glowing smoke bubbling out of the chimney pots rose only a few feet before cascading down the gabled roof to become a low-lying fog. Matt was surprised to see a black shape suddenly swoop through the smoke, only to be followed by another and yet another. Large bats fluttered around the twin chimneys and the three towers, feasting on clouds of ghostly moths seemingly drawn to the pale green smoke. Matt had seen the occasional brown bat before, but never so many and never as big as these.

As Matt gazed up in wonder at the fluttering forms, he noticed something strange out of the corner of his eye. There were no candles in the small attic windows, yet he thought he had spied a pale figure looking at him from one of the darkened windows. He looked back at the window, but the ghostly shape had vanished as quickly as it had appeared. It sent a shiver up his spine.

Walking slowly over to the Hawthorne's gate, Matt admired the fantastic cobwebs that covered their fence, bushes, and even the lower branches of the trees. They appeared to be real spider webs, not the thick, cottony, store-bought stuff he'd seen at the neighbor's houses. Each one was outlined in diminutive droplets of dew and hosted what looked like a large black spider sitting smugly at its center. Matt was impressed; the webs looked expensive, and it must have taken a lot of effort to drape them so realistically.

The gate creaked mournfully as Matt opened it. Thirteen of the most intricately-carved jack-o-lanterns he'd ever seen lined the front walk. Each had a different expression, some friendly and some almost terrifying, and every one worthy of wonder and envy. They were so incredible that Matt thought Gwyneth, her mother, and great-aunt must surely have worked all day on them.

The fog grew thicker. Matt looked into the darkness on either side of the walkway where the mist lay like a ghostly shroud upon the ground. It almost hid the fairy rings of large, white toadstools that had sprouted among the teepees of dried corn stalks and giant pumpkins at least a yard across. To his right, what looked like a real skeleton hung suspended by a hangman's noose from a lower branch of the huge oak in the corner of their front yard. To his left, another pair of realistic skeletons sat hand in hand in the small gazebo next to the fence between their houses. Clearly, Matt thought, the Hawthornes went all out on Halloween.

The covered porch was lined with more of the marvelous jack-o-lanterns. Cobwebs hung from the newly painted gingerbread trim and between the ornately-turned spindles of the recently-repaired railing. Leaning over to take a closer look at one of the webs, Matt jerked back in shocked surprise. Both the big black spider and its web were real! Turning in amazement, he went to the windows for a better look at the colored candles; they were real with flickering flames burning yellow, orange, red, or green.

Chapter 7 – Trick or Treat

Matt shook his head in admiration before looking back at the cheap decorations of his own home. He knew his father would never have allowed actual candles in windows with curtains, and he would never have approved of spending extra for special trick candles with colored flames. Wishing his father could afford better decorations, he reached up, lifted the heavy gargoyle-shaped doorknocker, and dropped it loudly on the old oak door.

There was a long, loud creak as Gwyneth slowly opened the door wide, giving Matt his first good look into the Hawthorne House as she stepped out on the porch. Yet in spite of his curiosity about the house, Matt found his eyes drawn to Gwyneth. She wore a tall black witch's hat, an elegant, black, Victorian gown with long, flowing sleeves that stopped just high enough to reveal her old-fashioned, black, buckled shoes and a glimpse of her orange and black striped stockings.

"Welcome, young vampire," Gwyneth said, holding out a small cauldron filled with homemade candy. "I'm afraid we ah fresh out of blood, but hopefully these candies will satisfy youah cravin's." She smiled warmly at Matt, who suddenly realized Gerallt's older sister wasn't merely pretty. She was beautiful.

"Er, thank you," Matt stuttered. "Are, uh..., Gerallt and Gareth ready? We're going trick-or-treating together."

"Just a second, young vampire; I shall see," she said, stepping back inside the house and closing the door. The muffled sound of her calling her brothers was immediately followed by the sound of their feet running and jumping down the staircase.

"Hi, Matt!" Gareth said, throwing open the door to join Matt on the porch.

"Happy Samhain!" Gerallt added as he quickly walked out and carefully closed the door behind them before Matt could get more than a glimpse of candles and stairs inside the darkened foyer. The boys were dressed identically as wizards from some fantasy movie or TV show. Each wore a tall conical hat and a heavy, dark-blue velvet cloak that reached to the ground. Each also held a long, wooden wizard's staff topped with a large crystal in one hand and a thin, black, metal cauldron for their candy in the other. However, what surprised and impressed Matt most was that they both had a live animal perched on their shoulder.

"Matt, say hello tah Nightwing," Gerallt said. The large crow sitting on Gerallt's shoulder cocked its head sideways to get a better look at Matt. Its black feathers sparkled a deep iridescent purple as the moon briefly shown from behind the rushing clouds. It greeted Matt with a friendly "Caw caw!"

"And this is Shadow," Gareth said, pointing to the large black squirrel sitting contentedly on his shoulder. "He's coming trick-or-treatin' with us!" Shadow stared solemnly at Matt and then lay down, wrapping his bushy tail around Gareth's neck. Although apparently satisfied that the young vampire's diet did not include squirrels, Shadow's shiny black eyes nevertheless remained warily on Matt.

Chapter 7 – Trick or Treat

"Wow!" was all that Matt managed to say. Dogs and cats, he could understand. Maybe even a pet guinea pig or gerbil, but crows and squirrels? "I've never known anyone who owned a crow or squirrel before. I didn't even know you could buy them." Matt had often watched the gray squirrels that lived in the old oaks lining Hawthorne Drive, but they were small compared to Shadow. "Do they bite?" Matt asked. "And how do you know they won't fly or run away?"

"Don't worry, Matt," Gerallt answered. "We've had them foah years, and they'ah very tame. Nightwing likes tah ride around on my shoulder, and if she flies off, it's just because she loves tah fly. She'll either come back tah me, or I'll find her sittin' on my windowsill when I return."

"And Shadow will just fall asleep on my shoulder if he gets bored," Gareth added, leaning forward so that Matt could get a better look at his pet.

"He's kind of big for a squirrel, isn't he?" Matt asked, slowly extending the back of his hand rather than his fingers in case the squirrel chose to bite a stranger. Having decided that Matt was a decent sort of vampire, the squirrel trustingly presented his neck for petting.

"Come on, Matt," Gerallt suggested. "I can't wait tah find out how Hawthorne compares with Deeah Isle when it comes tah candy." Stepping off the porch into the thick swirling fog, he solemnly held up his staff and intoned "*Magna Dea, fac, quaesumus, ut lux sit!*" The fist-sized amethyst crystal at its end gave off a soft purple glow to light the path before him.

Gareth likewise raised his staff and repeated the words *"Magna Dea, fac, quaesumus, ut lux sit!"* The somewhat smaller quartz crystal began to glow with a pale white light.

Matt assumed Gerallt and Gareth had flicked hidden switches to turn on the lights in their staffs. Matt hurried to join the two brothers who were striding purposefully into the night.

An hour passed. Gerallt, Gareth, and Matt were rapidly being weighed down with candy, small coins, and the occasional popcorn ball. Many people were intrigued by the boys' unusual pets. Meanwhile, there was also a small but steady stream of children visiting the Hawthorne House, although many of them demanded that their parents, or an older sibling, accompany them up to the town's infamous "haunted house." Yet Gwyneth answered each "trick-or-treat" with a smile, a handful of homemade chocolates and other candies, and a kind comment regarding the wearer's mask or costume. Overall, it was turning out to be a wonderful Halloween, with many parents admiring the amazing decorations and the obvious improvements that had been made to the Hawthorne House.

Then trouble approached.

Standing on the porch, Gwyneth could hear them coming long before she could see them through the fog. Colin O'Connell, Clayton Cartwright, and Dylan Jones were sauntering down Hawthorne Drive, argu-

Chapter 7 – Trick or Treat

ing noisily over who had collected the most candy and loudly wondering whether it was time for some Halloween tricks instead of treats.

"There's the Hawthorne House," Clayton said, looking up at the mansion rising above the thickening fog. "And isn't that Matt Mitchell's house next door?" he continued, pointing at the modest two-story house to its left.

"Yeah," Colin replied. "I think we've finally found the place for our toilet paper and rotten eggs. Time for a little payback, eh Clayton?"

"Yeah, payback," Colin's toady, Dylan, agreed.

Clayton glanced down at the dirty cast covering his right hand and index finger and nodded cruelly. Although the black eyes he got from his broken nose had mostly faded, the hatred that still smoldered there made him look like a monstrous, rabid raccoon.

In short order, the three boys removed rolls of toilet paper from their trick bags and covered the lower branches of the oak trees in front of Matt's house with wide white ribbons.

"Okay," Colin said, as he admired their handiwork. "Now let's use the eggs next door." Then the three young vandals packed up their arsenal and strode up to the front gate of the Hawthorne House.

"Wow, look at those decorations," Clayton said, pointing at the candles and the pale green smoke rising from the twin chimneys. "And it looks like they're giving out candy this year. Let's go and get some before we egg the place."

"Sure, Clayton," Colin said, looking appreciatively at the candles with the colored flames. "Besides, I want a closer look at those lights."

"Wow, these spider webs are really realistic," Clayton observed as he walked up the path. "And these pumpkins are crazy. It'll almost be a shame to smash them."

"Damn, those spiders are huge," Dylan noted nervously, trying to stay close behind the two older boys without letting them know how scared he was getting. "And those skeletons look real!"

"Aw, back off, Dylan," Colin said, pushing the smaller boy back. "I'm not your mama. Besides, those are just expensive decorations. Nobody has real spiders and real skeletons."

They slowly climbed up the steps of the porch, and Colin was about to knock on the door when Dylan got a good look at the spider webs on the porch railings. "Shit, they're real spiders!"

Before the older boys could react, Dylan was off the porch and running as fast as he could back down the path to the street and safety. Colin and Clayton turned just in time to see Dylan duck behind a tree on the far side of the fence. The two boys looked at Dylan cowering in fear, looked back at each other, and laughed. "Hey, Dylan, stop being a baby and get back here!" Colin yelled.

Both remaining boys had their backs to the door and didn't notice when it quietly opened behind them. Gwyneth stood there with a witch's wand instead of the candy cauldron in her hand.

Chapter 7 – Trick or Treat

"The doah's ovah heah, boys," Gwyneth said, smiling grimly at the bullies' backs. "What ah you dressed as? Juvenile delinquents?"

"We're too old for kiddy costumes...," Colin snapped, turning around to see Gwyneth standing there in her witch's hat and old-fashioned black dress. "I see you aren't wearing a costume, either. What did you do? Borrow that dress from your grandma?"

"You know, if you ah goin' to insult someone," Gwyneth answered coldly, "then you should at least get your insults right. The dress is mine, not my great ahnt's." Looking over at Clayton standing there with his candy bag out, she asked, "Well, aren't you goin' tah say it?"

"Uh ... say what?" Clayton asked, surprised by the unexpected question.

"Trick-or-treat," Gwyneth said, shaking her head with scorn. "It's Halloween, isn't it? And you're heah for candy, aren't you?"

"Uh ... Trick-or-treat?" Clayton answered.

"Okay, I choose trick," Gwyneth replied, raising her wand and aiming it at the two boys in front of her. *"Magna Dea, fac, quaesumus, ut vespertiliones veniant!"*

Clayton took a startled step backward and turned to join Dylan out in the street. "Hold it, Clayton!" Colin commanded, grabbing the bigger boy by the arm. "You don't scare us," he said to Gwyneth. "The stories about Old Lady Hawthorne being a witch are just something to scare little kids. She's no witch, and neither are you. You can't hex us."

"Are you so sure, Colin O'Connell?" Gwyneth asked.

Colin was about to ask her how she knew his name when a dozen large bats suddenly swooped onto the porch and began flapping rapidly around Colin and Clayton's heads. Clayton let out a yelp, yanked his arm loose from Colin's grasp, and made a run for the street. Colin held his ground for an instant until a bat landed on his shoulders. Then he too broke and ran.

The boys had barely made it halfway to the gate when Gwyneth again waved her wand and whispered *"Magna Dea, fac, quaesumus, viam lubricam! Magna Dea, fac, quaesumus, ut sacci eorum scindant!"*

Both boys' feet slipped out from under them, and they landed with a crash on their bags containing the rotten eggs. Simultaneously, their candy bags flew up in the air, ripped, and dumped their contents in front of several small children who had just entered the gate. The little ghosts, goblins, and princesses made a mad scramble for the candy scattered at their feet, while Colin and Clayton limped angrily out into the street, leaving the sulfurous stench of rotten eggs trailing behind them.

The jack-o-lanterns along the Hawthorne's sidewalk smirked as the three vandals vanished back into the darkness from which they'd come. The mess from the broken eggs and toilet paper on the tree in front of the Mitchell's house had vanished as if they had never existed.

Chapter 7 – Trick or Treat

It wasn't long afterward that Matt, Gerallt, and Gareth finally turned toward home. As they moved farther out into the neighborhood, the fog that had faded away returned and grew thicker with each homeward step they took. The full moon now loomed large and orange over the steeply-gabled roof of Hawthorne House. Matt's bag and the brothers' cauldrons were overflowing with candy, and their legs and feet were tired as they trudged up Hawthorne Drive to stop in front of their homes.

"We did really good, didn't we?" Matt asked, hefting his heavy bag. "I think a lot of people gave us extra candy because of Nightwing and Shadow."

"Ayuh," Gerallt answer, gazing appreciatively at the candy nearly overflowing his black cauldron. "Hawthorne's not Deeah Isle, but it's not half bad eithah. This'll keep us in candy for weeks."

Gareth's face practically glowed as he sat down on the curb to sample some of his treats.

"Do you want to come in?" Matt invited. "We can have some hot chocolate, sort our candy, and trade for our favorites."

Gerallt looked up at the moon, gauging the time. "I'm afraid that'll have tah wait 'til tomorrow. It's almost time for ah Samhain celebration." He looked down at his brother, who was finishing off a large candy bar. "And, Gareth, you'd bettah wipe that chocolate off your face befoah Mothah sees you. You know you'ah not allowed tah spoil youah appetite before the feast."

"Aw, Gerallt, it's only one piece," Gareth complained, wiping his mouth with the sleeve of his cloak.

"You know Mothah's already upset, tryin' tah make everythin' tonight perfect for Fathah," Gerallt said, going through the gate to their house. "Come on, Gareth, let's go. See ya, Matt. It was great!"

"Bye, Matt," Gareth repeated, waving as he followed his brother up the front walk. "Thanks foah lettin' me come along with you!"

"Okay... Uh, see you both tomorrow," was all Matt could think to say as he watched them walk past the jack-o-lanterns and up the stairs to their porch.

Gwyneth opened the door and bent down to place a plate of apples and Halloween cookies at her feet for any hungry spirits that might come by. She waved briefly to Matt and then led her brothers inside for the Hawthorne family feast and Samhain celebration. Matt paused a few minutes to admire the Hawthorne's amazing Halloween decorations once more before turning back to his own home with its cheap, store-bought decorations.

Matt's house was dark and quiet when he walked in the front door. Tina was spending the night at her friend's Halloween party, and his father was sitting in front of his computer at the dining room table, working on a program he'd brought home from work. Matt went up to his room and dumped his candy onto the bed. He started to sort it into piles, but he couldn't keep his mind on his candy.

Chapter 7 – Trick or Treat

All that Matt could think about was how strange the Hawthornes were and what it must be like to be Gerallt, living in the Hawthorne House and having a crow for a pet. And how it would be to celebrate Halloween as some kind of weird, religious holiday with a special feast for the dead. He wondered what it must be like to believe that your father's spirit would somehow rise from the ocean's depths to visit you one night a year. Most of all, Matt wished his mother could visit him that night, just like Gerallt thought his father was going to visit him. Matt didn't believe in ghosts, but maybe he could at least dream they existed. So he put away his candy, got ready for bed, and wished with all his might he would see his mother in his dreams.

As Matt slept, he dreamed he was walking along the Oregon coast when his mother called him home for dinner. However, this time, no nightmare prevented him from reaching the safety of his seaside cottage and the security of his mother's embrace.

Thus, Matt didn't see the candlelight coming from beneath the shades of the Hawthorne's dining room windows as they held their Halloween feast. And he didn't see the soft flickering of green light in the third-floor windows of the round tower where they secretly observed their sacred Samhain Sabbat.

Chapter 8
Inside Hawthorne House

It was a crisp autumn afternoon, a few days after Halloween. The squirrels in the large oak trees lining Hawthorne Drive were enjoying the beautiful Fall weather as they gathered the acorns they needed to last through the long, cold Indiana winter. Matt and Gerallt had just arrived home from school, and Matt was the first one back outside after dropping off his schoolbooks in his room. He was leaning against a tall oak tree in front of the Hawthorne House when Gerallt burst out of the door and ran up with a huge smile on his face.

Before Matt could even say "Hi," Gerallt surprised him by exclaiming, "Matt, you know how my mothah and great ahnt have this thing about nevah havin' anyone ovah tah ah house? Ahnt Vivianne is always complainin' she needs her peace and quiet, and Mothah just nevah feels up tah seein' anyone and always makes a big deal about how much work it would be tah prepare for entertainin' a guest..."

"Uh huh."

"Anyway, I've been askin' and askin' them foah a couple of weeks now, explainin' how you'ah my best friend. And it's not like you'ah some important guest that they have to fix up the house foah, and you don't really care what the house looks like. Besides, those ah just excuses tah justify keepin' outsidahs out, and I've been ovah tah youah place lots of times, and it's

Chapter 8 – Inside Hawthorne House

just not fair not bein' allowed tah have you ovah tah my room. I promised them we'd be as quiet as a couple of mice in a house full of cats, that we wouldn't be any bother at all, and they wouldn't even know we were there."

Gerallt stopped just long enough to take a quick breath before continuing.

"Well, I walked in as Ahnt Vivianne was talkin' tah Mothah, and I heard her remarkin' how you've been a great help with the doah yard this fall. I asked them again, and they both finally said ayuh! You can come ovah this evenin' for an hour after suppah if I get my homework and chores done by then."

Matt could hardly believe his ears. After weeks of not being allowed to set foot inside the front door, he had begun to resign himself to never seeing the inside of the infamous Hawthorne House.

"I need tah head right back in and start on my homework and chores," Gerallt continued. "I'll come ovah tah get you as soon as we've cleaned up after suppah, say around 7:30. See you then!" With a rush, Gerallt ran back through the gate and into his house before Matt could say a word.

Visions of what the inside of Hawthorne House might look like filled Matt's head. Although everyone in town called her "Old Lady Hawthorne" and half of the children believed she was a murderous witch, Vivianne Hawthorne had never been anything but kind to him. Still, there was no denying that the Hawthornes were by far the strangest people he'd ever met. If Gerallt could be believed, they were all 'witches,' even if Matt still wasn't exactly sure what he meant by that.

Before dinner, Matt followed Gerallt's example and quickly finished his homework and chores so there would be no reason for his father to refuse to let him go. At dinner, over plates of homemade stir-fried chicken and Chinese vegetables, Matt raised the topic. "Dad, you know how I've never had a chance to see the inside of the Hawthorne House?"

Sam looked up from some documentation he'd brought home from work. Tina also looked at Matt with interest.

"Well," Matt continued, "Gerallt's invited me over to his house for an hour this evening after dinner."

"Are you sure it's okay with his mother and Mrs. Hawthorne?" Sam asked. "She has made it quite clear ever since we moved in that she never allows anyone inside her home."

"Yeah, Dad. Gerallt got it okayed and everything. He even said his great-aunt called me a good worker."

"But what about Matt's chores and homework?" Tina interrupted. "I don't want to get stuck doing his chores on top of my own, especially while he's out with a friend on a school night."

"Already done," Matt said, glad he'd anticipated one of them would raise the issue, and happier still that he'd done most of his chores. "All I have left is cleaning up after dinner, and I can do that now and still be done by 7:30. That's when Gerallt's coming over to get me. I can go, can't I?"

Chapter 8 – Inside Hawthorne House

"Okay, Matt," Sam said, "but make sure you're not a bother to anyone, and you're back by 9:00. Remember, it's a school night, and you need to be in bed and ready to fall asleep by 9:45."

Even though he wasn't quite finished eating, Matt jumped up, carried his dirty dishes to the sink, and started putting away the food. Having completed his half of the after-dinner chores, he headed outside to wait for Gerallt.

The sun had set, and the weather was turning colder, with dark clouds rolling in from the west. After ten minutes that crept by like thirty, the front door of the Hawthorne House opened. Gerallt stepped out, saw Matt standing by the gate, and waved him in from the cold. Matt ran to the door where Gerallt, his mother, and his great-aunt stood waiting on the porch.

"Matt," Vivianne Hawthorne said, "I'd like tah introduce you tah my niece Gwendolyn, Gerallt's mothah."

"Pleased to meet you, Mrs. Hawthorne," Matt said, trying to be on his best behavior. He briefly shook her hand when she offered it.

Gwendolyn Hawthorne was tall and slender like Gwyneth, with long, straight black hair. She was also as beautiful as her daughter, or rather would be if only sadness hadn't left its mark on her. Although Gwendolyn looked nothing like her aunt Vivianne (having married into the Hawthorne family), both women wore nearly identical black dresses: old-fashioned, floor-length, with a high neck and long, flowing sleeves that partially covered the backs of their hands.

"Nice tah finally meet you, too," Gwendolyn said. "Gerallt's told me so much about you. I'm glad he has found such a good friend."

Matt followed Gerallt and the Hawthorne women into a corridor dimly-lit by oil lamps on tables and numerous wall sconces, each holding a long white candle. Oblong mirrors appeared to duplicate each candle so that one burned a few inches in front of the wall while its reflection burned just as brightly. The flames flickering in the draft from the open door gave the foyer a warm golden glow, and the air held the smell of lavender, cinnamon, and other less-common spices.

A straight, narrow staircase led steeply up to the second floor, while two large portals with pocket doors on his left and right, opened into the darkened parlor and dining room respectively.

"Here, let me take youah coat," Gerallt's mother said, after carefully closing, locking, and bolting the front door behind them. Matt handed her his jacket, which she hung on a beautifully-carved, antique coat tree by the door.

To his left, Matt caught a glimpse of the parlor where a small crackling fire in its corner fireplace dimly illuminated several overstuffed chairs and Tiffany lamps with beaded fringes along the bottom of their shades.

"Come on, Matt," Gerallt said, heading for the stairs. "Let's go up tah my room."

Matt followed Gerallt up two narrow flights of stairs to his friend's bedroom at the top of the

Chapter 8 – Inside Hawthorne House

stairwell. Because the doors to the other bedrooms and bathrooms were closed, all he could see of the second and third floors were hallways that looked nearly identical to the downstairs foyer, with its oil lamps, candles, and high-patterned ceiling.

"Well, what do you think?" Gerallt asked, as he led Matt into his bedroom.

The first thing Matt noticed was the cheerful little fire in the stone fireplace in the far-left corner of the room. Several candles burned brightly on their reflective wall sconces, while two oil lamps sat on a small oak desk and two more sat on either end of an antique chest of drawers, added their light to the fire's warm glow.

"This is sweet!" Matt answered in awe, looking at the flames which were crackling merrily in the fireplace. "I can't believe you have your own fireplace. Dad won't even let me have a candle in my room."

Matt's eyes rapidly adjusted to the relatively dim light in Gerallt's room, and it soon seemed entirely natural that there were no electric lights in the Hawthorne House. He glanced around the room, taking in its antique furniture, the tall narrow windows, and the high ceiling. Unlike Matt's bedroom, there was no clutter, and everything was clean and in its place.

Matt was somewhat taken aback by the lack of electricity. However, the presence of Nightwing, Gerallt's pet crow, more than made up for the absence of a TV, stereo system, computer, or any visible toys, electronic or otherwise. She was sitting on a big bird stand over a large litter box to catch her droppings. A water bowl and pie tin containing dry cat food, peanuts, corn, and raisins sat on the floor in a nearby corner. Matt walked over to take a closer look at Nightwing, and the crow cocked her head to one side and stared silently back at him.

"You can pet her if you want," Gerallt offered. "Just don't make any quick movements, and keep your hands away from her head and beak."

"Thanks," Matt said, moving his hand slowly so as not to startle the crow. Nightwing remained still as Matt ran the tips of his fingers gently down the bird's back. "Sweet! I didn't know feathers were so soft and smooth," "Does she do any tricks?"

"Quite a few," Gerallt answered, reaching down to pick up a raisin and holding it out so she could take it. Nightwing looked at the raisin with mild indifference before eventually accepting it as proper tribute from her "pet" boy. "Crows are really intelligent, but she does have her little quirks. She likes tah hide food and other things around the room. It's annoyin' tah get intah bed and find pieces of dry cat food under youah pillow. Still, it's a lot bettah than it was when I first got her. I tried to give her a more natural diet. You won't believe where I would find her hidden worms, beetles, and pieces of rottin' fruit."

"Ugh," Matt said. He stepped over to the tall, narrow window on his left and pulled back the old lace curtains. "I was wondering which room was yours. Hey, you can see my bedroom window on the second floor, down there on the right." Matt said,

Chapter 8 – Inside Hawthorne House

pointing down across their darkened yards to his house.

"I know. Sometimes you leave youah curtains open, and I can see you watchin' TV or playin' with youah video games. It makes my room feel kind of empty and borin' by comparison." Gerallt paused, a little embarrassed by the envy he had let creep into his voice. "So, what do you want tah do first? I have some games in my bottom desk drawer. We could play cahds or maybe dominoes or chess."

Gerallt walked over, opened the bottom drawer to his desk, and then looked back at Matt with a mischievous grin on his face. "I know what we can do," he said, pulling out a small, wooden box and opening it to reveal a deck of very old and strange-looking cards. "This was Fathah's first Tarot deck from when he was our age. Do you want me tah use it tah foretell youah fortune?"

"Sure," Matt answered, getting into the "spirit" of the evening, even though he didn't actually believe in fortune telling. "So, what do we do?"

"Well, first I want you tah shuffle the deck a few times until you feel comfortable with it. Then cut the cahds, and give them back tah me," Gerallt said, as they sat down facing each other on the hardwood floor.

"Now what?" Matt asked, after shuffling the deck three times, cutting it, and handing it back to Gerallt.

"Okay. Now, I am goin' tah lay out the first ten cahds, one by one, on the floor, in a traditional pattern called the Celtic cross spread. The first two will form a cross, the next four will form a circle around the cross, and the last four will form the staff. As I lay each cahd down, I'll tell you what the position represents and what the cahd signifies. Got it?"

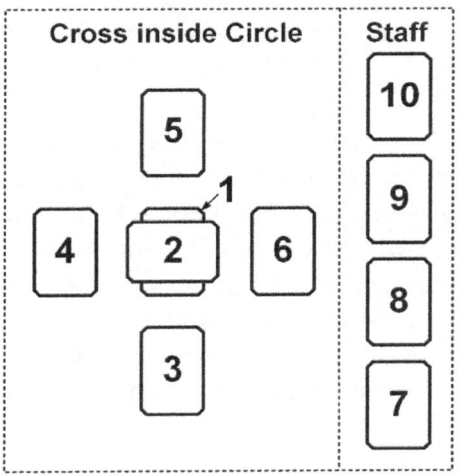

"I think so," Matt said, looking uncertainly at the cards in his friend's hands. "Go ahead."

Gerallt began by drawing the top card from the deck, turning it over, and placing it face up in the center of the floor in front of Matt. "This first cahd in the spread represents your immediate problem." The card bore the image of a seated man who appeared to be wearing the robes of a pope. "This cahd is called the Hierophant, and it symbolizes education. So, it looks like your primary problem is related tah school."

Gerallt drew the next card from the deck, turned it over, and placed it crosswise on top of the first card.

Chapter 8 – Inside Hawthorne House

The card carried the image of a medieval peasant holding a wooden staff, standing behind six more staffs stuck into the ground. "The second cahd represents the forces that oppose you in solvin' youah immediate problem. This is the seven of Wands. It stands for aggression. I guess it's safe tah say this card signifies our 'good friends' Colin, Clayton, and Dylan."

"Next, I'm goin' tah draw four cahds that will form a circle around the first two," Gerallt said as he drew the next card and placed it face up below the first two cards. The card showed a sad figure in a black cloak standing over five golden goblets on the ground. "The third cahd represents the ultimate source of youah problem. The 5 of Cups means bereavement and loss. This cahd must symbolize the death of youah mothah."

"The fourth cahd represents the past, somethin' you should let go of." Gerallt drew a card showing a dog baying at the crescent moon and placing it face up to the left of the first two. "Ah, the Moon cahd. It denotes fear. The cahd seems tah be tellin' you tah overcome your fear of Colin and his gang."

Gerallt turned over a card and placed it face up above the first two cards. It bore a medieval woodcarver carving one of eight disks, each inscribed with a pentacle. "The fifth cahd represents youah beliefs, assumptions, and even youah delusions. The eight of Pentacles signifies knowledge. This cahd is tellin' you youah belief that magic isn't real is a delusion." Gerallt grinned. "Maybe you don't know as much about magic as you think you do."

Gerallt drew another card and placed it to the right of the first two cards to complete the cross part of the spread. It bore a large yellow sun, its golden rays radiating down onto a field of sunflowers. "This sixth cahd represents the future and completes the circle. The Sun cahd stands for enlightenment. Maybe I'll get you tah believe in magic after all." Gerallt smiled.

"Don't count on it," Matt said, grinning back at Gerallt, who ignored the remark and continued with his reading of the deck.

Gerallt drew another card and placed it face up to the bottom right of the others. "The seventh cahd forms the base of the staff, a column of four cahds tah the right of the circle and cross. This cahd represents how you see yourself." The card bore the ugly image of Mephistopheles with large curling horns and cloven feet, sitting over two figures bound in chains. "The Devil is a very negative cahd that typically means hopelessness and bondage. Maybe you see yourself stuck heah in Indiana without hope of evah returnin' tah the coast. I know that's the way I sometimes feel about evah going home tah Deeah Isle."

Gerallt drew a card with three swords piercing a large red heart over a background of clouds and rain. He placed it face up to the right of the first six cards, just above the seventh. "The eighth cahd is the second cahd in the staff and represents the environment you find yourself in. The three of Swords signifies heartbreak, loneliness, and betrayal. The death of youah mothah has hurt everyone in youah family. Her death is building walls between you, youah sister, and

Chapter 8 – Inside Hawthorne House

youah fathah, leaving you lonely. And you might even feel youah fathah betrayed you when he took you away from youah home."

Gerallt drew a card with a single wand being held by a hand emerging from a cloud and placed it face up above the sixth and seventh cards of the staff. "The ninth cahd represents your hopes and feahs. The Ace of Wands signifies confidence and courage. This cahd means you'll find the confidence and courage tah face youah problems and solve them, even though you feah you won't be able tah."

Gerallt drew one last card holding the image of ten golden goblets in the arc of a rainbow over a joyous family. He placed it face up above the ninth card to complete the staff. "And the tenth and final cahd represents the outcome of youah problem. This is excellent. The ten of Cups means joy, peace, and family. It looks like things will work out just fine in the end for you, Tina, and youah fathah." Gerallt laid the remaining cards down on the floor and smiled smugly at his friend. "Well, Matt, what do you think of that? Looks like the cahds know you pretty well, don't they?"

"Nice job," Matt replied, looking down at the pattern made by the strange-looking cards. "Not that I really believe a word of what you said, but it was definitely interesting. You made it sound so convincing I almost believed you. But how do I know you haven't just used what I've been telling you about myself and made it all up as you went along?"

Before Gerallt could reply, there was a soft knock on the door, and Gwyneth walked in, carrying a silver platter with homemade sugar cookies and cups of hot spiced apple cidah. "Mothah thought you two might like a snack." She sat the tray down on the floor beside them.

"Great, Gwyneth. Thank you," Gerallt said.

"Yeah, thanks," Matt added as he took a cookie and the cider.

Instead of leaving, Gwyneth wavered, first looking down at the Tarot cards on the floor and then over at her brother. "I see Gerallt's been tellin' fortunes. Well, Matt, what did you learn?"

"That if Gerallt's right, we won't have to put up with the bullies at school forever," Matt answered with a grin.

"I should hope not," Gwyneth said, smiling with relief that Gerallt was restricting himself to the Tarot deck. "I would like tah think the two of you will graduate sooner or later." She paused to let the jibe sink in. "Did the cahds make any predictions about Gareth?"

"No...." Gerallt said, unsure where his sister's question was leading.

"Well, I can predict that Gareth would like tah be invited in. Ever since the day with the seagulls, he's talked about nothing except how Matt came tah his rescue. You know, it wouldn't hurt for you tah ask him tah join the two of you every now and then."

"Okay," Gerallt said. "Send him up. We could use another person for the next game anyway."

"Wise decision. Mothah always notices these sorts of things." Gwyneth stuck her head out into the

Chapter 8 – Inside Hawthorne House

hallway and called, "Gareth! It's okay. You can come on up."

Instantly, they heard a pair of feet flying up the stairs, two at a time. Gwyneth opened the door fully, and Gareth raced in, his stockinged feet sliding on the smooth hardwood floor. "Can I really play too?" he asked as Gwyneth left, closing the door behind her.

"Sure, Gareth, you can play, too," Gerallt answered as he carefully placed the Tarot deck into its box. "Put this back in my bottom drawer and bring over the Ouija board."

Gareth put the box away and pulled out a large, flat, wooden game board. The alphabet was written across its center in two arcs of ornate letters, underneath which were written the digits from 1 through 9 followed by a zero. A figure of the sun labeled with the word "yes" was printed in the top left corner, while a figure of a crescent moon labeled with the word "no" was in the upper right. The words "good bye" were centered at the bottom of the board. Gareth also brought over what appeared to be a flat triangular piece of wood.

The Secrets of Hawthorne House

"The Ouija board is a little like a Tarot deck," Gerallt explained as the three boys sat down on the floor in front of the board. "Both are used for divination, but the Ouija board gives you more information because it will actually answer your questions."

"So how does it work?" Matt asked, looking skeptically at the board in front of him.

"You use an Ouija board tah contact someone from the Spirit World and ask questions. This is the planchette," Gerallt said, holding up the triangle of wood. "We place it on the board, and we all lightly rest our fingertips on it. Then one of us asks the spirits a question. With any luck, a spirit will move the planchette around the board tah give us its answer."

"If you say so," Matt said skeptically.

"Well, actually, that's exactly what a lot of New Age pagans believe," Gerallt said with a chuckle. "But this is really just a simple board game we'ah going tah play for fun. People don't realize they ah subconsciously moving the planchette to spell out messages from beyond. This is just a poor imitation of a real Ouija board."

"Okay," Matt said, wondering how much longer his friend was going to continue pulling his leg. "So, what does the real Ouija board do?"

"It predicts the future," Gerallt replied with a straight face. "And you don't move the planchette; you don't even touch it. It moves itself. Ahnt Vivianne has a real one hidden downstairs in the library. Maybe one day, she'll allow me to show it tah you."

Chapter 8 – Inside Hawthorne House

"Good one, Gerallt." Matt laughed. "Once again, magic is real; I just have to wait to see it." He reached out and placed his fingertips lightly on the waiting planchette. "Okay, let's play."

When Gwendolyn entered the room 20 minutes later, the boys were asking silly questions about the future and laughing as each one secretly tried to move the planchette to spell out the most outrageous answers possible. "Time tah go, Matt," she said. "And Gareth, it's time for you tah get ready for bed."

Matt walked over to say goodbye to Nightwing as Gerallt put away the Ouija board. While Gareth stopped at the second-floor bathroom to brush his teeth before bed, the older boys continued down to where Gerallt's mother and great-aunt stood waiting for them by the door. Matt made sure to thank them both for letting him come over, especially on a school night.

Matt put on his jacket and walked outside into the dark and freezing air. Heavy clouds carried the threat of the year's first snowfall, even though it wasn't expected to stick. Matt glanced back at the Hawthorne House as he stepped onto his porch. Somehow, the old house next door didn't seem spooky at all.

Chapter 9
Colin's Revenge

"What's up, Colin?" Clayton asked, as he and Dylan followed Colin through the cafeteria after the three had picked up their lunches. "Why aren't we sitting at our usual table?"

"Yeah, Colin," Dylan added. "Why do we have to eat all the way over here?"

Ignoring their questions, Colin continued until he'd reached his goal, an empty table in the corner farthest from the cafeteria monitor. "This'll do," he said to himself, placing his tray on the table. He took a seat with his back to the wall that was covered by a huge mural of a bald eagle, the school's mascot. While the others sat down opposite him, Colin carefully scanned the large room that was packed with students on their lunch break. "We have unfinished business," he finally answered, pointing briefly across the room to where two figures dressed identically in black sat by themselves at a table near the door that led out to the rain-drenched football fields.

"What do you mean?" Clayton asked, turning around to look where Colin had pointed.

"Yeah, I don't see anything," Dylan said.

"Look again," Colin commanded his cronies. "Surely, you can see Witch-Boy sitting there with his sorcerer's apprentice."

"Oh, I see 'em," Clayton said. "But what can we do if Hawthorne's going to hex us as soon as we try

Chapter 9 – Colin's Revenge

anything? Jeez, Colin, I'd like to get even with him as much as you." He looked down at his right hand, where his index finger was still in a splint. "But I don't need any more magic."

"Nor do I," Colin replied grimly, remembering the smell of the seagull poop and the rotten eggs on Halloween. Suddenly, he wasn't so hungry and angrily shoved his tray to the side. He leaned over the table and whispered, "So here's what we're going to do...."

English class was nearly over. Having finished and handed in their assignments, Gerallt and Matt were sitting quietly, discussing their plans for the evening while waiting for the bell to ring.

"So, what do you think?" Matt whispered when he saw that the teacher was busy at his desk answering another student's question. "Do you think it's too soon for me to come over again? If it is, you can always come over to my place."

Gerallt was about to answer when someone walked up from behind, shoved himself between them, and suddenly fell with a loud thud on the floor. Dylan was sprawled at their feet, holding his leg and rocking back and forth as if his shinbone were sticking out of his pants.

"Ow! My knee," Dylan screamed at the top of his lungs. "Gerallt, I told you I don't have any more money!"

"What the...." Gerallt said, jumping up out of his chair to stare down at Dylan.

"Don't hurt me! I'll give you the money tomorrow! I promise!" Dylan wailed, crawling backward toward the teacher's desk, while still holding his leg as if it were about to fall off. "Keep him away from me!"

"What's the meaning of this?" Mrs. McKinney, the English teacher, demanded as she rushed up to place herself protectively between Dylan and Gerallt.

"I saw the whole thing," Colin offered from his desk in the back of the room. "Dylan was just walking up to hand in his assignment when Gerallt tripped him and shoved Dylan as he was falling."

"I nevah," Gerallt protested, turning around to face his new accuser.

"Yes, you did!" Clayton said from his desk next to Colin. "Mrs. McKinney, Gerallt's been forcing kids he doesn't like to give him their lunch money and threatening to hex us if we don't pay him."

"I did not!" Gerallt shouted, looking back and forth between Colin and Clayton.

"Did too! Why else would I be paying you every week since you did this to me?" Clayton said, raising his hand so that everyone could see the splint on his finger. Murmuring in agreement, several students seemed ready to accept any accusation against a Hawthorne.

Meanwhile, Dylan lay whining and whimpering on the ground, and Mrs. McKinney could feel the situation rapidly spinning out of her control. "Mr. Hawthorne, you will take yourself immediately to

Chapter 9 – Colin's Revenge

Principal Tanner while I take Mr. Jones to the school nurse."

"But..." Gerallt objected.

"No but's," Mrs. McKinney interrupted. "Go now. I will deal with you later." Turning around, she bent down to lightly touch Dylan's leg. Dylan winced in pain.

Giving a defeated look at Matt, Gerallt slowly picked up his things and headed for the door.

"Excuse me, Mrs. McKinney," Matt said, as Gerallt left the room, hoping to explain that they were talking and that Gerallt couldn't have done what the others said.

"Not now, Mr. Mitchell. I have to escort Mr. Jones to the nurse's office."

"But, Mrs. McKenney, Gerallt didn't..."

"Mr. Mitchell," the English teacher interrupted. "think carefully before you say another word. I may not see you and Mr. Hawthorne whispering when my back is turned, but there's nothing wrong with my hearing. If you try to help your friend by lying, you'll give me no choice but to send you to the principal, too."

Matt nodded. The end-of-class bell rang, and Matt picked up his belongings and headed off to gym class. *I'll stop by the office after school*, he thought, *and explain to the principal what really happened.*

By the time Matt dropped off his books at his locker and made it to the gym, the next bell had already

The Secrets of Hawthorne House

rung. The first boys were heading out onto the gym floor just as he entered the boys' locker room. Matt opened his locker, took out his PE clothes, and turned to find Colin and Clayton standing behind him. Glaring menacingly, the pair silently blocked his escape until the last boy had left the room.

"So, where's your witch friend now?" Colin asked with a sneer. "I don't see any seagulls. Do you, Clayton?"

"Nope, no seagulls here," Clayton answered, looking stupidly around the locker room. "What about you, Matt? Do you see any seagulls?"

"What do you want, guys?" Matt asked, stalling for time while he tried to figure out how to get past them and out of the locker room.

"We have some unfinished business, you and me," Colin said, taking a step forward.

"Me, too," Clayton added, glaring down at Matt, whose back was now up against his locker.

"Come on, guys," Matt said, hoping to hear someone's, anyone's, footsteps entering the room. "I don't want any trouble."

"Now that's funny, ain't it?" Colin replied with a definite edge to his voice. "Cause you're definitely going to get some. Right, Clayton?"

"Right," Clayton answered, smiling like a lion standing over a defenseless antelope. "It's payback time."

Suddenly, Matt heard the sound of footsteps rapidly approaching.

Chapter 9 – Colin's Revenge

The three boys turned to see Dylan running into the locker room.

"Great performance, Dylan," Colin said, as Dylan hurried over to join the others. "Definitely Oscar material."

"Yeah," Clayton said. "I thought you might have actually hurt yourself."

"It went just like you said it would, Colin. And look." Dylan proudly held up a piece of paper as if it were a trophy. "I even got a note from the nurse saying I don't have to do any exercises today."

Colin nodded to Dylan, and the two silently moved to approach Matt from opposite sides. Soon he was totally trapped, cornered between the bench and the row of lockers, with Dylan on his left, Colin on his right, and Clayton directly in front of him.

Filled first with fear, followed by resignation, and finally anger, Matt clenched his fists and prepared for the inevitable attack. *Well, if I'm going to be beat up*, he thought, *I may as well go down fighting. I can't take them all, but at least I can give that little shit Dylan something real to cry about this time.*

"Now!" Colin exclaimed. As Clayton and Dylan lunged at him, Matt immediately spun to his left and hit Dylan's nose with all his strength. Colin's toady yelped and fell backward between the bench and the lockers with blood pouring from his nose. Unfortunately, Matt had turned his back on Colin, who quickly grabbed him from behind. Matt struggled to free his arms from Colin's vice-like grip, but it was no use. Suddenly, Clayton's good hand, balled into a fist, connected solidly with Matt's stomach. Gasping for breath with the wind knocked out of him, Matt could only stand there as Clayton struck him four more times in rapid succession.

"That's what happens to people who side with a Hawthorne," Colin hissed in Matt's ear. "And this is for hitting Dylan. "Stop!" Colin shouted at the top of his lungs. "Matt! Get off him! You're killing him."

Matt struggled to break free as Colin dragged him out from behind the bench and away from Clayton and Dylan. It was hopeless. He could barely breathe from being hit, and Colin's grip was too tight to break.

Matt heard the sounds of shouting and running feet coming from the gym. The class, led by Mr. Armstrong, the gym teacher, poured into the locker room to see Dylan lying on his back, moaning for real as blood streamed down his face and onto the concrete floor. Colin still held Matt who clenched his fists in rage and frustration.

"Who started this?" Mr. Armstrong demanded, walking over to help Dylan to his feet.

Before Matt could find the air to answer, Clayton answered, "Matt jumped Dylan just as he walked in. He said something about teaching Dylan a lesson for ratting on Gerallt last period in English class. Matt was on top of Dylan, beating the crap out of him when Colin ran up and grabbed Matt from behind and started yelling at him to stop. Matt kept trying to get at Dylan, so Colin had to hold him until you got here. I'd have tried to help Dylan myself, but my broken

Chapter 9 – Colin's Revenge

finger...." Clayton held up the splint on his right hand and made a gesture as if he were helpless to do anything.

"Is that what happened?" Mr. Armstrong asked, looking at Colin.

"Yes, sir," Colin answered. "Is Dylan okay?"

"But..." Matt managed to say.

"I've heard enough, Mr. Mitchell!" Mr. Armstrong interrupted. "Go straight to the Principal's office and wait for me. I'll see you there just as soon as I see Mr. Jones to the nurse's office."

Matt looked around the room, didn't see a single sympathetic face, and realized that arguing would be pointless. Colin, Clayton, and Dylan had set him up just like they'd set up Gerallt. Seething with rage at the injustice of the situation, Matt stormed out of the locker room and headed for the office.

Gerallt was still waiting outside the principal's office when Matt arrived.

"Matt!" Gerallt whispered, smiling with gratitude as his friend sat down. "I'm glad you decided tah come and tell Mr. Tanner what really happened. I can't believe how well they set me up. I was really startin' tah worry."

Matt didn't return the smile. "Sorry, Gerallt. Mrs. McKinney got on my case when I tried to tell her. The bell rang, and I didn't know what to do, so I went to gym class. I made a big mistake of putting off coming here until after school."

"So, what are you doin' heah?" Gerallt asked quietly, glancing up at the clock. Only 20 minutes had passed since Dylan had fallen.

"Colin and Clayton trapped me in the locker room until Dylan arrived," Matt whispered. "It was obvious they were going to beat me up, so I was ready when they made their move. I managed to hit Dylan before Colin grabbed me from behind, and Clayton began punching me in the guts with his left hand. Then, the three put on this big act for Mr. Armstrong, claiming that I was the one who started it by jumping Dylan. He bought it hook, line, and sinker."

"What a pissah!" Gerallt muttered. "We've been had, but good."

"Yeah," Matt agreed, hanging his head. "They managed to separate us so that it ended up three to one. Now, no one's going to believe anything I say."

"It must have been Colin," Gerallt surmised. "He's the only one of the three smart enough tah have come up with somethin' like this. Dylan wouldn't dare try tah tell the others what tah do, and Clayton's numb as dirt."

"Yep," Matt agreed, correctly assuming that 'numb' was the Maine colloquialism for dumb. "They blindsided us good. I certainly didn't see it coming."

"Well, there's goin' tah be somethin' comin' their way," Gerallt answered angrily, his voice edging louder. "I'm definitely goin' tah get Colin for this! And Clayton and Dylan, too!"

"Step into my office, gentlemen," Principal Tanner ordered, walking past them to open his door. Both

Chapter 9 – Colin's Revenge

boys had been so involved in their conversation that neither had heard nor seen him coming. "I've just come from talking with Mrs. McKinney and Mr. Armstrong. I've also seen Dylan Jones who, thanks to you two, is once more in the nurse's office, this time with a bloody nose to go with his injured knee. And if that weren't enough, I understand that you, Mr. Hawthorne, have been extorting money from your classmates under threat of witchcraft. And just now, I overhear you making more threats against Dylan, as well as Colin O'Connell and Clayton Cartwright, who apparently have done nothing more than tell their teachers what you did." He stopped to glare across his desk at the two boys, neither of whom dared to look back at him.

"Well," Mr. Tanner demanded, "What do you have to say for yourselves?"

Matt and Gerallt looked at the principal, at each other, and then back again. The situation looked so bad, neither boy knew where to begin.

"Okay, Mr. Hawthorne. You first," Mr. Tanner said. "What happened in English Class?"

"Well... Matt and I were talkin' when Dylan suddenly pushed in between us, fell, and started yellin' at me."

"So, you and Mr. Mitchell were talking in class," Mr. Tanner observed.

"Er... ayah," Gerallt conceded. "Then Colin and Clayton lied about what happened. All three did. I didn't trip Dylan, and I nevah took money from anyone."

"So, you would have me believe that Dylan injured himself, all three of them lied about you, and you're totally innocent of everything except talking in class," Mr. Tanner observed.

Gerallt nodded.

"That's right, Mr. Tanner," Matt said. "I saw the whole thing. They set Gerallt up. Dylan wasn't really hurt; he was just faking it to get Gerallt in trouble."

"So you say," Mr. Tanner replied. "Well now, let's discuss what happened in the locker room, shall we? I suppose you're going to tell me Dylan was also faking his bloody nose."

"No," Matt answered, angry again at the memory of Dylan bragging about what he'd done to Gerallt. "I hit him. But it wasn't my fault!"

"Oh, it was an accident then?" Mr. Tanner asked. "He just accidentally hit your hand with his nose."

"No," Matt replied, worried about where the conversation was heading, but having no idea how to stop it. "I hit him, but Colin, Clayton, and Dylan had me trapped and were getting ready to beat me up. They planned the whole thing in English class so that I'd be alone, and Gerallt couldn't protect me with his..." Matt stopped mid-sentence when he realized that he was about to say the 'm' word.

"Protect you with his what, Mr. Mitchell?" Mr. Tanner asked, smiling. "His magic?" The principal looked across from Matt to Gerallt and back. Both boys squirmed in their chairs, but neither said anything. "I think this has gone on quite long enough, don't you? I'm going to have to call your parents and

Chapter 9 – Colin's Revenge

ask them to come in. You can retake your seats outside in the hall. And close the door behind you."

Once Gerallt and Matt left, Mr. Tanner opened the school directory, looked up Sam's work number, and placed the call. Although the principal's voice was too muffled for the boys to understand, the tone was clear.

"We're doomed," Matt said.

"Doomed," Gerallt agreed.

Chapter 10
The Principal's Office

After looking up the number, Mr. Tanner picked up his phone and dialed Matt's father. "Mr. Mitchell? This is Principal Tanner from Hawthorne High."

"Yes?" Sam said. "What's wrong? Is Matt or Tina hurt?"

"No, they're fine," Mr. Tanner replied. "But Matt's been in a fight, and he may also be involved in something significantly more serious. I have him sitting outside my office. Could you please come in now? I think we need to deal with this right away."

"Uh... Okay," Sam answered, worried about his son but also about what his boss would think of him leaving in the middle of the afternoon. "Give me ten minutes to reschedule a meeting, and I'll drive right over."

"Perfect, Mr. Mitchell. And one more thing."

"Yes?"

"Gerallt Hawthorne is also involved. The boy lives near you, doesn't he?"

"Yes, just next door."

"Well, it appears his mother didn't leave a phone number. Would you mind stopping by and asking her to come, too? Given the boys' close friendship and what has happened today, I think it would be best if both of you were to take part in resolving this."

Chapter 10 – The Principal's Office

"Okay. I'll stop by and let her know what you've said. We'll be there as soon as we can."

Ten minutes later, Sam pulled up in front of the Hawthorne House. He hurried up the front walk, raised the antique doorknocker, and dropped it loudly on the old oak door. When no one answered, Sam knocked again. He was about to knock a third time when he heard faint footsteps and the unlocking of several locks. The door opened a few inches to reveal Vivianne Hawthorne peering over the sturdy security chain that prevented the door from fully opening.

"Why, Mr. Mitchell," she said warily. "What brings you by on a weekday afternoon?"

"Is your niece at home?" Sam answered. "I had a phone call from the high school and need to speak with her."

"What happened? Are Gwyneth and Gerallt okay?" Worry washed over the old widow's face.

"Yes. They're fine." Sam replied, sorry that he had unnecessarily worried the old woman. "It's Gerallt. Apparently, there was a fight at school, and both he and Matt were involved. Mr. Tanner, the principal, asked me to tell Gerallt's mother. He wants us to come to the school right away."

"Oh, dear!" Vivianne Hawthorne exclaimed. "Just a minute. I'll go get her. We'll be right back." With that, the door closed and the footsteps rapidly receded.

It wasn't long before the door opened again, and the Hawthorne women, wearing long and heavy cloaks against the cold November air, joined him on the porch.

"Mr. Mitchell, I'd like you tah meet my niece, Gwendolyn."

"What happened, Mr. Mitchell?" Gerallt's mother asked, ignoring the introduction. "My ahnt said somethin' about a fight. Are the boys all right?"

"Please call me Sam," Mr. Mitchell replied, unable to help noticing how beautiful Gwendolyn was, and even more surprised to notice that he noticed. "I'm not really sure myself what happened, but the principal did say that the boys are okay. Anyway, he called me at work and asked me to tell you that they are in some sort of serious trouble and that he wanted us to go to the school right away to discuss it."

Sam paused, looked around to see if any other car were parked along the street. "Do you have a car? If not, I can take you in mine."

"I'm afraid not," Gwendolyn answered. "I'd greatly appreciate the ride."

"Would you like me tah join you, dear?" Vivianne Hawthorne asked tentatively. "Or maybe I should go instead if you're not feelin' well enough."

"No thanks, Vivianne," Gwendolyn replied wearily. "He's my son. I will handle it."

Matt's father and Gerallt's mother drove off, leaving a worried Vivianne Hawthorne on the porch as threatening gray clouds rolled down from the north. After a final glance at the gathering storm, she returned inside, locked the door, and sat down in her darkened parlor to wait.

Chapter 10 – The Principal's Office

The boys were still sitting in the chairs outside the principal's office when their parents arrived.

Gwendolyn rushed up to her son and sat down in a chair next to him. "Gerallt, what's going on?" she whispered angrily, leaning over so that only Gerallt could hear. "Mr. Mitchell told me you were in a fight." Meanwhile, Sam walked up and asked Matt the same question. Before either boy could answer, the door to the principal's office opened, and Mr. Tanner stepped outside.

"Please follow me, Mrs. Hawthorne and Mr. Mitchell," the principal requested. "I've asked Mrs. McKinney, the English teacher, and Mr. Armstrong, the gym teacher, to join us in the conference room. Boys, wait here. I'll send for you shortly once we've had a chance to talk with your parents."

Gerallt and Matt were left to stew in their own juices while Mr. Tanner led their parents into the school's conference room. Gwendolyn and Sam sat down at the large table opposite the principal. The English and gym teachers soon joined them and took the seats on either side of Mr. Tanner. It made Gwendolyn and Sam feel like defendants awaiting judgment before a tribunal.

After brief introductions, Mr. Tanner said, "I want to thank you for coming on such short notice, Mrs. Hawthorne and Mr. Mitchell. Ordinarily, I'd just have one of the secretaries set up a conference in a day or two. The potential seriousness of today's events, however, made me feel it was important to talk with you before deciding what to do about your boys." He glanced at the English teacher at his left. "Mrs. McKinney, would you please tell them what happened in your class this afternoon?"

"Your sons have English with me right after lunch. It was near the end of class, and Gerallt and Matt had already turned in their assignment for the day. I was speaking with another student when I heard someone fall to the floor. I looked up to see Dylan lying on the ground in front of your boys' desks, holding his leg and crying out in pain. Originally, I thought that he'd accidentally tripped, but he immediately accused Gerallt of tripping him as he passed between your boys. More importantly, Dylan also accused Gerallt of deliberately hurting him because he had not been able to pay Gerallt the money he demanded."

"But Mrs. McKinney, my son would nevah do such a thing," Gwendolyn exclaimed. "I can't believe it."

"Yes, I understand," Mrs. McKinney continued. "Parents often have a hard time believing what their children are capable of. However, Dylan's accusation was substantiated by two other boys in my class. They saw Gerallt trip and push Dylan, and they complained that Gerallt has also been forcing them to give him their lunch money. They said Gerallt had threatened to put a spell on them if they didn't pay him."

"Oh, no!" Gwendolyn gasped, the color draining from her face.

Chapter 10 – The Principal's Office

"Yes," Mrs. McKinney said. "Naturally, I sent your son here to the office while I escorted Dylan to the nurse's station."

"Mrs. Hawthorne," Mr. Tanner said, "perhaps now you realize the seriousness of the situation. Gerallt is no longer in middle school. He's growing up, and his actions can have the most serious of consequences. Assault, extortion, and possible experimentation in the occult are matters that I could potentially turn over to the local police."

Stunned, Gwendolyn sat there as if turned to stone. Finally, with great effort, she asked, "Surely, isn't there some other solution? He's nevah done anythin' like this before."

"Well, that's why we're here," Mr. Tanner replied. "While we cannot allow Gerallt to continue extorting money or to injure other students, we also want to do what's best for him." Mr. Tanner turned to the teacher to his right. "Now Mr. Armstrong, let's hear what happened in gym class."

"Class had just started, and Matt had not joined us out on the gym floor. I heard a boy in the locker room yelling for Matt to get off Dylan. I ran back to the locker room and found Dylan lying on the ground with a bloody nose. Another boy was holding Matt's arms behind his back so that he couldn't continue hitting Dylan. According to Dylan, Matt was waiting for him when he got back from the nurse's office and started to beat him up for telling on Gerallt. Two of their classmates said they heard the noise and went back into the locker room. When they saw Matt sitting on top of Dylan hitting him, one of them grabbed

Matt from behind and held him until I arrived. I sent Matt here to the office and escorted Dylan back to the nurse's station."

Never having had any serious problems with Matt, Sam was finding it hard to grasp what he was being told. "Are you sure it wasn't just a typical kids' fight?" he asked hopefully.

"Mr. Mitchell, it was hardly a fair fight," Mr. Armstrong replied. "While Matt isn't huge, Dylan is one of the smallest students in the school and had just been injured. And we usually don't have to drag one student off of another."

"So now you know what happened," Mr. Tanner continued. "The question is why. The teachers and I have been concerned about both of your boys, even before today. Except for each other, they are loners who don't seem to have any other friends. Then there's also the matter of their clothes."

"Clothes?" Gwendolyn asked, her brows knitted in confusion. "I don't understand."

Mr. Tanner briefly glanced at Gwendolyn's plain black dress before continuing. "We don't have a dress code here at Hawthorne High. Nevertheless, it is worrisome that in the last few weeks, Matt has begun to imitate Gerallt by dressing totally in black. Their antisocial, Gothic, and now violent behavior may be symptomatic of serious depression or worse. Have your sons ever mentioned hurting others, or possibly themselves?"

"No, never!" Sam blurted. Gwendolyn could only shake her head.

Chapter 10 – The Principal's Office

"I note that you are both single parents who have recently moved into town from out of state. I'm sorry if this next question stirs up painful memories, but how well have your sons handled being separated from your former spouses? Divorce can be very hard on any child, and it can sometimes be even worse on a teenager who is struggling with making the difficult transition to adulthood."

"My wife died last June in an automobile accident," Sam whispered, clearly remembering the terrible moment when the doctor had turned off her ventilator, and her breathing stopped.

"And my husband passed away last May. There was a fiah..." Gwendolyn added in a dull monotone.

"Oh, I'm sorry, I didn't realize," the principal stammered. "Then maybe that is where we should look for the underlying cause of your sons' behaviors. Perhaps they see themselves as kindred spirits. Death can be traumatic, especially to a child, and it can lead to antisocial behavior, depression, drug use, and even violence. It might also explain your sons' interest in witchcraft and the occult."

Gwendolyn visibly flinched at Mr. Tanner's final words.

"And how are things at home with the boys?" the principal continued. "Have you noticed any change in their routines? Are they becoming withdrawn from the family, spending all their time together rather than with you and their other siblings?"

"I guess," Sam replied, realizing just how much time he'd been spending in the office, working in the evenings and on weekends. He realized he didn't know what Matt was doing other than having Gerallt over and working weekends at the Hawthorne House. "I'm not really sure."

Gwendolyn had been spending so much time sitting alone in her room that she had even less idea what her son had been up to. She dropped her head as her anger quickly turned into darkness and despair.

"I want you both to understand we take violence and theft very seriously here at Hawthorne High. If they were seniors rather than freshmen, we'd expel them and might even involve the police."

Gwendolyn gasped.

"However, this is their first serious offense. If the two of you can commit to working with us to make sure that this doesn't happen again, I think we can let the boys off with a one-week in-school suspension and a stern warning. During that time, we are going to keep them separated and keep a close eye on them here at school. Can I count on you giving the boys sufficient restrictions to get their attention? If we all work together, I think we can get them back on track to becoming good students and citizens. Does everyone agree?"

Gwendolyn and Sam nodded solemnly. Swept up by the swirling tide of events, they felt as though they had no choice but to agree.

"Well, it's settled then. I'll go and ask the boys to come in. Once I've told them what their punishment will be here at school, then you can take them home where I'm sure you have much to discuss. The day's

Chapter 10 – The Principal's Office

almost over, and I'd prefer they didn't ride the bus home together today."

With that, he rose, left the room, and swiftly returned with Matt and Gerallt. The boys sat down next to their parents and looked anxiously across at the principal and their teachers.

"Well, boys, Mrs. McKinney, Mr. Armstrong, and I have discussed today's events with your parents, and we've all come to an agreement. Despite the seriousness of what you've done, I've decided this time not to expel you because this is your first major violation of school rules. However, if there are any more occurrences of extorting money or attacking your classmates, do not doubt that you will be expelled."

Mr. Tanner paused briefly for the full weight of what he had said to sink in. "I have decided to give you a one-week in-school suspension. Instead of going to your regular classes, you will be doing your assignments under the watchful eye of Mr. Armstrong. He will be reporting directly to me on your behavior. You will not sit together, and you will not talk to each other until your suspension is over. Is that understood?"

Both boys hung their heads and nodded.

"When I ask you a question, I expect to hear an answer, gentlemen," the principal said. "Is that understood?"

"Yes, Mr. Tanner," both boys replied.

"As the day is almost over, I am permitting your parents to take you home. I'm sure that they will also have something to say to you when you arrive."

Chapter 11
Grounded

The short ride home from school in the Mitchell's minivan was silent and very uncomfortable for everyone. Sam and Gwendolyn were too embarrassed by what they'd heard in the principal's office to speak in front of each other. They were buried in thought, worrying about what to say to their sons once they got them home and behind closed doors. Still in a state of shock, Matt and Gerallt were feeling too betrayed and depressed by what had happened to talk. To everyone, the short drive seemed to last forever.

Sam parked in front of their houses, and the two boys and their parents silently stepped out into the cold November wind. The bare branches of the old oak trees standing beneath the gray cloud-covered sky mirrored the mood of the people below. The first few flakes of snow began to fall.

"I want to thank you, Sam, for stoppin' by on youah way tah school," Gwendolyn said, pulling her coat closer around her neck. "And for lettin' us ride with you. There are times when not ownin' a cah can be very inconvenient."

"You're quite welcome," Sam said, trying to ignore the wind and the steadily increasing snow. "I'm just sorry we had to meet under such circumstances."

After a short and awkward pause, Gwendolyn continued, "Well, Gerallt and I'd bettah go. I guess each of us will be havin' a long overdue talk with ah sons."

"Wait, Gwendolyn," Sam said, as she started to turn. "Since this involved both Matt and Gerallt, I think the two of us should get together and discuss it. That way, we can be consistent in how we deal with them and let each other know if we see something we think the other should know."

"Ayuh, you're probably right," Gwendolyn replied, her mind more on what she was going to say to Gerallt than on what Sam was saying.

"Then how about getting together for lunch tomorrow while the boys are at school?"

"What?" Gwendolyn replied. "I'm not sure I could have the house ready tah have anyone over so soon."

"That's okay," Sam continued. There's a little Chinese place I usually eat at that's fairly quiet. We should be able to talk there. I'll pick you up tomorrow around noon."

Before Gwendolyn could think of another excuse, Sam turned and marched Matt up the front walk and into their house.

"Well," Sam said, as he and Matt sat down at the kitchen table. "I must say I was shocked when Mr. Tanner called me at work today to tell me you had been in a fight. I'm very disappointed in you. And it certainly didn't help to hear your PE teacher say the boy you beat up was much smaller than you. How could you have lost your temper so much you had to be pulled off him?"

Chapter 11 – Grounded

"But, Dad, that's not what really happened! I was just trying to protect myself."

"Matt, you don't protect yourself by continuing to hit someone when they're down. You could have seriously hurt the boy."

"But Colin, Clayton, and Dylan had me cornered in the locker room so they could beat me up. I only managed to hit Dylan once before Colin grabbed me and Clayton started punching me. I was the one who was attacked!"

"Are you trying to tell me you were beaten up by the boy you told me had a broken hand?" Sam asked incredulously. "Matt, how can you expect me to believe you when there were so many witnesses against you? You don't have a single mark on you, and you and Gerallt sent that poor Dylan kid to the nurse's office twice in just one hour. I know it's important to have friends and to stick up for them, but you can't let your friendship with Gerallt be an excuse to be a bully."

Matt couldn't believe what he was hearing. "We're not the bullies; they are!" he shouted in frustration and anger. Not able to remain sitting, Matt jumped up and continued. "Mom would have believed me; why won't you?" he demanded, looking down at his father.

Sam just sat there, his shoulders bowed as if he bore the weight of the whole world upon them. "Matt, enough," he replied softly. "It's time now to stop lying. I'm sorry, but the evidence against you is overwhelming." He paused, shaking his head with sorrow. "At first, I thought it was great that you'd found a friend. I ignored it when you started dressing all in black and began avoiding Tina and me. I guess it's really my fault. I've been way too busy with my new job to spend enough time with you and keep track of how you were doing. But that's going to stop right now."

"But, Dad..."

"Enough!" Sam shouted. "Things are going to change around here. To begin with, you're grounded for a week. The only time you can leave the house is to go to school. And you'll have no TV, video games, computer, music, or anything else until the week is up."

"But..."

"And you and Gerallt need a cooling off period until Mrs. Hawthorne and I can decide what's best for you. I don't want you talking to him on the bus or at school. Now, go to your room; you need to seriously think about what you've done."

Matt didn't know whether to scream or cry. Anger, frustration, and betrayal surged through him like storm waves crashing on a rocky shore. Before he knew it, he was standing in his room, the slam of his door still echoing in his ears.

Gerallt was hardly in the door when his mother demanded, "*Magna Dea!* How could you misuse youah gift from the Goddess? Do you want tah bring her wrath down on you, on all of us?" She shook her head in disbelief. "You know how critical it is for us tah nevah use or mention ah gifts in front of

Chapter 11 – Grounded

outsidahs! What if they learned who and what we are? And tah extort money from the othah kids at school? It had tah be Matt. He must have put you up tah this, seducin' you with all his electrical marvels. I should have known it was a mistake tah evah let you go ovah there."

"But Mothah," Gerallt countered when she paused briefly to take a breath.

"Don't you 'but Mothah' me," she continued. "Ahnt Vivianne has worked hard her entire life tah hide who she is from the outsidahs. And what happens the first month we're heah? First, you break one boy's nose and fingah, and now you're caught extortin' money, and almost break another boy's leg when he doesn't pay up. *Magna Dea*, are you possessed? I should nevah have stopped home-schoolin' you."

Gerallt was tempted to try once more to explain what happened. However, looking into the fury of his mother's face, he realized it was hopeless. Arguing would only increase her anger and his punishment. He hung his head and waited for her to hand down his sentence.

"First, hand over youah amulet," she demanded. "There will be no moah gift from the Goddess foah you until you prove you can be trusted."

Gerallt quietly unbuttoned the top of his shirt and pulled out the round golden amulet hanging from its sturdy silver chain. The large green gemstone in its center glowed briefly as the amulet changed hands and recognized its new master.

"Now, Gerallt, go up tah your room and stay there. I'm groundin' you tah your room for a full month. And don't you dare let me see you outside of it except foah school, youah chores, the bathroom, and meals. In fact, you can go without dinner tonight. Maybe that will help you realize just how dangerous the situation is that you've put us all in."

Gerallt was left with no choice but to turn and slowly climb the narrow stairs to his bedroom. He walked sadly over to Nightwing. Seeming to sense Gerallt's dismal mood, the crow cawed a mournful greeting.

It wasn't long afterward that the school bus arrived with Tina, Gwyneth, and Gareth. Tina rushed up to Matt's room. "I heard you were in a fight in gym class with Colin O'Connell and Clayton Cartwright," she said, looking at her brother with a mixture of concern and sympathy. "Then when you weren't on the bus, I was afraid they'd really hurt you. Are you okay? What happened?"

Matt told Tina how Colin, Clayton, and Dylan had set up Gerallt and him. "And worst of all, Dad doesn't believe me. He grounded me for a week.

"Wow! Everyone knows they're the school's worst bullies, but this is evil, even for them. You must have done something big to piss them off like this."

"I've tried to stand up to them, but I don't think I was their real target. I think they were mostly angry at

Chapter 11 – Grounded

Gerallt, and since I'm Gerallt's only friend, they decided to get me, too."

"Well, I'll go talk to Dad and tell him what I know about Colin, Clayton, and Dylan. Hopefully, he'll listen to me."

"Thanks, Tina. It's good to have at least you believe me."

"Don't worry, Baby Brother. The kids at school know Colin and his gang are liars. Meanwhile, I know how to cheer you up. I think I'll fix your favorite dinner tonight: spaghetti with meat sauce."

At the Hawthorne House, Gareth burst into Gerallt's room.

"I was worried when I didn't see you and Matt on the bus home," Gareth said, looking up at his big brother. "Then, I overheard that stupid Clayton kid tell some other kids that you'd been expelled for stealin' kid's money and threatenin' tah put a spell on them. And now Mothah's down in the study whisperin' with Gwyneth, but she won't tell me anythin'. So, what happened?"

Gerallt sat down and told his brother everything.

"That's not right!" Gareth exclaimed when Gerallt had finished his story. "That Dylan's evil, and I'm glad Matt hit him. He deserved it."

Gareth and Gerallt talked and played cards until Gareth had to go downstairs for dinner. Four hours later, Gerallt was bored and beginning to get really hungry. There was a quiet knock on his door.

"May I come in, dear?" Vivianne asked through the closed door.

"Sure," Gerallt replied, glad for the company.

"I thought you might like a little somethin'," Vivianne said, bringing in a covered tray holding leftover fried fish and potatoes from dinner. "I think youah mothah may be overreacting a dite tah what happened today. So, let's just let this be our little secret, shall we?"

"Thank you!"

"Gareth and I had a little talk, and he told me what you said about Colin, Clayton, and Dylan. I haven't trusted those juvenile delinquents evah since they started damagin' my property and spreadin' lies about me."

"What did they damage?" Gerallt asked with concern.

"Oh, nothing much, really," Vivianne replied. "Just the usual kinds of things you might expect from such kids. They soaped my windows one Samhain, and they left a burnin' paper bag of dog...," she hesitated. "Well, you know, dog droppin's, on my porch. Then, they graduated tah peltin' the house with rotten eggs and throwin' stones at the greenhouse windows. So I prayed to the Goddess for a little plague of flies, and they left me alone for quite a while. I thought they'd decided there were easier and safer targets until Gwyneth told me they came back on Samhain tah egg the house."

"So, can you talk tah Mothah for me?" Gerallt asked hopefully.

Chapter 11 – Grounded

"I already did, but she's not yet in the mood tah listen. You'll just have tah live with being grounded until she cools down. Then, I'll see if I can talk her intah reducin' your sentence to somethin' a little more reasonable."

"But I didn't do anythin'!"

"Maybe you did, and maybe you didn't," Vivianne answered skeptically. "Or perhaps you only did some of what your mother said she heard from youah teachers and principal. And if you did do somethin', maybe Dylan deserved it. Anyway, I wasn't there. I have tah listen tah both you and your mothah and then make up my own mind about what actually happened."

"I guess that's fair," Gerallt grudgingly replied, looking over at his great-aunt with growing respect. "But I didn't do anythin' this time, I swear."

Vivianne nodded and stood up. "Just put the tray under youah bed when you're done with it, Gerallt, and I'll take care of it tomorrow. Good night."

"Good night, Ahnt Vivianne. And thanks."

Chapter 12
What to Do?

Bringing more wind than snow, the night's storm left brown leaves poking their heads up through their thin white blanket. Matt and Tina made a point of going out early to wait for the Hawthorne children, but they didn't appear until the bus had rounded the corner. Gwyneth led Gerallt as if she were guarding a prisoner being transferred between cells.

"Hello, Gerallt," Matt said as they approached.

"Excuse me, Matt," Gwyneth interrupted as she motioned her brothers to board the bus. "Gerallt's been grounded, and Mothah has asked me tah ensure that the two of you do not talk or sit togethah." She followed Gerallt onto the bus, found a pair of empty seats, motioned Gerallt in, and sat down next to him. He shrugged his shoulders apologetically as Matt walked past to take a seat near the back of the bus.

After storing their winter coats in their lockers, Matt and Gerallt met in the detention room. Having already heard about the previous day's events on the school's grapevine, the older girl and two boys who were there glared up at Gerallt with a mixture of dislike, fear, and curiosity as he and Matt entered the room. The two friends were about to sit next to each other in the back of the classroom when Mr. Armstrong, the detention teacher, spoke up.

"Mr. Hawthorne and Mr. Mitchell, you will please select seats up front on opposite sides of the room,"

Chapter 12 – What to Do?

Mr. Armstrong commanded. "As this is your first time here, let me explain the rules. There will be no talking and no goofing off in this room. You will read your textbooks and work on your assignments. If you have any extra time, you may read a book, but no graphic novels or comics. Do I make myself clear?"

"Yes, sir," the boys answered as they moved back up to the front and sat down where they were told.

About an hour later, Gerallt raised his hand, got permission to go to the restroom, and left. Matt waited a full three minutes before raising his hand and doing the same.

"So Gerallt, how'd it go when you got home?" Matt asked, as he entered the nearest boys' bathroom to find his friend washing his hands.

"Not good. Mothah got ugly on me and grounded me tah my room for a whole month. I can't leave it except tah go tah school, do my chores, eat, and... go tah the bathroom," Gerallt answered, smiling at the irony of their location as he gestured around the boys' restroom. "How about you?"

"I thought I had it bad," Matt answered, shaking his head with disbelief at Gerallt's harsh sentence. "I'm grounded too, but only for a week, and I get the run of the house. I can't watch TV, play video games, listen to music, or use the computer, though."

"Mothah has also forbidden me tah talk tah you."

"Same here, so we have to be careful so that no one catches us together."

"It gets worse. Back on Deeah Isle, I nevah needed money, and now that I'm heah, I've never had the opportunity tah buy anythin'. Since Mothah thinks I have no use for the lunch money, she thinks I'm just kifing it tah give tah you."

"What? Your mom thinks I've talked you into stealing for me? That's terrible."

"Ayuh. It's a honkin' pissah!"

"We got to do something! I can't have your mom thinking I'm responsible for this mess we're in."

"Agreed. But what do you think we should do?" Gerallt asked, after looking around to make sure that they were alone. "She took away my amulet, so we can't count on Colin, Clayton, or Dylan having any more 'unfortunate' accidents. At least, not until we can prove we're innocent."

"What do you mean, she took away your amulet?"

"It's a long story, and we don't have the time now," Gerallt replied. "I have tah get back before Mr. Armstrong comes lookin' for me. Any moah problems heah, and Mothah will start home-schoolin' me again foah sure. And if she does that, I don't know how we'll evah get together again. I'd bettah go. We can try meetin' heah again this afternoon. I'll talk tah you then."

"It won't be necessary. I was afraid that we'd both be grounded, so I brought you this," Matt replied, pulling a small walkie-talkie and some extra batteries out of his pants pocket. "It's not very good and will only reach about a hundred yards, but that should be plenty good enough for us to talk to each other from our rooms tonight. What time do you finish dinner?"

"About seven or so, I guess. Why?"

Chapter 12 – What to Do?

"As soon as you're back in your room, go to your window. I'll be watching. We can talk then."

"But how do I use it?" Gerallt asked, as if he were holding some alien artifact.

"It's easy," Matt explained. "First, you turn it on by sliding this tiny switch on the top. Then this little green light will come on. After that, all you need to do is squeeze this trigger to talk and remember to release it to listen. When the light starts to flicker, and you can't hear me very well anymore, then you'll have to change the batteries. Just slide this back, take the old ones out, and replace them with the new ones, so they line up the same way the old ones did. I just put in new batteries so you probably won't have to worry about replacing them for a week or so. That's all there is to it."

"Thanks, Matt. I think I got it. Anyway, I'll see you back in detention. Talk tah you tonight!"

As Matt and Gerallt were unpacking their sack lunches at school, Sam was pulling up in front of the Hawthorne House to pick up Gwendolyn so they could discuss their sons over lunch. This time, she had been waiting and watching from the parlor window, so she joined him before he had walked halfway up the walk. Returning to his car, it didn't take long to drive the short distance to the restaurant.

Sam and Gwendolyn pulled into the parking lot of a small shopping center that had seen better days, where the Mandarin Dragon was nestled between an auto-parts store and a used-clothing store. The small family-run Chinese restaurant was a long-time fixture of the neighborhood. It had changed little since Sam had left Hawthorne to attend a small liberal arts college in Oregon, where he had met his wife. Taking Gwendolyn's coat and hanging it next to his, Sam led her past the big brass Buddha and red-paper lanterns to a booth in the corner where they could talk privately. The place was dimly lit and nearly empty so that the staff slightly outnumbered the patrons who had braved the cold to temporarily leave work and enjoy an authentic Chinese meal.

Once Sam and Gwendolyn sat down, there was an awkward pause. Neither of them knew where to begin.

As the silence lengthened, Sam cleared his throat and said, "So, Gwendolyn, I forgot to ask you yesterday. Do you like Chinese?

Gwendolyn looked nervously around the dimly lit room at the red paper lanterns and the murals of fantastic mountains and strangely dressed women playing bamboo flutes. "Hard tellin'. I've nevah had it befoah."

Then Sam remembered Gerallt's description of the typical Hawthorne meals and nodded. "That's okay. When we had Gerallt over for dinner, he told us that you eat a lot of fish, but rarely anything spicy. Seafood is a very popular part of Chinese cuisine, so I'm sure you'll enjoy it. I often eat here for lunch and know most of the dishes. Why don't I order for the two of us this time?"

Chapter 12 – What to Do?

Gwendolyn looked up with relief from her menu with its faded pictures of unfamiliar dishes with strange names like Triple Delight and Moo Goo Gai Pan.

"What the kids and I usually do is order one entrée per person, and then we share. There's always more than enough food, and that way, each of us can sample several dishes."

He motioned to the young waitress who had been waiting patiently for them to decide.

"Mr. Mitchell, so good to see you again. What can I get for you today?"

"I think we'll start with some egg drop soup to warm us up from the cold. Then, we'll have an order of Crab Rangoon as an appetizer. And finally, the shrimp fried rice, scallops with snow peas, some steamed rice, and a couple of extra plates so we can share."

"Very good," the waitress replied. "And to drink?"

Sam looked over at Gwendolyn who shrugged her shoulders.

"A pot of jasmine tea, I think," Sam said, and the waitress left to place their order.

There was another brief pause until the waitress returned with their tea. She also placed a napkin and a pair of disposable chopsticks in front of Sam and some silverware rolled in a napkin next to Gwendolyn.

"What ah those?" Gwendolyn asked, looking over as Sam unwrapped his chopsticks.

"Oh, these are chopsticks, the traditional way to eat Chinese food," Sam said, raising them so that Gwendolyn could see that they were nothing but long, straight, and thin sticks of sanded wood. "I guess not many people here use them, so ordinarily one has to ask for them. But I like to learn about other cultures, and I've eaten here enough that they know to bring them now without asking. Anyway, you hold them in your hand like this and use a scissoring motion to pick up your food. Would you like to try?"

Gwendolyn imagined making a fool of herself by dropping most of her food in her lap. "No thanks, Sam. I'll be satisfied tah just watch you demonstrate this time."

Once again, the conversation stalled, and as Gwendolyn was studying the décor, Sam took the opportunity to look closely at her for the first time. Whereas he had hidden the pain of his wife's death by moving inland and burying himself in his work, Gwendolyn had instead buried herself in grief. She was quite pale from having sat in near darkness for the six months that had slowly passed since her husband's untimely death. The contrast of her white skin and her raven hair was striking. For the first time since his wife had died, Sam was alone with a woman, and although they were here to discuss their sons, he found that he couldn't completely ignore her beauty, touched though it was by the depths of her sorrow. He also couldn't stop himself from wondering what she'd look like if only she would smile. Sam was sure that it would light up her face like sunlight on freshly fallen snow. Then she looked back at him before quickly

Chapter 12 – What to Do?

glancing away with embarrassment, and he realized that he had been staring with mingled admiration and concern.

"I'm sorry," he apologized. "I didn't mean to stare, but I couldn't help admiring you."

"Why thank you, Mr. Mitchell. But remembah, we ah heah tah discuss our sons," she replied nervously. Yet her face also held the hint of a smile at the unexpected compliment.

"Yes, of course," Sam agreed, forcing his thoughts back to the topic at hand. "Did Gerallt tell you his version of what happened?"

"Ayuh, though he still argued that he was totally innocent in spite of all we heard in the principal's office. And your son?"

"The same. Matt maintains that he and Gerallt were set up by some bullies at school. He wouldn't confess, so I had to ground him a week to give him a little time to reconsider his actions."

"Only a week?" Gwendolyn exclaimed with a mixture of surprise and disapproval. "But surely Matt deserves more than that for convincin' Gerallt tah steal foah him."

"What?" Sam asked, his voice also raising a notch. "No one at school said anything about Matt being involved in extorting lunch money. Did Gerallt blame Matt for that?"

"Well, no," Gwendolyn conceded. "But why else would Gerallt do it? He's nevah needed money, and anyway, there's nothin' foah him tah spend it on."

"In my experience, all teenagers think they need money, and there's no end to the ways they can spend it," Sam replied, remembering the last time he had taken his children to the mall. "Besides, Matt's been making all the money he needs working for your aunt."

"Well, my children do not need money, and the only thing I can think of is that Matt seduced Gerallt with all of his modern electronic toys and gadgetry. I'm sorry now that I let him come ovah and spend the night."

"Now wait just one second," Sam said. "Matt's a good kid, and I've never had any real problems with him before. And the way the principal made it sound, Matt's heart was in the right place, even if he wasn't using his head. The gym coach said that Matt got into the fight in the locker room because he was standing up for Gerallt. Maybe if your son hadn't got himself into trouble, then Matt wouldn't have had any reason to get in trouble either."

Their argument was about to escalate out of control when the waitress arrived with their soup, the Crab Rangoon, and a small bowl of sweet and sour sauce.

Embarrassed by having raised their voices, both parents quietly turned their attention to their soup as they tried to regain their composure and think of some way to salvage their meeting. Watching Sam pick up a crab puff with his hands and dip it into the reddish sauce, Gwendolyn tentatively did the same.

Chapter 12 – What to Do?

"Let's start over," Sam said, as the silence became unbearable. "We're here for the sake of our sons. Okay?"

"Ayuh," Gwendolyn finally said, changing the subject. "This egg soup is quite good though its slimy texture may take some getting used tah. And the crab Rangoon is very strange, both familiar and yet oddly unrecognizable. I'm not acquainted at all with some of its spices and flavorin's."

"I hope you like it," Sam said, relieved that Gwendolyn had not become so angry that she had demanded to be immediately driven home. "Gwendolyn, I'm sorry if we've gotten off on the wrong foot. The important thing is that we do what is best for our sons, and we'll succeed better with them if we work together."

"Sam, of course you're right," Gwendolyn reluctantly agreed. "I didn't mean tah take it out on you. It's just that this was so unexpected and so unlike anything Gerallt's evah done before. I don't know what tah do."

"I'm not sure I know what to do either, but if we work together, hopefully we can do what's best for our boys. You said that you thought I was being lenient, only grounding Matt for one week. What did you do to Gerallt?"

"Given the seriousness of his actions, I felt I had no recourse but tah ground Gerallt tah his room for a full month," Gwendolyn answered. "It's not just him forcin' other children tah give him their lunch money. It's also the way he did it. By drawin' attention to the name Hawthorne and magic, he rekindled hateful rumors about poor Ahnt Vivianne. And to do it while we've been forced to rely on her kindness for the roof over our heads and the food on our table. It's simply inexcusable."

"You mean the stories some of the neighborhood children say about your aunt being a witch? Surely you don't think anyone takes such stories seriously?"

"But I do take those stories seriously. They ah one of the reasons Ahnt Vivianne has been a recluse foah the last fifty years. It was bad enough that her husband ran off with her best friend, but tah add the further indignity of sayin' that she murdered him and put a hex on her former friend is just mean and hurtful."

"I agree. I heard those rumors when I was a kid, so I made it clear to Matt and Tina to never spread such stories. Surely you've never heard of him being anything but polite and helpful to her."

"No, I haven't," Gwendolyn grudgingly conceded. "Nevertheless, it has always been a very serious subject in our family. And Gerallt had absolutely no business drawing attention tah the topic."

Their conversation was once more interrupted when the waitress arrived with their entrees. Again, Gwendolyn copied Sam who had dished up some shrimp fried rice followed by some white rice which he covered with a hearty portion of scallops and snow peas.

"Still," Sam said, "aren't you afraid that by being so strict, you might make him feel that his punishment doesn't fit his crime? If he gets too angry, he might

Chapter 12 – What to Do?

forget that you love him and are doing this for his own good. Sometimes, if children think the punishment is excessive, they feel justified in doing what they're being punished for."

"Mr. Mitchell, he's my son. I must do what I think is best."

"Please, Gwendolyn. Call me Sam. I'm not suggesting that you shouldn't. Of course, you must do what you think is best." He paused for a moment, letting her have a chance to taste the food. "Okay, let's try another approach. Principal Tanner raised the issue that the boys have each lost a parent recently and that their actions may be a symptom of a resulting depression. That got me thinking. I've been very busy with my new job, and I haven't been spending enough quality time with Matt since we moved here. How about you? Has your relationship with Gerallt changed since your husband died?"

"Well, I used tah spend quite a bit more time with my children every day when I homeschooled them. But these last few months, I just haven't been able tah cope with the stresses of teachin' them on top of everythin' else. And yet, that hasn't stopped me from worryin' about all of the negative influences in the world outside of our home."

"Although I don't know him well, Gerallt seems to be a smart young man. Certainly, I can't imagine trying to teach Tina and Matt while running a household and bringing in an income."

"Well, I know I've let Gerallt spend a lot of time by himself recently. Apparently, I haven't been keepin' an eye on him as much as I should."

"So, one thing that we can agree on is that we should both spend more time with our sons."

"Ayuh, of course."

"And what about the principal's observation that the boys may be suffering from depression? I've been wondering if I shouldn't take Matt to see a therapist. I've been worrying about his choice of music and his wanting to wear nothing but black."

"And what is wrong with wearin' black?" Gwendolyn demanded. "My entire family wears black. Ah you questioning our traditions and heritage?"

"Not at all," Sam said, trying to reassure her. "It's just that it's not our tradition and that wearing nothing but black is sometimes a symptom of kids thinking nothing but dark thoughts."

"Well, it doesn't mean that to us. And for Matt, it probably only means that he admires Gerallt and wants to be more like him. Besides, even if he were sufferin' from depression, I know many herbs and potions that would be appropriate to use."

"Well, I'm not so sure that natural remedies will be as effective as antidepressants, but then again, I'm no doctor. Anyway, we must each decide for ourselves what to do for our sons. I would just like for us to work together to help them get over this."

"Ayuh, Sam. That's the important thing." Gwendolyn paused to take a bite of one of the large sea scallops. "I think I like Chinese food. I've nevah had shrimp and scallops served like this before. I used tah cook them quite often when my husband, Medwyn..." Gwendolyn stopped mid-sentence, her face suddenly

Chapter 12 – What to Do?

ashen. The memory of cooking over a wood-burning stove reminded her of flames and her husband's death in the awful fire that swept through his fishing boat.

"I'm sorry, Gwendolyn," Sam apologized. "I didn't mean to dredge up any painful memories. I just thought that it might make you feel more comfortable having seafood." Sam paused, and the silence grew uncomfortable. "I've tried to forget the ocean, but I can't. There are just too many good memories mixed in with the bad."

Hoping to change the topic, Sam continued, "I was thinking. While it makes sense for us to keep our boys separated for a while, I'm not sure that we should keep them apart for too long. They've become best friends, and they need a chance to talk things over. Maybe we can slowly bring them back together under controlled conditions. Perhaps, sometime next week, I could have your entire family over for dinner. That way, we can all get to know each other better."

"I'm not sure. I'll have tah think about it and discuss it with my ahnt. Still, it does sound appealin' tah get out of the house and be able tah talk to anothah adult. Don't get me wrong; I like Ahnt Vivianne. It's just that I get lonely for the voice of someone moah my own age."

"I know what you mean. I talk to the other programmers at work, but it's always work-related, and they're all fresh out of college and so young. It would be nice to spend time with someone who understands what I'm going through. We've both recently lost someone we loved, and we're single parents who are new to the community. I'd like to be able to spend time with you, especially under better circumstances where we don't have to discuss our boys getting into trouble."

"Ayuh," Gwendolyn replied. "I think I'd like that, too. It's been so long since I've had the opportunity tah talk tah anyone othah than Ahnt Vivianne and the children. I've felt so alone since Medwyn's death. I guess I'd forgotten what it was like tah speak with anothah adult who understands what it's like to have children. Ahnt Vivianne has been really kind tah us since we've moved in, but she's from another generation. She's nevah had children of her own, and the two of us just don't seem tah have all that much in common." She smiled briefly before looking self-consciously back at her now empty plate.

So, Sam began to see Gwendolyn as a kindred spirit with whom he might eventually share his painful memories and maybe even his hopes for the future.

Chapter 13
Matt's Marvelous Plan

As soon as dinner was over, Matt ran up to his bedroom and got out his walkie-talkie. Moving his chair next to his window, he sat down and waited for Gerallt to signal him that it was safe to talk.

After about twenty minutes, Matt saw Gerallt wave an oil lamp briefly in front of the window and then disappear He returned holding something in his hand.

"Hello, Gerallt," Matt spoke softly into his walkie-talkie. "Can you hear me?"

"Ayuh, I hear you!" Gerallt replied excitedly. "This is honkin' great! So how are you holdin' up bein' grounded?"

"Not so bad. Tina's been pretty nice, fixing me special dinners, and I have some books I've been meaning to read. How about you?"

"Gwyneth is givin' me the silent treatment. Gareth and Ahnt Vivianne sometimes stop by foah a while, but then they're gone, and it's just Nightwing and me. I'm going tah go crazy if I have to stay in heah foah a whole month."

"What about your mom?"

"She's the worst. The only time Mothah talks tah me is tah give me a lecture about how important it is for us tah not draw attention tah ourselves. That the Goddess's gifts must remain hidden, and we can nevah evah give anyone a reason tah associate us with them. As fah as she's concerned, I've let everyone down: her, Ahnt Vivianne, the whole family."

"But you're innocent! We both are."

"Ayuh. Colin, Clayton, and Dylan really got us good. We can't let them get away with this. But, what ah we goin' tah do?"

"I'm not sure. Since I can't think of a way for us to prove we're innocent, we need to find a way to prove they're guilty. What we really need is to get them to confess. Is there some way we can scare them into confessing?"

"No way. Mothah would kill me if I threatened them. Anyway, it would just make them look like they're telling the truth about me threatenin' tah hex them. Besides, she made sure I couldn't, even if I wanted to."

"What do you mean, making sure you couldn't? What did she do?"

"Mothah confiscated my..." Gerallt paused. "Anyway, she confiscated somethin', and I can't do anything without it. If I tried tah sneak out of my room tah find out where she hid it and she caught me, she'd ground me forevah. She'd homeschool me foah sure. We'ah just going tah have tah do somethin' else."

"Like what?"

"What about usin' some of youah gadgets, like this..., this..., what did you call this thing, again?"

"A walkie-talkie."

Chapter 13 – Matt's Marvelous Plan

"Oh yeah, a walkie-talkie. So, isn't theah some electronic thing like this that we can use tah record them confessin' what they did tah us?"

"Well, I suppose we could use the microcassette recorder my dad let me have. It's small enough I could hide it in my pocket. But how are we going to get them to confess? With the in-school suspension, we can't even get close to them. And there's another problem. Even if we got them to confess, they'd just say we forced it out of them. Besides, they're not likely to confess in front of us, anyway."

"I got it!" Gerallt exclaimed. "You know how they always eat lunch at the same table in the cafeteria. Maybe we can hide it undah the table and record them talkin'. They're always braggin' about what they've done when they think no one's listenin'."

"Good idea! I could duct tape it to the underside of the table. Sooner or later, they're bound to say something useful."

"But how are we going tah do that? We're stuck in the detention room, and the cafeteria's crowded by the time we get there. They'll already be sittin' at the table, or if we somehow managed tah get there before them, they might still see us around theah table and get suspicious. We really need someone who'd hide it foah us. Gwyneth's on Mothah's side so she certainly won't. How about Tina?"

"Sure, she'd do it. I'll ask her tonight. Oh wait... we still have a problem. She'll have to hide it there early so she won't be seen. But the tape recorder can only record for thirty minutes. It might run out of tape before lunch starts. I'm going to have to rig up some kind of timer for it."

"Can you do that?"

"I think so. I have a small, mechanical alarm clock. I should be able to hook it up to the recorder. Then when the alarm goes off, it will start recording instead of ringing."

Matt heard the muffled sound of someone climbing the stairs outside his bedroom door. "Someone's coming. I'll talk to you tomorrow."

Matt hid his walkie-talkie under his mattress and returned his chair to his desk. Then he got to work. The small alarm clock and microcassette recorder were in an old shoebox Matt used to keep things he eventually wanted to take apart to see how they worked. Setting them on his desk, he took out a screwdriver, soldering iron, scissors, and duct tape. An hour later, he'd wired the alarm clock to the tape recorder and mounted both in a small box that he'd made out of pieces cut from the shoebox. It wasn't pretty, but it was small, relatively flat, and it worked when Matt tested it. Now, all he needed was to borrow the duct tape and explain the plan to Tina.

A few minutes later, Matt knocked on Tina's bedroom door.

"Come in," Tina said.

Matt walked in to see her lying on her bed, reading her French textbook. "You busy?" Matt asked, not sure where to begin.

Chapter 13 – Matt's Marvelous Plan

"Not really," Tina answered, putting down the book as she got up from her bed. "So, what's in the box, Baby Brother?"

"Well," Matt answered, forcing himself to not point out that she was only four minutes older. "Gerallt and I have been using my walkie-talkies to discuss what to do about Colin, Clayton, and Dylan."

"Ingenious, but you'd better be careful not to let Dad find out. He's still worried that Gerallt's a bad influence on you. If you don't watch out, he could do more than just ground you."

"Yeah, I know. But we need to prove we're innocent, and the only thing we can think of is to get them to confess they set us up."

"You're probably right, but somehow I don't see them doing that anytime soon. So, what's your plan? And you still haven't told me what's in the box."

"Well, I wired the guts of an old alarm clock to my microcassette recorder so it will start taping instead of ringing when the alarm goes off. If I set the alarm for lunchtime, and we hide it under the table where Colin, Clayton, and Dylan always eat, it might record them talking about what they did to us. So, what do you think?" Matt handed the box to Tina.

"Not half bad, Matt," she said, with reluctant admiration as she looked over his invention. "This just might work. But how are you going to hide it if you're stuck in the detention room all day? Oh... When you said 'we,' what you really meant was me. So, what do you want me to do?"

The next day after the children had left for school, Gwendolyn and Vivianne were sitting in the parlor discussing what to do about Gerallt.

"I don't know what tah do with him anymoah," Gwendolyn confided. "Every time I talk tah him, he just gets ugly and won't listen. I don't know what else I can take away from him, and I'm just about at my wit's end. He won't confess, and until he admits his guilt, I don't see how I can trust him to not misuse his amulet."

"It might be that Gerallt just needs more time," Vivianne suggested. "Besides, I've talked tah him several times, and I'm not at all convinced he's as guilty as you think. I know his accusers. Colin, Clayton, and Dylan are bad seeds. Why I wouldn't put it past them tah have planned the whole thing just tah get Gerallt and Matt in a gaum."

"I don't know. The principal and the two teachahs seemed very sure of themselves. And I don't trust Matt. He's an outsidah, and he could easily have tempted Gerallt with his electronic wonders tah violate our laws and traditions. Gerallt could have been extortin' money for Matt in exchange foah some modern marvel or other."

"I don't think so. I've watched Matt closely foah the last couple of months, and he's not like the othah boys. He's worked hard and been respectful. In fact, I've grown tah like him. More importantly, I trust him. In fact, he's reminded me that there are good kids, even among the outsidahs. He's earned plenty of

Chapter 13 – Matt's Marvelous Plan

money workin' foah me. It doesn't make sense he'd risk his job just tah push Gerallt intah extorting a few dollars from his classmates. I really think blamin' Matt's a red herring."

"I want tah trust Gerallt, but I've got tah know foah sure, and the uncertainty is killin' me. I've been thinkin' that maybe I should search his room. Then if I find the money or some electronic plaything, I'll know foah sure he's guilty and can confront him with it."

"I'm not sure that's wise, deah. This situation has already strained youah relationship with Gerallt, and he's at an age where a certain amount of rebellion is natural. You don't want tah totally destroy his trust and drive him away."

Gwendolyn looked puzzled. "So, what should I do? I've got tah do somethin'."

"Perhaps there's another way. Maybe I should be the one tah search his room. Then, if I find anythin', you can say it was my idear. That way, you won't be breakin' his trust."

"I guess if you really think it's best."

"I do." Vivianne left her niece and headed up the two flights of stairs to Gerallt's room. Opening his door, she pulled a short wand of polished oak out of a pocket in her dress and waved it at the dresser. "*Magna Dea, inveni, quaesumus, quod absconditum est!*"

Nothing happened.

Next, she walked over to Gerallt's desk and repeated the incantation. Once again, nothing happened. With growing relief, she turned and waved her wand over his bed with the same results. Finally, she stepped up to his closet, a tall antique oak wardrobe that stood along the wall just inside the door.

This time when she intoned the incantation, the tip of the wand glowed and shot out a green ray of light that illuminated the top of the wardrobe. With a mixture of worry and resignation, she dragged Gerallt's desk chair over to the wardrobe, climbed up, and peered over the top. She saw a small wooden box that didn't belong there.

Vivianne hesitated a moment and then lifted its lid to see the battered old walkie-talkie and extra batteries Matt had given Gerallt. Then she smiled with relief and closed the box, carefully replacing it and the chair where she found them. She headed down to where her niece sat, waiting and worrying.

"Did you find anythin'?" Gwendolyn asked nervously, as Vivianne reentered the parlor. "Did you find the money? Or anything electronic?"

Vivianne Hawthorne gazed down with concern at the worried expression on her niece's pale face. Deciding that what she found was not worth worrying her niece about, she replied, "No, deah, there's nothin' in Gerallt's room that doesn't belong theah."

Gwendolyn looked relieved. Maybe Gerallt was telling the truth after all.

Chapter 14
An Unexpected Anthem

While Vivianne was searching Gerallt's room, the children were at school, where Tina was putting her brother's plan into action. Excusing herself from class, Matt's sister headed for the cafeteria instead of the girl's restroom. It took only seconds to duct-tape the modified microcassette recorder to the bottom of the table where the three bullies always ate. On her way back, she paused briefly outside the detention room's open door and gave Matt and Gerallt the thumbs up before heading back to class. Now they could only wait and hope that their plan would work.

The lunch bell rang, the alarm clock reached its set time, and the hidden tape recorder silently started recording. Seven minutes later, Colin, Clayton, and Dylan arrived, carrying their trays and their bad attitudes.

"You know what?" Colin asked, as he looked around the crowded cafeteria with a pleased expression on his face.

"No. What?" Dylan asked, as Clayton sat down and immediately began shoveling a fork full of mashed potatoes into his mouth.

"I think the cafeteria's been looking better the last couple of days, don't you?" Colin continued, as he took a bite of pizza.

"I don't know," Clayton replied, looking up from his plate to glance around the room. "Looks the same to me."

"Yeah. So, what's different?" Dylan asked.

"It sure looks a lot better to me now that witch boy and his friend are eating their lunches in the detention room." Colin chuckled and took a second bite of pizza. "Even the pizza tastes better. Ah, revenge is sweet."

"Yeah, it sure is," Clayton agreed between mouthfuls of meatloaf and more mashed potatoes. He formed his right hand into a fist and smiled at it, feeling great now his splint had finally been removed the previous afternoon. "It would almost be worth getting in trouble, just to be able to sit in there with them and watch 'em stew."

"I know what," Dylan interrupted. "Let's go by after lunch. We can taunt them from the hallway. With any luck, maybe one of them will lose it and be suspended for another week."

"Nah, I don't think so," Colin replied, though he smiled at the thought of seeing the helpless rage on their faces. "We'd better not risk it. If one of the teachers catches us, we could end up in front of the principal instead of them."

"Not if we're halfway careful, we won't," Clayton argued. He looked around to ensure that the lunch monitors were across the room and out of earshot. "Heck, the teachers are dumb as dirt. They never even suspected what we did to Gerallt and Matt. And Mr. Tanner's the dumbest of all, buying that ridiculous

Chapter 14 – An Unexpected Anthem

story about us giving them our money. Besides, Colin, your last plan worked just the way you said it would. I bet if you came up with another one, we could get the two of them expelled this time."

"Maybe you're right, Clayton," Colin agreed, pleased at having his ego stroked as well as at the prospect of having Gerallt out of the school forever. "But no matter how stupid our teachers are, they can still get lucky if we get careless. I think we'd better wait a while before we try to frame the two of them again."

"Okay," Clayton reluctantly agreed. "But now that my hand's okay again, I'm itching for something fun to do with it."

"It must have been frustrating, only being able to hit Matt with your left hand," Colin said in mock sympathy, as he looked around the room again. "Okay, guys, do you see the nerds over there on the other side of pig girl?"

"Jeez, Colin," Dylan said. "It's hard to see anything on the other side of her."

"Good one, Dylan," Clayton said. "Okay, Colin, I see them. What about 'em?"

"Well, Science Club is meeting today after school. How 'bout we see if any of them are walking home afterward? Maybe some of them will pay us to ensure no 'unfortunate accidents' happen to their precious science fair projects."

The rest of the lunch period went much the same with the three young delinquents dividing their time between evil plans, putdowns, and petty acts of meanness. In the noisy cafeteria, they never noticed the quiet click as the microcassette recorder stopped when its tape ran out. They were long gone when Tina once again left class, this time to retrieve Matt's hidden tape recorder.

After returning home from school, Tina quietly carried her backpack up to Matt's room and returned to him the little box containing his tape recorder and alarm clock. Matt thanked his sister, who went back downstairs to keep an eye on their father while Matt went straight to work.

Starting the recorder, Matt waited impatiently for Colin, Clayton, and Dylan to arrive with their lunches. He couldn't believe his luck as he listened to their inadvertent confessions. After transferring the entire recording to his computer, Matt opened a sound-editing program so he could cut it down to just the good parts. They had been such blabbermouths there was little for him to delete. Once he had the final version of the recording, it didn't take long for him to burn a CD with only the incriminating evidence on it. He popped out the CD, labeled it "Homework" in case his father should wonder what it was, and placed it in its crystal case. Then he hid it in plain sight on his desk next to his schoolbooks and went downstairs to do his chores. He could hardly wait until after dinner for Gerallt to signal him so that he could play it for his friend and they could discuss what to do next.

Chapter 14 – An Unexpected Anthem

After dinner, Matt returned to his room and sat by his window to wait for his friend's signal. Time passed, and the lamplight eventually appeared in the window on the back corner of the third story of Hawthorne House.

"Hello, Matt," Gerallt called over the walkie-talkie. "Did it work? Did you get anythin'?"

"You won't believe it," Matt replied. "We got everything. They talked about setting us up and how stupid they think the principal and teachers are. They made nasty comments about other students and even planned to force some kids in Science Club to give them money in exchange for not destroying their science fair projects. Just listen." Then Matt quietly played the new CD on his stereo, holding the walkie-talkie up to the speakers so Gerallt could hear what Colin and his gang said.

"That's honkin' savage! Have you played it foah youah fathah yet?"

"No, I thought you should hear it first. Besides, I'm kind of worried."

"About what?" Gerallt asked with surprise. "You've done it. All we need tah do now is tah play it for Principal Tanner, and everything will be okay. What could possibly be a problem?"

"I'm not sure we should do that. I think I remember something from some TV show where someone said it was illegal to record other people without their consent. And Colin, Clayton, and Dylan sure didn't give us permission to record this. We might get in even worse trouble if the principal finds out what we did. And I don't want to risk getting Tina in trouble, too."

"But this is crazy! We can't just ignore it. That recording proves we're innocent."

"I know. We have to use it; we just need to be smart and careful about how we use it. Somehow, we have to play it so that no one knows we had anything to do with it."

"Well, we cahn't be the only ones Colin and his gang have picked on. They made fun of lots of people on the tape. And they were plannin' tah get the Science Club kids. Anyone could have recorded them."

"That's it!" Matt said, having a stroke of inspireation. "I think I know who we can get to help us."

"Who?"

"You know the big girl that always sits by herself in the back of the bus?"

"You mean the honkin' robust one? Sure. What about her?"

"Well, she runs the audiovisual equipment at assemblies and games."

"So?"

"Well, Colin, Clayton, and Dylan are constantly teasing her, and they even teased her on the recording. I'd bet she'd be happy to get back at them by 'accidentally' playing it instead of the National Anthem at the basketball game tomorrow night. That way, we'll be home because we're grounded, and no one could ever blame it on us or even know we had anything to do with it."

Chapter 14 – An Unexpected Anthem

"That's perfect! But how are we goin' tah talk tah her without anyone noticin'? We'll still be stuck in the detention room, and the bus is too crowded; someone could overhear us."

"I'll ask Tina to do it. She'll be so pissed off after she hears what they said, she'll be glad to help us."

Matt said goodnight and put his walkie-talkie back in his desk. Then he took his CD player with the new CD to his sister's room and played it for her.

"What do you think?" he asked after the recording was finished.

"That those three idiots are disgusting pigs!" Tina exclaimed. "Let's go down and play it for Dad."

"No, not yet," Matt countered, smiling slyly. "I've got a better idea."

"Like what?"

"You know the big girl that rides on our bus?"

"Sure. Sarah Duffy. She's in a couple of my classes. Why?"

"Well, Colin, Clayton, and Dylan are constantly teasing her, and she usually runs the audiovisual equipment at assemblies and games. She'll probably be playing the National Anthem right before the basketball game tomorrow night."

"Oh, Matt, that's evil," Tina said with a wicked smile. "I love it! And you're right. I bet she'll love to accidentally play your CD instead of the National Anthem. You want me to ask her, don't you?"

"Would you?"

"Oh, I wouldn't miss it for the world! Too bad you and Gerallt will be stuck home during the game. You'll miss all the fun."

"Not really," Matt said. "That'll give Gerallt and me perfect alibis. Besides, since they never go to the games, the best part will be on Monday when the three of them show up at school. I can't wait to see their faces when they learn that they confessed in front of most of the school and even publicly insulted the principal and teachers."

The following day, Tina took the CD and stayed after school to talk with Sarah Duffy. Then she left to hang out and have dinner with a friend before going to the game. Thus, Tina didn't have a chance to speak with her brother until she arrived home later that night. When she finally returned home, she rushed up to Matt's bedroom where he was waiting anxiously to hear how things went.

"Well, Tina, what happened?" Matt asked excitedly, as his sister entered the room. "Did she play the CD? Were Colin, Clayton, and Dylan there? What did everyone do when they heard what the three of them said?"

"Hold on a second, Baby Brother!" Tina interrupted. "One question at a time."

"Okay, so what happened?"

"Well, I stayed after school to talk to her while she was getting the sound equipment ready for the game. I let her know what we did and gave her the CD. Once

Chapter 14 – An Unexpected Anthem

she listened to it, there was no way she wasn't going to play it. It seems that Colin and his gang have been teasing her for years."

"Great! I was worried she'd be too afraid to do it. So then, what happened?"

"Well, when it came time for the National Anthem, your recording of Colin and his cronies started playing over the loudspeakers. It took several seconds for anyone to react. Then, Principal Tanner and some of the teachers began walking as fast as they could for the sound booth. The recording abruptly stopped, but everyone at the game had heard enough to know who was talking and how the three of them had set you and Gerallt up. Everyone began talking and whispering and laughing about what they'd heard. It was amazing!"

"Excellent! What about Colin, Clayton, and Dylan? They weren't there, were they?"

"Matt, you know how much they hate the jocks. They'd have been bored stiff at the game. And seeing how none of them has any other friends, I doubt it if anyone will call them up to warn them. I bet everyone's just waiting 'til Monday to see the look on their faces when they learn what happened."

"You're probably right. But what about the teachers and Principal Tanner? How'd they react to hearing themselves being called stupid in front of the whole school?"

"They tried to act as if nothing happened, but you could tell they were really pissed off, especially the principal, the English teacher, and the gym coach. I sure wouldn't want them mad at me like that."

"So, do you think we're going to get away with it? Did they give Sarah a hard time?"

"Not really. I talked to her later, and she did great. Sarah said someone must have switched the CDs on her, and anyone could have done it because they aren't locked up or anything. Between being pissed at Colin and his gang and feeling guilty for what he did to you and Gerallt, I doubt the principal cares who switched the CDs. And as Sarah said, they don't have any real evidence to go on, and anyone could have done it. Besides, everyone knows the two of you couldn't have been involved because you've either been in the detention room at school or grounded here at home. I bet the whole school's going to be talking about this mystery for months. You did good, Baby Brother. Real good."

"And you too, Sis. I couldn't have done it without you."

"You're very welcome. It's been fun taking that trio of bullies down a few notches. But now there's one thing I want you to do."

"What's that?"

"The next time you see Sarah, I want you to go up and thank her in person. We couldn't have done it without her help.

"You're right. I will. I owe her big time." Matt paused to look at his phone. "It's getting late, and I bet Gerallt's going crazy waiting for me to call him on my walkie-talkies. See you in the morning."

Chapter 14 – An Unexpected Anthem

"Tell him hi for me. Goodnight," Tina said, closing the door behind her.

Matt rushed over and signaled Gerallt, who'd been sitting anxiously by his window. Once Matt had told him the great news, both went to sleep content in the knowledge that their suspension and grounding would soon be over.

Chapter 15
Freedom

The following Monday morning, the sun rose into a clear blue sky, to shine brightly on a thin new blanket of sparkling snow. Gerallt, Matt, and Tina smiled secretively to each other when the Hawthorne children joined the twins under the oak's bare branches. They didn't have to wait long for the school bus to pull up in front of their houses. Walking down the aisle, Matt and Gerallt surreptitiously glanced over to where Clayton was sitting, but the bigger boy showed no signs of having heard anything at all. After taking his seat, Matt looked back to where Sarah Duffy sat in the back of the bus. She smiled brightly at him, and he nodded back his thanks. Soon, the four conspirators walked into the school with high hopes for a great day.

It was only upon arriving at Hawthorne High that the change in people's attitudes became obvious. Several students stopped, stared, and snickered as Clayton passed by. It took a while for it to dawn on him that anyone might actually be laughing at him behind his back. When he finally demanded one of the offenders tell him what was so funny, the smaller boy promptly acted dumb. Clayton had no choice but to let him go when a nearby teacher took notice. Clayton was consequently in a foul mood when he arrived in the first-period history classroom.

Chapter 15 – Freedom

Still having three more days of suspension to serve, Matt and Gerallt were sitting in the detention room and didn't get to see Clayton and his minions being sent to the principal's office. The two friends could only open their books and wish they could have secretly seen the three bullies' faces as they listened to the principal replaying Matt's CD. Principal Tanner promptly suspended them for a week and called their parents to come and take them home.

Some thirty minutes after school started, Principal Tanner entered the detention room and asked Matt and Gerallt to pick up their things and follow him. The two grinned at each other as he led them down the hall and back to his office.

"Well, gentlemen," the principal began after closing his door behind them. "I take it you've heard about what happened at the basketball game last Friday."

"Er... no sir," Gerallt lied, hoping that the principal wouldn't think that he and Matt had been talking with each other. "I couldn't be there because Mothah grounded me tah my room for a whole month because of what you told her."

"And my dad grounded me for a week," Matt added. "But my sister Tina went to the game, and once she got home, she told me someone played a recording over the loudspeakers of Colin, Clayton, and Dylan confessing."

"So, the two of you are telling me that you were both home and neither of you had anything to do with this?" he asked, looking closely at each of the boy's faces as he held up Matt's CD.

"Yes sir," both boys answered.

"And when I talk to your parents, they will each tell me you were at home during the game?"

"Yes, sir," they repeated.

"Okay," Principal Tanner conceded. "Then I believe I owe you two an apology. Gerallt, you are clearly innocent of extorting money from other students. And Matt, you were only defending yourself during the fight in the locker room. And finally, I see no reason to link you two to the unfortunate incident with the switched CD at the basketball game. Your in-school suspensions are hereby rescinded, and I think that the two of you have earned the right to hear this." He put the CD into the stereo on his bookshelf and played it for the boys, who tried their hardest to act as though they were hearing it for the first time.

"But what about our parents?" Matt asked, once the recording stopped. "They still believe what you said about us, and now they don't trust us anymore. We were both grounded, and Gerallt's mom really came down hard on him."

"Well, Mr. Mitchell, I'll call your father at work and let him know you are innocent and that Colin, Clayton, and Dylan set you up. Mr. Hawthorne, since your mother doesn't appear to have a phone, I'll write a letter explaining what actually happened that you can give to your mother." The principal paused, looking guiltily from one boy to the next. "I made a mistake, and I am very sorry for suspending you for something that you didn't do. I just hope you'll remember how strong the evidence was against you.

Chapter 15 – Freedom

Please believe me; I was only trying to do what I thought was right based on what I believed to be true."

Principal Tanner looked hopefully over at Gerallt and Matt, who accepted his apology with silent nods. However, neither boy was in the mood to say anything that might ease the principal's guilty conscience.

"Well, you two can head back to your regular classes," Principal Tanner continued after an uncomfortable pause. "I'll call your father now, Matt. And Gerallt, you can stop by after lunch and pick up the letter for your mother."

"What about Colin, Clayton, and Dylan?" Matt demanded. "They caused us both a lot of grief, and you let them get away with it."

"Well, they've each been suspended and sent home for a full week. I made it very clear to their parents exactly what they did to you. And the teachers and I will be watching them closely when they return. I also made it perfectly clear to them that they'll be expelled if they ever try anything like this again. Satisfied?"

Both boys let the principal twist in the wind for several seconds before looking at each other, nodding, and answering. "Satisfied," they chorused.

Principal Tanner gave Matt and Gerallt notes for their teachers to allow them back into class. They left the office and headed to their regular classes, happy and relieved that their plot hadn't been traced back to them.

"I really want tah thank you, Matt," Gerallt whispered as they walked down the hall. "I thought it was hopeless and that I'd be stuck in my room for the whole month. Your recording device was savage!"

"It was kinda awesome, wasn't it?" Matt said with a grin, giving his friend a playful pat on the back. "But you know what, Gerallt? It's like when you jumped over the fence to help me when Colin was going to beat me up. It's what friends do. Besides, it got me out of my room, too!"

The rest of the school day was perfect. Not only were Colin, Clayton, and Dylan gone, the three bullies were also the source of a lot of laughter and the butt of more than a few jokes. Best of all, several students even said 'Hi' to Gerallt as they walked by.

Matt's father and Gerallt's mother and great-aunt were waiting on the steps of the Hawthorne House when the school bus pulled up to the curb. They all rushed out to meet the boys on the sidewalk.

"I'm so sorry," Gwendolyn apologized, hugging her son and giving him a big kiss on his forehead as he stepped off the bus. "When Sam got the principal's call, he drove straight home from work and told me everythin'."

"Ah, Mothah, not in front of the kids on the bus," Gerallt complained, though he didn't pull back from her arms.

"And I'm also very sorry," Sam said, giving his son a quick but heartfelt hug. "I should never have doubted you."

Chapter 15 – Freedom

"I told you that you couldn't trust the three juvenile delinquents who accused Gerallt and Matt," Vivianne Hawthorne told her niece as she smiled at both boys. "They're bullies and liars and will come tah a bad end one day."

Meanwhile, Tina and Gareth were all smiles seeing their brothers' vindication. Even Gwyneth looked guilty, gave Gerallt a hug, and whispered, "Sorry I was so rough on you."

"It's okay, Gwyneth. I understand," he said, imagining just how upset his sister must have been. The potential ramifications of the accusations could have been catastrophic.

"Well, kids, I believe Gwendolyn and I should definitely do something special to make it up to you for not believing you and punishing you when you were innocent," Sam said. "Now that you aren't grounded anymore, what would the two of you like to do?"

"I know," Matt said. "Gerallt and I are tired of being cooped up. Let's go out to eat and see a movie."

"Sounds good to me. What do you think, Gwendolyn?" Sam asked. "It'll be my treat."

Gwendolyn hesitated, unsure what to do or say. She glanced over at her aunt, who seemed equally at a loss. "But Sam, it's a school night," she finally said. "I'm sure the boys have lots of homework tah catch up for all the time they've missed."

"We're not behind, Mrs. Hawthorne," Matt argued. "We had plenty of time in the detention room to do our class work and almost all our homework."

"Well, then, it's not going to be a problem," Sam said, as he turned to Matt and Gerallt. "We can go out tonight. You boys promise to do the rest of your homework when we get back?"

"Of course, Dad," Matt answered.

"Absolutely, Mr. Mitchell," Gerallt agreed.

"See, Gwendolyn," Sam said, smiling at Gerallt's mother. "Come on, it will do you good to get out of the house and enjoy yourself."

"But Sam, Vivianne and I have been peelin' and cuttin' up vegetables all afternoon. We're starting a cauldron of stew this evening so that it can simmer all night and be ready for us tah start cannin' tomorrow mornin'."

"Well, it's only 3:15," Sam said, looking at his watch. "The kids can drop off their books, you can put away the vegetables, and we can leave in thirty minutes. We can have an early dinner and be done in time to catch a movie and still get home by seven. That should give you plenty of time to finish making the stew and for the kids to finish their homework."

Having run out of excuses, Gwendolyn turned to her aunt. "Vivianne, what do you think?"

"I don't know," she answered, her voice a mixture of uncertainty and fear. "It's been so long. I don't know if I can handle it. There will be so many, so very many..."

"Mr. Mitchell," Gerallt said softly to Matt's father, "Ahnt Vivianne hasn't been out of her house in years. As much as I would like tah see a movie at a real theater, I don't think she can stand bein' around so

Chapter 15 – Freedom

many people. Even eatin' out could be a problem if there are lots of people at the restaurant."

"Mrs. Hawthorne," Sam said, turning to Gwendolyn's aunt. "I'm sorry. I guess I got carried away. We can skip the movie tonight. But if we leave soon, we'll beat the dinner crowd, and the restaurants should be practically empty. It will just be us having a good time among friends and family."

"Mr. Mitchell," Vivianne said, steeling her courage. "Your son is a good boy. He has been a good worker for me and a good friend tah Gerallt. Both boys have suffered, and you are right. They deserve a celebration. I wouldn't feel right standin' in the way. Let's go, Gwendolyn, and we can finish up the stew when we return."

"Are you sure, Ahnt Vivianne?" Gwendolyn asked. "We can always stay home if you feel it will be too much."

"No, Gwendolyn. I think I can manage. Besides, when was the last time the Hawthorne family had a real reason to celebrate?"

"Uh, Dad..." Matt said, "I hate to be the one to point it out, but how are we going to get there? There are eight of us, and our minivan only seats seven."

"Oh no," Vivianne groaned. "I didn't think of that. You can't expect me tah ride in one of those infernal machines. Not with all the crazy people on the road. It isn't safe."

"Sam," Gwendolyn said. "When my ahnt was Gerallt's age, her parents were killed in a cah crash. She hasn't ridden in one since."

"Not a problem," Sam said, working hard to save the afternoon. "I know a nice little restaurant that's only four or five blocks away. Everyone meet back here in front of the house in thirty minutes." With that, Sam shooed Matt and Tina inside before anyone else could come up with another reason not to go.

Half an hour later, the Mitchell family was on the sidewalk at the gate in front of the Hawthorne House. The Hawthornes met them at the gate.

"Okay, Mr. Mitchell," Vivianne said. Somehow, she managed to seem both uncertain and determined at the same time. "Let's go befoah I change my mind."

With that, Matt's father turned right and led the group past his house and down Hawthorne Drive to Miguel's Cantina, a small family-run restaurant. The restaurant's sole waiter pushed three small tables together. Sam politely pulled the chair out at one end of the table for Gwendolyn to sit down. By the time she had, Vivianne and the children had already taken the three chairs along each side. Sam had no choice but to sit in the seat farthest from Gwendolyn at the opposite end of the table.

Being so early, the restaurant was empty, and they had the waiter entirely to themselves. After bringing in bowls of chips and salsa, the waiter took their drink orders and left to give them time to decide what to eat. Except for Gerallt, the Hawthornes had never had Mexican food before. They quietly looked at the chips

Chapter 15 – Freedom

and salsa with some trepidation while Gerallt and the Mitchells immediately dove in.

"Don't worry," Matt said, noticing that the Hawthorne's weren't eating. "It's just *pico de gallo*. It's not spicy."

Gareth took a chip, dipped it into the sauce, and took a bite. "Hey, this is wicked good," he said, smiling. The others picked up chips, and soon everyone was digging in with gusto.

"Matt and Gerallt," Sam said, "since this is really your celebration, how about the two of you deciding what we'll be eating tonight? You can order a table full of food, and then we can share, just like when we have Mexican at home."

"Great, Dad," Matt said. "Let's get plenty of tacos and burritos."

"And some refried beans tah go with the chips," Gerallt added, remembering how good they went together. "But, Matt, you'd bettah order the rest. Tacos, chips, and beans are all I've evah had."

"Okay, Gerallt. Dad and Tina, how about some guacamole for the chips and maybe some cheese enchiladas?"

"Sounds good to me," Matt's father agreed.

The waiter returned with their drinks, took their order, and left.

"Everyone," Gerallt began, speaking to the rest of the Hawthornes, "just wait 'til you taste the Mexican spices. Mothah, you'll have tah' find out what they ah so we can have them at home."

The waiter brought the food, and in minutes everybody was diving in as if they'd all skipped lunch. Soon, several lively conversations wove a colorful tapestry of topics from favorite classes at school to memories of living by the sea. Gareth told a joke he'd heard that day at middle school, and Vivianne laughed although everyone else mostly chuckled, having heard it many times before.

Matt happened to glance over at Tina and was shocked by what he saw. His sister was smiling, genuinely smiling, as she talked to Gwyneth about their classes at school. More importantly, her appetite had returned! Tina had loaded her plate with tacos and enchiladas, which she was actually eating. Something had changed. Hopefully, she would finally gain back the weight she'd lost in the months since their mother had died. Matt smiled, having one less concern to worry about.

Looking down the table, Sam watched Gwendolyn as she listened to Tina and Gwyneth comparing their classes and teachers. It dawned on him that this was the first time he'd ever seen her truly happy. He thought she was beautiful, now that a radiant smile had replaced her usual expressions of worry and sadness. She glanced down the table and noticed him gazing intently at her. For an instant, she smiled warmly back, and Sam experienced emotions he had not felt since before his wife had died. Realizing what he was doing, he quickly looked away, feeling a mixture of guilt, confusion, and happiness. Gwendolyn became intensely interested in Tina's descripttion of the school dance the coming Friday night.

Chapter 15 – Freedom

While everyone else was eating and talking, Sam and Gwendolyn were strangely quiet and often stole brief glances at each other when they thought the other was not looking.

Eventually, the food disappeared from the table, and only a few broken tortilla chips remained untouched in their baskets. The conversation slowed when the waiter brought the bill and gave it to Sam. Then it died as a couple with two small rambunctious children arrived and were seated by the waiter. Their young boy turned around in his chair, pointed at the Hawthornes in their black clothes, and asked quite clearly, "Mommy, who are those people in the funny clothes?" Vivianne and Gwendolyn glanced nervously at each other.

"I think it is time to get back, don't you?" Sam asked, picking up the bill. To avoid waiting for the waiter to run his credit card, he placed sufficient bills on the table to cover dinner and the tip. He hurried to help Gwendolyn put on her coat while the others prepared to leave.

While they were in the restaurant, the temperature had dropped drastically. The cold north wind had begun to blow as they stepped out into the dusk, and the first tiny flakes of snow were falling. The dense, rapidly moving clouds softly glowed with the reflected light from the town below.

After talking so much over dinner, everyone seemed to have run out of words as they walked toward home. Matt and Gerallt were followed some distance behind by Tina and Gwyneth. Sam found himself walking with Gwendolyn just behind Gareth and Vivianne, where they could ensure that the older woman would not be left behind. "I didn't realize that it was supposed to snow this evening," Sam said several minutes later, trying to make conversation to fill the awkward silence.

"Me, neither," Gwendolyn said, her teeth beginning to chatter. "It's nippy now that it's breezed up. I wish I'd thought tah bring a stockin' cap and warmer coat."

Sam looked over. Her coat was short and thin, and she was blowing into her bare hands in a vain effort to keep them warm.

"Here, take my gloves. I don't really need them," Sam lied as he took his off and handed them to her.

"Thank you, Sam," Gwendolyn said, as they continued to walk. She smiled up at him as she gratefully slipped her small hands into his large leather gloves.

Then Sam noticed her cheeks and the tip of her nose and ears were turning red. "Here, you'd better put this on too." He stopped, pulled off his woolen scarf, and placed it around her neck and over her head so that it covered her ears. "There, that's better."

"But Sam, ah you sure you'll be warm enough?"

"I insist," he replied as they turned and started walking again. The others had continued on, leaving the pair some distance behind. Strolling side by side, their hands touched. Without a word, he took Gwendolyn's hand in his, and she didn't pull it back. The rest of the way back, Sam hardly noticed the cold at all.

Chapter 15 – Freedom

Sam and Gwendolyn turned the corner onto Hawthorne Drive just in time to see their families entering the Hawthorne House front door. A few minutes later, Sam and Gwendolyn were stepping onto the porch that wrapped around the front and side of the old mansion. They dropped their hands and stepped inside. Everyone was waiting for them in the parlor, where the children were warming themselves in front of the fireplace.

Vivianne Hawthorne was in the octagonal turret that formed the corner of the parlor facing the street. Its tall narrow windows looked out on the gathering dusk. She glanced back and forth between her niece and Matt's father as they walked up to her. "Well, Sam, I'd like tah thank you foah taking us out tonight. That must be the first time I've left the house in ovah forty years. I'd forgotten everythin' pleasant outside my doah. More importantly, I'd forgotten that outsidahs need not be feared."

"I'm glad you enjoyed yourself," Sam said, not knowing exactly how to take her use of the word *outsiders*. "Hopefully, you won't wait so long before venturing out again. In fact, I would be happy to have you and your family over for dinner sometime soon." He turned to Gwendolyn, who smiled up at him. "And it's been especially nice to see you smile this evening."

"Ayuh, and you too. We've both been through a lot this last year, and this is the first time I've felt good since Medwyn died. It is nice tah know there are still reasons tah smile."

"You know, you're right," Sam agreed. "I've wasted far too much time buried in my work and not enjoying the simple pleasures of spending time with friends and family."

Soon, Matt and Gareth followed Gerallt upstairs to his room. After a few minutes, Tina headed home to start on her homework, and Gwyneth and Vivianne went back to the kitchen to continue working on the stew. Sam and Gwendolyn remained in the parlor, lost in conversation and didn't notice as the hours passed. Eventually, Vivianne came in bearing mugs of hot chocolate and freshly-baked brownies.

"I'd like to thank you again, Sam," Vivianne said. "Evah since the first day Matt came ovah lookin' foah a job, I've felt a change comin' ovah me. It's been as if I'm finally wakin' up from a deep dreamless sleep. I realize now that I'd let feah and distrust turn my beautiful old home intah a prison as I turned intah a miserable old recluse. When Gwendolyn and her wonderful children came, I started tah see I still had things to be thankful foah. And, now I get tah know you and your lovely daughtah, Tina. I guess I've been wishin' for a good reason tah get out of the house, and this was it. Why I feel twenty years youngah. Thank the Goddess, I woke up and realized that theah's moah to life than sittin' alone in my parlor, rockin' in front of the fireplace with my nose in a book."

"It's been my pleasure," Sam said. "Everyone seemed to have a great time." Sam noticed the grandfather clock ticking quietly in the corner. The hands pointed to 8:30. "Goodness. Is it that late? I'm going to have to get Matt home so that he can finish

Chapter 15 – Freedom

his homework. And what about your stew? I've kept Gwendolyn in here all this time."

"Don't worry about it, Sam. Gwyneth helped me finish it. Besides, it was more important that you've had some time tah talk, just the two of you. You've both been worryin' too much and haven't had enough time talkin' with anothah adult."

"Yes. It's nice not having the other programmers at work being the only adults in my life. Still, I'm afraid it's time to go. I'd better go up and get Matt; he'd stay the night if he could."

"That's okay, Sam," Gwendolyn said. "I'll get him. I was goin' up anyway."

A few minutes later, Gwendolyn and Matt came down the stairs. Matt left for home and his homework, while Gwendolyn walked Sam to the door.

"Thank you again for the gloves and scarf," she said, handing them back to him. "They were nice and warm."

"You're welcome," Sam said, as he put on his coat. He stood there self-consciously for a few seconds, looking around the foyer at the old paintings and not knowing quite what to say. The candles in their holders on the walls flickered, casting moving shadows down the hall. "Gwendolyn, I'm glad you decided to come tonight," Sam said, finally breaking their awkward silence.

"Me too, Sam. Me too."

They stood silently again, neither one making a move to open the door.

"I guess I'd better go then," he said.

"It is getting late," she agreed.

More silent seconds passed before he turned to the door, put a hand on the knob, turned quickly back, and kissed her lightly on the lips. A second later, he was out the door and marveling at what he had done.

Everyone was soon in their respective homes, their doors shut against the dark and snowy night. Vivianne and the children were sleeping in their warm beds, dreaming pleasant dreams as whirlwinds of snow whipped through the oak trees lining Hawthorne Drive. However, it was a long time before Sam and Gwendolyn fell asleep.

Chapter 16
Modron and Miracles

The gathering winds marked the edge of a huge snowstorm that moved slowly from Indiana into Ohio. During the dark hours before dawn, the storm swiftly dumped half a foot of powdery snow on the houses, lawns, and streets of Hawthorne. With another eight to ten inches forecast by late-afternoon, school was canceled for the day. Upon waking and learning of their good fortune, the Hawthorne and Mitchell children eagerly looked forward to enjoying a day spent building snowmen, throwing snowballs, and sledding down the gentle slopes of a nearby hill.

Even more than he wanted to enjoy the snow, Gerallt wanted to privately thank Matt again for everything he'd done to prove their innocence. So shortly after breakfast, he bundled up and headed next door to his friend's house.

"Isn't it great?" Matt asked, as he led Gerallt into his room. "Back in Oregon, we always had to go up into the Coastal Range to see this much snow."

"Ayuh, it's nice," Gerallt agreed, although he'd often seen similar snowfalls from the nor'easters that had blown through Maine. "You know, Matt, with everythin' that happened yesterday, I nevah got a chance tah really thank you foah the fantastic way you captured Colin, Clayton, and Dylan's confession. I'd nevah have been able tah wire an alarm clock tah a tape recordah like you did."

"Aw, Gerallt, it wasn't really that hard. For as long as I can remember, I've been taking things apart to see how they worked. Most of the time, I can even put them back together again. We were just lucky that I had an old alarm clock and a microcassette recorder to work with. If I only had the new ones with circuit boards instead of mechanical parts, I don't think I could have done it."

"Well, anyway, I really wanted tah thank you. I'd have gone crazy if I'd had tah remain in my room foah the whole month."

"That's okay, Gerallt. Besides, you were the one that gave me the idea to secretly record their conversations. So, is everything back to normal at home?"

"Even bettah. Mothah totally trusts me now. And last night was the first time I can remembah seein' her smile since Fathah died. I think she likes your fathah."

"I think Dad likes her, too. Did you notice the way they both kept glancing at each other when they thought no one was looking? And it's the first time I've seen him ignore his work since we got here."

Matt paused, suddenly remembering what Gerallt had said when they were trying to figure out how to trick Colin, Clayton, and Dylan into confessing. "So, did your mom ever give you back whatever it was that she confiscated from you?"

"Yes..." Gerallt replied warily.

"So, what was it?"

"I'm sorry, Matt, but it's a secret. I can't tell you."

"Well, so is what I did to the alarm clock and tape recorder, not to mention the help we got from Tina

Chapter 16 – Modron and Miracles

and Sarah," Matt said, frustrated and beginning to become angry. "The whole last few days have been full of secrets, and now you're trying to tell me that you don't think I can keep a secret?"

"No, it's not that. You just don't know what you'ah askin' me tah do. This is a lot more than just a secret between friends. It's even more than a Hawthorne family secret. You're asking me tah go against our customs, tah break a code of secrecy that's been drilled intah me every day for as long as I can remembah."

"Gerallt, either you trust me, or you don't," Matt said. Then he smiled. "Besides, now you have to tell me. You can't give something that kind of a buildup and then just leave me hanging. Come on. Show me."

Gerallt hesitated and then made his decision. "I guess you've earned that right given everythin' you did tah get it back for me." He undid the top button of his shirt and pulled out an amulet that was securely attached to a sturdy silver chain around his neck. About two inches across and a quarter inch thick, it was a heavy golden disk engraved with strange symbols around a large, green gemstone at its center. "This is my gift from the Goddess. My amulet is what enabled me tah break the chair and control the seagulls."

"Whoa," Matt whispered. After stepping forward for a closer look, the look of awe on his face was replaced by one of skepticism. "Don't get me wrong. I know you're not lying, but you've got to prove that it's real. You have to show me some honest-to-goodness magic, something that's obviously supernatural and can't be confused with some weird coincidence."

Gerallt thought about it for a few seconds before replying, "Okay, Matt, but remembah. I'm dependin' on you. You've got tah keep it secret and nevah tell anyone. And I mean nevah, no matter what."

"I promise." Matt walked over to his bedroom door and locked it. "Besides, who would ever believe me? Heck, I won't believe it until I see it with my own eyes."

"Okay, Matt. So, what would convince you?"

"How about levitation? Can you make something of mine float right in front of my eyes?"

"Sure. That's one of the easiest things I can do. What do you want tah see float?"

Matt reached into his pocket and pulled out a coin. "How about this?"

Gerallt placed his thumb on the green gemstone in the amulet's center and intoned "*Magna Dea, fac, quaesumus, ut nummus ascendat!*" The coin slowly rose from Matt's hand until it hung suspended in the air a foot in front of his eyes.

"Whoa!" Matt said with a mixture of disbelief and amazement on his face. "Can I touch it?"

"Sure, but be careful. It'll get pretty warm if I keep it floatin' foah very long."

Matt reached up and gently touched the coin. "Hey, you're right. It's warm." He paused for a second. "What language was that? It sounds a little like Italian."

Chapter 16 – Modron and Miracles

"Latin. Now, look at this. *Magna Dea, fac, quaesumus, ut nummus verset!*" Slowly at first, the coin started to spin, twirling faster and faster until both sides merged into a blur. Matt could feel warm air from the coin blowing on his face. "*Magna Dea, fac, quaesumus, ut nummus descendant!*" The coin dropped to the floor, bounced once, before rolling under Matt's bed.

"That's amazing! So, how did you do it?"

"You don't understand. I didn't do it; the Goddess did."

"No. I'm serious. How did you do it?"

"I told you, Matt. I didn't do it. Even the amulet didn't do it. The goddess Modron did. Magic is really just another word for miracle."

"Like in the Bible kind of miracle?" Matt asked incredulously.

"I suppose so. Hard tellin' if what's written in the Christian's Bible really happened. All I know is that the Goddess is real because her gifts are real and her miracles are real. You just saw three of them yourself."

"But... But how does it work?"

"You saw how it works. When I hold one of Modron's sacred gifts, and I properly say one of her prayahs usin' the old language, the Goddess will answer my prayah. There are quite a few prayahs, but Mothah hasn't taught me all of them yet. But you have tah say it right. Your prayah will only be answered if the amulet accepts you, and you're touchin' it with your bare skin."

"I can't believe what I'm hearing," Matt said, shaking his head in disbelief. "It just doesn't make any sense. There has got to be some rational explanation; this violates everything I've ever learned in science class."

"So, how would you explain what you just saw?"

"I don't know. But I do know one thing. You have to tell me more about the amulet and the goddess... What did you call her?"

"Modron." Gerallt paused, nervously realizing that he'd already said too much, even though he really wanted to say more. "What I am about tah tell you is somethin' that we ah nevah permitted to share with outsidahs. If I am going tah say any more, then you have tah absolutely sweah that you won't breathe a single word of it tah anyone. You can't tell youah fathah, youah sistah, and foah the love of the Goddess, not anyone in my family. If the wrong person finds out, I could be shunned, cast out, or worse."

Although Matt wasn't sure exactly what being shunned or cast out meant, he could clearly see that Gerallt was telling the truth. His friend was obviously scared and really believed every word that he said. "Okay, I swear," Matt said solemnly.

"Not good enough. Not for this. You can't just sweah on nothin'. You have tah sweah on somethin', on somethin' important, on the most important thing that you can."

Matt thought for several seconds before answering. "I swear on the memory of my mother."

Chapter 16 – Modron and Miracles

Gerallt looked closely at Matt, searching for any hint of hesitation or wavering. He saw none. "Okay, Matt, I'm going tah trust you. Some of what I'm going tah tell you is history, and you can probably find it in a book. But most of what I am about tah share with you is written in the Holy Book of the Goddess and has been passed down from generation tah generation." Gerallt told Matt the story of his people.

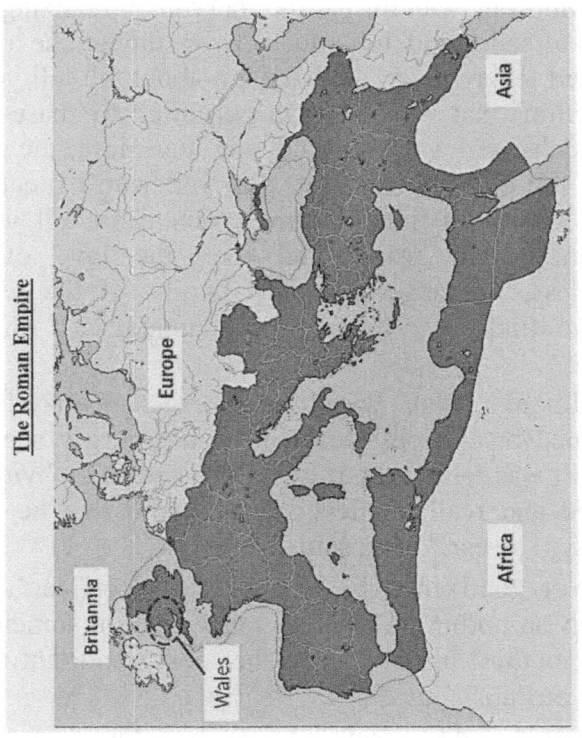

The Secrets of Hawthorne House

"My ancestors were Celts who lived in the Roman province of Britannia during the reign of the Roman Emperor Trajan. They lived in a small village in what is now Wales in the southwestern part of the United Kingdom. Like their ancestors befoah them, they worshiped the many Celtic gods and goddesses: Aeron, the god of battle; Belenus, the god of healing; Brigit, the goddess of fire; and Cernunnos, the horned god of fertility and wealth. But most importantly, they also worshiped Modron, the great mother goddess."

Gerallt briefly closed his eyes. When he opened them, he began to speak as if quoting word-for-word a story that he had heard countless times as a young child.

"It began durin' the summah of Trajan's ninth year as Emperor, or what is now known as 107 AD. Late one night, immense flashes of lightnin' and the great boomin' sound of rollin' thundah woke the people in the village. They went outside expecting tah see mighty Taranis, the god of thundah, wield his weapons across the clouds, but the moonless sky was clear and covered with stars. Tah their amazement, the people saw a Fae light in the woods. Most of them were frightened of the Fair Folk and ran back intah their huts tah hide. But a few of the bravest men and women gathered up their courage and went intah the dark forest hopin' tah see the fairies dance and sing. They followed the lights, but they found none of the Fair Folk when they reached the sacred oak grove on the shores of the nearby lake. Instead, they saw a beautiful woman whose gown glowed softly in the night as if woven from moonbeams and starlight.

Chapter 16 – Modron and Miracles

"The Great Goddess spoke to them saying, *I am Modron, and I have heard your prayahs. You who are brave shall be my druidae, and I shall teach you my secrets and the rituals you must perform for me. You shall bring me offerings as I command, and I shall give you sacred tokens of my power and protection. These gifts shall enable you tah perform miracles in my name.*

"And so it was as the Goddess said. The druids and druidesses made Modron offerings of the plants and animals she desired and did her biddin' in all things. In return, the Goddess gave them sacred wands and amulets, and she taught them the propah ways tah pray so that she would answer theah prayahs. The villagahs loved and worshiped the Goddess who cured them when they were sick, granted them good harvests, and protected them from outsidahs. She even saved them from some of the worst abuses of the Romans. The small village prospered and grew.

"Thus, it continued for many years until one fateful day in the year 212. The Goddess announced tah her druidae that the time had come for her tah return tah the other gods and goddesses in their eternal home in the Otherworld. She charged them tah guard her secrets, follow her rituals, and keep her sacred gifts safe, passing them down from mothah tah daughtah and from fathah to son until the day she would return. That night, she led her druids and druidesses back tah her sacred grove where she had first appeared. She said goodbye, and those who accompanied her fell instantly intah a deep and dreamless sleep. When they awoke, the Goddess was gone.

"After Modron left, life continued for a while almost as it had befoah. The druidae made their offerings and performed the rituals. They prayed to the Goddess with their wands and amulets, and the Goddess answered theah prayahs just as befoah.

"But all was not like it was befoah. Often, when the children grew sick, the druidae could not cure them. Sometimes the harvests failed, and the people endured great hungah. The villagahs prayed, but most of their prayahs went unanswered. The people who had worshiped the Goddess felt abandoned and grew afraid.

"Then, in the year 312, Christianity became the official religion of the Roman Empire, and worship of the pagan Celtic gods and goddesses was outlawed. Adopting the new faith, the people turned against Modron's druids and druidesses whom they had grown tah envy and feah because of their 'magical' powers. Finally, in the year 330, a new Christian priest came to the village and roused the people's angah against the old gods. The villagers cut down the oak trees in the sacred grove and burned the houses of Modron's followahs, forcing them to flee for theah lives.

"My ancestors were driven intah hiding, forced intah keepin' their deepest beliefs and sacred relics a secret from all around them. Evah since that day, we have remained apart from othah people, livin' in our own villages so that we could practice our faith in secret. For hundreds of years, we have hidden our true beliefs and sacred relics, and pretended to be good

Chapter 16 – Modron and Miracles

Christians around outsidahs to avoid bein' persecuted as witches."

Gerallt paused, remembering his parent's countless warnings to stay away from outsiders and never ever do anything that might divulge his people's existence. For centuries, these had been their two most unbreakable commandments. Yet, that was exactly what Gerallt had just done. He had placed his safety, the very safety of his people, in the hands of his best friend.

"Matt, outsidahs tortured several of my ancestors intah confessing they were witches before killing them. Some were drowned, some were hanged, and many were burned at the stake. We have good reasons for secrecy and will not speak openly or perform our rituals in front of outsidahs. We have suffered too many years of terrah because of it. That's why we live apart. We have grown self-reliant, able tah grow our own food and make our own clothes. Like the Amish and Mennonites, we druidae have learned tah live in the modern world but remain apart from it."

"Dru-ee-deh?" Matt asked, trying to pronounce the strange word.

Gerallt nodded. "I have shown you what only a very few outsidahs have ever seen, and now you know my family's greatest secret. Ahnt Vivianne, Mothah, and Gwyneth are druidesses. I am a druid, and Gareth and will be a druid when he comes of age. This amulet is one of the sacred gifts that the Goddess gave tah our ancestors nearly 2,000 years ago."

"Wow!" Matt said, staring at the amulet with its shiny gemstone surrounded by the ring of strange symbols. He remembered an old Indian-head penny that his grandfather had once shown him. Over the years, it had been worn down to the point where he could barely read the year the coin was minted or make out the individual feathers of the Indian's war bonnet. But the gold encircling the large green gem was smooth and shiny with no scratches obscuring the amulet's strange markings. "Hey, your amulet looks brand new."

"But it is. The metal doesn't tarnish and looks like gold, but it's extremely hahd and almost impossible tah scratch. Even so, our amulets and wands ah sacred gifts from the Goddess. That's why we take such good care of them." Gerallt paused to return the amulet to its hiding place beneath his shirt."

"So, what can you pray for? Can you pray for anything?'

"I know how tah pray for lots of things, but the amulet does have its limitations. Although my prayahs can float a coin, they can't lift a cah. And we can't change the original set of prayahs the Goddess gave us or add any new ones."

"Well," Matt said, "You've given me a heck of a lot to think about. You haven't convinced me that a Celtic goddess is answering your prayers, but you have proven that whatever is happening, it's real, and that you can actually control it. And you know what?"

"What?"

"I think we should definitely give Colin, Clayton, and Dylan a welcome back party when they return to school next week."

Chapter 16 – Modron and Miracles

"Me, too," Gerallt agreed. "So, what do you have in mind?"

Chapter 17
Gerallt's Revenge

The following week, during which Colin, Clayton, and Dylan were suspended, was by far the best one yet for Gerallt and Matt at Hawthorne High. More students were friendly, and their teachers seemed to be doing everything they could to make up for the previous week.

When Colin, Clayton, and Dylan finally returned from their suspension, Matt and Gerallt started the second phase of their revenge. This time it was Gerallt's turn to furnish the fun. He waited until the bus pulled up in front of the school and Clayton stepped off.

Gerallt touched the ancient amulet hidden under his shirt and quietly whispered, "*Magna Dea, fac, quaesumus, ut saccus eius scindat!*"

The bottom of Clayton's backpack burst open, dropping its contents into a large, slushy puddle. Even worse, Clayton's homework binder slid completely under the bus. While the other students looked on and clapped, Clayton had to get down on his hands and knees to retrieve his soggy belongings.

Thus, it was a wet and dirty Clayton who angrily stormed into American history class that morning. Plopping heavily onto his seat, he slammed his dripping book and binder under his chair. He turned to a smaller boy next to him and demanded a dry piece of paper. Then he pulled out an old pencil covered

Chapter 17 – Gerallt's Revenge

with tooth marks and began to print his name in big block letters. The point of the pencil broke.

Anticipating Clayton's next move, Gerallt reached under his shirt and whispered "*Magna Dea, fac, quaesumus, ut sella eius decrescat!*"

Clayton started to get up so that he could walk to the pencil sharpener, but his desktop seemed to have grown unusually tight against his belly. He tried to slide sideways, but his pants stuck to the seat and the desktop only held him tighter. In frustration, he gave the desktop a huge shove, and this time it was the back legs of his chair that buckled. The entire classroom heard his curse as Clayton and his chair crashed backward on the floor, leaving him looking like a monstrous overturned turtle with his legs flailing in the air. It took his teacher and two more from neighboring classes to pull Clayton from the wood and steel jaws of his desk and chair.

Once the end-of-class bell rang, Clayton stormed out, carefully followed by Gerallt and Matt who stayed well back from the bully. It didn't take long before Clayton found Colin and Dylan, who were waiting by a drinking fountain in the hall. He was about to tell them about his embarrassing rescue from the boy-eating chair when Dylan leaned over to get a drink.

Gerallt reached between the buttons of his shirt, whispered "*Magna Dea, fac, quaesumus, ut aqua in eum volet!*" A perfect parabola of water arced through the air onto the crotch of Clayton's pants.

"Arrgh!!!" Clayton screamed in exasperation, looking at the dark wet spot spreading down the front of his pants.

Colin and Dylan took one look and started laughing. Clayton gave them both a look that could melt steel, and the two shut up.

Carefully avoiding the curved path taken by the water, Colin also bent over for a drink. From his vantage point down the hall, Gerallt whispered the incantation once more. The water took an entirely different direction, this time toward Dylan who showed amazing agility by jumping backward out of the way.

Unfortunately for Dylan, however, he jumped directly into the path of several senior football players who promptly tripped and fell on top of him. They were not amused and not the least bit careful of whom or what they stepped on as they got up. After a few well-chosen curses, they told Dylan to stick his head in an anatomically impossible position and sauntered down the hall.

The second bell was about to ring, so Gerallt and Matt had to get to class and wait until lunch to continue with their revenge. They were waiting at their table when Colin, Clayton, and Dylan entered the cafeteria carrying their trays. This time Gerallt whispered, *"Magna Dea, fac, quaesumus, viam lubricam!"*

Clayton slipped, throwing his tray of spaghetti on Dylan's back in the process.

Chapter 17 – Gerallt's Revenge

"Jeez, you big clumsy idiot, look where you're going!" Dylan yelled, turning to face Clayton, who couldn't decide whether to feel angry because of what Dylan had called him or guilty about what he'd done. Clayton decided instead to just laugh at him.

"Watch out," Colin warned, pointing at the cafeteria monitor who had noticed the noise and was walking their way.

Colin swiftly sat down at their usual table, while Clayton went back to get more food, and Dylan left to remove the remains of spaghetti from the back of his shirt. Not waiting for the others to return, Colin took a bite from his pizza and opened his milk carton.

"*Magna Dea, fac, quaesumus, ut lac eius coagulet!*" Gerallt whispered, as he and Matt observed Colin from their table at the far end of the cafeteria.

Colin took a swig from the carton and immediately spewed a mouthful of milk across his table and part of the next. Several nearby students made disgusted sounds but became far more disgusted when Colin poured the rest of his milk in large coagulated globs onto his tray. Colin quickly grabbed Dylan's pop bottle to wash the curdled milk out of his mouth, but Gerallt was too quick for him.

"*Magna Dea, fac, quaesumus, ut aqua in eum volet!*" Gerallt whispered, as Colin twisted off the bottle cap.

The bottle's contents sprayed over Colin's face, shirt, and pants. Cursing in disgust, he slammed the nearly empty bottle down on his tray and stormed out of the room to the sound of clapping and jeers from several students at nearby tables.

At their table across the room, Gerallt and Matt quietly chuckled as they watched Colin leaving the cafeteria just before Clayton returned to find the now empty table with its trays covered with pop and curdled milk. As they went to pick up their afternoon books from their lockers, the boys agreed that it had been a most memorable and enjoyable lunch.

In English class, several students stared and chuckled at Dylan, who entered the room with the back of his shirt and pants still wet and stained from his unsuccessful effort to remove the remains of Clayton's spaghetti. Dylan scowled at Clayton, who was already sitting at his desk. Clayton shrugged his shoulders in a vain attempt to imply that it wasn't his fault. Looking a bit green from the curdled milk and with his shirt spotted by the pop, Colin ignored the other two as he joined them in the back of the classroom.

"Okay, everyone. Let's settle down, shall we?" Mrs. McKinney said, as she looked around the room for the cause of the chuckling. She scowled at Colin, Clayton, and Dylan before continuing. "Take out your copies of Steinbeck's *Of Mice and Men*, and read the first chapter." Clayton raised his hand. "Yes, Mr. Cartwright. Is there a problem?"

"Uh..." Clayton stammered.

"Yes, Mr. Cartwright. Out with it."

"I can't, Mrs. McKinney. I don't have my book with me."

Chapter 17 – Gerallt's Revenge

"And why is that?"

"Because the door to my locker's stuck."

Colin and Dylan also raised their hands.

"And I suppose you two don't have your books with you, either," Mrs. McKinney suggested, eying the pair skeptically. "What's the matter? Are your locker doors also stuck?"

"Yes ma'am," both boys answered sheepishly.

"Do you actually expect me to believe that all three of your lockers chose the same day to jam?"

The three boys looked uncomfortably at one another. "Uh... Yes, ma'am."

"Enough of this nonsense! The three of you can spend an hour in detention tomorrow after school for coming to class unprepared. In the meantime, you can borrow classroom copies."

"But, Mrs. McKinney, our lockers really are..." Clayton protested.

"I said *enough*! One more word from you, Mr. Cartwright, and I will make it two hours."

Gerallt did his best to stifle his smile as Clayton angrily retrieved the three books and returned to join the others.

Matt looked over at Gerallt and silently mouthed the words, "Was that you?"

Gerallt grinned back, nodded, and whispered, "Between classes this morning."

Midway through the class, Mrs. McKinney said, "Okay everyone, take out your pens and a sheet of paper. You have until the end of the period to answer the following questions about the chapter you've just read. What are the similarities and differences between the book's two main characters, George and Lennie? What is their relationship, and how they feel about each other?"

Gerallt raised his hand to his chest, slipped his fingers between the buttons of his shirt, and whispered *"Magna Dea, fac, quaesumus, ut stili eorum perfluant!"*

Seconds later, everyone in the class heard Colin, Clayton, and Dylan muttering and slamming their hands on their desktops.

"Now, what is it?" Mrs. McKinney demanded in exasperation.

"It's our pens," Colin answered. "They're leaking ink all over our hands." The three boys raised their ink-stained hands in proof.

"Okay, you three. I've had all of your shenanigans I'm going to take. Just one more, and all three of you will have earned yourselves a day of in-school detention. Now go and wash your hands, but I want you all back here in your seats in five minutes. Is that understood?"

The three nodded and stormed out of the room, only to return five minutes later with ink stains still on their hands. The remainder of the class passed without a hitch.

After the bell rang, the five boys joined their classmates in the boy's locker room to dress for gym class. Mr. Armstrong stood in a corner with his arms crossed over his chest, making sure there would be no

Chapter 17 – Gerallt's Revenge

repeat of the incident that got Matt into trouble. Once everyone was dressed and outside on the gym floor, Mr. Armstrong began the class by having everybody do a few stretching exercises. A moment later, Clayton bent over to touch his toes, and the whole class heard the loud rip of the back seam of his gym shorts giving way. Matt glanced questioningly over at his friend, but Gerallt shook his head.

"It wasn't me," he whispered to Matt. "Maybe he just ate too much while he was home last week."

The coach sent Clayton back to the locker room to change while he had the rest of the class run several laps around the floor. After a long series of calisthenics, the period ended with the rope climb. Most of the students, including Matt and Gerallt, had no problems making it to the top of the pair of ropes hanging down from the ceiling. Then, it was time for Colin and Dylan, who had waited until last.

Standing behind the other students, Gerallt whispered "*Magna Dea, fac, quaesumus, funes eorum lubricos!*"

The two began to climb their ropes. The boys steadily worked their way up and were near the top when first one and then the other one slipped several feet down. They started back up again, but the same thing happened.

"What's wrong up there?" Coach Armstrong asked, as Colin and Dylan hung suspended like a pair of angry spiders.

"It's my rope, Coach," Colin replied. "It's slippery near the top."

"Mine, too," Dylan said.

"Did anyone else think that the ropes were slippery?" the coach asked, looking around at the rest of the students, who shook their heads. The coach glanced at the gym's large wall clock. "Well, come back down if you can't make it. We're about out of time anyway. Okay, everyone to the showers."

To hide the existence of his amulet and protect it from theft, Gerallt never showered at school. Instead, he merely whispered a silent prayer to remove the sweat from his clothes and body. Thus, Gerallt remained in the locker room with Clayton, who had already changed out of his gym clothes. Coach Armstrong stood in a corner, keeping a watchful eye on Clayton to ensure he didn't bother Gerallt, while Colin and Dylan joined Matt and the other boys in the steaming showers.

Colin and Dylan had barely finished soaping up when their water suddenly turned ice cold. They both gave out high-pitched screams and jumped out of the icy water. Yet no one else's water had changed temperature. The two bullies gingerly stuck their hands back under the water, which was now nice and warm. When they stepped back under the water's flow, it had once more turned as frigid as a winter's frost. This happened twice again, even after Colin had shoved a nearby student out from under his warm spray. Both Colin and Dylan were covered with soap suds as they walked back into the locker room to dry off and dress. Colin gave Gerallt a look that could have boiled ice, but Gerallt merely smiled.

Chapter 17 – Gerallt's Revenge

By the middle of the last class of the day, Colin couldn't take any more. After silently signaling Clayton and Dylan, Colin asked his teacher for permission to leave the room. A few minutes later, Clayton and Dylan also excused themselves and met Colin in the boys' restroom. Thus, none of the three was there to notice that a few minutes later Gerallt also excused himself and left the room.

"So, Colin, what's so important it can't wait 'til school's out?" Clayton asked. "You know we're going to get in trouble if a teacher catches us in here cutting class."

"Yeah, Colin," Dylan added. "My father's already furious at me for getting suspended. We've got to be really careful until everything blows over."

"We've got bigger things to worry about than our parents, Dylan. Don't you guys see what's going on? Having this much bad luck in one day just isn't natural. Gerallt's got to be hexing us." Colin pulled a half-empty pack of cigarettes out of his pocket and lit one.

"Jeez, Colin," Dylan said. "Put that out. If a teacher catches us smoking, Tanner will expel us for sure."

"Ah, Dylan, stop being such a wuss. We need to figure out some way to get Gerallt off our backs. If we don't, he's going to keep doing this to us 'til..." Colin stopped mid-sentence when a shower of green sparks spewed from the end of his cigarette. "What the..." he exclaimed as he dropped the blazing cigarette on the concrete floor while the other two looked on with a mixture of amazement and terror. It continued to burn furiously like a Fourth of July fireworks fountain.

"Quick," Colin yelled as he turned toward the sink. "Get some water to put the damned thing out!" While Clayton joined Colin in carrying handfuls of water to douse the brightly burning cigarette, Dylan decided he'd had enough and ran to the door.

"Oh God," Dylan cried, "The door's stuck! I can't get it open!"

"Forget the damned door!" Colin commanded, as he and Clayton threw water on the blazing cigarette. "Get over here and help us put out the fire before anyone comes in."

The instant the water hit the cigarette, the sparks went out, only to be replaced by billowing clouds of white smoke.

"Oh, no," Clayton cried, as he rushed back to the sink. "We need more water. We've got to put it out!"

Colin stamped on the cigarette, scattering tiny bits of tobacco that continued to smoke like dozens of minuscule chimneys.

"Okay, enough of this!" Colin shouted. "We've got to get out of here before anything else happens."

All three boys rushed to the door, but no matter how much they pulled on the handle, it stubbornly refused to open.

"This is insane," Colin said. "I'm going back to try again to put the damned thing out." But he couldn't find the remains of the cigarette because the smoke had thickened to the point where he could hardly see his hands in front of his face.

Chapter 17 – Gerallt's Revenge

Colin had barely started searching for it before the sprinklers turned on, drenching everything and everyone in the room. Yet strangely, the clouds of smoke cleared as soon as they were touched by the spraying water. In less than a minute, Colin, Clayton, and Dylan were totally soaked.

"Now what?" Clayton asked, looking down at the squashed remains of the cigarette that was slowly floating toward the drain in the center of the floor. "Mooching lunch money off nerds is one thing, but this... How in the hell can we fight against all of this?"

"We don't," Dylan said firmly. "We don't. I don't know about you two, but I'm never going to say or do another thing that might piss Gerallt off. He really is a witch."

"But..." Colin started to say.

"But nothing, Colin!" Clayton shouted. "It's your fault we got suspended, and it's your fault we're in here getting drenched. And it'll be your fault if this gets us expelled. If you want to do anything more to Gerallt or Matt, you can do it by yourself."

"Right!" Dylan said.

Upon hearing Dylan agree with Clayton, Colin exploded. He shoved Dylan who slipped and fell backward onto the watery floor. Having had enough, Clayton stepped up to Colin and shoved him right back. Colin lost it and took a swing at Clayton, hitting him on the chin. But the blow only further infuriated Clayton, who roared with rage as he jumped on Colin, wrestling him to the ground. Dylan, having scrambled to his feet, piled on top of the pair, so that all three boys were rolling around on the water-covered floor.

The sprinklers stopped, and the door opened. It was a member of the varsity football team, who took one step onto the flooded floor and cursed. Then he noticed the three drenched and angry boys sprawled on top of each other in the water. He laughed and exited back into the hallway.

Embarrassed by having been seen, Colin, Clayton, and Dylan jumped up to stand in the middle of the room with water dripping off their hair and clothes. The bell rang, signaling the end of the school day.

"Okay, you two," Colin said, "Let's get out of here before anyone else sees us." Gathering up the last shreds of his drenched dignity, Colin led his minions out to the crowded hallway and into the laughter and stares of the other students.

Gerallt and Matt made sure that they were waiting near the school buses when the three finally shuffled outside.

"Well, well, what do we have heah?" Gerallt asked. He looked at the three boys standing there dirty, wet, and freezing in the cold November afternoon. "What do you think, Matt? Shall we give them somethin' really special tah top off theah day?"

"I don't know," Matt said. "They look to me like they've had about enough for one day. Besides, we have to save something for tomorrow. And the day after that."

"And the day aftah that," Gerallt agreed.

Chapter 17 – Gerallt's Revenge

Clayton looked utterly overwhelmed, while Dylan looked terrified enough to run like a rabbit if Gerallt said "Boo!" Colin merely looked defeated.

"Okay, guys, you win," Colin said. "What do you want?"

"You know, Matt," Gerallt said. "That's just not the first thing I wanted tah heah."

"You're right, Gerallt. I think a little groveling would be appropriate before we discuss the terms of their unconditional surrender."

"Ayuh," Gerallt agreed. "I think some heartfelt apologies are in order."

"I'm sorry," Clayton said.

"Me, too!" Dylan added. "Please don't do anything more."

Colin nodded sullenly.

"No. Somethin's still not right," Gerallt observed. "Oh, I got it. You're still standin'. Get down on your knees and repeat after me."

Clayton and Dylan immediately knelt down onto the cold hard sidewalk.

"You too, Colin," Gerallt commanded.

Colin reluctantly got down on his knees.

"Now repeat after me," Gerallt said. "We sweah that we will nevah bother Matt Mitchell, Gerallt Hawthorne, or anyone in their families ever again."

The three bullies repeated, "We swear that we will never bother Matt Mitchell, Gerallt Hawthorne, or anyone in their families ever again."

"And we sweah we will stay away from the Hawthorne and Mitchell houses forevah."

"We swear we will stay away from the Hawthorne and Mitchell houses forever," the three bullies chorused.

"And one last thing," Matt added. "We swear we will never bully anyone ever again."

"We swear we'll never bully anyone ever again."

"Do you know what will happen if we ever catch any of you violating what you just swore?" Gerallt asked.

"No," a terrified Dylan answered.

"You don't evah want tah find out," Gerallt answered sternly. "Now get up and get out of heah."

The three bullies scrambled to their feet and ran as fast as they could for their buses.

"Well, Matt, do you think that will work?" Gerallt asked.

"Probably not forever," Matt replied. "But I doubt that they'll give us any trouble for a *very* long time."

"Good, because I'd just as soon not have tah deal with them again. In fact, I think it's much too nice a day tah even think about them anymoah."

"You're right. So, after we finish our homework and chores, where do you want to meet: your place or mine?"

"How about mine? I think it's about time I showed you a few moah of the Hawthorne secrets."

Chapter 18
Spending the Night

It was very early Saturday morning when Matt's alarm woke him from a pleasant dream. He lay in bed, enjoying its fast fading memory. He had been hiking with Gerallt along his favorite trail in the coastal hills above the beach cottage where he had grown up. Gerallt had been just about to share some Hawthorne family secret when the alarm rang.

Rubbing sleep from his eyes, Matt suddenly realized that he hadn't had a nightmare about his mother's death in weeks. He smiled, jumped out of bed, and swiftly dressed.

Today was finally the day when Matt was going to be allowed to spend the night at the Hawthorne House. Matt grabbed his sleeping bag and the backpack he'd packed the night before with a second set of clothes for Sunday. Silently closing his door behind him, he rushed downstairs for a quick breakfast of Frosted Flakes and orange juice. His father and Tina were still asleep as Matt headed next door to where Gerallt was just finishing his own breakfast, a thick slice of home-baked bread and his great-aunt's raspberry preserves.

Darkness was just beginning to give way in the east as Matt walked outside. The last of the fallen leaves lay scattered over the lawns and sidewalks of Hawthorne Drive. The old oaks raised their naked branches into the dark and dreary November sky as if praying for the swift return of springtime. Matt ignored them as he walked by, and their only answer was the cold North wind.

Matt was about to lift the old, iron knocker when he noticed a small flickering light moving behind the stained-glass panels that bordered the heavy oak door.

Gerallt opened the door and motioned Matt inside. "Come in," he whispered. "No one's up yet. Let's take youah stuff up tah my room."

Matt walked in, and Gerallt bolted the door behind them. The house was strangely cold, as dark and silent as a crypt. Matt glanced left into the parlor, which usually had a pleasant fire in the fireplace, but the few remaining embers from the previous evening gave neither heat nor light. The room was gloomy, and the oil lamp in Gerallt's hand cast deep, ominous shadows behind the overstuffed chairs. Matt couldn't help but remember the scary stories he'd heard about the Hawthorne House being the home of the town's "infamous witch."

Gerallt quietly led Matt up two flights of stairs to his bedroom. The candles on the stairway walls were out, and none of the oil lamps on the hallway tables was lit. Matt was glad to enter Gerallt's room, where a small cheery fire warmed the air and added its light to the candles in their wall sconces and the two oil lamps on his friend's desk.

"That's bettah," Gerallt said, as he entered the warm room. "You can put your stuff on the floah by my chestahdrawahs."

Chapter 18 – Spending the Night

Matt dropped his backpack and sleeping bag between the dresser and the old oak wardrobe where Gerallt hung his clothes. Then he walked over to warm himself in front of the fire. "Do you always let your house get so cold at night?" Matt asked, rubbing his hands before the flames. "It's freezing out in the hall."

"It's not so bad once you're used tah it," Gerallt answered. "And it saves lots of money. No sense heating the house when no one's up tah notice. Besides, everyone has a nice thick comforter, and we can always add moah wood to our fireplaces if our bedrooms get too cold. That reminds me. The first one up has tah get the furnace going."

"Same at my home in the winter. I turned up the thermostat before I left. Where's yours?"

"Thermostat?" Gerallt asked, sounding like he'd never heard the word before.

"You know. The thing on the wall that you use to set the temperature."

"Oh, technology. You'll have tah tell me how it works sometime. We don't have one heah. Come on, I'll show you."

Gerallt silently led Matt back down to the first floor. This time, the boys turned left and headed back toward the kitchen and the stairs that continued down into the basement. Gerallt opened the old door, revealing shadowy steps that dropped down into total darkness. Holding the small oil lamp in front of him, Gerallt calmly started down. He reached the bottom before realizing that Matt still stood frozen at the top of the stairs.

"Come on, Matt. You can help me shovel the coal," Gerallt said, looking back up at his friend.

"But Gerallt..." Matt paused, his breath visible in the freezing air that rose up from the basement. The sight of his breath brought shivers to his back as fear tightened his throat and his heart began to pound. How could he admit to his friend just how much he dreaded the dark with its unseen terrors? The weak light from the oil lamp's flickering flame did little to decrease the darkness.

"Oh, Goddess," Gerallt blasphemed. "It's just the down cellah. There's nothing much down heah but the furnace and the coal you're going tah help me with." Gerallt took one step back up the stairs. "Do you need me tah climb back up there and hold your hand?"

Unwilling to further shame himself in front of his friend, Matt steeled his courage and started down the stairs. Doing his best to ignore the darkness, he kept his eyes centered on the lamp's tiny flame. The old wood creaked with each step he took.

"That's more like it," Gerallt said, as he turned to his right and headed past the stairs toward the coal chute and the old black furnace.

Not wanting to be left behind, Matt hurried to catch up with his friend.

Lifting the furnace's heavy iron handle, Gerallt opened its door and looked in. "Good," he said. "There are still some embers left ovah from last night. I hate it when the furnace is cold, and I have tah

Chapter 18 – Spending the Night

restart it from scratch." He poked the remaining embers with an iron rod and shoveled a small amount of coal on top of them. "So, what was that all about? You're not really scared of the dark, ah you?"

"I can't help it," Matt admitted. "One afternoon when Tina and I were seven or eight, we found an old abandoned house in the woods near our home. The floorboards were rotten and broke when I stepped on them. I fell down into the basement. The stairs back up broke when I stepped on them, and I couldn't climb out. Mom had warned us never to go near it, and Tina was too scared to tell her what happened. I was trapped down there with tons the spiders and other bugs for what seemed like forever." Matt shuddered at the memory. "It wasn't until after dark when Mom finally got Tina to tell her and Dad where I was. You know, Gerallt, this is the first time since then that I've gone into a basement."

"*Magna Dea*! No wonder the down cellah scares you," Gerallt said, with a tone both understanding and sympathetic. "Let's get you some light down heah." He walked over to the wall, took a candle from its holder, and lit it with the flame of his oil lamp. "Heah," he said, handing the candle to Matt. "I'll light some moah, and then we can finish shovelin' the coal intah the furnace and go back upstairs."

"Thanks, Gerallt," Matt said, holding the candle a few inches in front of his eyes. He cupped a hand behind the flame, protecting it from nonexistent drafts while hiding most of the basement behind his fingers.

After lighting several more candles, Gerallt took the bellows down from their hook on the wall and blew strong blasts of air on the few glowing coals that had lasted through the night. The embers burned brighter, and small yellow flames appeared. Before long, Gerallt had a roaring fire going. He added two more shovels of coal, closed the door, and adjusted the vent to provide a steady flow of air to the fire. The small glowing openings glared like angry red eyes against the black iron of the ancient furnace. "Come on, Matt. Let's head back up tah my room."

Matt glanced nervously around the basement as he quickly walked back to the base of the stairs. The walls were made of thick brick, broken only by the stone foundation under the west fireplaces and an extensive root cellar that covered the southern wall. Matt was somewhat surprised to see that the basement was only half the size of the house, lying just under the parlor and library and only reaching back as far as the staircase. Matt hurried up the stairs as Gerallt blew out the candles one by one.

Back at the top of the stairs, Gerallt went to the downstairs bathroom to wash the coal dust off his hands, leaving Matt in the hallway outside the open door to the kitchen. While the boys were in the basement, Gerallt's mother and great-aunt had come downstairs and were discussing their plans for the day. As it was the first time Matt had seen the Hawthorne kitchen, he stuck his head inside and looked around.

Like the rest of the ground floor, the spacious kitchen had a high ceiling covered in decorative antique tiles. A steaming cauldron of water hung over a fire in the corner fireplace. Gerallt's mother stood at

Chapter 18 – Spending the Night

the nearby counter, cutting up meat and vegetables for the stew that would be simmering all day. To her left stood a huge cast-iron stove where Gerallt's great-aunt stood with her back to the boys. An old Shaker broom hanging on the wall above the back door made Matt wonder; was it merely decoration or was it something more? He decided he'd ask Gerallt about it once they were alone.

"Go on in," Gerallt said. "Good mornin', Mothah, Ahnt Vivianne. What's foah breakfast?"

"Buckwheat pancakes," Vivianne answered, not looking up from the big bowl she was stirring with a long, wooden spoon. She turned around and noticed Matt standing behind Gerallt. "Oh, good mornin', Matt. You hungry? We've plenty of batter, and I can always make moah if we need it."

In spite of having already wolfed down a bowl of cereal, Matt found the thought of sharing pancakes and maple syrup with his best friend and his family irresistible. "Yes, Ma'am."

After breakfast, Gerallt took Matt on a tour of the house. "This is the library," he said, leading his friend past the downstairs bathroom and into the room across the hall from the kitchen.

"Whoa," Matt exclaimed as he stepped through the door. Except for a reading nook in the middle of the wall to his right, the walls were lined with dark oak bookshelves that ran all the way from the floors to the room's high ceilings. Hundreds of old books, most of them bound in leather, filled the shelves. Stepping up to the nearest shelf, Matt scanned the titles and authors. Although he recognized a few of the more famous writers such as Poe, Shakespeare, and Byron, most of the books were written by people he'd never heard of. Matt walked slowly along the wall, and it soon became clear that the books were organized by the languages in which they were written: Spanish, German, French, and even Latin. "You weren't kidding when you called this the library. Dad likes to collect science and computer books, but his collection wouldn't fill half of even one of these bookshelves."

"Ayuh, it is pretty amazin'," Gerallt conceded, closing the door behind them. "These ah my great-grandfathah and grandmothah, Henry Hubertus and Rhiannon Hawthorne." He pointed at a large portrait of a well-dressed, if somewhat severe-looking, middle-aged couple. The man who had built Hawthorne House had the confident look of someone who'd never known want, whereas his wife's face had the haunted, lonely look of someone who had lost her way in life.

"They met when he visited Deeah Isle while on a huntin' and fishin' trip tah Maine," Gerallt continued. "Accordin' tah my mothah, Rhiannon had nevah been tah the mainland before, and Henry Hawthorne was the very first outsidah she'd evah known. Apparently, it was love at first sight. It took a while, but he was used tah getting' his own way. Eventually, they convinced her parents and more importantly the colony's eldahs tah let them marry and move away from the island. He built this house foah her."

Chapter 18 – Spending the Night

"Man, they must have loved to read," Matt said, gazing at row after row of leather-bound books.

"I guess there wasn't much else tah do in a small town like this," Gerallt said.

Matt looked around the room. There was the old leather chair in front of the corner fireplace where a person could read a book in the candlelight of a brass chandelier suspended over his shoulder. Then he noticed a stand with a huge book opened on top of it. "What's this?" Matt asked, walking over to take a better look.

"Don't touch that!" Gerallt exclaimed, running over to put himself between Matt and the book. He continued in a whisper, "Henry Hawthorne didn't own all the books in the library. This book is one of the very few things my great-grandmothah Rhiannon Hawthorne was permitted tah bring with her from the island. It was a weddin' gift from the eldahs so she could properly raise her children in the ways of the Goddess. That book is not for outsidahs tah read or touch. I'll tell you more, but not heah and not now."

Gerallt led Matt to the parlor that shared a wall and fireplace with the library. The first thing that Matt noticed was the alcove that formed the base of the house's octagonal tower. Vivianne's rocking chair sat in its center, facing outward so that she could sit and observe the world outside. Five tall, narrow windows in the turret, as well as two more on the wall facing Hawthorne Drive, provided considerable light to the room. Each of these windows was topped by a square of stained glass with a large yellow H inside green leaves on a blue background.

The room looked as though it hadn't changed since the 1920s. It was filled with overstuffed couches and chairs with doilies on their arms. The walls were hung with numerous paintings darkened with age and sepia-toned photographs of various members of the Hawthorne family. The mirrors of antique silver wall sconces reflected the flames from white candles, while Tiffany oil lamps sat on the small, round tables near each chair and couch.

Several of these Art Deco lamps were in the form of beautiful brass fairies whose large, stained-glass wings would glow when the lamps behind them were lit. Others were more traditional with stained-glass shades with small, beaded tassels dangling from the edge. It was easy for Matt to imagine Gerallt's great-aunt sitting in this room, watching the changing world outside her windows while her life remained frozen in this time capsule of a room.

"Come on, Matt," Gerallt said, leading Matt across the hall. "This is our dinin' room."

Matt looked around the room, so different than the Mitchell's simple dining room with its small table that was often obscured by pieces of mail and other things that were waiting to be put away. The Hawthorne's spacious formal dining room held a long table that could comfortably seat ten people. Their table was covered by an elegant, white linen tablecloth, laid out with five place settings of gold-rimmed dishes, each monogrammed with the letter H, polished antique silverware, beautiful leaded-glass goblets, and four fat, multi-wicked candles on heavy silver candlesticks.

Chapter 18 – Spending the Night

Overhead hung a massive chandelier made from hundreds of cut-glass crystals surrounding dozens of tall white candles. The dining room had an enormous stone fireplace in the far-left corner that mirrored the one in the parlor. An alcove forming the base of the round tower extended from the far-right corner of the room. In its center stood a waist-high, brass, Art Deco plant stand in the form of a slender nude, her arms raised high over her head to support a huge potted fern.

On the wall opposite the row of tall narrow windows stood a massive ornately-carved china cabinet displaying two rows of the gold-rimmed monogrammed plates. The final noteworthy items were oil paintings of the six steam locomotives that had once belonged to Gerallt's great-grandfather, Henry Hubertus Hawthorne, the railroad baron who had built Hawthorne House.

"Wow," Matt said. "Do you eat here every night?"

"Of course," Gerallt responded, confused by his friend's question. "Where else would we have suppah besides in the dinin' room?"

"Well, at home, we usually eat dinner watching the TV in our living room."

"But why don't you eat in the dinin' room?"

"Dad brings stuff home from work so he can finish it in the evenings. I guess that our table has sort of become his desk. Besides, there's always something good to watch on TV."

"But then when do you sit down together and talk about your day?"

Matt thought about it for a second, remembering the family dinners back in their cabin by the beach. "I guess we haven't done much of that since Mom died."

Gerallt nodded. "Ayuh, I know what you mean. We talk about school and other things, but the one thing we nevah talk about is Fathah." He paused, suddenly no longer interested in showing Matt his new home. "Let's head back up to my room. We can talk." He paused again before continuing. "About anythin'." With that, Gerallt turned around and led his friend upstairs.

Chapter 19
Tina and the Tree Branch

It was a cold and gloomy Saturday evening when the old grandfather clock slowly struck nine. After the last chime had died away, the parlor fell silent. The only sounds were the crackle of the fire, the somber ticking of the clock, and the soft, rhythmic creak of Vivianne's antique rocker, her favorite chair in her favorite place to think.

Although Vivianne had tried to hide it from her niece, she was deeply troubled. The money she had inherited from her parent's estate and the little money that her husband had left behind had lasted fully three-quarters of a century. Now, it was finally reaching its end. Although Vivianne didn't regret inviting Gwendolyn and her three children to come and live with her, the four extra mouths to feed only worsened her finances. If she couldn't think of a way to find more money soon, her funds would not last another six months, eight at the most if they were lucky and saved every penny they possibly could.

Vivianne had already been forced to sell the most valuable of her mother's jewelry as well as several valuable paintings. Soon, she would have to start selling her rare books, something she feared she would be unable to bear. Losing her parent's beloved books would be like losing her mother and father all over again. Often when she sat in the library, she could feel their comforting presence. These books and the pleasant memories they evoked had been the only

The Secrets of Hawthorne House

things that had kept her from going insane during the fifty years she'd spent as a recluse after her worthless husband disappeared with her best friend.

A car that Vivianne didn't recognize slowly drove up Hawthorne Drive and stopped next door in front of the Mitchell's house. The headlights turned off, but no one got out into the wintry mix of sleet and frigid northwest winds. After a couple minutes, the car backed up until it was parked in front of Hawthorne House.

Strange, she thought. No one got out of the car, and it was too dark to see who might be inside.

"Ahnt Vivianne," Gwyneth said, as she entered the parlor ten minutes later. "Do we have any eucalyptus and willow bark? Mothah thinks Gareth might be catchin' a cold and wants to make him a poultice."

"Of course, dear. They'ah in the herb pantry." As Gwyneth turned around, Aunt Vivianne called out "But before you go, come over heah and take a look outside. A car stopped in front of the Mitchell's house, but then it backed up, and now it's parked out front. Whoever it is, they'ah just sittin' inside."

"It's probably Tina. Matt mentioned she was going tah a friend's birthday party this evenin'. I bet one of her friends drove her home, and she's just waitin' for the sleet tah let up before gettin' out of the cah."

"Well, they've been sittin' there for a while now. And if Tina's waitin' for the sleet tah stop, she's goin' tah have a long wait. The barometah has been droppin' all afternoon, and these old bones can feel a big storm a-comin'. The way they ache, I bet we'll

Chapter 19 – Tina and the Tree Branch

have a foot of snow come mornin'. But if it is Tina, why did the cah back up and stop where it did?"

Just then, the passenger door opened a few inches, and the interior light came on. For a couple of seconds, Vivianne and Gwyneth could clearly see the car's two occupants. One was indeed Tina, but the driver was a rather large boy wearing a Hawthorne High letterman's jacket. Holding a struggling Tina with one arm, he roughly reached past her and yanked on her door, slamming it shut and plunging the interior back into darkness.

Both Vivianne and Gwyneth reacted instantly, drawing their wands, but Gwyneth was much younger and faster. She pointed her wand at the old oak standing over the car and yelled "*Magna Dea, fac, quaesumus, ramum ruinam!*" There was a loud crack, and a large branch broke off the tree and fell, crashing onto the hood of the car. Seconds later, Gwyneth had unlocked the front door and was running toward the car when the passenger door flew open, and Tina stumbled out.

"Tina, this way!" Gwyneth yelled, throwing open the gate. She gave the boy a glare that would have horrified him had his attention not been entirely directed at the massive branch laying across the deeply dented hood of his father's car. Putting her arm protectively around the younger girl's shoulders, Gwyneth led a terrified Tina into the house.

"Ah you okay, deah?" Vivianne asked, as she sat Tina in a chair in front of the fire and placed a warm shawl around Tina's shoulders. "He didn't hurt you, did he? Were we in time?"

Sobbing, Tina shuddered but was too upset and frightened to speak.

"Gwyneth, go and tell your mothah what's happened. And ask her tah make us a calmin' tea. Chamomile and lemon balm with a couple of dried passion flowers should do the trick." Vivianne turned her attention back to the young girl sitting there, shaking despite the warmth of the fire.

"There, there, deah girl. You're safe and among friends who are more than able tah protect you from the likes of that boy outside. Now take a deep breath and let it out."

Tina looked up at Vivianne and breathed a sigh of relief. The unpleasant smell of beer was faint but unmistakable.

"Again, deah. A big deep breath this time, and then let it all out. There, that's bettah."

Gwyneth returned, followed shortly by her mother, who carried a tray with an antique silver teapot and four fine china cups. Gwendolyn poured the tea and handed a steaming cup to Tina. No one spoke until everyone had had a sip and Tina had finished hers.

"Now, deah, we all want tah help, but first we need tah know what happened this evenin' so that we can give the right kind of help."

Tina looked anxiously at the three generations of Hawthorne woman gathered around her. "What... what about Dad? Are you going to tell him what happened?"

"Now, don't you go worryin' about youah fathah," Vivianne answered. "Foah now, this will be a secret

Chapter 19 – Tina and the Tree Branch

just among us women. No need tah get the menfolk involved, not if you don't want us tah."

"I don't," Tina said quickly. "I don't think he'd understand."

"Well, you might be surprised at what your fathah would understand, but that is a topic foah anothah day," Gwendolyn said. "Right now, deah, we really do need tah know what happened that has caused you tah be sittin' heah, havin' a nice cup of tea among friends."

Tina nodded but remained quiet.

"I know this might be hard tah talk about," Vivianne said, "I'll tell you what. I'll start, and you can interrupt me any time I'm wrong."

"Okay, I guess," Tina said, beginning to feel warm, safe, and much calmer as the tea took effect.

"Well, Matt told us you were goin' tah a birthday party, but it wasn't really a birthday party, was it?"

Tina shook her head sheepishly.

"So, several older boys and girls wah havin' an unsupervised party, probably at the home of one of them whose parents wah away," Vivianne continued. "There was music and dancin', and there was also drinkin', beer by the smell of it. One of the boys spent the whole evenin' with you, maybe even the one you wah hopin' tah see theah. He told you how pretty you ah—and you ah quite a pretty girl—and tried tah get you tah drink with him.

"You didn't want him thinkin' you wah a child, and so you let him talk you intah it. But you didn't like the taste and only drank a little. And then, when it was getting' tah be time tah go home, he offered tah drive you, and you accepted.

"Neither of you wanted youah fathah tah know you wah alone with a boy, and he didn't want you tah go in right away, so he backed up the cah so your fathah couldn't see you. You wanted tah spend more time with him, so you talked foah a while. And everythin' was goin' fine until he decided he wanted moah than just talk." Vivianne paused. "Does that about covah most of the evening?"

"How... how did you know?" Tina asked, amazed at how well the old lady had described her evening."

"You are not the first young girl tah be seduced by an older boy. Such parties have taken place for time out of mind and will almost certainly continue long aftah we'ah all dead and gone. The important thing is that we stopped him before he could do permanent harm. And we did stop him in time, didn't we? He didn't have his way with you, did he? That would necessitate a call tah the police foah him as well as an altogether different tea foah you."

"Oh God, no!" Tina exclaimed, when she realized what Vivianne was asking. "He wanted to. We kissed, but then he tried to put his hand down my top. I told him to stop, but he wouldn't. He started forcing his other hand up under my dress. I struggled and almost got out, but he reached over and yanked my door shut so I couldn't. He was so strong. Then..."

"And then the branch fell." Vivianne shook her head and sighed. "It's a shame so many young men are obsessed with sex. Some can't understand why

Chapter 19 – Tina and the Tree Branch

anyone would reject them, and they see failure as a weakness. It's clearly time tah teach this boy that no means no. Who is this boy who can't keep his hands to himself?"

Tina paused. "I don't want to cause any problems, especially if Matt finds out and tells Dad. Can't I just ignore him, and we all forget about the whole thing?"

"Tina, I'm afraid that boys like that do not forget. He will keep aftah you, and if you continue to ignore him, he may even brag to his friends that you couldn't resist his *charms*. And theah ah the othah girls tah considah.

"Such boys rarely stop unless someone stops them. You might well have not been the first, and if we don't do somethin', you almost certainly will not be the last. No, we must stop him before he causes irreparable harm tah someone and even tah himself should the police have tah get involved. So, Tina, tell us the name of this boy."

Tina paused. When she finally answered, her voice was little more than a whisper. "Brad O'Connell."

"I know him," Gwyneth said. "Brad's one of Colin O'Connell's cousins. He's a junior in some of my classes. He's a big football jock, kind of handsome if you'ah intah hunks with moah muscle than brains. Thinks he's the Goddess's gift tah anything in a dress. I'll talk with him and make sure he learns that no means no. Once I'm done with Mr. Hands, he won't be makin' the same mistake again."

"But what if someone overhears you?" Tina asked. "And what if Brad lies and brags that I gave in to him?"

"Don't worry. I'll be discreet. Believe me, when I get through with him, he'll want to forget this evenin' evah happened."

"Thank you, Gwyneth. I really appreciate it."

"Well, now that we have taken care of Mr. O'Connell," Vivianne continued, "there is only one more thing to discuss. Although there is absolutely no excuse foah what he tried tah do, it is unfortunately all too common. This time you were lucky. You won't always have friends nearby, and you certainly can't count on a tree branch fallin' on your attacker's cah.

"That is why you must learn tah protect yourself, physically if you have tah. But bettah than fightin' is avoidin' the fight in the first place. While I am in no way blamin' you for what he tried tah do, your poah judgment tonight put you in unnecessary dangah. Next time, you should not lie tah your fathah. Don't let anyone, especially an older boy, talk you intah drinkin', and definitely don't let a boy you barely know drive you home."

"Yes, Mrs. Hawthorne. I won't."

"There's no need to be so formal, deah. Call me Ahnt Vivianne. Everybody else does."

"Yes, Mrs. Haw... Aunt Vivianne." Tina paused, suddenly realizing that something didn't quite add up. Looking intently at the old lady, Tina continued. "Wait a minute. You've said several times that you stopped him, but it was the branch. When it fell on the

Chapter 19 – Tina and the Tree Branch

car, he let go of me, and I was able to open the door and get away. So why are you saying that *you* stopped him?"

"Why deah, Gwyneth prayed tah the Goddess tah keep you safe until she could get tah you. And the Goddess looked down and, in her mercy, answered our prayahs. She commanded that old tree tah drop the branch on the boy's car."

At first, Tina didn't know what to say. The three Hawthorne women obviously meant well. They offered her sanctuary in their home, and Gwyneth had run to her rescue. However, their talk about prayers and goddesses making tree branches fall made her nervous. Finally, she said, "I appreciate everything you did for me, really I do. But it's late, and I need to get home. I told Dad I would be home thirty minutes ago." She started to get up, then stopped. "You don't think Brad's still out there, do you?"

"Not if he knows what's good for him, he isn't. But Gwyneth will escort you safely home, regardless."

They all went to the windows and looked out. The spot where the car had parked was empty except for the fallen branch.

Gwyneth put on her coat, selected a large umbrella from the umbrella stand next to the door, and walked Tina to her front door.

"Ah you goin' tah be alright?" Gwyneth asked, as Tina pulled out her house key.

"I think so. And thanks again for coming to my rescue. I don't know what I would have done if you hadn't come running."

"You're very welcome Tina. But the next time you want tah go tah a party, invite me along. It would be fun to go out together, and I'll make sure that no one forces you tah do something you shouldn't."

"Thank you, Gwyneth. I will."

Chapter 20
The Inadvertent Investiture

It was barely three weeks until Christmas, and as the holiday break drew near, so did the final tests of the fall semester. Gerallt was having trouble in Physical Science, and the final was worth one-fourth of the class grade. He'd been worrying about the test and knew he needed to ace it if he were going to bring his grade up to a solid B, his mother's lowest acceptable grade. Although Matt was in Honors Biology instead of Physical Science, he excelled in all types of science and had volunteered to help Gerallt study for the coming test. Both boys were in Matt's room, where Matt was asking his friend questions that were likely to be on the test.

After a couple of hours, they took a short break and went downstairs for a snack to bring back up to Matt's room. As they sat on Matt's bed eating potato chips and drinking colas, neither of them was particularly eager to start studying again. Gerallt felt like his brain would explode if he stuffed it with just one more fact or formula, and Matt was confident that Gerallt could ace the test in his sleep.

Gerallt finally asked, "So, do you want tah do somethin' else? I'm as ready for the test as I'll evah be."

"Definitely," Matt answered. "What do you want to do?"

The Secrets of Hawthorne House

"I don't know. Since you've been helpin' me, why don't you decide? Just anything but physics."

"Anything?" Matt asked, perking up. "My choice?"

"Sure. Why not? What do you want tah do?"

"Do you have your amulet with you?"

"Always. Why?" Gerallt raised his hand to feel the hard form of the amulet resting next to his skin under his shirt. "You want me tah show you anothah miracle?"

"That would be sweet, but I'd rather learn how to use it myself."

"But, Matt," Gerallt replied, frowning. "This isn't like one of your games that anyone can play. The amulet is one of the ancient holy gifts that Modron entrusted tah us, and only druidae can use it."

"So, what would happen if I were to try to use it? Would your goddess strike me down with a bolt of lightning?"

"No, that would be Taranis, the god of thunder," Gerallt answered, a bit miffed by Matt's flippant attitude. "Nothin' would happen. Modron knows you'ah not a druid and would just ignore youah prayah."

"Then I guess there wouldn't be any harm in you letting me try, would there?"

"I guess not," Gerallt conceded. "You'll probably just keep buggin' me about it until I show you, anyway. Lock your doah so that no one walks in on us. I'd be skinned alive if this ever got back tah my mothah."

Chapter 20 – The Inadvertent Investiture

Matt got up and locked his door. "Satisfied?"

Gerallt nodded. "Okay, sit heah on the floor facin' me." As Matt sat down, Gerallt took a coin from his pocket and placed it on the rug between them. He pulled his amulet from under his shirt and held it in his hand. "Okay. I'm goin' tah teach you one of the simplest prayahs, the prayah for levitation. I'll do it first so you can see, and then you can try. I'm goin' tah ask the Goddess tah make the coin float up intah the air." Slowly and carefully pronouncing each syllable, Gerallt said, "*Magna Dea, fac, quaesumus, ut nummus ascendat!*"

The coin slowly rose until it floated between them.

Gerallt said, "*Magna Dea, fac, quaesumus, ut nummus descendant!*" and the coin slowly settled back down onto the rug. Gerallt lifted the amulet over his head by its sturdy silver chain and placed it carefully around Matt's neck. "Now it's your turn. Hold the amulet in your hand and repeat what I am about tah say exactly the way I say it. Concentrate on having the coin rise up until it's floatin' between us. Okay?"

"I guess so," Matt replied, a little uncertainly.

"Okay. Repeat after me. *Magna Dea, fac, quaesumus, ut nummus ascendat!*" Gerallt said, speaking slowly and clearly.

"MAG-nuh DAY-uh, fact, KWEI-sue-moose, ut NOOM-moose..." Matt stopped before the end when he couldn't remember the last word.

"Not bad for a first try," Gerallt said, smiling encouragingly at Matt. "Let's try again. *Magna Dea, fac, quaesumus, ut nummus ascendat!* And remembah, it is MAG-nah, not MAG-nuh and fahk, not fact."

After several more tries, Matt finally managed to repeat the words perfectly while picturing the coin rising in his mind. The coin still stubbornly refused to move.

"See, I told you. Even though you said the prayah properly, the Goddess knows you aren't really a druid and has denied youah request."

Gerallt reached out his hand to take back his amulet, but Matt wasn't yet ready to admit defeat. He had an idea. "Gerallt, maybe it's just because I don't know what I am saying. Heck, I don't even know what language I'm speaking."

"It's Latin, the language the Roman invadahs spoke when Modron first appeared tah my ancestahs during the reign of the emperah Trajan. In English, the prayah is *Great Goddess, we beseech Thee, make the coin ascend*. But She didn't ignore youah prayah because you didn't understand the translation word foah word. Lots of children don't fully understand the Latin words when they first receive theah gift and learn theah first prayahs. Modron ignored your prayah because you aren't a druid."

Matt repeated the first prayer, this time concentrating on its meaning as well as its pronunciation, but the coin still refused to move.

"Satisfied?" Gerallt asked, holding his hand out again to take back his amulet.

Chapter 20 – The Inadvertent Investiture

"Uh..." Matt replied, thinking furiously while still holding the amulet. "Did you have to do anything when you received the amulet? Some ceremony or something?"

"Sure. When you turn thirteen, youah parents hold your Rite of Investiture. You receive your first gift, usually an amulet, and your ceremonial robes. And theah's a big feast with everyone in the colony."

"Maybe I just can't do it because I haven't gone through the ceremony. Is there something that someone says to make you a druid?"

"Of course. It's only been a couple years since I was invested." Gerallt thought silently for a moment. "Okay, I remembah now."

"Well, maybe you need to say that, too," Matt suggested.

"Well, clearly it's important, or it wouldn't be part of the ceremony," Gerallt conceded. "But that's not the reason. You'ah an outsidah."

"Maybe," Matt said, "but maybe not. Let's try it."

Gerallt thought for a few seconds before he reluctantly agreed. "If we do this, if I say the words, will you give up and believe me? The Goddess is not goin' tah be fooled by this. She'll look intah your heart and know you don't really want tah become a druid in her service."

"I still think it's worth a try. Have you ever heard of someone going through the ceremony and not being made a druid?"

"No."

"Then you don't really know for sure. It's like in science. If no one has ever performed an experiment, you don't know for sure how it will turn out. You might be able to guess from what you know, but you might be wrong. If you have a question about how something works, you have to run the experiment and see what the universe answers."

"Well, that might be the way science works, but this isn't a matter of science. It's a matter of faith. I am a druid, a priest of Modron, and I know my Goddess and her sacred gift. You should trust me," Gerallt replied, beginning to feel a little angry and exasperated by Matt's stubbornness. "Let's do this and get it over with. But when you still can't raise the coin, I want you tah give me the amulet and stop tryin' tah be somethin' you aren't. If you truly want tah have the power, you will have tah believe in the Goddess and vow tah serve her. And that's just somethin' I don't see you ever being able tah do."

"Let's just try this, Gerallt, and I'll stop bothering you. At least for today, though I can't promise that I won't think of another thing to try tomorrow."

"Matt, you're hopeless," Gerallt answered, shaking his head. "Okay. It's a long and involved ceremony, but here's the prayah that officially makes you a druid. Touch the amulet." Once both boys were touching the amulet, Gerallt intoned: *"Magna Dea, comproba, quaesumus, hunc puerum druidam tuum!* There, I have just prayed tah the Goddess tah accept you as her druid. Try floatin' the coin again."

Matt looked down at the coin and carefully said, *"Magna Dea, fac, quaesumus, ut nummus ascendat!"*

Chapter 20 – The Inadvertent Investiture

The coin slowly rose into the air to hang, suspended between Matt and Gerallt. At that moment, no one would have been able to tell which of the two was more surprised: Matt that the coin had levitated or Gerallt that the Goddess had answered Matt's prayer.

"Son of a..." Matt cursed.

"*Magna Dea!*" Gerallt whispered, shocked, confused, and angry. "I don't believe it."

"Neither do I," Matt added.

"Matt, do you know what this means?" Gerallt asked.

"Sure. That you don't know as much about the amulet as you thought." Matt grinned, thinking of how amazing it was to perform real, honest-to-goodness magic.

"No, Matt. It means you ah a druid of Modron. It means that you have duties and responsibilities tah the Goddess. You need your own amulet. You need to be taught the prayahs. Most importantly, you need tah believe. *Magna Dea*, what have I done? What am I goin' tah do? I can't teach you. I'm goin' tah have tah tell my mothah, and she's goin' tah kill me! I'll be banished foah certain..."

"Hold on a second," Matt interrupted. "Let's stop and think for a minute. You don't really have to tell her, do you? At least, not right now."

"Well, maybe not immediately, but I don't see how I can not tell her. I don't know. This has nevah happened befoah, at least I don't think it has, and I don't know what tah do."

"Well, I do. You're not going to tell your mother until we've had a chance to think it through," Matt argued. "I can't believe you made me a druid just because you said some Latin while we were both holding this amulet. Maybe Modron didn't do this. In fact, I just realized what this reminds me of. Some smartphones come with built-in thumbprint readers so they won't work without the right thumbprint. Maybe you just programmed your amulet to accept my thumbprint or DNA. Maybe your amulet's some kind of advanced alien tech..."

"Matt, stop it!" Gerallt exclaimed, grabbing the amulet from Matt's hand. "We're not talkin' about a computer heah. This is a sacred gift from the Goddess. What you just said is blasphemy, and I can't listen tah it. I got tah go." Gerallt got up and headed for the door.

"Wait, Gerallt. I'm sorry. I didn't mean to offend you or do anything sacrilegious. I don't want to argue..."

However, Gerallt had already unlocked Matt's bedroom door and left. By the time Matt jumped to his feet and reached the top of the stairs, Gerallt was gone, having slammed the Mitchell's front door behind him.

"Matt, is everything okay?" Matt's father asked from the living room as his son slowly descended the stairs. "You two get in an argument?"

"It's nothing, Dad," Matt replied, hoping he wasn't lying although he knew he was. He just hoped Gerallt would not do or say anything that couldn't be undone

Chapter 20 – The Inadvertent Investiture

or unsaid. He turned around and headed back to his room. Matt knew it was going to be a long night... for both of them.

The next day, Gerallt was uncharacteristically silent as the Hawthorne and Mitchell children waited for the school bus. Matt tried several times to start a conversation, but Gerallt only responded with single words like ayuh, no, maybe, and uh-huh before lapsing into silence. When the bus arrived, and the boys boarded, Matt sat down in their usual spot. He slid over to make room, but Gerallt just walked past and took a seat near the back.

Tina noticed and took the seat next to Matt. "What's wrong, Baby Brother? Did you and Gerallt have a fight or something?"

Matt looked at Tina but didn't have a clue what to say. It wasn't as if he could tell her that Gerallt had a magic amulet. And he certainly couldn't tell her about the stupid experiment he'd talked Gerallt into or that his friend was convinced he was a blasphemous druid of the goddess Modron.

"It's personal. I can't talk about it. I promised."

"Well, I hope the two of you work it out soon. You've been inseparable since the day you met, and you'll both be miserable if you don't."

Matt nodded in agreement but was still no closer to figuring out what to do about it. He thought that maybe he should walk up to Gerallt and apologize, but he couldn't lie and say he believed in the miracles of an ancient Celtic goddess. Faith might be adequate for religious believers, but his love of science and engineering told him that having faith was nothing more than believing in the unbelievable when there was insufficient evidence to back it up. Matt wished he could talk about it with Tina and his father, but he couldn't. He'd promised Gerallt that he wouldn't tell a soul about their secret.

The rest of the day was just as bad as the bus ride. Gerallt ignored him in the classes they shared and made a point of sitting with his sister during lunch. Gerallt sat with his back to Matt, and every time Matt looked over at them, Gwyneth was looking at him with a worried look on her face.

During the bus ride home, Matt decided that he couldn't stand it anymore. As they all got off the bus, Matt pulled his friend aside and said, "Gerallt, I can't take this silent treatment. We need to work this out before it goes too far."

Gerallt waited until everyone else had gone inside before speaking. "You know how I feel about what happened, and you made it perfectly clear how *you* feel. I don't know what else tah say. Accordin' to our beliefs, a druid who stops believin' in the Goddess is an apostate who must be shunned and banished from our people."

"But Gerallt, how can you call me an apostate if I never really believed in your goddess in the first place? You can't banish me or shun me; we're best friends. Besides, if you keep this up, your family is bound to pressure you into telling them why you're avoiding me."

Chapter 20 – The Inadvertent Investiture

"Maybe you have a point. It's so honkin' crazy; I don't know what tah think. I've always been the black sheep of the family, the one with the least faith, but seein' the Goddess accept you and grant you control of the amulet is really upsettin'. I guess I didn't realize how much I truly believed deep down inside. How can an outsidah pray tah the Goddess and have his prayah answered? But, if there's no Goddess, then what is the amulet and how does it work?"

"I don't know, Gerallt. But if we work together, I bet we'll learn. Just give it some time, and we'll figure it out."

"I guess," Gerallt answered dubiously.

"Anyway," Matt continued, "I didn't mean any disrespect when I suggested that your amulet was like a computer and the ceremony was like getting a user ID and password. I certainly didn't mean to offend you or belittle your beliefs. As Mom always said, 'your beliefs are yours, mine are mine, and neither of us has the right to tell the other what to believe.'

"My mom was always very spiritual," Matt said, "sort of a mix of Native American and pagan beliefs. Dad's different. He was a Baptist until he went to college and began to question how he'd been raised. Now, he's an atheist. If they could get along, so can we."

"I hope so," Gerallt said. "I'm tired of hidin' from outsidahs, livin' in the past, and waitin' for the Goddess tah return while the rest of the world passes us by."

Matt shuddered, trying to imagine how it must feel to have your parents drill that fear of murderous outsiders into you as a little kid. He wondered what his Native American ancestors must have felt when they heard the white invaders say that the only good Indian was a dead Indian. For as long as he could remember, his family hadn't celebrated Columbus Day. Instead, they spent the day remembering the slavery and genocide that Columbus had brought to the European's so-called New World.

"So, are we still friends?" Matt asked.

Gerallt paused for a few seconds, then smiled. "Friends."

"Great! Come on, let's race. First one done with his homework and chores gets to go to the loser's house and pick what we're going to do."

The boys turned and raced for their front doors. Matt won, but only barely and only because he didn't have to open a gate.

Chapter 21
Laid Off

A few days later as their school bus pulled up in front of the Hawthorne House, Matt and Gerallt were having a good-natured argument about which of Matt's games was the best. Matt preferred to play alien first-person shooters, while Gerallt really liked the car-racing games.

"Hey, you two," Gwyneth said, as she walked past the boys. "You'd bettah pay attention if you don't want a long walk home."

Looking up, the boys noticed where they were and rushed down the aisle to the laughter of the students still on the bus. Tina was already inside her front door, and Gwyneth and Gareth were halfway to Hawthorne House by the time Gerallt and Matt got off. They were still deep in discussion as Matt opened his front door, and they went in.

The boys were on their way upstairs to Matt's room when they heard his father call. "Matt, could you come down here, please?"

Matt and Gerallt walked back to the Mitchell's small dining room where they saw Matt's father and sister sitting at the table.

"Hello, Mr. Mitchell," Gerallt said.

"Hi, Dad. What are you doing home so early? You never get off work until after six."

"Hello, Gerallt," Sam said, ignoring his son's question. "I need to talk privately with Tina and Matt for a little while. Would you mind going home and coming back later?"

"Sure, Mr. Mitchell," Gerallt replied. "Matt, come over and get me when you'ah done, okay?"

"Sure. See you then."

Sam waited until he heard Gerallt close the front door before speaking. "You'd better sit down, Matt. I have something important to tell the two of you."

'Okay," Matt said, sitting next to Tina. It dawned on him that his father didn't look well. He looked tired and beaten down. In fact, his father looked noticeably older than he had the previous evening. "Are you sick?"

"No, Matt. I'm not sick, though goodness knows, I've felt better."

"What's wrong?" Tina asked, nervously glancing at Matt with a look that silently asked, *Do you know what's wrong with Dad?*

Matt shook his head, and the twins both gave their father their full attention.

"You know how I've been working extra-long hours lately," Sam said. "It's been because our project's several months behind schedule and way over budget. Everyone on the team's been working so hard to get us back on target, but nothing has seemed to help. Management way underbid the contract and left it to us to make some sort of miracle happen..." He trailed off.

"So, what did they say?" Tina asked. "They already have you working most evenings. Are they going to make you work weekends, too? Do you

Chapter 21 – Laid Off

know how much longer you're going to have to be working like this?"

"No, I'm not going to have to work weekends. No one will. The customer canceled the project."

"Oh, Dad," Tina said, "All those long hours you've been working. And they're not even going to use any of the software you've written? That's terrible."

"Maybe canceling the project will turn out to be a good thing," Matt said, trying to look for a silver lining. "Now you can get back to working normal hours and not have to bring work home every night. So, what are they going to have you do next?"

"That's the problem, Matt. Nothing. The company's too small, and this was our biggest project. With the economy as bad as it's been, there aren't any other projects out there, especially not in this area. Except for a couple of people who've worked there for years, they laid off everyone else. If they don't get another project soon, the company's going to go out of business altogether. And the icing on the cake is that they're in such bad financial shape that they couldn't even give us two weeks' notice. I get my last partial paycheck on Friday, and then that's it."

"Oh, no," Tina groaned, as the full significance of the situation sunk in. "Dad, what are we going to do?"

"I don't know, Princess, I just don't know," Sam answered sadly. "First thing tomorrow morning, I'll go apply for unemployment. I'll start looking for work, but you have to realize that Hawthorne's too small to have many programming jobs. And I'll be competing against more than a dozen of my former coworkers who are all in the same boat. There are a couple large companies down in Fort Wayne that might be hiring, and I'll try looking in all the neighboring towns. Until I find something more permanent, I'll see if I can get a substitute teacher job teaching science, math, or computers."

"You'll find something, Dad," Tina said, when her father paused. "We'll be okay. You'll see."

"I hope so," Sam answered, smiling sadly and reaching across the table to lay his hand on his daughter's. "Still, we can't count on my finding anything right away, and the trip here took almost all of the money we had left after paying for your mother's medical bills and funeral. We've been living paycheck-to-paycheck since we got here. I don't see how I'm going to pay the rent and utilities, put gas in the car, and put food on the table, let alone deal with the dozens of other expenses that empty our checking account each month. Starting tomorrow, we're going to have to start cutting back everywhere we possibly can."

"Like what?" Matt asked nervously.

"Well, we start by giving up eating out. It's cheaper to cook at home, although we'll all probably have to get used to eating meals mostly made from bulk foods like rice, beans, and pasta. Our cable TV and Internet bills were already more than we could afford. Now, I'm going to have to cancel cable for the foreseeable future. I'd cancel the Internet too if I didn't need it for email and applying for work online. Meanwhile, we'll just have to get by watching all of the old DVDs we have."

Chapter 21 – Laid Off

"Dad, I can probably get a few more babysitting jobs," Tina offered. "It won't be much, but I should be able to get enough work to help."

"Thank you, Tina. That's the spirit!" Sam beamed at his daughter. They both turned to Matt, who knew he had no choice but to make his own sacrifice.

"Okay, Dad," Matt said, with a sigh. "You can have the money I make helping Mrs. Hawthorne. Maybe that way, we can still order pizza now and then."

"It's a deal, Son," his father said, offering his hand. "While I'll need to spend most of it on gas and groceries, you can buy pizza Since it's your money, you can choose the toppings, and the garlic breadsticks will be on me."

Sam looked at his children with a mixture of relief and pride. "I really appreciate how you two are stepping up to help out. I've been dreading having to tell you the bad news ever since my boss told everyone this afternoon. I know it will be hard for a while, but we'll get through this somehow. I promise."

Matt and Tina nodded, not knowing what else to say. After their meeting ended, the three went their separate ways. Sam sat in his recliner, opened his laptop, and began searching for jobs. Tina went upstairs to start on her homework, and Matt went next door to see Gerallt. They were all thinking the same thing, the one thing they had all left unsaid. What if there were no nearby jobs, and they'd have to move away, far from Hawthorne Indiana and far from the

Hawthorne family that had become such an essential part of their lives?

Matt's father began by applying for unemployment, but the weekly checks were only for $140 because he had worked so little in Indiana. It was not nearly enough to live on. For the next few weeks, Sam applied for a programmer job at every company from Gary and South Bend to Fort Wayne. However, the only responses he received were form letters from human resource departments saying they'd keep his resume on file, but there were no positions currently open.

Eventually, Sam managed to line up a couple of interviews, but they went nowhere. The interviewers asked him a few questions about his experience and knowledge of the latest technologies, knowledge that he lacked. Between his age and limited work experience, he was politely told that they would contact him if a suitable position became available. It never did. The results were no different when he applied for a substitute teaching job at every school district within 50 miles. Thanks, but don't call us; we'll call you.

Discouraged and becoming desperate, a month later he was forced to take a job managing a local fast-food place for just a couple of dollars above minimum wage. It was a heavy blow to his self-esteem and confidence, but it did put food on the table and pay the utilities. Unfortunately, there wasn't

Chapter 21 – Laid Off

enough left over to pay all of the rent, and Christmas presents were out of the question.

The eviction notice came just a little over a month later, and the threat of actually becoming homeless crept closer every day. It was time for another family meeting.

Instead of eating dinner in front of the TV, Sam had the twins set the table in the dining room. After everyone had finished their mac and cheese, but before Matt and Tina could disappear into their rooms, he said, "Kids, I've got something important we need to discuss."

"What's up, Dad? Did you finally find a second job?" Matt asked hopefully.

Sam shook his head sadly, and Tina gave him a worried look.

"You know that my so-called *manager* job doesn't bring in nearly what I made programming."

Both kids nodded.

"Well, the truth is that it only adds up to a little over $900 a month, and that just hasn't been enough. The bottom line is that I haven't been able to pay all of the rent. We're being evicted."

"No," Tina whispered. Matt was speechless.

"Yes, and I just don't know what we're going to do." Sam hung his head and tears started falling on the tablecloth. "I'm so sorry," he continued, sure that he was failing them as a father.

Tina got up and gave her father a hug. He clung to her arms as if they were a lifejacket, and he was a drowning man.

Matt sat there, looking at his father and sister, too shocked to move. All he could think of was that the only time he ever saw his father cry was when his mother had died. Slowly, he got up and went over to hug them both.

Later, Matt walked over to the Hawthorne House. Once in Gerallt's room, Matt shut the bedroom door and turned to his friend.

"Gerallt..." he began, not sure how to start.

"Ayuh," Gerallt said, when Matt fell silent. "What chuppta?"

"Gerallt," Matt tried again. "We're being evicted, and Dad doesn't know what we're going to do. His current job doesn't pay enough, and he hasn't been able to find a second one. We're going to have to move somewhere else, but we don't have the money to even do that. I don't know what's going to happen to us."

"What a honkin' pissah!" Gerallt said, shaking his head with shocked disbelief. Then a smile lit his face. "I know. The carriage house. You can move intah the carriage house. It's not much, but I'm sure Ahnt Vivianne will let you stay theah."

"Where?" Matt asked, confused.

"The carriage house," Gerallt replied, pointing out his window at the somewhat dilapidated, two-story

Chapter 21 – Laid Off

garage on the far side of the garden. "They used tah keep a couple of horses and a carriage theah. The drivah and his family lived upstairs in a little apartment. I checked out the place the first week we were heah. It's full of junk, and everything's totally covered in dust, but I bet it would look pretty good if we cleaned it up. And the best thing is that it'll be free and carryin' your stuff over should be easy."

"Do you really think your great-aunt would be okay with us moving in?"

"Of course. Why wouldn't she?"

"I don't know," Matt replied. "She's always kept to herself, and as you said, we're outsiders. Wouldn't this be breaking some kind of rule or something?"

"But you aren't just any outsidahs, you're you. Anyway, it's only the carriage house. It's not like you'ah actually movin' intah the house. Don't worry. I'll talk to her. She'll be happy tah help. Besides, there's no way Mothah wants your fathah tah move away, eithah. She's sweet on him."

"Jeez, Gerallt. I'm totally freaked out, and you're making a joke? Talk about bad timing."

"No, I'm completely serious," Gerallt replied. "You have no idear what my mothah was like befoah she met your fathah. Just sittin' up in her bedroom foah hours and hours, barely sayin' a word and cryin' any time anyone mentioned anythin' remotely related tah Fathah. But ever since we all went out tah eat togethah, it's been different. Haven't you noticed the way she looks at him?"

"Huh?" Matt looked at Gerallt in confusion. "Not really, but then I guess I haven't exactly been paying attention."

"Well, maybe you should keep youah eyes a little more open, 'cause youah fathah's been lookin' at Mothah the same way she's been lookin' at him. I think they've been havin' lunch togethah when we'ah in school, and Gwyneth thinks it's beginnin' tah get serious."

"Really?" Matt asked. Then he remembered how his father had looked at Gwendolyn and how he had been less depressed in spite of their financial troubles. "I think that's great. But now we have one more reason why moving away would suck. Gerallt, if you're right, then we can't move. If we do, then your mom and my dad will go back to the way they used to be, or worse. Hell, Dad's barely holding it together as it is."

"Don't worry. Mothah and Ahnt Vivianne will let you move in; I know they will."

"Well, I hope so. Otherwise, we may end up forced to move into a dump, a shelter, or worse yet, out of town."

Chapter 22
Moving In

Later that evening when Matt and Tina were in their rooms, there was a knock on the Mitchell's front door. Getting up from his computer where he'd been searching for jobs and sending off applications, Sam went to answer it. He was surprised to see Gwendolyn standing at the door with an antique ceramic jug under her arm.

"Gwendolyn, what a nice surprise. Come in," he said, taking her coat and smiling for the first time that day.

"Evenin', Sam," she said. "Gerallt told me the bad news, and I thought you might like anothah adult tah talk tah. That and some of my ahnt's hard apple cidah. She brews this herself from apples from her little orchard out back."

"Why, thank you. That might be just what I need," Sam said, motioning Gwendolyn to the living room couch while he left for the kitchen. A few seconds later, he returned with two glasses and sat down beside her. She poured generous portions of the golden cider for each of them. Sam took a drink, and it was like liquid sunshine, radiating a comforting warmth from his stomach to his skin.

Gwendolyn took a smaller sip and said, "You know, Sam, I understand what you'ah goin' through. When Medwyn died, so did our income. I'd have sold the boat, but the fire and sea took her. Oh, I still had some money from my candle shop, but there weren't that many flatlandahs last summah, and our savin's didn't last long."

Gwendolyn sighed, remembering how she felt when last of the money was gone. "We used tah have fresh fish every night, but that ended a few weeks after the accident when his fellow fishermen slowly stopped bringin' over fish from their catch. We were reachin' the bottom of my root cellah and nearly the last of the vegetables and fruit that I'd canned. I was at my wit's end. That's when Ahnt Vivianne asked us tah move in with her."

Taking another drink, Sam nodded, happy that Gwendolyn had found a safety net, even when he had none. "Yes, you've been very fortunate to have your aunt. It worked out well for everyone, what with your aunt living alone in such a large house." Sam paused, wishing he had a similar relative he could turn to.

"I've talked it over with Ahnt Vivianne, and we want you tah move in with us..." she said, pausing for a second before continuing. "Sam, I want you tah move in with us."

Sam was surprised, caught off-guard by their generous offer. "That's really nice of you, but your house doesn't have room for three more. Matt told me you are already using every room."

"I was thinkin' Matt could bunk with Gerallt. The two are practically inseparable anyway. As for you and Tina, you can stay in our carriage house. The drivah and his family had a small apartment on the second floah. You might as well get some good out of

Chapter 22 – Moving In

it; we're certainly not usin' it, except tah store some odds and ends that have been there for yeahs and yeahs. It'll be perfect. You and Tina can each have youah own room. There's a little combined parlor and kitchen area with a pot-bellied stove for heat and a small cast iron stove for cookin'. It even has its own bathroom. And you don't always have tah stay and cook there if you don't want tah. We can share the kitchen. I like tah cook, and best of all, we can all eat togethah." Beaming up at Sam, she paused to catch her breath.

"But Gwendolyn, that would be a huge imposition, having the three of us move in. I really don't want us to be a bother, what with your great-aunt having lived alone for so many years. Won't she have a hard time dealing with three more people, especially ones who aren't family?"

"Sam, it was her idear... Well, mine too," she added, a hint of a blush on her cheeks. "Besides, Matt and Gerallt are practically brothahs, Gareth idolizes Matt, and Gwyneth has begun tah take Tina under her wing. Sam, we've truly grown very fond of your entire family." The look in her eyes made it clear that she thought that her idea was a perfect solution for everyone.

Sam was torn between not wanting to be a burden, feeling like a failure for not being able to support his family, desperate for a place to live, and wanting to stay close to Gwendolyn. "Are you sure?"

"Absolutely."

"Then I guess you've got yourself three renters," Sam said, smiling.

"But Sam, you don't need tah pay rent. I know you'll need to save every penny until you get a bettah-paying job."

"Gwendolyn, I insist. At least, let me pay enough so I can pretend that I'm paying my own way. I'll cover our part of the groceries. I'll also be your chauffeur when you need to go someplace; it's only fitting since I'll be living in your carriage house. In fact, I'll help out any way that I can."

"Thank you, Sam. I was so afraid you might have tah leave Hawthorne tah look for work, and I'd nevah see you again."

Sam didn't remember either of them getting up, but there they stood, face to face, nearly touching, and suddenly so close he could feel her breath gently caress his lips. He put his arms around her and looked down into her beautiful emerald eyes. "Me too," he said, and they shared their first true kiss.

The next morning, Sam was up well before sunrise. By eight o'clock, he couldn't hold back any longer and ran up the stairs, taking them two at a time. "Wake up, sleepyheads," he shouted, knocking loudly on each of the twins' doors. "The sun's up, time's a wasting, and we have tons of work to do this weekend."

"But Dad, it's still dark," Tina groaned.

Neither Tina nor her father was exactly right as the sun was just beginning to creep above the horizon to brighten the overcast sky.

Chapter 22 – Moving In

"Dad," Matt moaned, trying to focus his bleary eyes on his alarm clock. "It's Saturday, I'm still sleepy, and I don't have to start work for another hour and a half."

"Come on, you two," their father yelled back. "Get up. I've got great news!"

"What happened? Did you get a second job?" Tina called back.

"Nope, Tina. Better! Now hurry up. We have a big day ahead of us."

Matt and Tina dragged themselves out of bed. They knew from experience that their father wouldn't leave them in peace until they did. Besides, they were curious.

A few minutes later, they came down the stairs and discovered that their father had set the table and placed a huge stack of steaming pancakes in the center.

"Jeeze, Dad," Tina exclaimed, "What's up? Did you invite the whole neighborhood for breakfast?"

"Well, I was waiting for you to get up, and... I don't know; I guess I might have gotten a little bit carried away," Sam replied.

"Ya think?" Matt chuckled, gazing at easily three times as many pancakes as they could possibly eat.

"Okay, Dad," Tina said, once she and her brother sat down. "What's this fantastic news that's better than your getting another job? Did we win the lottery or something? Cause if you did, I want to hear why you've been spending money on lottery tickets.

You've always called lotteries a tax on the numerically illiterate."

"No, we didn't win the lottery, and no, I haven't been buying lottery tickets with the money that we don't have."

"So, what's up?" Matt asked through a mouthful of pancakes and imitation maple syrup.

"Last night, Gwendolyn came by after you two had gone up to your rooms for the night," Sam said, smiling at the memory. "She really is an amazing woman," he continued, with a faraway look in his eyes. Realizing he had spoken that last thought out loud, he paused and began to blush. "Anyway, apparently Matt told Gerallt about my being laid off and the financial fix that put us in. He told his mother, she told her great-aunt, and now everyone knows we're running out of money and options."

"But Dad," Tina interrupted. "Not to be Captain Obvious, but why exactly is Matt blabbing about our finances and Gwendolyn knowing that we're broke a good thing?"

Matt was wondering the same thing but wisely kept his mouth closed, which wasn't difficult seeing as it was stuffed with pancakes.

"That is a good question," Sam said, a bit of a silly grin still on his face. "Naturally, being broke is certainly not something to be proud of, especially if you are trying to impress someone." Again, he paused, realizing he hadn't intended to say that last part. "But Gwendolyn and her great-aunt have a perfect solution to our eviction problem. You know

Chapter 22 – Moving In

that unused garage they have? Well, it's actually a carriage house with a small second-story apartment where the carriage driver lived."

"Yeah," Matt added between bites of pancakes. "Gerallt told me that it was full of dusty old junk."

"We're going to move in!" Matt's father said, as if they were moving into a palace instead of what amounted to little more than a cramped and cluttered set of storage rooms. "That way, we won't get evicted, and I won't have to worry about paying rent with the measly salary I'm making. Best of all, we won't have to move into a shelter or away from Gwen... from Hawthorne."

Tina and Matt gave each other a knowing look. Obviously, Gerallt had been right about how their father felt about his mother.

"Dad, even assuming the place is livable once it's clean, it's only got two bedrooms. You're not saying Tina and I have to share a bedroom, are you?"

"I'm not sharing a bedroom with Matt," Tina decreed, her arms folded over chest. "No way; you can forget about it."

"Don't worry, Tina. You'll get your own room," her father reassured her. "Matt's moving in with Gerallt."

"Sounds good to me," Matt said, happy to spend more time with Gerallt, not to mention not having to sleep with his father and sister in the garage.

The Secrets of Hawthorne House

Thirty minutes later, the Mitchells and Hawthornes stood at the door to the carriage house, a two-story rectangular brick building across the garden from Hawthorne House.

"I'm afraid no one's been in heah in fifty years," Vivianne said, placing a key in the rust-covered lock. It wouldn't budge.

"Here, let me help with that," Sam said. Taking the key, he inserted it into the lock and tried to turn it. Once more, the key refused to budge. "The lock's rusted shut. Give me a second while I run back home and get some WD-40. That'll loosen it right up."

"Try again, Sam, "Gwendolyn encouraged. "I'm sure you can do it." Sam tried again, and the key turned with a loud, metallic squeak. None of the Mitchells had seen her touch an antique locket at her throat or notice her lips moving silently.

Sam opened the door. Although it was nearly freezing outside, it seemed much colder as they all filed into the gloomy interior. The sky was overcast, and the weak sunlight barely made it through the dirt and cobwebs that covered the rows of windows lining both sides of the room.

Straight ahead, a narrow stairway led steeply up into the coachman's quarters. Across the room, they could dimly see the closed door to the tack room and a row of four empty horse stalls. A long-abandoned workbench and some shelves holding a few partially used cans of paint lined the wall to their right. The main area of the floor was bare, with the carriage having been sold long ago. The car that was wrecked

Chapter 22 – Moving In

in the accident that killed Vivianne's parents had never been replaced.

Used to running things after living so many years by herself, Vivianne immediately took charge. "Gerallt and Matt, run back tah the house and fetch us some of the spare oil lamps and a tin of oil from the down cellah. Tina and Gareth, go bring back every broom and mop in the house. Gwendolyn and Gwyneth, you can get a couple buckets of hot soapy watah and some old rags. Sam and I will head upstairs and see if we can get any watah out of the old pipes.

Once the others had left, Vivianne turned to Sam and said, "I've nevah seen the need for it myself, but you'll probably want tah have electricity installed. Just remember, you will have to cover the cost yourself. If not, we have several 2-gallon tins of lamp oil and plenty of boxes of candles so you won't want foah light foah at least a month or two. You will need tah purchase more firewood; I only bought enough tah last the winter with a small reserve. There just won't be enough for all of us, although I suppose we can spare some coal until you can arrange delivery of moah."

Vivianne and Sam made their way up the narrow stairs, following the footprints Gerallt and Gareth had left behind during their earlier explorations. The oaken steps were surprisingly sturdy after so many years of neglect. Upon reaching the top, they stopped to survey the challenge that faced them.

"Wow," Sam said, when his eyes had sufficiently adjusted to the darkness. Mounds of old furniture, steamer trunks, boxes, and yet more boxes filled the large open area forming the front half of the apartment. Clearly, the combined kitchen, dining room, and living room had become the final resting place for decades of things too good to throw away. The floor was piled high with things that at one time could have been worth keeping. For most, mildew and long years of neglect had stolen any value they once might have had.

"What do you want us to do with everything?" Sam asked.

"Most of it will likely need tah be put out for the garbage men or taken out tah the fiah pit and burned," Vivianne replied. "You might find some of it useful. Anything else of value will need tah be carried intah the down cellah. As I sort through this mess, you, Gerallt, and Matt can carry it where it needs tah go."

A few minutes later, Gerallt and Matt arrived with a tin of kerosene and several oil lamps. Tina and Gareth followed them up the stairs, their arms filled with brooms, mops, dust pans, and garbage bags. Last to arrive were Gwendolyn and Gwyneth, each carrying a bucket of soapy water and a bag of rags.

"Gwendolyn, deah, why don't you begin with the kitchen? You can see if the faucets work. Hopefully, we won't have to carry any moah watah in from the house." Turning to the children, Vivianne continued, "Gwyneth, you and Tina can start by gettin' the grime off the windows so we have more light tah work by. Gerallt and Matt, how about the two of you carryin' up a couple armloads of firewood so Sam can light the stove? It's as cold as a miser's heart in heah."

Chapter 22 – Moving In

Everyone got to work with Vivianne playing the role of general as she directed their battle against decades of dust and neglect. By lunch-time, a fire in the cast-iron potbellied stove had warmed up the little apartment. Gwyneth and Tina had cleaned the windows in the combined kitchen and living area. Sam and the boys had removed at least a third of the boxes and furniture that had been piled on the floor.

As Vivianne predicted, most of the removed items ended up in a pile by the garbage cans. The majority of the rest had been carried down into the basement of the main house. The remaining items had been moved downstairs to be cleaned, restored, and hopefully sold as antiques.

About 11 o'clock, Vivianne and Gwendolyn left to fix lunch, leaving Sam in charge. While most of the wooden furniture was salvageable, the mattresses and everything made from cloth were mildewed and moldy beyond repair. Sam, Matt, and Gerallt carried them down to the road for garbage pickup, while Gwyneth and Tina began cleaning the two now-empty bedrooms.

Ten minutes later, Tina stopped by the other bedroom to ask Gwyneth if there were any more newspapers she could use for cleaning the windows. When she opened the bedroom door, Tina could hardly believe her eyes. The windows were spotless, the dust was gone, and Gwyneth was almost finished with mopping the floor.

"Oh my God, Gwyneth! How in the world did you get so much done? I'm still working on the windows."

The Secrets of Hawthorne House

"Uh... practice?" Gwyneth answered, somewhat nervously. "Since movin' heah, Mothah has had me doin' the dustin' and washin' the windows." She smiled sheepishly. "Do you need somethin'?"

"Yeah, I ran out of newspapers. Do you have any left?"

"Ovah on the nightstand," Gwyneth replied, hoping that Tina wouldn't notice she hadn't touched her own stack of newspapers.

"Thanks, Gwyneth. Can you help me when you're done? I'm a lot slower than you are."

"Sure," Gwyneth answered, trying hard not to look unhappy at the prospect of having to help clean Tina's bedroom without using her gift from the Goddess.

Half an hour later, Gwendolyn climbed the narrow staircase to see everyone sitting on the floor, resting with their backs against the wall. The upstairs was completely empty. "Wow, you've been quite the busy beavahs since I left. I bet by suppahtime you'll have everything cleaned and ready for you tah move in. Anyway, I came out tah tell you that lunch is ready. Come in and wash up."

She paused, realizing how dirty everyone's clothes were. "But first, make sure you dust each other off. Why if dust were black, you'd look like a family of chimney sweeps. Ahnt Vivianne will have a case of the conniptions if you come in like that. In fact, while you're washin' up, I think I'd bettah find some towels tah cover the chairs before you sit down."

Chapter 22 – Moving In

"So, Sam," Vivianne said from her chair at the head of the table, "When do you think you and Tina will be movin' in?"

Caught with his mouth full of fried chicken, it took a few seconds before Sam could swallow and answer. "I notified the landlord yesterday and told him that we would be out in a week. I'd say if I work on it during the day, and the kids help in the evenings, we could probably move in three or four days."

"Great." Gwendolyn said, "That will give me time tah sew up some curtains. And we should put on a couple coats of paint; the old wall-paper is in bad shape, and a light color would brighten up the place."

"Once lunch is over," Sam said. "I'll drop by the hardware store and pick up some cheap curtain rods, paint brushes, and a gallon of their least-expensive white paint. Can anyone think of anything else I should get while I'm there?"

"Do you know anything about stained glass?" Vivianne asked.

"A little. It's something I have always been interested in, and I've watched several YouTube videos on it. Why do you ask?"

"One of the stained-glass windows in my bedroom is cracked and has a small hole in it. I've had tah put tape over it to keep the cold air out. Do you think you can fix it?"

"I don't see why not, although I don't think I can get what I'll need here in Hawthorne. Once we get done with the move, I'll drive down to Fort Wayne and buy the glass and other things I'll need."

"Thank you, Sam. It will be nice tah have a man around the house tah repair things."

"Think nothing of it. I'm glad I can help."

Sam glanced at his son, before turning to Gerallt. "Once we're done here, you can help Matt carry over his bed."

"I've been giving that some thought," Vivianne said. "We've been usin' the room next tah Gerallt's as a storeroom. There's no reason why we can't move everythin' in theah down tah the down cellah. That way, Matt can have his own room and still be close tah Gerallt."

"That would be great," Matt said. "I was afraid there wouldn't be space for my bed in Gerallt's room."

"But Ahnt Vivianne," Gwyneth said, "what about... you know, our things for *gŵyl lleuad lawn?*"

"There is plenty of room for the chest in the Sabbat room," Vivianne replied.

"*Gwill lyad laun?*" Sam asked, trying his best to pronounce the Welsh words he'd just heard.

"Our holy days," Gwendolyn answered, before rapidly changing the subject. "While you get the paint, we'll start cleanin' out the storeroom. There's not that much in theah. Matt will be able tah start movin' his stuff over tomorrow."

"But what about your computer, TV, and video games?" Tina asked, suddenly realizing there was no electricity in the Hawthorne House.

Sam looked at his son, hoping that Matt wouldn't make a scene about being forced to live without

Chapter 22 – Moving In

electricity. "We'll just have to rough it until I can afford to have electricity run to the carriage house. Besides, it will do us all good to take a break from TV and games for a while. Just think of it as roughing it like when we'd go camping."

"Don't worry, Dad. Gerallt and I will find something to do," Matt replied, giving his friend a knowing nod. Yes, Matt and Gerallt knew exactly what they'd do once the coast was clear.

Chapter 23
The Stolen Amulet

It was cold and cloudy that Saturday morning in late November. Although it had not snowed for a week, a few remnants of snow remained in the shadows on the north sides of the houses along Hawthorne Drive. Neither rain nor snow had been in the morning's forecast, but a swiftly moving layer of low gray clouds threatened to make the weatherman a liar.

An old white minivan drove past the Hawthorne House. It slowed and stopped before turning around to park in front of the Victorian mansion. As if made sick by the cold weeks of winter weather, the minivan shuddered and loudly coughed up a large cloud of smoke as its engine rattled and died. The van had seen better days. The long ladders on its roof rack were covered with a rainbow of splattered paint Long, brown patches of rust had eaten through the base of its metal body where salt and dirty slush had splashed up from the road. "Smith's Painting and Home Repair" was written in large black letters on its side.

Its driver was a man in his late forties. Like his van, George Smith had seen better days. His teeth were yellowed with tobacco stains. Smith's thin receding hair was a greasy black, and three days of stubble covered his chin. His clothes looked as if they had been slept in for days, and they had.

Letting his bloodshot eyes roam over the old Hawthorne House, Smith was surprised to see its

Chapter 23 – The Stolen Amulet

many recent improvements. He took notice of its new coat of paint and the repairs to the porch railing, angry that someone else got the work that should have been his. Leaning forward, Smith reached back and pulled a metal flask out of the hip pocket of his tattered overalls. He took a swig of cheap whiskey, wiped his mouth with the back of his hand, and returned the flask to its familiar hiding place. Then he looked up at the roof and the original gingerbread trim under its eaves. Noting that several pieces were missing or hanging loose, he smiled a predatory smile.

Smith got out of his minivan, walked up the sidewalk, and climbed the stairs onto the mansion's wrap-around porch. He stood for a minute, appreciating the obvious value of the narrow, stained-glass windows lining both sides of the old oak door. Lifting the ornate silver doorknocker, he let it fall with a deep, dull thud.

A few seconds later, he heard soft footsteps and saw a shadow approach through the stained-glass followed by the sound of four separate locks unlocking and the sliding back of a deadbolt. The heavy oak door slowly creaked open a few inches before being stopped by its thick safety chain. An old woman skeptically peered out, first at the man and then over his shoulder at his rundown minivan.

"Good morning, Ma'am," the handyman said, bowing slightly. "I was driving by and noticed that some of your gingerbread trim needs to be repaired. My name's George Smith, and I do home repairs and painting," he continued, waving vaguely back at the words painted on the side of his minivan. "Perhaps I could be of service." He opened his wallet and handed her an old business card, its edges bent and worn.

Vivianne Hawthorne didn't like the looks of the stranger, but neither did she like the looks of her broken gingerbread trim. It was the last major repair work before the outside of her house would be done. "How much?" she asked warily, remembering how rapidly her bank account had dropped since Gwendolyn and her children had moved in.

"Well, I usually charge $300 for a job like this," the handyman replied. Then, he noticed the worried look flicker across Vivianne' face. "But seeing as this is a slow time of year, I suppose I could possibly go as low as $200 if money's a problem." Smith was also growing desperate. His rent was nearly a week overdue, he was out of cigarettes, and he badly needed both beer and booze.

Vivianne looked at him with distrust, wondering if she had really detected the faint smell of liquor on his breath. "I'll tell you what," she finally offered. "I'll give you $100 tah do the front of the house, and if you do a good job, I'll give you another $100 tah do the back."

"Well, Ma'am, you've got yourself a deal," Smith agreed, smiling at the thought of earning enough money that he could finally pay his rent and have enough left to take care of his other needs.

Vivianne Hawthorne briefly watched as Smith sauntered back down the steps. Hoping that she hadn't made a mistake, she closed and locked the old oak

Chapter 23 – The Stolen Amulet

door before heading back to the kitchen to work on the large pot pie for dinner.

Meanwhile, the handyman got to work. He started by walking around the house, counting the pieces of trim that needed to be replaced. Using one of his long extension ladders, he climbed up and removed a piece to use as a pattern. Over the next hour, he used a carpenter's pencil to trace the trim's intricate pattern onto a piece of plywood that he'd spread across two sawhorses.

No sense paying for a solid piece of wood, Smith thought. *She'll never notice its plywood once I have it painted.*

Smith got out his jigsaw, plugged it into one end of a long, outdoor extension cord, and carried the other end to the porch in search of an outdoor outlet. He couldn't find one. Frustrated, he walked over to the door and knocked once more.

Returning to the door, Vivianne Hawthorne unlocked the locks, opened it as far as its chain would allow, and asked, "Ayuh, Mr. Smith?"

"Excuse me, Ma'am, but you don't seem to have an outdoor electric outlet. Would you mind plugging this in inside your house?" he asked, holding up the end of his electric cord.

"I'm sorry, Mr. Smith, but we don't have electricity heah. I'm afraid that you will have tah saw the wood somewhere else."

"Well, I'll be," Smith replied, scratching his head as she closed the door and relocked all of its locks. "I guess I'll just have to do this in the parking lot outside my apartment," he muttered to himself as he stared at the closed door before him. "Oh well, I need to buy some paint anyway." Packing up the plywood, sawhorses, saw, and extension cord, he drove off to the hardware store for some cheap paint.

Two hours later, the handyman returned with the new pieces of gingerbread and a couple gallons of paint that nearly matched the trim's original color. Soon, he was back on his ladder, nailing them up under the eaves along the front of the house.

Having rushed through breakfast and headed upstairs, Matt and Gerallt had no idea that Vivianne had hired a handyman to replace the broken trim under the eaves of Hawthorne House. They'd been so engrossed in Matt's secret lessons that at lunchtime they'd stopped just long enough to grab a couple of sandwiches to take back to Gerallt's room.

Smith had finished with the front of the house and had moved on to the back. The entire afternoon passed, as the handyman's ladder steadily moved closer to Gerallt's window.

Meanwhile, both boys were sitting on Gerallt's bedroom floor, facing the locked door with their backs to the windows. The small battery-operated radio that Matt had given Gerallt was sitting on his desk, playing just loud enough to make it difficult for anyone outside the door to hear what they were saying. The reason for their caution was that Gerallt was secretly teaching Matt how to use his amulet.

Chapter 23 – The Stolen Amulet

Gerallt tried not to think of what would happen if anyone in his family discovered what they were doing. It was bad enough that Matt was introducing Gerallt to the wonders of the modern world. That was merely against druidae culture and traditions. But teaching an outsider to use the sacred gift of the Goddess was entirely different; it was both a high crime and a heinous sin.

Matt was having trouble remembering the different prayers to the goddess, or magic spells as he preferred to think of them. He was also having trouble correctly pronouncing the Latin in which they must be spoken.

"Gerallt," Matt said, while practicing the levitation spell on a handful of pennies. "I just don't get how you do it. I can get the first one to float, but as soon as I try to make the second one rise, the first one falls."

"You've got tah concentrate more," Gerallt advised, taking the amulet. "*Magna Dea, fac, quaesumus, ut nummi ascendant!*" he intoned. One by one, the coins floated up to hang in the air in front of Gerallt. "*Magna Dea, fac, quaesumus, ut nummi descendant!*" The coins fell onto the floor. "Holdin' the amulet and sayin' the words are only parts of the prayah. You also have tah form a clear picture in your mind of exactly what you want the Goddess tah do. Otherwise, she won't grant your request. Try it again, and this time, try tah visualize all the coins floatin'. Close your eyes if it helps. And don't start worryin' about one fallin', or you'll see it fall in your mind, and then it really will fall." He handed his amulet back to Matt.

Matt held out the amulet and looked at the coins on the rug. He closed his eyes. *"Magna Dea, fac, quaesumus, ut nummi ascendant!"* he said, concentrating on getting the intonation just right. This time, several of the coins rose into the air to dance jerkily in front of him. Matt opened his eyes, and one of the coins began to fall. He closed his eyes, and the coin slowly rose again to join the others. This time when Matt opened his eyes, the coins continued to float. Eventually, their jerking stopped, and they slowly drifted in front of him like a small copper constellation.

There was no porch or balcony along the back of the house, so Smith had to use his longest extension ladder to reach the eaves of the Hawthorne House. The boys concentrated so much on Matt's training that the music in Gerallt's room masked the sound of the handyman moving his ladder next to Gerallt's window.

The sun was dropping behind a thick, gray blanket of clouds as Smith slowly climbed up to where he was even with Gerallt's window. Pausing to catch his breath, he glanced inside. Sitting on her perch in the corner next to the window, Gerallt's pet crow Nightwing cocked her head sideways to stare at the surprised handyman. Intrigued, Smith leaned over and looked deeper into the darkened room lit only by several small candles. With the clouds hiding the sun, the handyman cast no shadow into the room that

Chapter 23 – The Stolen Amulet

could have given his presence away to the two boys sitting on the floor with their backs to the window.

At first, Smith only thought it strange that the boys would have a pet crow. Just as the growing cold and darkness were convincing him to continue his climb and paint the last few pieces of trim, Smith saw something far stranger than Nightwing. Several small objects appeared to be floating in front of one of the boys. The objects flickered as they slowly rotated in the dim candlelight. Matt shifted slightly, and the handyman suddenly saw Gerallt's golden amulet glittering in the boy's hand. Fearing that he was having another hallucination from his longtime daily diet of beer and booze, Smith leaned back, closed his eyes, and hung tightly to the cold aluminum rails of the extension ladder.

There was a knock on the door.

Inside their room, Matt whispered "*Magna Dea, fac, quaesumus, ut nummi descendant!*" and the small cloud of coins rained onto the carpet.

The old-fashioned doorknob started to turn. "Come on, you two. Open this door!" Gwyneth called when the locked door wouldn't open.

Matt quickly hid the amulet in his shirt pocket, as Gerallt jumped up and unlocked the door.

Gwyneth opened the door and walked in. "I've called you three times already, and you would have heard me if you didn't have that infernal thing in heah," she said, looking at the radio with annoyance. "Suppah's on the table, and we're all waitin' for you." Noticing the pennies scattered on the floor, she gave the two a quizzical look. "What have you two been doing in heah all day?" she demanded.

"Nothing," they both replied simultaneously.

Gwyneth looked from one to the other. She noticed their guilty expressions and was about to ask them again.

"Hurry up, or we'll start without you!" Gareth yelled up the stairs.

Gwyneth paused for a second before turning and heading back downstairs.

Realizing that it had been hours since they'd eaten their small lunch, the boys needed no further encouragement. They jumped up and headed for the door. Following Gerallt out into the hallway, Matt stopped and pulled Gerallt's amulet out of his pocket. In his rush to get downstairs, Matt thoughtlessly laid it on Gerallt's desk instead of giving it back to its owner. Shutting the door behind him, Matt followed Gerallt down to dinner.

When Smith opened his eyes and looked back in through the window, the room was empty. He was about to chalk it all up to one of his occasional alcoholic hallucinations when he saw Gerallt's amulet lying on the desk. Its golden surface and emerald-like jewel glittered in the candlelight. The handyman listened, but the room was utterly silent. Intrigued by what he saw, he wondered what the amulet might be worth.

With the practiced stealth of a jungle cat, Smith silently lifted the window and carefully crawled inside. He walked over to the desk and picked up the

Chapter 23 – The Stolen Amulet

amulet. The green gemstone in its center sparkled, and the gold-colored metal glowed warmly in the candlelight. It was surprisingly heavy, much too heavy for costume jewelry.

Behind him, Nightwing felt the cold enticing breeze on her feathers. The stranger's presence made her uneasy, and she flew soundlessly outside.

Pocketing the amulet, Smith climbed back out the window, closing it behind him. The handyman quickly finished painting the last piece of trim. Lowering his ladder, he carried it and the paint back to his van. In a rush to leave with the stolen necklace, he stowed them away, not even bothering to clean his brushes. Finally, he headed for the front door and his money.

Matt and the Hawthorne family were in the middle of dinner when Smith knocked on the door. Vivianne looked across at Gwendolyn, who had gone outside and inspected the work when the handyman was three-fourths done. When Gwendolyn nodded her approval, Vivianne got up, gave him a check, and returned to the dining room as the handyman drove off into the dark.

"Who was that?" Gerallt asked, once his great-aunt had returned to the table.

"Just a handyman who repaired and painted the trim around the roof," she answered.

"You might have known that if you paid more attention tah what goes on around heah," Gerallt's mother added with a smile. "You've been up in your room so much that I barely recognize you anymore.

By the way, just what have you two doin' up there all day?"

"Just talking," Gerallt answered, with a hint of a guilty expression.

Unnoticed by her mother, Gwyneth gave both boys a searching look.

After a short drive, Smith pulled his battered old minivan into the parking lot of the Shadyside apartments. Originally a cheap motel built during the 1950s, it had since been converted into a two-story complex of cheap, one-bedroom apartments that had seen better days. Now, it served as low-cost housing for people who typically leased their apartments on a month-by-month basis.

Unlocking his door, Smith entered a room that looked more like a junkyard than a place to live. The initial overwhelming smell was of stale beer and dirty socks. However, that was instantly followed by the smell of old pizza and rotting Chinese food coming from piles of dirty dishes that overran the small sink and covered every available surface.

The handyman stepped into his private garbage dump, turned on the lights to reveal pile after pile of dirty clothes, and locked the door securely behind him. Shoving more dirty clothes onto his already filthy floor, he flopped down onto the old lumpy couch in front of the TV.

Smith reached into a pocket of his paint-covered coveralls and pulled out the amulet the boy had been

Chapter 23 – The Stolen Amulet

holding. Lifting it up, he examined it under a ceiling light that served as a mass graveyard for dead flies and cockroaches. The metal of the heavy golden object looked particularly smooth and shiny on the handyman's dirty, rough hands. A strange script surrounded a large green jewel in the center.

"Jeez, this thing looks real," Smith muttered, turning the amulet over to examine its back. Both the front and the back were covered with a strange, otherworldly script. "Maybe it is real."

Groaning with sore muscles from climbing up and down his extension ladder, Smith walked over to the tiny kitchenette. He opened the nearly empty refrigerator and pulled out his last beer from where it sat between two bowls holding what appeared to be biology experiments gone bad. He opened the can, took a long, appreciative swig, and walked back to where he'd left the amulet lying on his dirty coffee table.

"Maybe, just maybe," he said, remembering how the coins levitated when the boy had held the amulet.

Sheepishly, he pulled out a handful of small change from his pocket and dropped them onto the coffee table next to the amulet. Then picking up Gerallt's sacred relic, he held it in front of him just as he remembered Matt doing.

"Float," he said to the coins.

Nothing happened.

"Rise up!" Smith commanded, sounding like a preacher from his distant youth attempting to energize a congregation made sleepy by a long and boring sermon.

Still, nothing happened. The amulet ignored him.

"It was probably just my eyes," he muttered angrily, drinking the last of his beer and throwing the can on the floor where it joined its brethren in a mountain of empties.

"What I need is a drink," he said to the silent amulet. "But I don't have any money, and I can't cash the old woman's check until Monday. Besides, I don't think I want a unique piece like you on me if the cops happen to show up looking for stolen property. I think I'm just going to have to stop by the pawn shop before going to the liquor store."

Smith pocketed Gerallt's amulet and left, carefully locking his door to keep his worthless possessions safe from the other thieves in the apartment complex.

Only a block and a half away, Peter's Pawn Shop stood sandwiched between a bail bondsman and a bankruptcy lawyer. The handyman looked into its barred window, noticing a camera that he'd stolen the previous week. Passing under three brass globes, the traditional symbol of pawn shops, he entered the door. His legs broke a beam of light, and a buzzer sounded, announcing his entrance.

The proprietor, Peter Henderson, a portly man with the cunning eyes of a wolf peering out of the fat jowls of a pig, entered from the back room. Standing behind a glass counter containing a collection of used watches and assorted jewelry, he looked at the handyman who regularly arrived with property of

Chapter 23 – The Stolen Amulet

uncertain origin. "What do you have for me this time?"

"This," Smith replied, placing the heavy amulet on the glass counter in front of the pawnbroker.

The pawnbroker picked up the amulet. He was surprised by the weight of what he had initially taken for a piece of gaudy costume jewelry. He took out his magnifying loop and looked at the gold-colored metal disk with its large, green gemstone. He looked for the tiny imprint of a number followed by the letter K that would symbolize the number of gold karats. But there was none. Smith considered that it might be foreign and too old to have the stamp. With the amulet's strange script and unique design, it wasn't like anything he'd ever seen. "I'll have to take this into the back and test it to see what it's made of.

"Okay," the handyman answered. "You haven't stiffed me yet, at least not too much." He grinned uncomfortably, hoping that he'd finally stolen something valuable enough to make up for the risks he'd been taking.

The pawnbroker took the amulet to a cluttered desk in the back room and looked closely at the jewel under his microscope. It wasn't glass, but it didn't seem to be a natural or synthetic emerald, either. In fact, he didn't quite know what to make of it.

Smith took out a small vial of nitric acid and touched its wetted glass stopper to the back surface of the amulet. The metal didn't dissolve, and no spot of blue copper nitrate appeared, which implied that the purity of the gold was very high. Still, something about the color of the metal seemed odd. The pawnbroker took out a steel stylus and tried to engrave a tiny scratch on its edge where no one would notice. But the metal of the amulet remained perfectly smooth. Because gold is soft, that meant that the gold content couldn't be very high. Possibly, it contained platinum in addition to the gold. Whatever it was, it was valuable, even if only for the value of the metal and the strange green gemstone.

"It's costume jewelry," the pawnbroker lied upon returning to the counter in the front of the store. "Good quality costume jewelry, but costume jewelry, nevertheless. Still, it's fairly unique and will not be easy for me to get rid of. I can't just put it here in my case; I'll have to take it down to Indianapolis. The most I can give you is 50 dollars for it."

"Well, I don't know. It's got to be worth five times that just for the gold," Smith countered, hoping to have gotten at least twice that amount."

"It's not gold, just gold plating over lead," Peter replied. "Still, George, I'll tell you what I'll do. Since you're such a regular supplier, I'll give you $75. But that's my final offer."

The handyman knew he was getting cheated, but he also knew he had no other way of getting rid of the piece. Besides, he could feel the nearby liquor store calling him. "Done," he said, holding out his hand.

The pawnbroker counted out three twenties, a ten, and a five. Pocketing the money, Smith quickly left, disappearing into the night from which he'd come. An hour later, he was snoring, passed out on his couch with a half-empty bottle of cheap whiskey sitting open on the coffee table.

When dinner was over, Matt and Gerallt headed back upstairs. Entering his room, Gerallt suddenly noticed that Nightwing was not sitting on her perch. He looked over to the top of his wardrobe, but Nightwing wasn't there either.

"Where's Nightwing?" Gerallt asked. Both boys searched the room, but Nightwing was nowhere to be found.

Matt noticed the amulet was not on Gerallt's desk where he had left it in his haste to go down to dinner. "Gerallt, the amulet's gone!"

"What?" Gerallt demanded, looking at his desk. The ancient, carved wooden box, in which he kept his amulet when he wasn't wearing it, was there. He opened the box, but the amulet was gone. "How did you know it wasn't in its box?"

"We were in such a hurry to eat that I forgot to put it back," Matt answered sheepishly. "I just left it lying on top of the desk. I'm sorry!"

Both boys looked around the room, hoping that Nightwing had knocked it behind the desk or had merely hidden it somewhere. Neither crow nor amulet was to be seen.

"Look at this!" Matt said, pointing at the window ledge. There was a partial handprint in fresh paint along with some paint smudges from Smith's overalls.

"The handyman!" both boys exclaimed.

"He must have kifed it," Gerallt said, having deduced Smith had stolen it. "And Nightwing must have escaped when he entered through the open window."

"He must have seen it lying on your desk," Matt added, feeling very sorry and responsible. "I should have put it into its box so it wouldn't have been lying out in the open for him to see."

"*Magna Dea!*" Gerallt swore. "You don't suppose he saw you practicin' with it, do you? What ah we goin' tah do? Mothah will have a fit when she learns that it's gone."

Gerallt paused as the magnitude of the situation hit him. "Mothah will realize I was showin' it tah you. Matt, if she finds out that I've been teachin' you, she'll have no choice but tah report what's happened tah the High Coven." Gerallt's fear was rapidly approaching panic. "They'll come and find the thief. They'll retrieve the amulet," he whispered.

"Isn't that good?" Matt asked, trying to find something, anything positive about the situation. "Sure, you'll get in trouble, but it won't be the end of the world. At least, you'll get your amulet back."

"No, Matt, I won't. The High Coven will keep it, and I'll nevah get another. They'll force everyone tah shun me, to cast me out!"

"No, they won't," Matt said, "because we won't tell your mom. We can't. We'll have to get your amulet back ourselves."

"But how?"

Chapter 23 – The Stolen Amulet

"First, we have to find out who the handyman is and where he lives."

"I know," Gerallt said. "We'll ask Gareth. He was always watchin' the othah people who worked on the house. Maybe he got a good look at him and what he drove."

They ran down the stairs and barged through the door into his brother's room. "Gareth, you busy?" Gerallt asked.

"Not really," Gareth said, looking up from a book he was reading. "Oh, hi, Matt! What are you two up tah?"

"Nothin' much," Gerallt lied, hoping that Gareth wouldn't notice how worried he was. "You remembah the handyman who worked on the outside of the house today?"

"Sure. A skuzzy looking man with an old minivan. Kind of creepy. Why?"

"He left his hammer on the porch," Matt lied. "I was going to call and tell him about it. You don't happen to know his name or anythin', do you?"

"No," Gareth answered, "but his truck had the name of his business written on it. It was 'Smith Paintin' and Repair' or something like that. He gave Ahnt Vivianne his business card, and I think she left it on the sideboard in the kitchen. You can ask her. She'd know."

"Thanks, Gareth. I will," Matt said as he and Gerallt headed down the stairs for the kitchen. Sure enough, the old business card was still on the counter where Gareth had seen his great-aunt leave it. Matt pocketed it, and the boys headed back up to Gerallt's room.

"516 West Main Street, Apt. 13," Matt read. "That's downtown, maybe 10 or 12 blocks away. It shouldn't take us more than 20 minutes to walk there if we leave now."

"But first, I have tah get somethin'," Gerallt said. "Wait heah. I'll be right back."

Gerallt snuck down the hall and quietly entered the Sabbat room. It was the room where the Hawthorne family held their weekly Sabbat ceremonies to worship the Goddess Modron and ask for her blessings. Strictly forbidden to outsiders such as the Mitchells, the Hawthornes rarely entered it except during the family's ritual observance of the Sabbat. Still, Gerallt listened outside the door for any indication of someone's presence. Satisfied that the Sabbat room was empty, he silently opened the door and slipped inside.

The family altar to the Goddess stood in the middle of the room where the Hawthornes could link hands and form a sacred circle around it. On top stood the goddess's golden chalice, the traditional golden sickle used to cut mistletoe growing on oak trees, the incense brazier, and the most sacred and powerful relic of them all. It was the small statue of the Goddess holding a tiny piece of the starstone that she had given her loyal servants.

Gerallt approached the ancient, heavy wooden chest that held the family's ritual robes and religious relics. Then hesitating for a second, he breathed a

Chapter 23 – The Stolen Amulet

silent prayer for forgiveness before opening it. Reaching in, Gerallt searched through the chest's contents and quickly found what he was looking for. He pulled out a wooden box, the lid of which was carved with a symbol representing the sacred gifts that the Goddess Modron had given to her faithful servants.

Gerallt opened the ornately-carved reliquary and found what he was looking for: two wands and three amulets like the one the handyman had stolen. He took one of the amulets and hid it in his pocket before closing the box and returning it to its place in the wooden chest.

Gerallt paused before taking the borrowed amulet out of his pocket. As only the most senior member of the coven was authorized to bind a gift from the Goddess to its owner, what Gerallt was about to do was not just forbidden. It was a grave sin. Hoping that the Goddess would understand and that his mother and great-aunt would never discover his transgression, Gerallt slowly reached out and gently rested his fingertips on the base of the statue.

Although the room was quite cool, the statue was warm, almost hot to the touch. An electric current made Gerallt's fingers tingle as he said the prayer that bound the borrowed amulet to him. Withdrawing his hand, he returned the amulet to his pocket and smiled. Now, he knew that it would conduct his prayers to the Great Goddess.

Stopping at the door, Gerallt paused to listen for footsteps in the hallway. Hearing only silence, he left the Sabbat room, shut its door, and quickly returned to his own room.

"Gerallt, where did you go?" Matt asked, once Gerallt had closed the door.

"Tah get this," Gerallt answered, holding up the amulet he'd borrowed. "I thought I'd probably need anothah one if we're goin' tah get mine back again. Let's go befoah it gets any later."

Gerallt and Matt headed downstairs, but they were stopped before reaching the door.

"Where do you two think you're goin'?" Gerallt's mother asked as they were putting on their coats.

"Just for a walk," Gerallt answered as he opened the door.

"Oh, no you don't," Gwendolyn answered. "You haven't even started youah papah foah English class, and it's due Monday."

"Mothah, I can do it tomorrow."

"No, you'll start it tonight. Show me that you have it half done, and you can go out for a few minutes. But not long. It's getting' really nippy out."

"But Mothah, by then it will be too late."

"Too late for what?"

The boys looked at each other. "Never mind," Gerallt answered as they turned and headed back upstairs to start on their homework.

"We'll just have to get it tomorrow," Matt said, once he closed the door to their room. "Besides, we need to make a plan." Matt paused and then smiled. "I know. Tomorrow, I'll call him on the phone and

Chapter 23 – The Stolen Amulet

pretend that I need him to do some work. I'll send him on a wild goose chase. Once he's gone, we can sneak into his place and find your amulet.

Chapter 24
The Secret Search

The next morning, Nightwing woke up Gerallt and Matt by tapping her beak on the window. After letting his crow into the room, Gerallt made sure to lock both of his windows. After Gerallt showed his mother his completed homework, the boys called the handyman. Unfortunately, there was no answer because Smith was still sleeping off the drinking he'd done the previous evening. The boys walked over to the Shadyside Apartments where the handyman lived.

"Now what do we do?" Gerallt asked, looking at the Smith's old minivan parked in front of the ground floor apartment with the number 13 on its door. "He's still inside. We cahn't search his apartment when he's still in it."

"You're right," Matt replied. "We'll just have to get him out." He pulled out his phone and redialed the number on the card. This time, he let the phone ring until the call ended. "No answer."

"Try again."

After two more tries, a groggy voice answered. "What?"

"Do you do repair work?" Matt asked, lowering his voice to sound more like his father's.

"Yeah," the handyman replied, trying to gently shake the cobwebs from his head without worsening his hangover headache.

Chapter 24 – Recovering Gerallt's Amulet

"I have a spare bedroom that I want to turn into a home office. I need some bookshelves and additional electrical outlets installed. Could you come over and let me know how much it would cost?" Matt continued, hoping that his voice sounded sufficiently mature to fool the handyman. He needn't have worried. Smith's greed made his answer certain.

"Sure, when can I come out and give you an estimate?"

"Could you come out right away? I have something I want to do later today," Matt answered.

"I'll be right over," Smith said. "Where do you live?"

"We're up at Tri-Lakes. Just head north on 33 until you get to County Line Road. Then turn left and go over 'til you see the signs for the lakes. We're at 25 Bait Road. It's a white house; you can't miss it." Matt continued, making up the address. A friend at school had told him how his uncle had taken him fishing at the lakes, but all Matt could remember was that it was near the edge of the county.

"Okay, I'll be there in about 20 minutes," Smith replied. "See you then."

Matt hung up, and it wasn't long before they saw the apartment door open and a disheveled man walk over to his minivan and drive away. The boys walked over and knocked on the door to make sure that no one else was home.

Now it was Gerallt's turn to act. He reached under his shirt and intoned "*Magna Dea, fac, quaesumus, ut ianua eius aperta stet!*" There was a soft click as the door unlocked. After looking around to see if anyone was watching, Gerallt opened the door and looked inside the empty apartment. The first thing to hit them was the disgusting smell.

"What a pig," Matt said as they entered, looking at the piles of dirty clothes, dirty dishes, empty bottles, and beer cans. "I hope he hasn't hidden it too well. I really don't want to touch any of this garbage."

"I think there's a searchin' spell," Gerallt said, "but my mothah hasn't taught it tah me yet. It would have come in wicked handy."

The boys started to search the apartment. At first, they were careful to put things back where they found them. However, as time passed without finding the amulet, they started to get sloppy, and then frantic. They looked under the couch cushions, in the clothes closet, dresser, and nightstand, beneath the bed, and under the mattress. They searched the kitchen, looking in the cupboards and drawers, behind the few pots, pans, and dishes that weren't covered in the remains of the previous meals, in the refrigerator, and even the freezer. Finally, Matt and Gerallt had no choice but to dig through the piles of dirty, smelly clothes.

"Okay, Gerallt, we have got to stop and get out of here," Matt said in frustration. "He has to have it on him or hidden in his minivan. Let's head over to the gas station, get a couple of sodas, and wait for him. Besides, my hands stink, and if I don't wash them right now, I'm going to scream."

Chapter 24 – Recovering Gerallt's Amulet

"But what if it's still heah? There has tah be someplace we missed." Gerallt argued.

"We have to leave now!" Matt countered. "He could get back any minute and find us here. And he's not going to be in a good mood after the wild goose chase I sent him on. And besides, if he's willing to sneak into your house and steal things, who knows what he might do to us if we're still here when he gets back."

Gerallt wasn't happy about leaving, but he didn't want to find out what Smith was capable of either. Taking one last frustrated look around the apartment, Gerallt joined Matt who stood waiting at the door. Matt opened it a crack, looked out, and saw that the minivan was still gone. Pushing the button on the inside doorknob to lock it, Matt joined Gerallt as the pair headed down the street to the gas station to wait.

Meanwhile, Gerallt's mother and great-aunt were sitting in the parlor of the Hawthorne House. Vivianne Hawthorne was reading a book from the family library.

"Vivianne," Gwendolyn said, "do you have any spare cloth? Gareth's had a growth spurt, and his shirt sleeves and pants legs are startin' tah look a dite short. I would like tah start sewin' him some new pants and shirts before the kids at the school start teasin' him about it."

Vivianne looked up from her book and nodded. "I should have enough." She thought for a minute. "You know, Gareth will be 13 next June, and Summah Solstice will only be a week after his birthday. We need tah start preparin' for him to receive his first gift from the Goddess. He'll need a new robe, and we will need to do somethin' special for him at the feast."

"Do you have a suitable amulet for him, or will we have tah ask the High Coven for one?"

"I was thinkin' of giving Gareth my first one." Vivianne smiled at the fond memories it evoked. "I keep it in the reliquary in the Sabbat room. The amulet's small and not very powerful, but it will be perfect for a novice."

"Can I see it?" Gwendolyn asked, remembering her own first amulet.

Vivianne led her niece up to the Sabbat room on the third floor. Once inside, she lifted the heavy lid of the ancient oak chest and began searching through the ritual robes, candles, herbs, and caldron for the small wooden reliquary that held the family's spare wands and amulets.

"Heah it is," Vivianne said, opening the box. "*Magna Dea*!" She exclaimed.

"What's wrong?"

"One of the amulets is missin'." Vivianne turned back to the open chest. "It must have fallen out. Just a second, and I'll find it." One by one, she started taking out the contents of the chest and placing them on the floor. But as she removed the last item, the chest stood empty. "It's not here," was all that she could say.

Chapter 24 – Recovering Gerallt's Amulet

"Is there anywhere else that you could have left it?" Gwendolyn asked. "Perhaps somewhere in youah bedroom or maybe in the library?"

"No, I have always kept all of the Goddess's gifts in the reliquary, and now it's gone. I can hardly dare to even think such a thing, but someone must have taken it. But how and when? And who?"

"It had to be the handyman!" Vivianne exclaimed. "I knew the instant I saw him that I couldn't trust him. But I just thought that he might try tah get my money without doin' the work. I didn't think he would steal from me."

"But how'd he get it?" Gwendolyn asked. "You always keep all of the windows locked, and you nevah let the man inside."

"Well, if he didn't steal the amulet, who did?"

"Hard tellin'," Vivianne answered. "Except for Gareth, we already have our own gifts from the Goddess. It's not as if any of us needs another one, especially given how weak the missing amulet is compared to our own. And Gareth wouldn't dare try tah get his hands on his amulet before Summah Solstice, especially knowin' what I would do tah him if I caught him with it. *Magna Dea*! Besides, he can't even use it because he hasn't been through his investiture yet. The Great Goddess would ignore his prayahs. It just makes no sense!"

After replacing everything into the chest, Vivianne led her niece back to the parlor. Sitting down on her rocking chair in the room's octagonal tower niche,

Vivianne stared out of one of the Gothic windows at the oaks lining the street.

Both women sat silently for a few moments, as the gravity of the situation sank in. Losing a sacred relic was unheard of. To have one stolen was unthinkable.

"Well, it has tah be someone who's had access tah the house. I hate tah think it, but you don't suppose Matt might have taken it, do you?"

"I falsely accused him once, and I'm not going tah make that mistake again," Gwendolyn countered. "Besides, he's always with Gerallt. And I can't believe he would risk their friendship. The two of them are inseparable."

Without wishing it, Vivianne was suddenly reminded of her former husband, John Carter, who had married her for her money. Once he'd found out she didn't have the enormous fortune that inheriting the Hawthorne House had implied, he'd run off with her best friend. She liked and trusted Sam, but she couldn't help but wonder. He had been in the house for supper and had briefly excused himself to go upstairs unescorted to use the bathroom when the one on the first floor one was occupied. Furthermore, she also knew that he was becoming desperate for money now that he'd lost his job. "Well, that just leaves Sam," she finally found herself saying.

"Vivianne, I can't believe I just heard you say that," Gwendolyn said, anger and betrayal welling inside her. "You know how we feel about each othah. No matter how badly he needs money, he would nevah steal from us."

Chapter 24 – Recovering Gerallt's Amulet

"I know, Gwendolyn," Vivianne said. "It's just that I don't know what tah think. Someone took it. And you know what that means. I'll have tah tell the High Coven. And when they come heah to investigate, they are not going tah like what they see: the children in public school instead of being taught properly heah at home, Gerallt befriendin' an outsidah, and you fallin' in love with one. We'll be lucky if they don't force me to sell my house and move us all back to The Colony."

Gwendolyn's blood ran cold. "We can't move away. Not now. There has to be another way."

"Maybe I did misplace it," Vivianne finally said, but she didn't really believe it. "We'll just have tah look until we find it."

"There he is," Matt said, as the handyman's minivan drove past them and into the parking lot of the Shadyside apartments. Even from their vantage point in front of the gas station across the street, Matt and Gerallt could tell that Smith was furious. They watched him slam his minivan door, stomp over to his apartment, unlock its door, and then slam it shut behind him. What they didn't see was Smith flopping down on his couch and finishing the half-empty bottle of whiskey from the previous night.

"Come on," Gerallt said, heading toward the parked minivan.

"Wait a second," Matt advised, worried that the handyman might quickly reappear.

"He's not going anywhere," Gerallt countered. "If he were, he wouldn't have come back heah first." With that, Gerallt started across the street, and Matt had no choice but to follow his friend.

Gerallt walked up to the white minivan, reached under his shirt to where Gareth's future amulet hung, and commanded, "*Magna Dea, fac, quaesumus, ianua eius aperta stet!*" The van door clicked softly as it unlocked. Without a second thought, Gerallt climbed inside and began to search the back of the van for his own missing amulet. "Come on, Matt, before someone sees us!"

Followed Gerallt in, Matt began to search the front of the van. They checked the glove compartment, under the seats, and in the tool boxes in the back. After ten minutes of hurried searching, they had to face the truth that the amulet wasn't in the van.

"Now what do we do?" Matt asked. "It's not here."

"*Magna Dea!*" Gerallt swore, throwing some rusted tools back into their box. "He must have it on him. We're goin' tah have tah confront him and demand that he give it back."

"Are you crazy? Sneaking around is one thing but confronting him face to face is something else. We know he's a thief. What if he's a kidnapper? Or worse?"

"Matt, I told you. I have no choice. If I don't get it back, I may nevah get another one. We're not talking about getting grounded for a month. The High Coven might send me away to one of our colonies where I'll

Chapter 24 – Recovering Gerallt's Amulet

nevah see anyone but other druidae for the rest of my life."

Matt considered their options but couldn't think of anything better. "Okay, Gerallt. I'm with you. Let's do it."

Gerallt rang the handyman's doorbell. Nothing happened. Gerallt rang it again, and still, nothing happened. He knocked on the door but was met only by silence.

"Do you think he left again while we were in his van?" Matt asked hopefully. "He could have gone for a walk or something."

"Only one way tah find out," Gerallt answered as he tried the door. It was locked. "*Magna Dea, fac, quaesumus, ianua eius aperta stet!*" Gerallt twisted the doorknob, and it opened.

Matt and Gerallt entered the darkened apartment, closed the door, and turned to see the sleeping handyman. Smith lay sprawled on the dirty couch, the empty whiskey bottle lying on the floor beneath his hand. He snored loudly while a trickle of drool dribbled down his unshaven chin.

"Yuck!" Matt whispered, as he watched the dangling drool vibrate with each snore and snort.

Ignoring the sour stench of the whiskey on Smith's breath, Gerallt carefully checked the pockets of the unconscious handyman's overalls for his missing amulet. Not finding it there, he tried looking for it around the handyman's neck. When that didn't work, he said, "Matt, help me turn him over so I can check his back pockets."

Matt stepped forward, warily watching the snoring Smith for any signs of waking. But as he stepped up to the couch, there was a solid thump as Matt's kneecap caught the edge of the coffee table. Although neither that sound nor Matt's stifled yelp woke the sleeping handyman, the resulting crash of a whiskey bottle on the floor did.

"Wha...?" the handyman asked, as his eyes opened to see Gerallt leaned over him. "Who are you?"

The stench of Smith's foul breath nearly made Gerallt retch as he recoiled.

Smith made an ineffectual grab at Gerallt but closed his eyes as the sudden movement caused his head to pound. "Who are you?" he hissed. "And what are you doing here?"

"Where's the amulet you kifed?" Gerallt demanded.

"What?" Smith groaned.

"The amulet. The amulet you stole from me!" Gerallt said, as he reached under his shirt. He pulled out the borrowed amulet and held it out in front of him like a weapon.

"What the?" Smith slurred, his gaze now on the amulet in Gerallt's hands. "But I already sold that... I thought I sold it." Then, remembering the whiskey he had bought with the money from the pawnbroker, he continued. "Yes, now I remember. I sold it last night." He groggily looked from the amulet to Gerallt and then Matt. The memory of the two boys levitating coins in the third-floor bedroom at the Hawthorne House slowly began to come back to him. "You! But

Chapter 24 – Recovering Gerallt's Amulet

how..." He tried to sit up, but his head pounded even harder, and he dropped back onto the couch.

"Tell me where you sold it!" Gerallt demanded.

"I ain't telling you squat!" Smith said.

"*Magna Dea, fac, quaesumus, ut lux sit!*" Gerallt commanded, aiming the borrowed amulet at Smith. A brilliant green light blazed out of its central gemstone and into the drunken man's eyes.

Smith cried out in pain as the bright light seemed to stab directly into his brain. "Stop!" the man cried, throwing his hands over his eyes. However, the brilliant light passed easily through his hands and closed lids. "Stop!" Smith begged, writhing in pain.

"Then tell me where you sold it!" Gerallt demanded.

"At the pawn shop! Peter's Pawn Shop; it's just down the street. Stop! Please stop!"

The green light dimmed and flickered out, as Gerallt stood triumphantly. "Do you know what will happen if you ever steal from me again?" he demanded, as the drunk lay moaning on the couch, holding his hands over his eyes.

Smith slowly shook his head, trying not to increase the pounding in his head.

"I will come back," Gerallt threatened. "And next time, I won't stop until you'ah blind!"

"No, please! I'll never bother again. I swear," Smith pleaded, looking at Gerallt through the tears of his bloodshot eyes.

"Let's go, Matt. We're done here."

The two boys walked outside into the winter sunshine. Gerallt slammed Smith's apartment door for good measure and smiled grimly when he heard a faint groan from the beaten man inside.

Matt looked at his friend with new respect and awe. "You know, Gerallt, I'm glad we're friends. I'd hate to have you as an enemy." He paused for a second. "You wouldn't actually blind him, would you?"

"Of course not," Gerallt answered, somewhat shocked that Matt could think he was actually capable of intentionally injuring someone. "I just said that tah scare him intah leavin' us alone. Even so, the light might not have been bright enough tah hurt enough if he didn't have such a wicked buzz on."

"Still, you can be really scary sometimes. Now I can see why people could be afraid of witches."

"I'm a druid, Matt, not a witch," Gerallt said. "But I see your point. It's just that he made me so honkin' ugly. When I think of what he did and what it could have meant, I guess I just lost it."

"Well, we're not home free yet," Matt reminded his friend. "We still need to get it from the pawn shop. Let's go."

Matt led Gerallt down the street to the shop with the three large, copper globes hanging over the door. They looked through the solid metal bars covering the picture window in front, but the amulet wasn't there. A buzzer announced their entry when their legs broke the light beam that guarded the entrance.

Chapter 24 – Recovering Gerallt's Amulet

Peter Henderson was sitting at his desk in the back room where he had been examining Gerallt's amulet. So far, he had verified that the green gemstone was not glass, crystal, emerald, or peridot. In spite of several tests, he also couldn't figure out what the metal was. After making a few calls, Henderson was getting ready to close his shop and drive down to Indianapolis, where he was going to sell the amulet to a fence who specialized in stolen jewelry.

Pushing himself back from his desk, the portly pawnbroker stood and walked to the front of the shop. The boys were busily looking at the glass cabinets that held rings and other jewelry that had never been claimed by their former owners.

"Can I help you?" Henderson asked, frowning at his potential customers. Kids their age rarely bought anything.

"Yes, we're looking for a birthday present for our grandmother," Matt lied. "She used to live overseas and likes old, foreign stuff. Do you have any costume jewelry that's not too expensive?"

"I have some estate jewelry that may fit the bill," he said, pulling out a tray containing antique broaches, necklaces, and rings.

The boys looked over the tray, but the amulet wasn't there.

"She really likes unusual things," Matt continued. "Do you have anything else?"

"Except for some rings and watches, that's everything," the pawnbroker lied, putting the tray back under the glass counter.

Matt and Gerallt looked at each other and headed back outside. The buzzer seemed to be taunting them as they left.

"Now what?" Gerallt asked, as they once more stood outside the shop.

"You know, Gerallt, your ability to unlock doors may be useful. Let's look around back." Matt said, leading his friend to the rear of the shop. Sure enough, the pawn shop had a locked back door.

"Okay," Matt said. "Here's what we're going to do. I'll go back in and try to keep the guy busy. Wait a few minutes until I'm back inside, and he's had time to leave the back room. Then unlock the door, get the amulet, and go."

"I'll count tah one hundred and open the door."

"Okay," Matt replied. "But watch out when you go in. He may have another of those light sensors at the back door."

They nodded to each other, and Gerallt started to count silently. Matt quickly returned inside and walked to the counter farthest away from the back room where Gerallt would be. It held cameras, phones, CD players, MP3 players, and even a portable DVD player. "Excuse me," Matt called to the pawnbroker in the back room.

"Yes?" the heavyset man asked, as he slowly walked back to the counter. "Changed your mind and decided to buy something for yourself?

"I have lots of DVDs and need a DVD player for my room," Matt answered. "What do you have?"

Chapter 24 – Recovering Gerallt's Amulet

The pawnbroker pointed to a shelf on the wall behind the counter. "I have several. Do you just want a DVD player or do you want one that also plays Blu-rays?" The pawnbroker set three machines on the counter.

"How much are they?" Matt asked, trying to sound interested.

While the pawnbroker tried to convince Matt to buy the more-expensive Blu-ray player, Gerallt used his borrowed amulet to unlock the back door. He slowly opened the door and peered inside. Listening carefully, he could hear Matt and the pawnbroker in the next room discussing the pros and cons of the different DVD players.

Carefully stepping over the light beam Matt had warned him about, Gerallt walked into the backroom and quietly closed the door behind him. He looked around the cluttered room with its shelves containing the former possessions of people whose luck had left them. He did not have to look for long. His amulet lay right in the middle of the pawnbroker's desktop.

With a mixture of joy and relief on his face, Gerallt scooped up his amulet and placed it around his neck. He looked through the partially open door to the front of the shop and listened. Matt was doing his best to stall for time. As quietly as he could, Gerallt went to the backdoor, turned the knob, and forgot to step *over* the light beam...

The burglar alarm went off.

Gerallt bolted out the back door and sprinted down the alleyway. Meanwhile, the pawnbroker had reached the backroom and realized that the amulet was gone. Henderson charged out of the back door and ran after Gerallt as fast as his weight would let him. Matt, who had run out the front door when the alarm sounded, reached the cross street just in time to see Gerallt briefly turn to face his pursuer, raise his amulet, and intone *"Magna Dea, fac, quaesumus, viam lubricam!"*

Henderson felt his feet slip out from under him, and he landed on the concrete with far more force that he had thought possible. The air had been knocked out of him, and it took a few moments until he could sit up. By then, Matt had joined Gerallt, and both boys were several blocks away. The pawnbroker looked up just in time to see them vanish around a corner. Lying on the ground, trying to catch his breath, the pawnbroker cursed. He couldn't report the amulet's theft to the police because Smith had almost certainly stolen it. With an additional curse, the pawnbroker forced himself to stand before slowly hobbling back to his shop.

Matt and Gerallt ran all the way home. Out of breath but victorious, they finally stopped in front of the Hawthorne House and leaned against the old oaks.

"What happened?" Matt eventually gasped out between breaths. "I heard the alarm go off... I thought you'd be caught for sure."

"I almost was," Gerallt replied, grinning back at Matt. "I didn't realize that I had tah turn off the alarm tah leave. I just opened it, and the alarm went off. The next thing I knew, I was runnin' down the alley as fast as I could with him chasin' me. All I could think of

Chapter 24 – Recovering Gerallt's Amulet

was tah use my amulet tah make him slip so he couldn't chase me anymore."

"Well, it sure worked. I've never seen anyone that big fall so hard."

"Yeah, I feel kind of sorry about that. He didn't know it was mine. Still, I had no choice. I had to get it back."

"Don't worry, Gerallt," Matt said. "I doubt he was really hurt, and besides, the amulet was yours to begin with. Now you can just put the other one back, and no one will ever know it was gone. We got away with it."

With the amulet once more around his neck and safely hidden beneath his shirt, Gerallt opened the gate and led Matt up on the porch. He was about to open the front door when his mother opened it.

"Hello, Motha," Gerallt said, surprised to have the door open just as he was reaching for the doorknob.

"Hello, Mrs. Hawthorne," Matt said, following Gerallt into the house.

However, Gerallt's mother did not continue onto the porch as the boys expected. Instead, she asked, "So, where were you two this mornin'? I stopped by the carriage house tah talk tah Matt's fathah, and you weren't there."

"We decided tah go for a walk," Gerallt replied. "We went to the park and then downtown for a while. Matt bought us some snacks So, did you have something for us tah do?"

"No, I was just wonderin' where you were," Gwendolyn replied. "Matt, would you mind goin' up to your room for a little while? I have something I need tah discuss privately with Gerallt."

Matt looked briefly at Gerallt, who shrugged. "Okay, Mrs. Hawthorne. See you later, Gerallt."

Once Matt had gone upstairs, Gwendolyn led her son into the parlor. "Gerallt, I need tah ask you a few questions."

"Is something wrong?" Gerallt asked, taking a seat in the velvet-covered chair opposite his mother.

"Yes. I'm afraid there is. How well do you trust Matt?"

Surprised by the unexpected question, Gerallt replied, "He's my best friend, Mothah. I totally trust him."

"Even though he is an outsidah?"

"Ayuh, even though he's an outsidah. Like I said, he's my best friend. Why are you askin'? What's wrong?"

"Gerallt, I was talking to Ahnt Vivianne today about how Gareth is getting older, and that he's goin' tah need his own gift from the Goddess for his investiture."

Gerallt's heart sank as it suddenly became clear where his mother's questions were leading. He struggled to keep the look of guilt and rising panic off his face.

"Ahnt Vivianne told me she had an amulet that would be just right for Gareth. However, when we went upstairs so that she could show it tah me, the amulet was gone."

"Gone? Wait. What's that got tah do with Matt?"

Chapter 24 – Recovering Gerallt's Amulet

"I really don't like thinking this, but he's the only outsidah that has free run of the house. I'm worried that Matt might have taken it."

"No way! Matt's no thief, and besides, I'm always with him. There's no way he could have taken it."

"Okay, Gerallt," she said. "You wouldn't happen tah know anythin' about the missin' amulet, would you?"

"Of course not. I have my own; what would I do with another?" Gerallt said.

"Okay, Gerallt. But this is important. I had tah ask. If Ahnt Vivianne doesn't find the missin' amulet, she's goin' tah have tah inform the High Coven. They'll send someone tah investigate, and they'll find out that I've sent you children tah public school and that you're friends with an outsidah. They'll find out that we've let a family of outsidahs move in with us. The repercussions could be severe."

"I understand. But it wasn't Matt or me. Can I go now? I have to feed Nightwing and make sure she has fresh watah."

When his mother nodded, Gerallt took ran up the two flights of stairs. But on reaching the third floor, he passed his own room and walked straight to the door of the Sabbat room. He listened for a second but heard only the faint voices of his mother and great-aunt drifting up from the parlor. Hoping that Gwyneth wouldn't leave her bedroom, he quietly opened the door to the Sabbat room and stepped inside. Ignoring the family altar, he went straight to the large wooden chest and dropped the borrowed amulet on the floor behind it. Hoping his mother and great-aunt would think that the amulet had accidentally fallen off the chest when someone had opened it, Gerallt walked out and knocked on Matt's door.

"What was that all about?" Matt asked, as he let Gerallt in.

"Ahnt Vivianne discovered that the amulet I borrowed was missing. Mothah's really upset. She even wondered whether you might have kifed it."

"Oh, no! What are we going to do?"

"Nothin'. I already took care of everything. I told her there was no way you would have taken it."

"So, what did you do?"

"I left it on the floor so that when they find it there, Ahnt Vivianne will think she accidentally dropped it."

"Hopefully, that will work. I hate to think that your mom actually thought I might have taken it."

"It'll be okay, Matt. Don't worry."

"Okay. So, what do we do now?"

"Well, now that I have my amulet back, how about learning another prayah to the Goddess?

Several hours later, Vivianne decided to search the Sabbat room a second time. Gerallt didn't hear until that evening that the missing amulet had been found.

Chapter 25
Searching for Treasure

It was a quiet midwinter Sunday morning in Hawthorne House, and Gareth was bored. He'd tried, although neither very hard nor successfully, to talk himself into studying for his upcoming Social Studies test. Instead, he was lying on his bed with his pet squirrel, Shadow, reading a popular science book that he'd borrowed from the school library. In actuality, he was waiting for Matt and Gerallt to finally wake up and pass his open door on their way down to breakfast. Both boys were still asleep after having stayed up for hours and hours after Gareth had gone to bed.

Meanwhile, Matt's sister Tina had been in Gwyneth's room all morning. Tina was giving Gwyneth advice about clothes and makeup, while Gwyneth was telling Tina about life on Deer Isle.

Back in the Mitchell's small apartment in the carriage house, Sam was going through the want ads. Meanwhile, Gareth's mother and great-aunt were working downstairs in the kitchen baking half a dozen loaves of bread for the coming week. In short, it was a typical Sunday morning in Hawthorne House.

Gareth's conscience had nearly convinced him to get out his textbook when the wonderful smell of fresh-baked bread drifted up the stairs and into his room. Studying for his test never stood a chance against hot bread and his great-aunt's blackberry jam.

Gareth was downstairs before Shadow could do more than chatter his annoyance at being left so abruptly.

"Mornin', Motah, Ahnt Vivianne," Gareth said as he entered the kitchen. "The bread smells great. Is any ready yet?"

"Good mornin', Gareth," Vivianne said, without turning around from the counter where she was kneading dough for a pan of cinnamon rolls.

"Good mornin'," Gareth's mother added, as she placed whole wheat dough into freshly greased baking tins and set them aside to rise. "I just took the first loaves out of the oven. You'd bettah let me cut it for you. It's hot, and I don't want you tah burn yourself."

Putting on oven mitts, she picked up one of the freshly baked loaves and rolled it out of its tin onto a cutting board. Using the mitt to hold the steaming hot bread, she cut two thick slices and set them in front of her youngest son. Butter and blackberry jam were already on the kitchen table, and Gareth quickly spread butter on one slice and jam on the other. The butter instantly melted, giving that slice a rich golden color that contrasted nicely with the deep purple of the jam.

While Gareth was eating, his mother opened the large, heavy door of the cast-iron stove and placed two tins of bread dough inside. Opening a second smaller door, she used a poker to stir the hot coals. Expertly judging the stove's temperature and the amount of wood needed to bake the bread, she added two pieces of split firewood from the pile stacked

Chapter 25 –Searching for Treasure

neatly next to the stove. "Vivianne, can I speak tah you for a second?" Gwendolyn asked softly.

"Certainly, deah," Vivianne said. She frowned, concerned by Gwendolyn's serious expression. "Is somethin' wrong?"

"Perhaps it would be bettah if we talked in the library," Gareth's mother answered, glancing meaningfully at Gareth.

"Of course." Wiping her hands on her apron, Vivianne hung it up on the wall.

The women headed for the library, leaving Gareth alone at the kitchen table. Their brief conversation had not gone unnoticed. Gareth's mother and great-aunt had barely closed the library door before Gareth raced up the stairs, half-eaten slices of bread in each hand.

Gareth lay down on the floor at the air vent connecting his bedroom to the library below. Through the grate, he could see the top of his great-aunt's head as she sat in her favorite reading chair. Although he couldn't see his mother, he could hear her footsteps on the hardwood floor as she paced nervously back and forth.

"Okay, child, tell me what's botherin' you," Vivianne said, her concerned voice rising clearly up through the vent.

"It's Sam. I just don't know what tah do."

"What's wrong? He hasn't done or said anythin' tah hurt you, has he?" The unwelcome memory of her former husband's infidelity rushed unbidden into Vivianne's mind.

"No, of course not!" Gwendolyn exclaimed indignantly. "Sam's always been the perfect gentleman." She paused, and when she continued, her tone conveyed a mixture of concern, worry, and more than a hint of fear. "It's the problem of his bein' laid off from work and not being able tah find a decent job. It has really started eatin' at him. I know he appreciates youah lettin' them move in, but he hates havin' tah rely on youah charity. It hurts his pride, especially since he can't afford tah pay you more than a token amount of rent."

"It's hardly charity tah let him and Tina move intah the carriage house. It's not like I've evah had any use foah the place. And Sam was the one who wanted tah pay rent; I invited them to move in as guests."

"But, Vivianne, it's not really about the rent. Bein' out of work keeps him from movin' on with his life. It's keepin' us from..." Gwendolyn paused, embarrassed at having given voice to her hopes.

"Oh," Vivianne said, with a smile that Gareth couldn't see from his perch at the vent. "I was wonderin' when he would finally open his eyes and realize what a prize he'd found in you. So, it is gettin' that serious? Has he proposed yet?"

"No, he hasn't proposed, Ahnt Vivianne," Gwendolyn replied, with a mixture of sorrow and embarrassment. "We've barely begun tah discuss how we feel. He clams up every time I start to mention it. *Magna Dea*, he can't even afford tah take me out tah lunch anymore!"

Gwendolyn sighed. "How can he think about startin' a new family and becomin' a stepfathah tah my children when he can't even support his own? And he knows stayin' in the carriage house isn't somethin' he can do forevah. Worse, I'm afraid that if he can't find work nearby, and soon, he's goin' tah feel like he has to take any job, even if it forces him to move out of Hawthorne, maybe even out of Indiana."

Gareth was so shocked that he almost dropped his last bite of bread. He had never considered that Matt might leave. With his nose nearly touching the vent's metal grill, he held his breath as he listened carefully to each word.

"I see, child. I suppose it is a possibility. Still, the man has tah work, and he has his children tah support. Sadly, men have a strange way of avoiding painful problems instead of talkin' them over with those who might actually help solve them."

"But Vivianne, how can I help him find work in the outside world? I know nothin' about workin' with computers."

"Surely, that is not the only thing he can do."

"He taught high school computers back in Oregon, but there are no openin's heah in Hawthorne, not even as a substitute teacher."

"So, what else would he like tah do?"

"Well, he has talked about makin' stained-glass windows. He really enjoyed repairin' the one that was broken. But tah do that for a livin', he would need lots of supplies and a proper place tah work. I'd lend him the money tah get started if I had any. We nevah needed much money back on Deeah Isle, and besides, it wasn't our way. Between the fish Medwyn brought home and our gahden, we nevah went without. The money he made went to pay taxes and buy the basics we couldn't make ourselves. After the cloth, leather, candle wax, and lamp oil, there was nevah much left ovah. Besides, Sam's pride would nevah let him accept money from me, even if I had some to give."

"Well, it will work out if the Goddess wills. You must have faith, and she will help you and Sam find a way."

"That's easy for you to say," Gwendolyn blurted out in frustration. "You've nevah had tah worry about money. Your fathah inherited his fathah's fortune and then used his gift from the Goddess tah make even more money. And you have the Hawthorne treasure. How can you possibly understand what it's like tah be poor?"

Vivianne Hawthorne slowly stood, her aged hands balled into bony fists as she strove to control her anger at the undeserved attack.

Realizing that she had gone too far, Gwendolyn covered her mouth with her hand, but it was too late. The words were out, and there was no calling them back.

Vivianne was about to remind her niece of the charity she had shown Gwendolyn and her children by taking them in. But the fire of her anger sputtered and burned out. She smiled at the irony of the situation.

"The great Hawthorne treasure? What treasure?" Vivianne sat back down in her old leather chair and

Chapter 25 – Searching for Treasure

gave her head a tired shake. "It's true that my parents left me this house. They also left me a good deal of stock and money, but the Great Depression took most of Fathah's wealth. After the stock market crash, the majority of his stock was worthless, and bank failures took most of his money. And if that were not enough, my good-for-nothing husband took all he could lay his hands on when he ran off with my best friend."

Vivianne sighed sadly. "Since then, I've been slowly emptyin' the remainin' bank accounts he didn't know about. I've had tah sell my fathah's coin collection, as well as the sculptures and most of the paintin's. Look around you, child. See all the empty places on these bookshelves? For the last 15 years, I have been sellin' the family's rare books one by one to pay for the property taxes and food."

"Ahnt Vivianne, I'm so sorry. I didn't know. I can't believe I said those terrible things."

"Don't worry, I don't blame you. I know it was your frustration speakin'. So you see, I also know what it's like tah not have the money I need. Frustration and I ah old friends."

"But, Ahnt Vivianne, my fathah used tah tell me amazin' stories about how incredibly wealthy his uncle was. How your fathah had his own railroad line. And how he ran liquor during prohibition. I heard him say that your fathah bragged he'd hidden most of his wealth. Fathah said the treasure was hidden right heah in Hawthorne House."

"Well, my fathah was known to brag about many things. Do you think I haven't heard those stories? When I was a little girl, Fathah told me I'd nevah have to worry about anythin'. And for years after he died, I looked. I've gone through every room, inch by inch. I've used the *Absconditum* prayah, but I nevah found anythin' of value. I have had tah learn tah accept it. I'm sorry, but there is no treasure. I can no more set up Sam's business than you can. All we can do is trust the Goddess. She will help us find a way."

While the women lapsed into an unhappy silence, their conversation had the opposite effect on Gareth. Jumping to his feet, Gareth practically flew up the steps to Gerallt's room.

Hearing feet pounding up the stairs, Matt barely had time to hide Gerallt's amulet in his pocket before Gareth barged into the room.

"Gerallt! Matt! You won't believe what I just heard!"

"What?" Matt and Gerallt both asked. Trying to appear innocent, they did their best not to look at the Tarot deck that hovered a few inches above Gerallt's desk.

Matt quickly closed the door, while Gerallt pushed his brother past the desk with one hand and grabbed the floating Tarot deck with the other.

"I was lyin' next to the floor vent in my room, listening tah Mothah and Ahnt Vivianne talkin' in the library. Mothah said she's in love with Matt's fathah, and she wants tah loan him money so he can start makin' stained-glass windows, but she can't cause she's broke, and Ahnt Vivianne can't either cause she's broke, too, and if he can't start makin' more money, then Matt may have tah move away, but there's this huge treasure hidden somewhere in the house, but Ahnt Vivianne doesn't know where it is. She's looked and looked and can't find it, but I know the Goddess wants us tah find it for them so that Mothah can marry Matt's fathah." Gareth finally stopped to catch a breath.

"What on earth are you talkin' about?" Gerallt demanded. "Slow down and start over."

"Like I told you, I was lyin' next to the floor vent in my room, listenin' tah Mothah and Ahnt Vivianne talk in the library, when I heard Mothah say she's in love with Matt's fathah, and she wants tah loan him money, but..."

"I heard all that." Gerallt interrupted. "What's this about a treasure?"

"The Hawthorne treasure! Don't you remembah? I remembah Fathah sayin' somethin' about it once. Ahnt Vivianne's fathah built this place and hid a honkin' big treasure in it somewhere. But her parents died in an accident, and they nevah told her where they hid the treasure. She couldn't find it and has given up looking for it. That's why we need tah look for it. Ahnt Vivianne said that the Goddess will help us find it."

"Are you sure you heard them right about the treasure?" Gerallt asked.

"And what's this about my dad marrying your mom and moving away?" Matt demanded.

"Mothah said they're in love, but your fathah won't talk about it until he has a good job. And Gerallt, I did hear them talk about the treasure. Come down and listen foah yourself if you don't believe me."

Matt and Gerallt followed Gareth down to his room, but by the time they got to the grate, the library was empty. Gerallt looked skeptically at his younger brother.

"I swear I heard it," Gareth protested. "I swear by the Goddess. Ahnt Vivianne said that the Goddess will help us find the treasure, and I believe her."

"Hmm..." Gerallt said. "I remember Fathah tellin' stories about his rich grandfathah hiding a huge treasure. That must have been Ahnt Vivianne's fathah. You know, maybe there is a lost treasure."

"Well, if there is, I say we look for it," Matt said. "I'm not going to sit here and do nothing when Dad might move us again. Not if there's a chance we can find the treasure."

Gareth looked expectantly at Gerallt, who eventually nodded his approval. "Okay, Matt. We look for the treasure. But where?"

"Mothah said it's hidden right heah in this house," Gareth answered.

"So where do we start?" Matt asked.

"The attic," Gerallt answered. "Nobody ever goes up there."

"Might as well," Matt said. "We can start at the top and work our way down to the basement. How do we get up there?"

"There's a trapdoor in the ceilin' just outside of Gwyneth's room," Gerallt answered. "When you pull

Chapter 25 – Searching for Treasure

down on a knob, part of the ceilin' drops down, and you can unfold a laddah."

"Great. Let's go," Matt said, heading for the door.

"Wait," Gareth said. "Mothah told us she didn't want us goin' up there and messin' with Ahnt Vivianne's stuff."

"We won't be messin' with her stuff," Gerallt argued. "We'll be looking for the treasure. But just tah be on the safe side, I think we shouldn't let Gwyneth catch us up there."

"But how ah we goin' tah do that?" Gareth asked. "I think the girls ah still in Gwyneth's room. They could come out any minute and see us."

Gerallt thought for a moment. "We need a way tah get them out of the room long enough foah us to get into the attic."

"I know," Gareth said. "I'll tell them that Mothah and Ahnt Vivianne ah bakin' bread, and they should go down and get some while it's still hot."

"Good idear," Gerallt said. "No one can turn down Mothah's bread when it's hot out of the oven. That'll give us enough time to get up into the attic, but what about when we need tah get back down?"

"I got an idea," Matt said. "Gareth, you can be our lookout. I'll give you one of my walkie-talkies, and we'll take the other one. Once we're up, we'll pull up the ladder and close the door. When we're ready to come down, I'll call you, and you can tell us when the coast is clear."

"Okay," Gareth said, proud that Matt had given him such an important task and happy that Matt was trusting him with one of his electronic gadgets.

"Wait here," Matt told the two brothers. "I'll go get them."

A few minutes later, Matt was back with the walkie-talkies, and the boys put their plan into action. Once Gwyneth and Tina headed to the kitchen, Matt climbed on Gerallt's back so that he could reach the knob and pull down the trapdoor. Matt and Gerallt were up the ladder and had pulled the door up just as Gareth heard the girls coming up the stairs carrying a plate of buttered bread.

Dimly lit by two small, round, dormer windows on each side, the attic took up the entire length and width of Hawthorne House. It had massive stone chimneys at each end and was packed with small boxes and all manner of items that had been stored there and forgotten in the hundred years since the house was built.

"This is goin' tah take forevah," Gerallt said, looking over the room's countless contents.

"Then I guess we'd better get started," Matt replied. "Let's start at one end and work our way to the other. We'll need to move everything to look for hidden trapdoors in the floor."

Matt and Gerallt searched through several steamer trunks and chests full of old clothes, boxes of old photographs, letters, and dishes. There were old lamps, plant stands, a gramophone, boxes of old records, and an antique birdcage. They also found boxes of tin toys and dolls, a three-story dollhouse that was a miniature version of the Hawthorne House, two cribs, a cradle, and a fancy, carved, wooden rocking horse. The boys looked for trapdoors under a dress form, a pedal-driven sewing machine, an umbrella stand made from an elephant's foot, several mounted animal heads, and quite a few things that they couldn't identify. What they didn't find was any hint of a treasure.

The boys were about to quit for lunch when they discovered a locked metal box roughly the size and shape of two small pizza boxes stacked one on top of the other.

"What do you think is in it?" Matt asked.

When Gerallt shook the box, he could feel something sliding back and forth and hear the shuffling of paper. "Hard tellin'. Could be anythin'."

"Only one way to find out."

"Let's take it to my room. Maybe we can pick the lock."

"Gerallt and Matt," Gareth's voice came from the walkie-talkie clipped to Matt's belt. "Mothah just called. Lunch is ready, and she wants us tah come down."

"Okay," Matt replied over his walkie-talkie. "We wanted to come down anyway. Is the coast clear? Where are Tina and Gwyneth?"

"They just went downstairs."

Gerallt lowered the trapdoor, and Matt followed him down the ladder. After stopping to hide the box under Gerallt's bed, the three boys headed downstairs to join the others for lunch.

After lunch, during which Gwendolyn had asked Gerallt and Matt how they had managed to get their clothes so dusty, the three boys returned to Gerallt's room to try to open the mysterious box.

The keyhole of the box's lock was relatively large, and it didn't take Matt long to pick it with a bent paperclip. Opening the box, Matt pulled out an old book bound in black leather and a stack of important-looking documents.

Gerallt looked at the first sheet of paper and said, "It's a stock certificate. One hundred shares in the Hawthorne Railroad Company. This must have been Great-Grandfathah's railroad."

"What do you think it's worth?" Gareth asked.

"Nothing," Gerallt answered sullenly. "It went bankrupt back in the Great Depression."

"Hey, they're all stock certificates," Matt said, shuffling through the rest of the papers. "There are quite a few more for your family's railroad company. The rest are for a bunch of companies I've never heard of. They're probably worthless too, but we should bike down to the library. We can use one of their computers to google the companies and see if any are still in business."

"Ayuh," Gerallt said. "I bet Ahnt Vivianne would have sold them if they were worth anythin'. Still, it wouldn't hurt for us to find out."

Chapter 25 – Searching for Treasure

"You're probably right," Matt said. "Still, people collect all sorts of things. I bet there are people who collect old stock certificates. Maybe we can sell them on eBay and make enough money to help pay for groceries or something."

"What's the book?" Gareth asked.

Matt opened it and flipped through the pages. Each one held a table in which every row was filled with handwritten dates and descriptions followed by columns of numbers. "It's a ledger book from 1929. Back before there were computers, companies used them to keep track of their finances. I think your great-grandfather used this one to keep track of his income and purchases."

"Let me see," Gerallt said. Matt handed over the book, and Gerallt flipped through several pages. "The handwritin's kind of hahd tah read, and some of the ink is faded."

"But what does it say?" Gareth demanded.

Gerallt skimmed several pages. "Mostly, it's just purchases. Groceries. Coal. Ice. Clothin'. Gas. It also lists payments of the chauffeur and maid's salaries."

"Didn't Mr. Thompson say the Great Depression started in 1929?" Matt asked.

"I think so," Gerallt answered, handing Matt the ledger book. "Wait a second. I'll look it up." Gerallt flipped through his American History book until he found what he was looking for. "Here it is. The Great Depression started on October 29th, 1929, when the stock market crashed. They called it Black Tuesday.

Anyway, that's the same year my great-grandfathah made this ledger."

"That's what I thought," Matt said. "Look at these entries he made during September and early October," he said, pointing to several places on the page. "There must be at least a dozen times when he sold some of his stocks. Each time, the amount he listed was more than a hundred thousand dollars. Here are two entries for more than a million dollars each."

"But Ahnt Vivianne said he lost most of his money when the stocks became worthless," Gareth said.

"Apparently not," Gerallt replied. "It looks like he sold a honkin' lot of his stock just in time."

"So, what did he do with all of that money?" Gareth asked.

"That has to be the Hawthorne treasure," Matt said.

"Maybe part of it," Gerallt replied. "But look at these entries. He bought a lot of gold bars and coins. It looks like he also bought several large parcels of land. And heah's an entry where he bought over 50 thousand dollars' worth of diamonds from Tiffany's."

"Wow," Matt said. "The treasure's real. And you know what? There's been tons of inflation since 1929. The gold and diamonds and property have to be worth a lot more now than when your great-grandfather bought them."

"We have to tell Mothah and Ahnt Vivianne," Gareth said.

"You're right," Gerallt agreed. "This is too important to keep to ourselves. Besides, we're going tah need everyone's help tah find the treasure."

The boys headed downstairs with the ledger. The great Hawthorne treasure hunt was about to begin.

For the next two weeks, the Hawthorne and Mitchell families searched every room of the Hawthorne House from the attic to the basement. They knocked on walls, ceilings, and floors hoping to hear the hollow sound of a secret hiding place.

When the Mitchells weren't with them, the Hawthornes used their gifts from the Goddess and said the prayer for finding lost or hidden things. By the end of the two weeks, everyone was tired, frustrated, and depressed. The search had slowly tapered off until they were forced to admit defeat. If the Hawthorne treasure existed, it was incredibly well hidden.

Despite not finding the treasure, the search produced three positive results. First, Matt was able to bring in over $100 by selling the worthless stock certificates to collectors on eBay. Second, they sold antiques worth several thousand dollars. Third and best of all, Vivianne was able to lend Sam the money he needed so that he could start making stained-glass windows.

Chapter 26
The Hidden Tunnel

The next morning, Sam awoke well before dawn. He'd been dreaming of making the most beautiful stained-glass windows. Now that he was awake, Sam couldn't get his mind off the money Gwendolyn's aunt had loaned him. He tossed and turned for another ten minutes, but sleep couldn't compete with his need to begin feeling useful again. Giving up on sleep, Sam dressed, grabbed some toast and coffee, and was on the road while everyone else still slept. As Hawthorne was too small to have a store selling stained-glass, he had to drive thirty-five miles south to Fort Wayne. With little traffic on a Saturday morning, Sam pulled into the parking lot of a mega-hardware store a quarter of an hour before it opened.

Having used his computer the previous evening to research stained-glass, it didn't take Sam long to gather up the wood, nails, frosted glass, and small fluorescent lights that he needed to make the light table on which he'd lay out and solder his stained-glass creations. He also bought sufficient wood and hardware to make several windows. Next on his list was the hobby store where he bought sheets of different colored and textured stained-glass, a glass cutter, rolls of copper foil and solder, a soldering iron, and several books of patterns. Being able to rapidly find what he needed made him feel like a prehistoric hunter who had skillfully tracked his prey, made the

Chapter 26 – The Hidden Tunnel

kill, and was now on his way back to the cave bringing meat to his hungry family.

In less than three hours, Sam was back at the carriage house. He carefully carried his supplies inside and headed over to the house to get Matt. Opening the back door, he stepped into the large, but crowded, kitchen where everyone was having a late breakfast.

"Morning, everyone," he called. "I'm back, and I have everything I need to start working on the stained-glass windows, that is, everything except for one thing."

"What's that?" Matt mumbled, his mouth otherwise occupied with a forkful of banana pancakes.

"You," his father answered, smiling. "We need to restack our stuff, so I can have a place to work. Right now, we barely have a path to walk from the door to the stairs. And the old workbench needs to be replaced or at the very least majorly repaired. I took a good look at it last night, and it will collapse if I put one more thing on it. So, I need your help once you're finished with breakfast."

"Okay," Matt said, without much enthusiasm. "As soon as I'm done, I'll put on some work clothes and come out. Ten minutes. Fifteen minutes tops."

A few minutes later, Sam headed out to the carriage house while Matt and Gerallt were on their way up to Gerallt's room. "I was planning on you helping me practice with the amulet," Matt moaned after the two had closed Gerallt's door.

"We can still practice this evenin'," Gerallt pointed out. "Don't worry. Helpin' youah fathah shouldn't take long, especially if Gareth and I help."

"So, what do you want us to do first?" Matt asked, as the three boys walked into the old carriage house.

Sam had already been busy moving the Mitchell's possessions into two of the horse stalls. By restacking the boxes so that the largest and strongest were on the bottom, he had managed to stack them higher and clear a fair amount of space.

"Okay boys, once we finish stacking the rest of the boxes out of the way, we need to clear the space where I'll be making the stained-glass windows. I need a place that's large enough for the light table, a new workbench for laying out and soldering the windows, and a storage cabinet for my glass and other supplies. I was thinking about the wall facing the house. There's a good window for plenty of natural light, and it gives me a fine view of the greenhouse."

Matt looked where his father was pointing and inwardly groaned. The spot was occupied by rickety cabinets and shelves covered in dusty cans of paint, rusted tools, and all manner of odds and ends. A heavy pile of old lumber lay on the floor under the shelves. Covered by cobwebs and a thick layer of dust, everything looked like it hadn't been touched in years. "So, what are we going to do with all this stuff?"

Chapter 26 – The Hidden Tunnel

"We'll move everything worth keeping into the remaining horse stall and carry the rest out for garbage pickup or to the burn pile. It will save us work if we sort it as we go. Just be careful about rusty nails. I don't want to have to stop and take someone to the doctor for a tetanus shot."

Sam, Matt, Gerallt, and Gareth divided the wall to be cleared into four equal parts, and each began to empty his fourth of the shelves and cabinets.

"What do you want us tah do with the paint cans, Mr. Mitchell?" Gerallt asked. "Most of them feel pretty light and don't slosh when you shake them."

"The paint probably dried up years ago. Still, we can't just leave it out with the garbage, especially if it is lead-based paint that might poison the groundwater under the landfill. Just stack it near the garage door for now 'til I can find out where we need to drop it off."

"What about the boards, Dad? Some of them are kind of banged up."

"You can carry the wood that's clearly not salvageable out to the burn pile. But be careful not to throw anything away that might be useful. Stack the rest of it together so I can sort it later. I might be able to use some of it to make window frames."

The job went surprisingly fast with four of them working together. They quickly fell into a rhythm of carrying something to where it belonged and then coming back for more.

"Okay, boys, it looks like the cabinets are too rickety to be worth saving, and the shelves will be in the way. Let's get rid of them next. Use your hammers to knock the boards apart.

Fifteen minutes later, Matt said, "Hey, Dad, look at this."

Everyone stopped to look where Matt was pointing. Removing the remaining pieces of a cabinet had revealed a large iron ring attached to the wooden floor. Matt had uncovered part of a hidden trap door.

"Where do you think it goes?" Gareth asked the question on everyone's mind.

"There's only one way to find out," Sam said. "Let's tear down the rest of this shelving so that we can open it." He used a hammer to tap under the shelves where they connected with their supports. Once the nails had been pulled out of the uprights, it was just a matter of lifting the boards and leaning them against the far wall.

Once they'd cleared the area, Sam gave the trapdoor a tug. It barely moved. Bracing his feet on either side of the trapdoor, he squatted and pulled. The thick and heavy door rose slowly, its heavily rusted hinges creaking loudly at having to move after so many years.

"Okay, everyone, stand back. This door is too heavy to just set down, and I don't want to risk crushing my fingers. I'm going to let it fall." When the others had moved back, Sam dropped the door, which hit the floor with a deafening boom.

Everyone stepped up to the hole in the floor and stared down into the darkness. A large wooden ladder led down into the small square room.

Chapter 26 – The Hidden Tunnel

"You don't suppose the treasure is hidden down there, do you?" Matt asked.

Each of them glanced quickly at the others. Everyone was grinning at the thought.

"Gerallt, would you mind running back to the house and getting a couple of flashlights?" Sam asked. "If you don't have any, bring back a couple of the oil lanterns and some matches."

Gerallt sprinted past the greenhouse on his way to the back door of the Hawthorne House.

"I think there's probably enough light to see down there once our eyes adjust," Sam said, growing impatient waiting for Gerallt to return. He lowered his feet over the edge and onto the ladder's top rung.

"Wait, Dad. That ladder's really old; we don't know if it'll support your weight. I'm lighter than you, so I should go first," Matt said, ignoring his fear of being trapped underground in the excitement of the moment. He descended into the tiny room, only six feet on each side.

The air was stale and musty, carrying the distinct smell of mold and rot. As Matt's eyes adjusted to the dim light coming through the open trapdoor. All four walls were covered floor to ceiling by narrow shelves filled with glass canning jars. They contained various foods that should have been eaten decades ago. Everything was covered in a thick layer of dust. "Dad, the ladder seems solid enough, especially if you're careful."

Just then, Gerallt returned, carrying an oil lamp in each hand. He was closely followed by Gwyneth,

Tina, Gwendolyn, and Vivianne, who joined Sam and Gerallt around the open trapdoor. The six of them blocked most of the dim sunlight from entering through the trapdoor, making the small room even darker.

Descending the ladder, Sam stopped about halfway so that Gerallt could hand him the two oil lamps, which Sam passed to Matt. Upon reaching the floor, Sam lit the lamps with matches that Gerallt had given him. Sam's and Matt's shadows lurched around the room like drunken sailors as they surveyed the room.

"It's a root cellar," Sam said. "Back before people had refrigerators, people would store things like potatoes, onions, and apples underground where it was cool. Apparently, the carriage driver's wife also used it to store the food she'd canned."

"Look at that," Matt said, pointing to the floor on the side of the room closest to the Hawthorne House. The two bottom shelves had collapsed, dumping their jars into a small puddle of water that had seeped through the wall. One of the jars had broken, and its contents now fed a large family of mushrooms.

Sam knocked his knuckles on the wall directly above the puddle and was rewarded with a low sound like that of a ripe watermelon. The sound's pitch was distinctly higher when he rapped on the wall several feet to either side. "It's hollow behind these shelves," he said, speaking loudly enough so that everyone could hear. "Matt, let's get these jars out of the way so that we can remove the rest of these shelves."

Chapter 26 – The Hidden Tunnel

A few minutes later, the remaining shelves over the puddle had been emptied, pulled from the wall, and passed up through the trapdoor. Sam and Matt studied the wall, checking for any sign of a hidden door or concealed mechanism to open it. However, the wall looked and acted just like any other wall. If there were a secret way through the wall, they couldn't find it. Impatient to get to the hollow space behind, they gave up their search, and Sam decided on a more direct approach.

"Gerallt, I think I saw a small sledgehammer and crowbar when we were moving everything out of the way. Could you find them for us?"

"Ayuh, Mr. Mitchell. I'll be right back." A few seconds later, Gerallt reappeared at the trapdoor and handed down the sledge and crowbar."

"Okay," Sam said to his son, "Stand back against the wall. There isn't much room to swing."

When Matt had backed out of the way, Sam took a mighty swing and hit the wall chest high just above where the water had leaked in. The sledgehammer hit the wall with a deafening thud. Its head had buried itself so that Sam had to wiggle the handle several times before he could pry it free. The splintered edges of several thin and narrow, horizontal wooden laths stuck out of a half-inch-thick layer of painted plaster.

Sam looked through the hole he'd made, but it was pitch black inside. He swung the sledge again, this time making a hole about a foot above the first one. Picking up one of the lanterns, he held it to the lower hole and looked through the upper one.

"Well, I'll be," Sam said, as he backed out of the way so that Matt could look.

"Don't keep us in suspense up heah. What do you see?" Gerallt called.

"There's a brick-lined tunnel," Matt replied, still looking through the hole. "It's blocked about six feet in by a brick wall with a door. There's a large puddle on the floor that's probably the source of the water that's seeped in here and rotted the lower shelves."

"Let's get this wall down," Sam said.

Matt backed away, and it wasn't long before his father had punched a narrow row of holes down the center of the wall from ceiling to floor. Sam started over, breaking the slats between the holes, splitting the wall in two. Using the sledgehammer was effective, but messy. The broken edges were jagged with long, vicious splinters.

"Heah, you'll need these," Gerallt called through the trap door. Sam and Matt looked up, and Gerallt tossed down two pairs of leather work gloves.

"Thanks, Gerallt," Matt and his father chorused.

After putting on the gloves, they carefully pulled the two halves of the broken wall, the backs of which were studded with dozens of rusty nails like a medieval torture chamber. Their backs also revealed the proper way to enter the tunnel. Sam had broken through more than a simple lath and plaster wall. He had also broken through a cleverly hidden door that had been barred from the inside.

Working on one piece at a time, Matt and his father carefully moved the two loose sections of wall to the

Chapter 26 – The Hidden Tunnel

side so that the nails were pointed away from the center of the cramped root cellar.

Having breached the first barrier, they stepped into the tunnel, splashing in the shallow black water. Reaching the brick wall blocking their way, Matt tugged on the rusty doorknob. The door creaked but remained closed.

"Let me try, Matt," his father said. Sam turned the doorknob and gave it a firm tug. Again, the door stubbornly refused to budge. Placing one foot where the brick wall met the floor, Sam wrapped both hands firmly around the doorknob, turned it, and pulled it as hard as he could.

For a second, the door held fast. Then with a mighty crack, the doorjamb broke free from the brick wall. Before he could let go, Sam slipped and fell backward onto the hard brick floor with both the door and its jamb falling heavily on top of him.

"Dad, are you all right?" Matt cried. He pulled on the door and doorjamb, but it was too heavy to lift.

"What happened?" Gwendolyn called.

"The door's come loose. It's fallen on Dad," Matt answered.

Gerallt immediately descended the ladder to help.

"I'm alright," Sam's voice finally called out from beneath the door. "Just got the wind knocked out of me."

With Sam pushing from below and Gerallt and Matt pulling from above, they lifted the heavy door still stuck fast in its jamb. After leaning it against the side of the tunnel, the boys helped Sam stand.

Sam's backside, as well as his pride, were bruised from his fall onto the tunnel's uneven brick floor. The backs of his shirt and pants were cold, wet, and filthy. He had also banged the back of his head, but he wasn't about to let a little knock on the noggin stop him. He strode to the rectangular hole and stared into the darkness.

Sam, Matt, and Gerallt could just make out a narrow brick-lined tunnel with a round vaulted ceiling. As far as they could tell, it headed in a straight line under the greenhouse and on to the Hawthorne House, roughly eighty feet away. Just beyond where the door had stood, there was another large puddle of water. A strong, earthy smell wafted out of the tunnel, and Matt and his father could hear the faint sound of dripping water. Roots, some of them quite large, had cracked the ceiling of the tunnel. Mold and slime covered the bricks, especially where cracks had let water seep through.

"Doesn't look too inviting, does it?" Sam asked. "I want you two to stay here while I take a good look at the ceiling. There's no telling how safe this is, and there's no sense in it crashing down on all three of us."

"What's goin' on down there?" Gwendolyn called. "We can barely hear you. Is everythin' all right?"

Sam stepped back into the root cellar and looked up through the trapdoor. Vivianne, Gwendolyn, Gwyneth, Tina, and Gareth stared down with a mixture of curiosity and concern. "I'm okay. Everything's fine. There's a tunnel that heads toward

Chapter 26 – The Hidden Tunnel

to the house. I'm going to take a lantern and check it out."

"You be careful, Sam," Gwendolyn said.

"Yeah, Dad, be careful," Tina added.

"Don't worry. I won't take any unnecessary chances. I'll tell the boys how it's going, and they can pass on my progress to you."

Sam returned to the door-shaped hole in the brick wall. "Okay, boys, you stay here, and I'll be back as soon as I've had a quick look around."

Sam paused for a second. Turning toward Matt and Gerallt, he spoke softly so that only they could hear, "If the roof does start to cave in, don't come rushing in after me. Yell up to Tina to call 911 and wait here for the fire department."

"Okay, Dad," Matt promised, knowing full well there was no way he wouldn't go into the tunnel if his father needed him.

Sam stepped through the open doorway and into the dark water that covered the floor of the tunnel. He pushed past thick cobwebs. Tangled tree roots dropped tiny avalanches of dirt on his head each time he brushed against them. The musty smell of decay and long abandonment grew stronger.

After a dozen paces, Sam stopped and looked back at Matt and Gerallt, who waited in the doorway. All he could see were the boy's small silhouettes. They blocked most of the meager light that had found its way through the dirty windows of the carriage house and into the abandoned root cellar. Sam's small oil lamp was the only thing holding back the darkness.

To Matt, it seemed as if the tunnel had simply swallowed his father. With Sam's back to them, the boys could just make out the faint glow of his lamp, hidden on the far side of his body. "Is everything okay, Dad?" Matt called.

"I'm okay," Sam replied. "It's just dirty." The flickering shadows from his lamp made it difficult to see anything that wasn't immediately in front of him. Several times, he stepped into puddles and felt ice cold water drip onto his head and shoulders.

Everything went well for roughly the first 50 feet of the tunnel. Then unexpectedly, Sam suddenly felt fear. The tunnel roof seemed to press down on him. Realizing that he was beginning to hyperventilate, he stopped and forced himself to slow his breathing. Without meaning to, he stepped backward, and the fear vanished as swiftly as it had come.

That's weird, Sam thought. *There's nothing down here but some roots and cobwebs. I'm just being ridiculous, letting the darkness get to me.*

"You still okay, Dad? What's going on?" Matt called. Matt's muffled voice seemed to be coming from much farther away than it possibly could have.

"Everything's fine," Sam called. He stepped forward, and the fear immediately returned. After fifteen feet, his dread had steadily risen to become an unnatural horror. The tree roots undulated like the tentacles of a monstrous jellyfish, reaching down to grab at him. He batted them wildly with his arms, so that dirt and droplets of water fell on his head and

Chapter 26 – The Hidden Tunnel

shoulders. Loose bricks that had fallen onto the floor seemed to move as though trying to trip him.

Then he saw the source of his fear. A few yards ahead, the black mouth of a cave appeared in the left wall of the tunnel. By sheer force of will, he took one step after another until with one final step, he could peer around the corner and into the darkness.

No more than ten feet away, stood a door from which all of the terror of the tunnel emanated, flowing out like a monstrous miasma. Sam knew that no treasure on Earth could be enough to make him enter or even touch that door.

Petrified, Sam didn't move, couldn't move. He heard something coming from behind the door. It was the clicking of beetles, large beetles, hundreds of beetles, millions of beetles... An unexplainable gust of wind came from everywhere. In spite of the oil lamp's chimney, its flame fluttered and died.

It was dark, utterly dark as though the very concept of light had ceased to exist.

The clicking of the beetles rapidly rose in intensity until it was nearly deafening. Sam panicked. He dropped the useless oil lamp and fled back down the tunnel toward the carriage house and safety. Seconds later, with his heart racing and his pulse pounding in his ears, Sam burst through the hole in the brick wall and into the root cellar. Ignoring Matt and Gerallt, he rushed past them and practically flew up the ladder into the old carriage house.

Matt and Gerallt glanced at each other and then looked at Sam, who stood staring down past them at the mouth of the tunnel as if expecting to see all the demons of Hell charge after him. He was very pale and breathed as though he'd just run a marathon. The boys looked down the tunnel but couldn't see anything that might explain Sam's strange behavior. They listened, but it was as deathly quiet as a long-abandoned crypt.

The boys climbed the ladder to join the others standing around Sam, who was bent over, still gasping for breath. He seemed on the verge of collapse. Tina found an old chair and helped her father sit down.

"What's wrong, Dad?" Matt asked, shocked at how his father was behaving. "You were quiet for a few minutes, and the next thing we knew, you ran past us. Did the tunnel start caving in?"

Matt's father would not take his eyes off the tunnel entrance. Slowly, he shook his head.

Gwendolyn knelt down beside him, pulled off his gloves, and took his hands in hers. "What happened, Sam?"

His eyes still locked on the mouth of the tunnel, Sam appeared not to have heard her.

Gwendolyn slowly placed her hand on his cheek and gently turned his head so that he was looking at her. "Sam, tell us what happened."

Upon seeing Gwendolyn, the overwhelming fear began to dissipate, leaving Sam exhausted, confused, embarrassed, and not knowing where to start.

"I don't... I don't know what happened." He slowly realized everyone was staring at him with a mixture of concern, worry, fear, and confusion. He was covered

Chapter 26 – The Hidden Tunnel

head to foot in a thick layer of dust and dirt. He wiped his filthy forehead with the back of his hand, leaving a sweaty streak of white skin showing through the grime.

"The tunnel's dirty," Sam said, lifting his hand as if needing to show some evidence of what he was saying. "It was hard to see more than a few feet because of the cobwebs and roots dangling down. It wasn't scary at first, just annoying. There are a few cracks in the ceiling, and a few bricks have been dislodged by roots, but I don't think there's any serious structural damage."

"So, what happened?" Matt asked.

"That's just it, Matt. I don't know. Everything was fine. I was making my way down the tunnel, and then suddenly, I started to feel scared, scared like I've never been before in my life. I can't explain it. I forced myself to keep going. I found a short side tunnel that was blocked off by a wall with a door. But something about that door terrified me. It was like some monstrous evil was waiting behind the door for me to open it. I know it sounds crazy; it sounds crazy to me, but that's how it felt."

"And then what happened?" Vivianne asked, her tone soft and comforting without the least hint of condescension or accusation of cowardice. "Is that when you ran?"

"No, I couldn't move... I was petrified. I was terrified of remaining, but even more terrified that whatever was behind that damned door would hear me and open it."

"And then?" she coaxed.

"I heard this terrible clicking sound coming from behind the door. Like a million hungry beetles, pushing against the door. It got louder and louder, and then... and then..." Sam buried his face in his hands.

"And then you ran," Vivianne said, saying what he could not. "Most understandable." She realized that Sam was shivering. "Sam, your back and feet are soakin' wet. We need tah get you warm before you catch your death."

Vivianne turned to the others. "Matt and Tina, take your fathah intah the house and sit him down in the kitchen in front of the fireplace. Gwyneth, you get Sam one of my older blankets and wrap it around him. Gwendolyn, brew Sam some mulberry tea; you know what tah add. After it's begun tah work, take him up tah Gareth's bedroom; a good dreamless sleep will do him a world of good. Now off with you; Gerallt, Gareth, and I can take it from heah."

As soon as the others had helped Sam back to the house, Vivianne turned to her two great-nephews. "Don't worry about Mr. Mitchell. He'll be just fine tomorrow morning."

"But what about the tunnel?" Gareth asked. "What could have scared him like that?"

"Nothing that you need be afraid of," Vivianne answered. "It appears that my fathah prayed tah the Goddess tah protect the hidden room from outsidahs. The only reason I can think foah him tah do that is that he hid somethin' very valuable there. Praise the

Chapter 26 – The Hidden Tunnel

Goddess, Gareth! I think Sam has found the Hawthorne treasure!"

Vivianne looked through the window to verify that the others had disappeared into the Hawthorne House. "Gareth, Gerallt and I are goin' tah go down and see what's in that room. Stand heah at the window and yell down tah us if you see Tina and Matt comin' back. Hopefully, we will have at least ten or fifteen minutes befoah they return."

"Yes, ma'am."

Gerallt descended into the root cellar and helped his great-aunt down the ladder. At the tunnel entrance, she removed her wand from its hiding place in the left sleeve of her dress and pointed it down the tunnel. "*Magna Dea, fac, quaesumus, et radices aranearum prosternite!*"

Instantly, a rustle came from the tunnel as the cobwebs and roots were ripped from the tunnel's ceiling. This was followed by the sound of them splashing into the puddles that dotted much of the tunnel's floor. "That's bettah," she remarked to Gerallt. "No sense getting dirtier than we need tah." Raising her wand, she continued, "*Magna Dea, fac, quaesumus, ut lux sit!*" Her wand began to glow like a thin fluorescent light. Holding her glowing wand in front of her, she strode confidently into the tunnel.

Unsure of what they might find, Gerallt pulled his amulet from under his shirt and followed her in the darkness.

Without the dangling roots and cobwebs, the tunnel lost much of its creepiness. In no time, they had passed the place where Sam had first felt the unnatural fear. They stood outside the door that had terrified Sam, but to them, it was only an ordinary door. The room behind it was silent.

Vivianne tried to open it, but the door stubbornly refused to move. She looked at the keyhole above the doorknob and smiled. "Gerallt, has your mother taught you yet how tah unlock a door?"

"Ayuh, Ahnt Vivianne." Gerallt put his hand to his amulet and prayed, "*Magna Dea, fac, quaesumus, ut haec ianua reseretur!*"

The lock clicked, and the door slowly swung open.

"Very good, Gerallt. Let us see what my parents have left for us."

Vivianne and Gerallt looked around the room. The small chamber held several crates, a small wooden table with two chairs, an antique roll-top desk, and a large metal chest.

Vivianne pointed her wand at two oil lamps on the table and said, "*Magna Dea, fac, quaesumus, ut lux sit.*" Small flames appeared inside the lamps' clear glass chimneys. They provided more than sufficient light to see clearly, especially after the darkness of the tunnel. "Theah, that's bettah," she said, returning her wand to its hiding place inside the left sleeve of her dress.

Gerallt lifted the lid of one of the crates. It was filled to the top with bottles, their brown labels faded with age. He read the label of one of them out loud. "Old Log Cabin Bourbon Whiskey. Distillers Corporation, Montreal, Canada."

Chapter 26 – The Hidden Tunnel

"I suspect you will find that the other crates will hold similar bottles," Vivianne said. "It seems some of the stories I heard about my fathah appear tah have been true. You might not believe it, but durin' the 1920s, America actually changed the Constitution tah outlaw the drinkin' of alcohol. They called it Prohibition. Of course, it didn't work. By makin' alcohol illegal, the only thing they accomplished was tah drive drinkin' underground and intah the hands of mobsters. I'm afraid my fathah was greedy and drawn tah easy money. I heard rumors that he hired drivers tah pick up the booze in Canada where it was legal, sneak it across the border, and deliver it tah speakeasies in Fort Wayne and Indianapolis. He must have used the tunnel and this room to hide it from the police."

Vivianne sat down at the desk and started opening its drawers. They were filled with letters, accounting books, and personal papers: potentially interesting reading, but hardly a treasure.

Vivianne walked over to the large iron chest in the corner. It was four-foot-long, two-feet-wide, and two-feet-deep. She tried to lift the heavy lid, but it proved too much for her. "Gerallt, can you help me open this?"

Working together, they lifted the lid and looked inside. A half-dozen large canvas bags, four small wooden boxes, and a black valise sat on top of several layers of large gold bars.

"Bless the Goddess!" Vivianne exclaimed. "It's Fathah's treasure!"

"We're rich!" Gerallt cried, gazing with amazement at the gold bars. After a few seconds, his curiosity drew his eyes to one of the large canvas bags. He opened its drawstring and pulled out a fist full of gold coins the size of silver dollars. "Wow!" With eyes nearly as large as the coins, he turned to his great aunt and said, "There must be hundreds of them in these bags!"

Vivianne placed the four wooden boxes in a row on the table. She opened the first box. It was full of diamonds that glittered in warm light from the oil lamps. "Oh, my!" she whispered.

"Savage!" Gerallt exclaimed.

The remaining three boxes held a king's ransom of rubies, emeralds, and sapphires.

Vivianne returned the box to the chest and set the valise on the table next to the gemstones. Opening it, she pulled out a stack of papers and handed Gerallt half of them. The two sat down and began looking through the documents. They were all stock certificates and deeds to various tracts of land. This time, the stocks were for prestigious companies that had survived the Great Depression, such as General Electric and Wells Fargo.

Gerallt picked up a box of gemstones and said, "I can't wait tah see Matt's face when I show him this."

"Not yet," Vivianne said, as she returned the papers to the valise and set it back in the chest.

"What?" Gerallt asked. "Why not?"

"Gerallt, Sam was the one who found the tunnel and the door tah the treasure room. He deserves tah be

Chapter 26 – The Hidden Tunnel

the one tah find the treasure, too. It's not his fault that he's an outsidah, and Fathah prayed tah the Goddess tah protect this room from outsidahs. It would be an insult tah his manhood if he knows that we can easily do what he could not."

"Oh. Okay," Gerallt said, disappointed at having to wait before spreading the good news. He reluctantly set the box back on the table.

"We've spent enough time here. Let's see where the tunnel leads before we head back," Vivianne said, as she led Gerallt out the door. Back in the tunnel, she paused to look back at the treasure room. Seeing several clear signs of their presence, Vivianne shook her head. "No, this won't do." She took out her wand and prayed to Modron, "*Magna Dea, redire, quaesumus, omnia ad pristinum locum!*"

The stock certificates and deeds returned to the Valise, while the handful of gold coins returned to the sack. After the four small boxes of gemstones, the valise, and the bag of coins had flown back into the chest, its heavy lid dropped down with a loud thud. Small whirlwinds of dust swirled across the floor and table, erasing Vivianne and Gerallt's footsteps and the other marks they had made. Seconds later, the door to the room closed, leaving Vivianne and Gerallt in the darkened tunnel.

The pair followed the tunnel as it continued toward the Hawthorne House. After about forty feet, the tunnel ended in a door. Pulling a lever to unlock it, Gerallt tugged on its handle, and the heavy door silently swung inward.

"It's the down cellah!" Gerallt exclaimed, looking into the basement of the Hawthorne House. "But we already searched it. How did we miss this door?"

"See how the outside of the door is covered with the same kind of bricks as the wall? The door would be invisible from the outside, and it's so thick that it's no wondah it didn't sound hollow when we knocked on it."

"But Aunt Vivianne, I don't see any mechanism for openin' the door from the down cellah side."

"I guess Fathah must have used some special prayah tah open it. No matter. Now that we know how tah get intah the tunnel from the carriage house, we can always open it from the inside."

Gerallt nodded.

"Okay, we had bettah head back before Matt and Tina return tah the carriage house and find us gone."

Closing the door to the basement, they retraced their way back through the tunnel. When they reached the root cellar under the carriage house, Vivianne extinguished the light of her wand.

"What did you find?" Gareth asked, as Gerallt and his great-aunt climbed the ladder.

"The treasure!" Gerallt exclaimed. "There was a chest full of gold bars and..."

"Gerallt," Vivianne interrupted. "Remembah what I said about keeping what we found a secret until Sam is able tah go back intah the tunnel. Gareth, Sam found the tunnel, so he deserves tah think he was the one tah find the treasure. Especially after being terrified by Fathah's protection prayah, I think it will

Chapter 26 – The Hidden Tunnel

help him get over what he just went through. So boys, can I count on you tah please keep this tah yourselves for a few more hours?"

Gerallt and Gareth looked at each other. Eventually, both nodded. "Ayuh, Ahnt Vivianne."

"Good, boys, I knew I could count on you tah do what's right. Now let's head back tah the house. I want tah make sure that Sam's okay and tell youah mothah and sistah what we found."

"But what about your prayah that cleaned out all of the tree roots and cobwebs?" Gerallt asked. "Won't Matt's fathah think it strange that they're gone?"

Vivianne smiled. "I guess that will just have to be one of the little mysteries of the Hawthorne House."

The next morning, Gwendolyn made a special tea for Sam, and soon he was raring to return to the tunnel and show her that he was not a coward. This time, Sam took Matt and Gerallt with him. In no time, they "found" the treasure room and returned carrying three of the small boxes of gemstones. Sam and Matt were so excited that neither one noticed the missing tree roots and cobwebs.

Chapter 27
Unexpected Announcements

Reflected and refracted by hundreds of cut crystals, the light from the chandelier's candles glittered like twinkling stars over the Hawthorne House's formal dining room. Together with the glow of the wall-mounted oil lamps and that from the fire crackling in the corner fireplace, they gave the place a comfortable warmth that could not be diminished by the wind-blown sleet pelting the windows.

Vivianne gazed at each smiling member of the Hawthorne and Mitchell families as they talked and ate the last few bites of their celebratory feast. With everyone stuffed with roast turkey, baked potatoes, sautéed vegetables, and freshly baked bread with butter and home-made raspberry jam, no one was in a hurry to eat some of Gwendolyn's made-from-scratch blackberry cobbler.

As heads of their respective households, Vivianne sat at one end of the table while Sam sat at the other. Gwendolyn naturally sat next to Sam. The two of them had spent far more time gazing into each other's eyes than eating the food that the Hawthorne women had made to celebrate the finding of the family's long-lost treasure. It warmed Vivianne's heart to see her niece's radiant smile now that Sam had entered her life. Gerallt and Matt sat next to each other, fanaticizing all of the things they would buy if only the treasure were theirs. Meanwhile, Gwyneth and

27 – Unexpected Announcements

Tina had their heads together, wondering whether there might be even more treasure buried somewhere on the property. Only Gareth looked back at his great-aunt, his expression one of curious expectation as if he knew that she was about to make an important announcement.

Vivianne gently rapped her spoon against her wine glass. The unexpected bell-like tone caused everyone to look at her.

"Now that we've all finished with our suppah, I have a couple of announcements tah make befoah we have dessert," Vivianne said, raising her glass. She waited until everyone had also raised their own glasses. "First, I would like tah propose a toast tah Sam, without whom we would have nothin' tah celebrate. He is the one who discovered the secret tunnel and is therefore the one who has solved our family's financial woes. Tah Sam!"

"To Sam," everyone chorused, raising their glasses and taking a sip.

"We Hawthornes owe a great debt tah Sam," Vivianne continued, "and as the matriarch of this family, I take our debts seriously. I can hardly enjoy our newly-found wealth while Sam continues tah face his own financial difficulties."

Vivianne paused briefly to enable everyone's curiosity to build. "For that reason, it is with deep gratitude and great personal pleasure that I hereby give Sam one-half of the Hawthorne family treasure."

The look of shock on Sam's face and the grateful smile on Gwendolyn's were worth far more to Vivianne than the gift's monetary value.

"But, Mrs. Hawthorne," Sam replied, "that is too much. I couldn't possibly accept such a generous gift."

"Sam, deah boy, of course you can. I insist. And it is high time that you start callin' me Vivianne. Since you and your children moved in, you've practically become a part of our family. I wouldn't have it tah give were it not for you." Vivianne smiled at her niece "Besides, I've seen the way you and Gwendolyn look at each othah. I'm not about tah let you continue feelin' unworthy tah court her merely because you're poor and she is the heir tah my estate. This way, no one will ever question whether you might be marryin' my niece for the money."

Stunned, Sam looked uncertainly at Gwendolyn. Only when she took his hand, smiled, and nodded encouragingly did he turn back to the elder Hawthorne. "Thank you... Vivianne. You have no idea what this means to me."

"But I do, Sam. It may have been more years ago than I care tah count, but I can still remembah what it was like tah be young and in love. So, it's settled. Half of the family fortune is yours."

The room erupted in clapping and excited words of congratulations as everyone started talking at once.

Again, Vivianne rapped her spoon against her wine glass. "I have one more announcement tah make," Vivianne continued once the others had settled down.

27 – Unexpected Announcements

The room instantly grew quiet as everyone turned their eyes on her.

"Yesterday evening, as I was goin' through the documents we found with the gold and gemstones, I discovered dozens of stock certificates. While many are worthless because the companies went bankrupt during the Great Depression, others are quite as valuable as the money and gold my father had hidden away. The documents also included several deeds tah properties my fathah owned, mostly tah tracts of land and buildin's that are being held in trust by the law offices of our family's lawyers. When they open on Monday morning, I plan tah find out why these deeds were nevah mentioned during the reading of Fathah's will. Regardless, given our financial situation, I intend tah sell the properties as soon as I can."

Vivianne paused to consider the importance of what she was about to say. "I found one deed, however, tah be of special significance. It seems that I own an estate outside of the town of Tofino, British Columbia."

"Where's that?" Gareth asked.

"On the Pacific Coast of Vancouver Island. The property includes some eighty acres of forest as well as several buildin's, the largest being a mansion that was once the favorite summah residence of Harold Hawthorne, my grandfathah and the man who built this house."

"Sweet!" Matt said, with a touch of envy in his voice.

"Sweet, indeed," Vivianne said, looking at Matt with sympathy. "I know that all of you moved heah tah Hawthorne, not because you wanted tah, but because you had tah. I also know that you lived in small coastal fishing towns: we Hawthornes came from Deeah Isle, Maine, while you Mitchells were from Port Orford, Oregon. But most important of all, I know that you loved livin' by the sea and that livin' this far from the ocean is not where you would choose tah live."

Everyone nodded in agreement except Tina, who had recently started dating a boy in her class.

"As for myself, Hawthorne holds too many bad memories foah me tah want tah live out my remainin' days heah. I have imprisoned myself in this house foah fah too long, and it's high time I break free. It's time tah make a fresh beginnin' somewhere new. I have therefore decided tah sell Hawthorne House and move tah Vancouver Island. More importantly, I want all of you tah come and live with me."

Matt broke the shocked silence by asking, "Can we, Dad? I miss the ocean and hiking in the coastal hills."

"And walkin' along the beach," Gerallt added.

"But where would we live?" Tina asked. "Is there another house for us?"

"There is, indeed," Vivianne answered. "The property includes an old lighthouse and a three-bedroom cottage for the lighthouse keepah. It's been empty evah since the province shut the lighthouse

27 – Unexpected Announcements

down back in the 1960s, but we clearly have more than enough money tah renovate it."

Vivianne paused briefly before continuing. "But I have a much bettah idear. The summah residence is considerably larger than this house so there will be plenty of room in it for everyone. It has eight bedrooms: one for each of us."

Gwyneth, who had been keeping count, asked, "But Ahnt Vivianne, what about the Goddess? Where will we hold Her Sabbats?" She paused suddenly, putting her hand over her mouth as she realized what she'd said in front of the Mitchells. They may be friends, even close friends, but they were still outsiders.

"It seems tah me that the lighthouse would make an ideal location tah hold the Sabbats, given its location and the view from the top," Vivianne said.

"Goddess?" Tina asked.

"Sabbats?" Sam added, looking questioningly at Gwendolyn, who looked to her aunt for guidance.

Vivianne paused, considering how much to say and how best to say it. "I was wonderin' when this day would come. And unless I am much mistaken, I believe that Matt already knows moah about our family's secrets than he has let on."

"Matt?" Sam said. "Do you know what this is about?

"Er...," Matt muttered, looking guiltily at Gerallt.

"Matt, do you or don't you know what Vivianne is referring to?"

"Gerallt?" Matt asked, with more than a hint of desperation in his voice.

Gerallt looked at his great-aunt, who nodded. He shrugged. "Go ahead, Matt. I guess it's not goin' tah be a secret any longer."

"Yes, Dad," Matt replied with relief. "I'm sorry, Gerallt made me swear I'd never tell a living soul what he told me. I promised."

Sam hesitated, unsure of how to react to his son keeping him in the dark about something that was obviously very important to the Hawthornes. "I understand. A promise to your best friend is not something that you should easily break."

"Okay. Dad, Tina, it's absolutely awesome!" Matt exclaimed. "You're not going to believe it. I know 'cause I didn't, not until I saw it with my own eyes. I'll have to show you; otherwise, you won't believe it's true."

Gwendolyn turned to her son. "Gerallt, you showed him? How could you have actually shown an outsidah your gift from the Goddess?"

"Ayuh, Mothah," Gerallt confessed. "I did. And more." Taking the chain holding his amulet from its hiding place under his shirt, Gerallt silently handed it to Matt."

Gwyneth gasped while Gwendolyn stared at her son with a mixture of shocked disbelief, anger, and fear.

Matt shoved his plate and silverware to the side. He took a coin out of his pocket and placed it on the table. Holding the amulet tightly in his hand, he softly

27 – Unexpected Announcements

said, "*Magna Dea, fac, quaesumus, ut nummus ascendat!*" The coin silently floated up until it hung in the air in front of him.

Gwyneth uttered a strangled cry of surprise, Gwendolyn moaned "Oh, no!" and even Vivianne let out a shocked "*Magna Dea!*"

"*Magna Dea, fac, quaesumus, ut nummus verset!*" Matt continued. The coin began to spin. After a few seconds, Matt finished his demonstration with "*Magna Dea, fac, quaesumus, ut nummus descendant!*" The coin dropped onto the tablecloth, rolled off the edge, and fell onto the floor.

"Dad, now do you see why I had to show you? You'd never have believed me if I'd just told you about Gerallt's amulet."

"What the heck just happened?" Sam asked, looking back and forth between his son, Gwendolyn, and Vivianne.

"More importantly," Gwendolyn added, "how is this even possible? He's an outsidah, and the Goddess answered his prayahs!"

"I kinda accidentally invested him," Gerallt confessed. "I thought the Goddess would know that he was an unbelievah and wouldn't answer his prayahs."

Everyone in the room turned to Vivianne, who was just as stunned and confused as the others. "I have no idear how this is possible. But it is not for us tah question the Goddess."

"But what about the High Coven?" Gwyneth whispered. "If they find out, they could strip us of the Goddess's gifts and banish us."

"Then, the High Coven must nevah find out," Gwendolyn said. "This will have tah be a family secret."

For the following hour, Vivianne and Gwendolyn told Sam and Tina the story of the arrival of the Goddess Modron, the selection of her druidae, the bestowing of her gifts, and the persecution that began once the Goddess departed. They talked about how the surviving druidae went into hiding and eventually dispersed to secret colonies including the one on Deer Isle where Gwendolyn and her children had lived.

Vivianne took a deep breath and turned to Sam and Tina. "And now you know what only a handful of outsidahs have evah learned. Tah save ourselves from torture and death, we druidae have safeguarded our secrets for centuries. The fate of my family is now in youah hands. Will you keep our secrets, or will you betray our trust? Will you come with us to Vancouver Island, or will you stay? What will you do?"

Sam looked from Vivianne to Gwendolyn and back again. After nearly a minute, he answered, "I don't know... I just don't know. This is a hell of a lot for me... for anyone to process. I'm going to have to discuss this with Matt and Tina, and I'm going to have to sleep on this."

"I understand," Vivianne replied. "Youah decision should not be made lightly, for it will have a lastin'

27 – Unexpected Announcements

impact on us all. May the Goddess guide youah feet ontah the correct path."

Sam turned to Gwendolyn, staring into her eyes as if seeking to see into her very soul. He turned back to his children. "Matt, Tina, come with me. We have to talk."

"Sam, I'm sorry," Gwendolyn said, as Sam stood up. "I should have been the one tah tell you. I wanted tah, but I thought we had more time."

"One more thing before you go, Sam," Vivianne said. "I meant what I said about givin' you half of the treasure. I won't hold it ovah youah head; half is youahs, regardless of youah decision."

Sam nodded his acknowledgment before looking at Gwendolyn. He paused as if unsure of what to say. Then he turned away. "Matt and Tina, we're leaving, now."

Tina got up first. "Yes, Dad," she said, as she followed her father out of the room.

Matt mouthed the words *I'm sorry* to Gerallt before hurrying after Tina and his father. The three grabbed their coats off the coat tree by the back door and walked out into the freezing rain on their way to the carriage house.

The Hawthornes stayed at the table in the dining room. The three empty seats mirrored the empty feelings of those that remained.

"I'm so sorry, Mothah," Gwyneth eventually said, as tears trickled down Gwendolyn's cheeks. "If I'd just kept my mouth shut and not mentioned the Goddess, none of this would have happened. This is all my fault."

"No, deah girl," Vivianne said. "You can't blame yourself for somethin' that would have had tah happen soon anyway. If anythin', it is my fault for announcin' the move so abruptly. Sam is a good man; I think he will come to understand and accept us if we give him time." She turned then to Gerallt and said, "I believe Matt told you that his fathah is not a religious man and thus does not believe in miracles."

"Yes, but he also said his mothah was a spiritual woman who held the beliefs of her native American heritage."

"As an unbeliever, Sam will find our faith and gifts especially hard tah accept. Still, if he could accept and love his first wife, then we have grounds tah hope he will learn tah accept us as who and what we are. We must all have patience with him. And Gwendolyn, you must not let fear or distrust make him forget his feelings for you or yours for him."

Opening the door to the carriage house, Sam lit an oil lamp to drive away the darkness. The dim light did nothing to brighten the gloom that chilled his heart. He led Tina and Matt upstairs, where they lit additional lamps and candles.

"Sit," he ordered, indicating the three chairs around the small circular table between the kitchen and living

27 – Unexpected Announcements

room. When they'd taken their seats, Sam and Tina stared at Matt.

"How long have you known?" Sam asked. His expression was grim, his tone serious.

"About two months, I guess," Matt answered guiltily.

"And you didn't think it was important enough to tell Tina and me?"

"Dad, that's not fair! Of course, I knew it was important. That's why I didn't tell you, either of you. Gerallt made me swear I wouldn't tell a soul before he said or showed me anything. And then, once I learned his secret, I understood why. You've got to remember that his ancestors were tortured to death because of it. Some were even burned at the stake. So many generations of his ancestors have lived in fear of being discovered that it's become a huge part of who they are. Gerallt took an incredible risk in telling me. I couldn't break his trust. I just couldn't."

Sam shook his head in frustration. "Matt, you've put me, put all of us into a hell of a predicament. I don't know whether to be proud of you for keeping your word or to ground you for life for keeping us in the dark."

"So, what will we do now?" Tina asked.

"I don't know," her father answered. "Vivianne's taken us in when we could have ended up living out of our car. And she just gave us so much money that I may never have to work another day in my life. On the other hand, this story about a goddess giving miracle-granting gifts sounds insane. I don't see how it's even remotely possible." Sam paused for a second, before turning to his son. "That amulet. What else can it do?"

"A lot of things," Matt answered "Gerallt used it to break the legs on a school desk of someone who was bullying him. He made a stream of water change direction. Stuff like that."

"That sounds like telekinesis," Tina said.

"Yeah, I guess so," Matt answered. "But the weirdest thing was how he saved us from getting beaten up by some bullies at school. He made a flock of seagulls poop on them."

"What paranormal power is that?" Tina asked.

"I haven't a clue," Matt answered. "And Gerallt told me that he's only learned a few of the prayers so far. His mother and great-aunt know lots more than he does, and they have this big book in the library that's full of them. He gave me the impression that his goddess can do just about anything."

"But an ancient Celtic goddess who answers prayers by performing miracles?" Sam asked. "I can't believe it."

"Dad, you saw what Matt did with the coin," Tina argued. "How do you explain what we saw?"

"I don't know," Sam said. "But just because I can't think of a rational explanation doesn't mean there isn't one. Matt, that thing you did with the coin. You have to tell me the truth. Was it real and not some kind of magician's trick that you and Gerallt cooked up?"

27 – Unexpected Announcements

"Dad, it's real. I swear it," Matt said. "I wouldn't lie about something like this."

"But..." Sam stopped when he saw the look of hurt on Matt's face. "Okay, Matt. I believe you. I don't believe that a goddess is granting your prayers, but I believe you. I don't know what it is, but apparently, it's real."

"I've thought a lot about this since Gerallt first showed me," Matt said. "I think I may know what's really happening. What if Modron wasn't really a goddess? What if she was only pretending to be a goddess? What if she was really an alien biologist studying life on Earth and using the locals to collect sample plants and animals for her? I think the amulet and other gifts are some sort of advanced alien tech that she left behind when she returned to wherever she came from, sort of as a reward for her helpers."

"I suppose that's possible," Sam grudgingly agreed. "As strange as that sounds, it makes more sense than miracle-performing relics from an obscure Celtic deity."

"But, Dad, please don't mention my alien tech idea to any of the Hawthornes. Gerallt and I had a huge argument when I suggested it. He called it blasphemy and got so upset and angry that I didn't know if he'd ever speak to me again."

"Ah," Tina said, remembering the boys' falling out. "I was wondering what happened between the two of you."

"Okay, Matt, I'll watch my tongue," Sam said. "No sense in my pouring gasoline on the fire. And besides, if there's one thing your mother taught me, it was that no one ever wins a religious argument by arguing. When you love someone, you have to accept her as she is and not try to make her into a reflection of yourself."

"Are you talking about Mom?" Tina asked, "or Gwendolyn?"

"I was thinking about your mother's spiritual beliefs, but maybe you're right. Maybe I'm just upset that Gwen kept this from me. I thought I knew who she was. Now, I don't know anymore. How do I know she isn't keeping other secrets from me?"

"Dad," Matt said, "you and Mom always told us we should never judge anyone without first imagining ourselves in their shoes and seeing the world through their eyes. To the Hawthornes, their secret is bigger than all of us. It's bigger than my friendship with Gerallt, and it's bigger than how you and his mom feel about each other. You can't blame her for not telling you. They're trusting us. What kind of people would we be if we didn't keep their secret?"

Sam looked at Tina, who nodded her agreement. "Okay, Matt. Their secret's been kept since the Romans occupied Britain. I guess there's no harm in helping them to keep it a while longer."

"Thank you!" Matt said with relief. "But what about Aunt Vivianne's offer to take us with them when they move?"

"We don't have to," Sam said. "With half the treasure, we could live anywhere."

27 – Unexpected Announcements

"I don't want to live just anywhere," Matt countered. "I want to move with Gerallt and his family."

"What do you think, Tina?" Sam asked.

"I don't know," she replied. "I do want to move back to the coast... I don't suppose we could move back to our old house in Port Orford?"

"Tina, we sold the cottage. It's not ours anymore. Vivianne was right about it being time for a new beginning. The only question is will it be with the Hawthornes or will we strike out on our own?"

"With the Hawthornes," Matt immediately answered.

"Uh... The Hawthornes?" Tina replied tentatively.

"Are you sure, Tina?" Sam asked.

Tina thought for a few more seconds. "The Hawthornes."

Sam looked at his children and smiled, "Then the Hawthornes it is. Let's go back and tell them their secret's safe with us and that we'll be moving with them to Canada."

Before Sam could stand, Matt jumped up, raced around the table, and gave his father his very best bear hug. "Thank you, Dad. I knew you'd make the right choice when you had a chance to think it through."

Tina soon joined Matt and her father for the family group hug. A few minutes later, the Mitchells headed back to the Hawthorne House and the beginning of their new life with the Hawthornes. It was going to be an amazing adventure.

Epilog

The following week, after Sam and Vivianne had sold a few of the gold coins, Sam bought a beautiful engagement ring and proposed to Gwendolyn. She, of course, accepted, and they decided to get married after the move to Vancouver Island. With their newly-found wealth, their applications to immigrate to Canada were quickly approved. What happened next is another story.

The story of Matt and Gerallt's adventures in their new home will be chronicled in the next book in this series.

Thank You

Thank you for purchasing and reading *The Secrets of Hawthorne House.*

The success of all books, but especially books by relatively new indie authors, greatly depends on their readers. Few potential new readers are likely to become aware of books, let alone purchase them, without sufficient book reviews and word-of-mouth recommendations. If you liked this book, then please help others enjoy it, too. Recommend it to your friends, both directly and via social media, and by taking a few minutes to write an honest review at your favorite e-book store and Goodreads.

If you post a review of the book, please email me at donfiresmith@gmail.com with a link to your review. To show my appreciation, I will send you a coupon for a free ebook copy of one of my other books.

Map

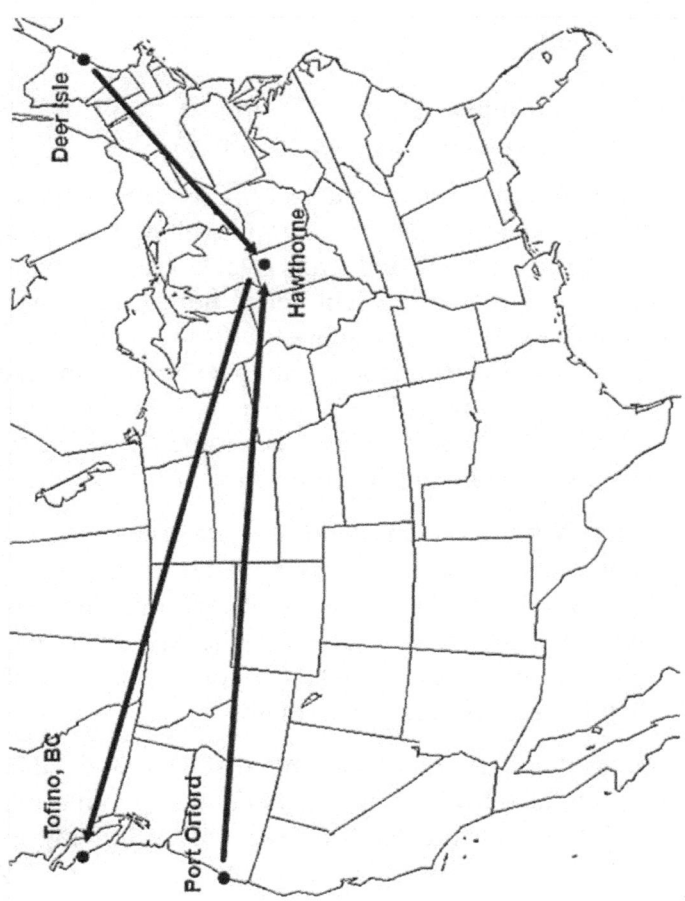

The Characters

The Mitchells

The Mitchell family is originally from Port Orford, a small fishing town on the southern Oregon coast.

- **Matt Mitchell** (15) is a boy of average height, build, and looks. He has straight blond hair and gray-green eyes behind small oval glasses. A loner due to his mother's recent death, he learns to face the bullies of his new school with the help of his friend, Gerallt Hawthorne. He loves the ocean and longs to return to his home in Oregon. With a keen interest in science and technology, he likes to take things apart and see how they work.

- **Tina Mitchell** (15) is Matt's fraternal twin, a popular, self-confident girl with an active social life. She is tall, slender, good-looking, and has long straight black that she inherited from her mother. She looks and acts a couple of years older than her age. She excels in math.

- **Sam Mitchell** (37) is the father of Matt and Tina. He taught Introduction to Computer Programming at the Port Orford High School before moving to Indiana. He moved with his children to Hawthorne, where he works as a software developer for a small company. He is tall, with sandy blond hair and medium build and small squarish glasses. He has kept himself very busy and somewhat distant since the recent death of his much-loved wife, Mary Mitchell.

- **Mary Mitchell** (35) was Sam's wife and the mother of Matt and Tina. She was one quarter Native American and a local artist and potter, with a spiritual and mystical side. She was killed by the town drunk's truck while she was walking along the roadside picking wildflowers for her pottery business. She was a tall, slender, and graceful woman with long, straight black hair, skin a shade too brown for the cloudy coastal climate, and hands that always seemed to have clay under the fingernails.
- **Midnight** is Matt's inquisitive black cat.

The Hawthornes

The Hawthorne family is originally from Deer Isle, a tiny fishing village on the central coast of Maine. They are secretly druids and druidesses who worship the Celtic Goddess Modron.

- **Vivianne** (VI-vee-ann) **Hawthorne** (73) is Gerallt's great-aunt. A recluse living in the Hawthorne House, she is considered a witch and murderess by the neighborhood children.
- **Gerallt** (GERR-alt) **Hawthorne** (15) is a lonely and somewhat somber boy who doesn't make friends easily. Gerallt is tall and slender with a pale face and straight black hair. More confident than Matt, there is a definite hint of mystery about

The Characters

him. He loves the ocean and longs to return to Maine.

- **Gwyneth** (GWIN-eth) **Hawthorne** (17) is Gerallt's mysterious older sister. She is tall and beautiful with emerald eyes and long, straight raven hair.

- **Gareth** (GAHR-eth) **Hawthorne** (12) is Gerallt's younger brother, a quiet boy who has lost his self-confidence since his father's death. He has not yet been invested as a druid.

- **Gwendolyn** (GWEN-doh-len) **Hawthorne** (37) is Vivianne Hawthorne's niece and mother of Gwyneth, Gerallt, and Gareth. She is a master herbologist and an artist who formerly made natural medications and sold scented candles, soaps, and oils. She has become quite depressed and withdrawn since her husband's death. Slightly shorter than her daughter, she is even more beautiful with emerald eyes and long, straight raven hair.

- **Medwyn Hawthorne** (42) was Gerallt's father, a fisherman who was recently lost at sea during a fishing accident.

- **Belladonna** is Gwendolyn's large black cat.

- **Nightshade** is Gwyneth's skinny black cat.

- **Nightwing** is Gerallt's pet crow.

- **Shadow** is Gareth's black pet squirrel.

The Hoosiers

The Hoosiers are from Hawthorne, a small town in Northeastern Indiana.

- **The Teachers at Hawthorne High School**:
    - **Mr. Marcus Thompson** (23) teaches freshman American History.
    - **Mr. William Tanner** (51) is the principal.
    - **Mrs. McKinney** (46) is the freshman English teacher.
    - **Mr. Jack Armstrong** (40) is the gruff, no-nonsense high school gym coach and detention teacher.
- **The Bullies:**
    - **Colin O'Connell** (16) is the leader of the sophomore bullies. He is large and cunning with blond hair and a cruel face.
    - **Clayton Cartwright** (17) is Colin's large and dull-witted thug, who has been held back two years at school.
    - **Dylan Jones** (15) is Colin's little toady.
- **Others:**
    - **Sarah Duffy** (17) is a shy, overweight girl who rides the school bus and volunteers to operate the video equipment at school.

- **George Smith** (45) is a shady handyman and thief who steals Gerallt's amulet.
- **Peter Henderson** (50) is the pawnbroker and fence who buys Gerallt's amulet from George Smith.

Celtic Gods and Goddesses

- **Aeron** was the Celtic god of battle.
- **Belenus** was the Celtic god of healing.
- **Brigit** was the Celtic goddess of fire.
- **Cernunnos** was the Celtic horned god of fertility and wealth.
- **Modron** was the great Celtic mother goddess and the source of the Hawthorne's sacred gifts including their amulets and wands.
- **Taranis** was the Celtic god of lightning and thunder.

Druidic Spells
(Prayers to Modron)

In this book, the Latin words are spoken in the traditional Latin of ancient Rome, which is not necessarily the same as current Latin pronunciation (for example, as spoken by a Catholic priest).

Druida (male singular), Druias (female singular), and Druides or Druidea (plural)
Druid, Druidess, Druids

Magna Dea!
(MAHG-nah DAY-ah!) Great Goddess!

Magna Dea, comproba, quaesumus, hunc puerum druidam tuum!
(MAHG-nah DAY-ah, kohm-PRO-bah, KWEI-sue-moose, hewnk POOR-uhm DRU-ee-dem TOO-uhm!) Great Goddess, we beseech Thee, approve this boy as your druid!

Magna Dea, fac, quaesumus, et radices aranearum prosternite!
(MAHG-nah DAY-ah, fahk, KWEI-sue-moose, eht RAH-dee-chays AH-rahn Yah-room PRO-stair-knee-tay!) Great Goddess, we beseech Thee, make the roots and spiderwebs fall down!

Druidic Spells

Magna Dea, fac, quaesumus, funes eorum lubricos!
(MAHG-nah DAY-ah, fahk, KWEI-sue-moose, FU-nace AY-oh-rum LOO-bree-kohs!) Great Goddess, we beseech Thee, make their ropes slippery!

Magna Dea, fac, quaesumus, ut aqua in eum volet!
*(*MAHG-nah DAY-ah, fahk, KWEI-sue-moose, ooht AH-kwah in AY-uhm WOE-let!*)* Great Goddess, we beseech Thee, make the water fly onto him!

Magna Dea, fac, quaesumus, ramum ruinam
(MAHG-nah DAY-ah, fahk, KWEI-sue-moose, rah-mum ree-nam!) Great Goddess, we beseech Thee, make the branch fall!

Magna Dea, fac, quaesumus, ut haec ianua reseretur!
(MAHG-nah DAY-ah, fahk, KWEI-sue-moose, ooht hike YAH-new-ah rehz-er-RAY-tour!) Great Goddess, we beseech Thee, make his door unlock! [Technically, reseretur means to unbolt a door.]

Magna Dea, fac, quaesumus, ut lac eius coagulet!
(MAHG-nah DAY-ah, fahk, KWEI-sue-moose, ooht lahk AY-oos ko-AH-goo-let!) Great Goddess, we beseech Thee, make his milk curdle!

Magna Dea, fac, quaesumus, ut lux sit!
(MAHG-nah DAY-ah, fahk, KWEI-sue-moose, ooht lukes sit!) Great Goddess, we beseech Thee, make light here!

Magna Dea, fac, quaesumus, ut nummi ascendant!
(MAHG-nah DAY-ah, fahk, KWEI-sue-moose, ooht NOOM-mee ah-SKIN-dahnt!) Great Goddess, we beseech Thee, make the coins ascend!

Magna Dea, fac, quaesumus, ut nummi descendant!
*(*MAHG-nah DAY-ah, fahk, KWEI-sue-moose, ooht NOOM-mee day-SKIN-dahnt!*)* Great Goddess, we beseech Thee, make the coins descend!

Magna Dea, fac, quaesumus, ut nummus ascendat!
(MAHG-nah DAY-ah, fahk, KWEI-sue-moose, ooht NOOM-moose ah-SKIN-daht!) Great Goddess, we beseech Thee, make the coin ascend!

Magna Dea, fac, quaesumus, ut nummus descendant!
(MAHG-nah DAY-ah, fahk, KWEI-sue-moose, ooht NOOM-moose day-SKIN-dahnt!) Great Goddess, we beseech Thee, make the coin descend!

Magna Dea, fac, quaesumus, ut nummus verset!
(MAHG-nah DAY-ah, fahk, KWEI-sue-moose, ooht NOOM-moose WEAR-set!) Great Goddess, we beseech Thee, make the coin spin!

Magna Dea, fac, quaesumus, ianua eius aperta stet!
(MAHG-nah DAY-ah, fahk, KWEI-sue-moose, ooht YAH-new-ah AY-oos ah-PEAR-tah steht!) Great Goddess, we beseech Thee, make his door open!

Druidic Spells

Magna Dea, fac, quaesumus, ut saccus eius scindat!
(MAHG-nah DAY-ah, fahk, KWEI-sue-moose, ooht SAHK-koos AY-oos SKIN-daht!) Great Goddess, we beseech Thee, make his bag rip!

Magna Dea, fac, quaesumus, ut sacci eorum scindant!
(MAHG-nah DAY-ah, fahk, KWEI-sue-moose, ooht SAHK-key AY-o-rum SKIN-dahnt!) Great Goddess, we beseech Thee, make their bags rip!

Magna Dea, fac, quaesumus, ut sella eius decrescat!
(MAHG-nah DAY-ah, fahk, KWEI-sue-moose, ooht SEL-lah AY-oos day-KRESS-kaht!) Great Goddess, we beseech Thee, make his chair smaller!

Magna Dea, fac, quaesumus, ut stili eorum perfluant!
(MAHG-nah DAY-ah, fahk, KWEI-sue-moose, ooht STEE-lee EH-o-room PEAR-flu-ahnt!) Great Goddess, we beseech Thee, make their pens leak! [Technically, the Latin word stili means writing sticks. The Romans did not have pens, but by concentrating on what he wanted, Gerallt made his intent clear.]

Magna Dea, fac, quaesumus, ut vespertiliones veniant!
(MAHG-nah DAY-ah, fahk, KWEI-sue-moose, ooht wes-per-tee-lee-OH-nace we-NEE-ahnt!) Great Goddess, we beseech Thee, make the bats come!

Magna Dea, fac, quaesumus, viam lubricam!
(MAHG-nah DAY-ah, fahk, KWEI-sue-moose, WEE-ahm LU-bree-kahm!) Great Goddess, we beseech Thee, make the path slippery!

Magna Dea, inveni, quaesumus, quod absconditum est!
(MAHG-nah DAY-ah, in-WHEN-nee, KWEI-sue-moose, kwoad ab-SCONE-dee-tomb est!) Great Goddess, we beseech Thee, find that which is hidden!

Magna Dea, redire, quaesumus, omnia ad pristinum locum!
(MAHG-nah DAY-ah, KWEI-sue-moose, OM-nee-uh ruh-DEE-ray aid Pre-STEEN-uhm low-kum!) Great Goddess, we beseech Thee, return everything to its original location!

Maine Accents and Idioms

Accents

The Hawthornes speak with a Maine accent that is particularly strong as members of the Deer Isle colony of druidae have limited interaction with outsiders.

Thus, the Hawthornes tend to pronounce the letter *r* at the end of words as *ah*. For example, ah (are), bettah (better), cellah (cellar), dooah (door), evah (ever), fathah (father), foah (for), hahd (hard), heah (here), mothah (mother), nevah (never), othah (other), suppah (supper), yahd (yard), youah (your), and you'ah (you're).

The word *to* is pronounced *tah*.

On the other hand, many words that end in the letter *a* get the letter *r* added at the end, so the word *idea* is pronounced as *idear*.

Mainers also drop the letter *g* at the end of words ending in the letters *ing*. Thus, the words *coming* and *going* become *comin'* and *goin'*.

Mainers typically broaden certain vowels, especially a and e sounds. For example, the words *aunt* becomes *ahnt* and *can't* becomes *cahn't*.

Finally, Mainers sometimes drag out one-syllable words so that they become two syllables. For example, the word *here* is pronounced as *hee-ah* and written as *heah* in this book.

Idioms

The Hawthornes use many idioms that are unclear to people who aren't from Maine. These include the following:

ayuh - yes
breezed up - windy ("It's breezed up today.")
buzz on - drunk ("He's got a wicked buzz on.")
cah – car
deah – dear (pronounced dee-ah)
dite - a little ("I'll have just a dite of pie.")
door yard - yard
down cellah – basement ("It's in the down cellah.")
fathah – father
flatlandah – anyone not from Maine
get in a gaum – get into trouble
gommy – clumsy ("He's just numb and gommy.")
heah – here (pronounced hee-ah)
honkin' - really big ("That's a big honkin' cah.")
idear – idea
intah - into
mothah - mother
nippy - cold ("It's getting nippy outside.")
numb - stupid
kife - to steal ("He kifed my amulet.")
pissah - great or terrible ("What a pissah!")
right out straight - busy
rugged - chubby
savage - awesome

Maine Accents and Idioms

suppah - dinner
tah - to
ugly - angry ("Now, don't you get ugly with me.")
wicked - very ("He is wicked numb.")
willie wacks – middle of nowhere

Family Trees

The following diagram shows the Mitchell and Hawthorne family trees. The white boxes represent regular people ("outsidahs"), while the other boxes represent druidae. The boxes of the main characters have thick borders. The deceased are indicated by tombstones.

410 Family Trees

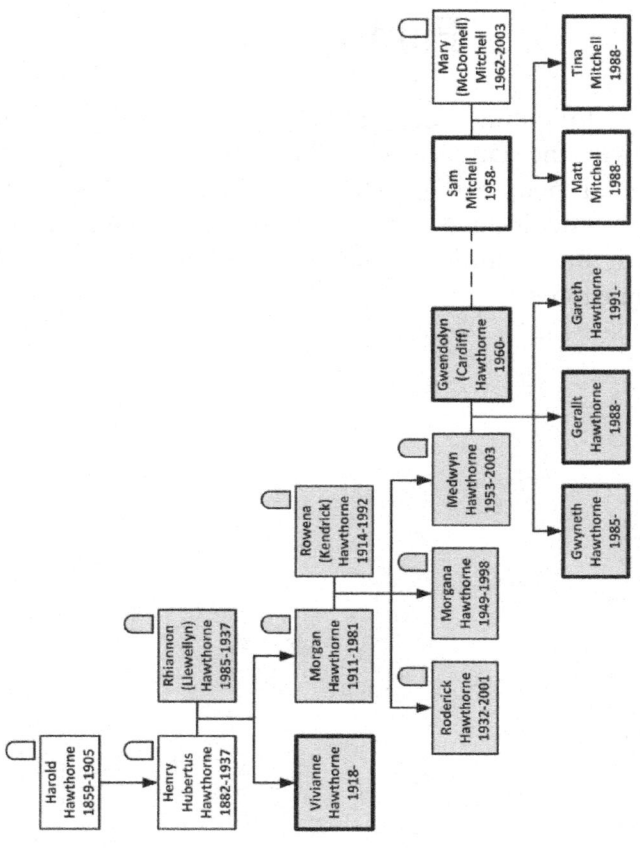

Acknowledgments

First, I would like to thank Rudy Parfaite, lead environment artist at the game company, Pretty Simple, who created the book's beautiful cover. He took my architectural drawings of the Hawthorne House and captured it beautifully in his original artwork. I would like to thank my copy editor, Donna Kelley, and my story editor, who wishes to remain anonymous. Both editors greatly improved the quality of the book. I also want to give a shout out to the many talented developers of the excellent Autocrit® (https://www.autocrit.com/) and Grammarly® (https://app.grammarly.com/) editing applications.

Finally, I would like to thank my beta readers who read early drafts of the manuscript and identified numerous issues for me to fix: Lisa Caudill, Chrystal Fenerty, Rebecca Firesmith, Philippe Lebacq, Melanie Savage, and Genelle Themann.

Dedication

For my wife, Becky, who encourages my writing, even when I make changes she doesn't like to manuscripts that she has already read.

About the Author

Donald Firesmith is a multi-award-winning author of speculative fiction including science fiction (alien invasion), fantasy (magical wands), and modern urban paranormal novels.

Prior to recently retiring to devote himself full-time to his novels, Donald Firesmith earned an international reputation as a distinguished engineer, authoring seven system/software engineering books based on his 40+ years spent developing large, complex software-intensive systems.

He lives in Pittsburgh, Pennsylvania with his wife Becky, his son Dane, and varying numbers of dogs and cats.

You can learn more about Donald by visiting his author website http://donaldfiresmith.com.

Don's magical wands and autographed copies of his wand lore book are available from the Firesmith's Wand Shoppe, which is on the Internet at http://magicalwandshoppe.com.

Other books by Donald Firesmith include:
Magical Wands: A Cornucopia of Wand Lore
Hell Holes 1: What Lurks Below
Hell Holes 2: Demons on the Dalton
Hell Holes 3: To Hell and Back

Cataloging-in-Publication (CIP) Data

Name: Firesmith, Donald.

Title: The Secrets of Hawthorne House / by Donald Firesmith.

Description: Second edition. | Pittsburgh : Magical Wand Press, 2019.

Summary: The life of a freshman at a new high school changes forever when a family of witches moves in next door. | Audience: Juvenile. | Language: English

Identifiers: ASIN B07GV2F814 (Amazon ebook) | 978-1726283151 (Amazon paperback) | EAN 2940161482247 (ebook) | ISBN 978-1987060690 (B&N paperback) | ISBN 978-1087866185 (Ingram ebook) | ISBN 978-1087866178 (Ingram paperback) | ISBN 978-0463294680 (Smashwords ebook)

Subjects: BISAC: Fiction / Fantasy /Contemporary. | Fiction / Fantasy / Paranormal. | Fiction / Mystery & Detective / Amateur Sleuth. | LCSH: American–Fantasy–Fiction. | American–Paranormal–Fiction. | American–Science Fiction–Fiction. | GSAFD: Adventure fiction. | Fantasy fiction. | Science fiction.

Made in the USA
Monee, IL
03 May 2024

57765164R00246